VISIBLE

VISIBLE

a novel

DARLENE CORBETT

WordCrafts

Scripture quotations taken from The Holy Bible, New International Version®, NIV® Copyright ©1973, 1978, 1984, 2011 by Biblica, Inc.® Used by permission. All rights reserved worldwide.

Cover concept and design by Mike Parker.
Front cover art © Forewer / Adobe Stock

Published by WordCrafts Press
Cody, Wyoming 82414
www.wordcrafts.net

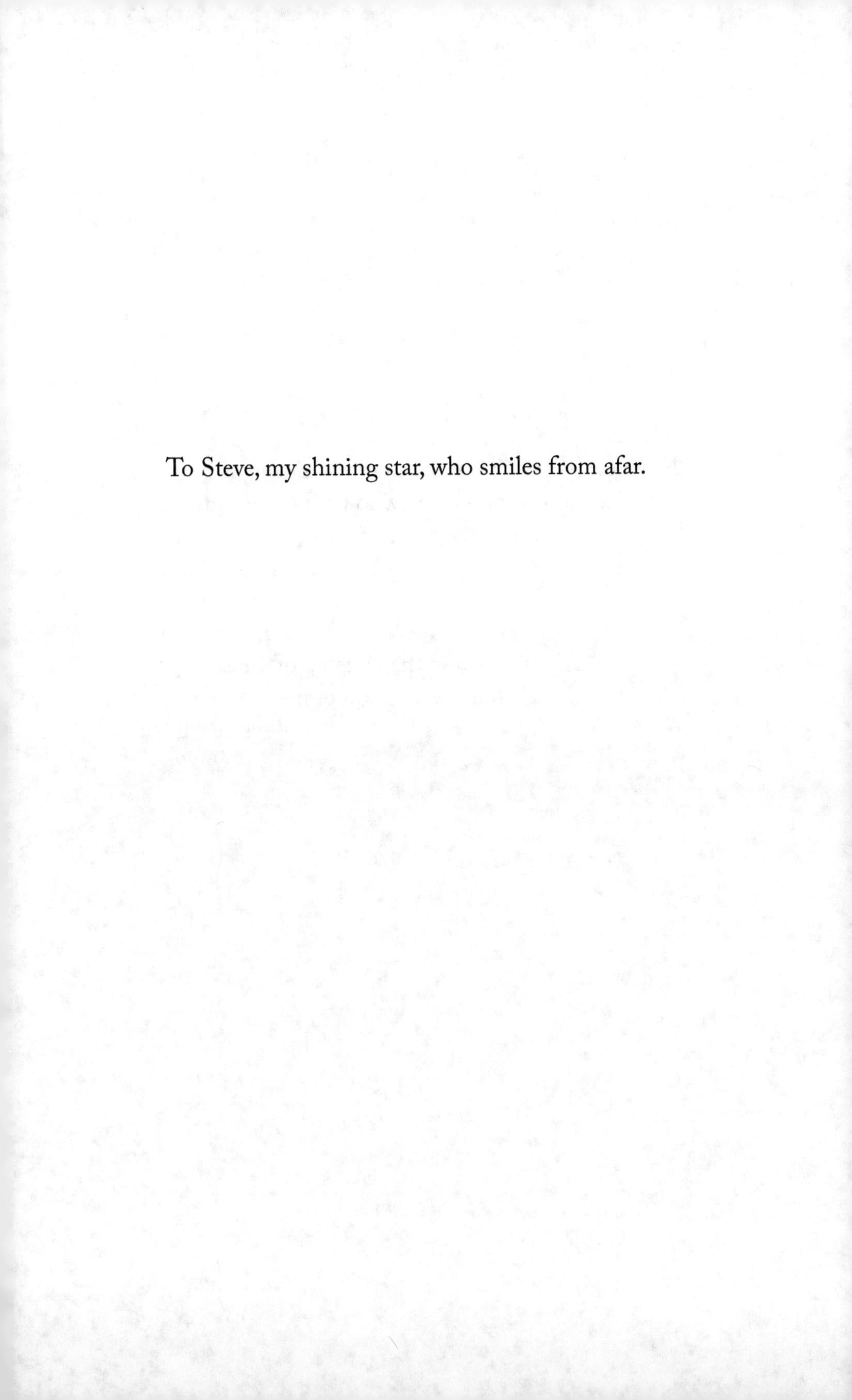

To Steve, my shining star, who smiles from afar.

"From everyone who has been given much, much will be
demanded; and from the one who has been entrusted with
much, much more will be asked."
~Luke 12:48 (NIV)

"Tradition is not the worship of ashes,
but the preservation of fire."
~Gustav Mahler

Chapter One

Session One—March 24th

Rachel Karem blew on a long bouncy ringlet positioned over her right eye and folded her arms into the layers of her cashmere sweater. Softness and warmth relaxed the taut steely coils puncturing her insides.

For thirty years, her practice flourished within the inviting, secure, teal-colored walls of a psychotherapy enclave.

But tonight? Less cozy.

What made the evening so raw?

Exhausted winter surprising newborn spring, with a snowy quilt and firm humph?

No.

Not having enough adipose tissue couched between epidural layers and muscles?"

No again.

Running on the colder side of body temperature?

Are you kidding?

With menopause bathing her in a swamp of heat?

An emphatic no.

Goosebumps flitted across her skin as a big chill enveloped her office, heightened by a humming vibration and shuffling feet. Unexpected and far icier than she expected.

And a single reprieve? Inhaling the eucalyptus-spearmint aroma she sprayed for their arrival. A refreshing delight. Rachel shut her eyes. "Ummm," she said out loud as the crisp aroma migrated deep into her lungs.

A chuckle emerged.

She snapped out of a momentary mindfulness.

Jason's dancing eyes caught hers. He leaned forward with his gold cross dangling from his neck.

"Ms. Rachel?" He closed his eyes and took a deep breath. "I can't get enough of it, yummy."

"Glad you still enjoy it after all these years."

"Yes, Ma'am." He said, with a salute.

Her eyes swept the room. The first session of a ten-week group journey. For a moment smiles painted on their faces. Maybe Jason's radiant words melted some of the freeze inside as spring's warmth wrestled with winter's cold outside.

A perfect reflection of the human condition. Whether group atmosphere or outside climate, God's in charge, not us.

Four of her long-term clients, strangers to one another, sat in a circle on colorful chairs with unique shapes and buttery surfaces. In the last few minutes, more than one of them glided their hands along the suede covering. A distraction or comfort for inner turmoil as they waited for the fifth member's arrival.

A Beyoncé song screeched from someone's phone. Heads popped up. Shalene bent down, opened her bag, and shut off her ringer.

"Sorry, I thought I had it on silent," she said in a strangled voice.

"No problem, my dear. It happens to everyone." Rachel waved her iPhone, clicking onto silent mode. "See, I forgot too."

Shalene relaxed her restrained expression and rewarded Rachel with a fleeting, one-dimpled, half-smile.

Rachel winked at her and regarded the other participants.

She adored all of them and prepared for the first session with a prayer.

"Please God, you've made me an instrument of hope. Guide me in this group experiment. I can't fail them with this one. They deserve the best."

Five special people. Successful but tortured.

She never forgot their first sessions.

Her gaze returned to Shalene.

An Ethiopian Queen. Silver strands threaded through glossy black hair, dominated by a white widow's peak.

The first time Shalene entered her office, she settled in the chair furthest from hers. With face pointed downward, she studied her ten tapering, bejeweled fingers. "You know. I'm here because my mother insisted."

Rachel nodded. "Not unusual even for adults. Sometimes setting up the initial appointment takes encouragement from a close friend or family member."

"Uh-uh. Well, I love my mother, but on certain things, we don't see eye to eye." Shalene twisted a couple of her rings. "Like me seeing you." Her eyes focused on her hands. "I'm sorry, but, well…"

A fog of hush crept into the room.

Rachel hated protracted silences.

How did others tolerate them?

"Shalene, your comfort and safety remain number one. This decision includes choosing the right therapist or even attending therapy."

Shalene pressed her legs together, grabbed the sides of the chair and stared at Rachel. "Okay, here goes. I'm not too keen on seeing anyone who looks like you."

Rachel raised her eyebrows. "Okay."

Careful, Rachel.

"So, what would work best for you right now?"

"I'll stay for this one meeting, and then, we'll see." Shalene offered a grin with a slight dimple emerging. "But just so you know, I twirl my rings because…" She tapped her stomach. "Inside somersaults."

Rachel smiled at her, which she continued to do every week for three years.

Now her eyes shifted.

Matt, a blue-eyed, massive version of the actor Kit Harington from the TV show Game of Thrones. His eyes, fastened to his phone, didn't flicker when he extended his tall legs, crossing and uncrossing them.

Four years ago, he sauntered into her office, dressed in a black pinstripe suit. His gaze circled the room before they landed on the Peel, a large chair that accommodated his size. He sat, lifting his creased pants, and pitched forward.

"Hi, um, may I call you Rachel or do you prefer Ms. Karem?" he asked, eyes steady on hers.

"Oh, Rachel suits me fine. How about you? Matt or Mr. Ryan?"

"Matt, of course," he said, with a forced laugh.

"Well, Matt, when you're ready, please tell me what brought you here today."

He loosened his tie, took off his jacket, and rolled up his sleeves. "Long day." Matt looked around. His eyes focused on the Renoir print of Dance at Bougival. "Nice office."

"Thank you."

"Are you acquainted with my mother, Sophia Ryan? She's also a therapist."

"I know of her."

"Yeah—and?" he asked, raising his eyebrows.

"And what?"

"Just curious about her reputation."

Rachel blinked. "Well, I've never met her, but from what I've heard, she's fabulous."

"Good. I thought so." He leaned back and reversed his position. "Um, my mother and I have a strained relationship. Long story which I'll explain at some point, depending on how far I go with everything." He paused, twisting his neck. "But, um, our situation connects to a relationship with a colleague of hers."

She waited as Matt's blue eyes searched hers.

"Matt, please tell as much or as little as you want."

Matt frowned and leaned forward. "Well, Rachel, I met a couple of therapists, and… I'll be honest. I'm a bit soured by the experiences." He tilted his head and crossed his legs. "Mind you even though therapists dominate the family." A half smile skidded across his face. "My sister, Desiree, Des, followed my mother into the profession. Even with that, unsure about the whole therapy thing."

"I understand, Matt. So, what would be helpful today?"

"Not sure and not sure how often or long I should attend these sessions, but for now I'll tell you about me."

Except for vacations, over the last five years, he'd never missed a session.

Rachel glanced at Yardley, a third-year law student who stared straight ahead. Red curly hair framed an oval alabaster face. No movements from her except clenching hands and steady blinks from large green eyes.

Two years ago, she wandered into Rachel's office, plopped on the planet, a smaller chair, and folded her arms. The layered clothing couldn't disguise her emaciated body.

Her gaze moved downward.

"Nice meeting you, Yardley."

"You, too," she said in a wispy voice.

"Have you been in therapy before?"

Yardley nodded without giving Rachel eye contact.

"Good experiences?"

Yardley shifted her wrist back and forth.

"I see. Some good, some so-so."

"Yes."

"Well, how about this? You and I evaluate each other, and I'll determine if I can help you or at least try."

Rachel nodded, her eyes soft.

"Never a guarantee. Right?"

"Right."

"And you can see how comfortable you are with me. How's that sound?"

Yardley's lips tilted upwards reaching her eyes. "That works for me."

With two hospitalizations and intensive outpatient in eighteen months, Yardley stayed, sometimes attending twice a week, and agreed to take the next step.

Rachel's eyes found Jason's again.

Four years ago, he entered her office, bigger than Matt. Shaved head, ebony skin, an Olympian God.

His hands smothered hers.

"Thank you so much for seeing me this soon."

"My pleasure, Jason."

"Although no emergency, I confided in my minister, and he pushed me to get the soonest appointment available."

"Based on the message you left on my voicemail, I understand why."

"Glad to sit here. Found God again and prayed for guidance. The minister said you're a God lady. A good thing. At least for me."

"Yes, Jason. Although I serve people with a variety of beliefs, I don't shy away if someone asks about my faith."

With his chin resting in his hand, Jason sighed. "Good. Cause lots to discuss."

"We'll go at your pace. How about that?"

"Terrific plan, Ms. Rachel. Already comfortable here."

"Ms. Rachel, or just Rachel, whatever you prefer."

"Well, if you can tell, I lived in the south, so I continue with the old-fashioned Ma'am and Ms. or Mrs."

"Should I call you Mr. Jason?" Rachel asked, offering an impish smile.

Jason roared. "No, Ma'am."

The beginning of Jason's journey.

Along with the others, she crossed her fingers, hoping this rung would help him leap over the obstacles, holding him back.

A familiar face emerged, silver coils, leaning forward. "And you? What about you?"

Rachel stiffened. Not about me right now. Doesn't matter anyway. No family since Sam. Can't control alienation. Tried. So work, besties, and pooches. Nothing else. Not so bad if I don't fail here.

She tried brushing the image aside, but it wouldn't budge.

Okay. Not so bad for now. Enough for you, Alexandra?

The image lifted her eyebrows.

No, I won't concede about the group. Not successful, my fault.

The coiled woman tilted her head and retreated.

We'll talk about it tomorrow.

Rachel glanced at the empty chair, one of the largest and the only one in a rose-peach shade. The Peel stood in regal display and awaited the last occupant's arrival. A perfect seat for Sapphire.

Not like her to not text or call.

Rachel rubbed her palms together and glanced out the window. An inky sky speckled with snowflakes, but no sign of Sapphire. She swallowed and considered the possibility of her bailing. Not her style, but even though Sapphire practiced as a therapist, you never know.

What therapist didn't have issues?

Rachel's stomach knotted even tighter. Seven minutes passed. Her iPhone, still in silent mode, displayed no text. A few more minutes.

She'd figure it out, and if she told her friends...

"Happens all the time, Rach."

But Sapphire promised.

"Just once," Rachel suggested as she did with the others. Although Sapphire grimaced the most, she said, "Okay, Rachel. Once and maybe more if you think it will help me share with others."

Screeching tires.

Rachel watched the frost-bitten Lexus slide into the parking lot. A car door slammed. Sapphire arrived.

Rachel exhaled like a deflating balloon.

The others looked toward the white, three-panel door, eyes darting back and forth.

Footsteps clicked along the entryway. With a slow movement of the knob, the door creaked, and a petite golden creature tip-toed into the office. Sapphire's glorious mane hung over half her face, covering one sparkling blue eye, unable to obscure her exotic appearance.

She dashed for the Peel, with her unique fragrance trailing, and peeked at Rachel, removing her pink, wool coat with careful precision. In a wispy voice, she said, "Sorry."

Rachel waved. "You're here." She embraced her with a smile.

Sapphire skimmed the other faces. "I didn't give myself enough time. My car didn't defrost fast enough, and the snow caused delays."

Except for Jason mouthing, "No problem," the others stopped for an instant and brought their eyes back to Rachel.

Rachel's smile extended to the entire group.

"Let's get started… Oh, first a reminder of the agreement you made about group confidentiality."

Three people yawned.

"Questions?"

Everyone shook their heads.

Rachel cleared her throat. "Who would like to begin?"

Ten eyes grasped hers, not looking anywhere else. An eerie stillness slithered into the room until a tapping from Sapphire's foot invaded the discomfort. Rachel glanced at her. Sapphire's hair disguised most of her downcast face, and her arms hugged her body.

"Hey, Rachel, maybe you can help us." Jason let out a timid chuckle, beads of sweat on his head. "Kind of tough getting started because we don't know each other or, I'll speak for me, what to say."

"I agree," Yardley mumbled.

"Yes, of course." Rachel swallowed. She observed the room and noticed the fringed lamps shining on their faces, impassive, wrinkled foreheads, and glares. Her stomach twisted.

Making them anxious in the first few minutes?

"You know me, Rachel Karem, and I've shared with each of you why I formed this group." No one changed their expressions.

"I'm situated outside of Boston and created this group, because, well…" she stumbled.

Repeating yourself?

"I'll say it again. I think group therapy might help you become more…" Rachel paused. "Um, visible."

Hmmm, I never mentioned that to them.

She inhaled a long breath. "So, let's try again. Please introduce yourselves, and what you hope to accomplish as a member of the group."

Tap, tap, tap.

Matt

Sea foam green. The palette of Rachel's interior created ocean breezes and rolling waves. Reminded him of Aruba and Bermuda. His eyes focused on the walls, waiting for someone to break the sullen mood suffocating the room.

Glad Rachel said something, but not a great start.

Jeez. What did she think? Everyone would hold hands and sing Kumbaya?

Nah.

She knew better. Looks like she might have jitters herself. She once mentioned she hadn't run a group in a long time.

Wow, if she shared a tidbit. Even after a simple revelation like that, he'd sit up straight, waiting for more.

And tonight? If these others think she would, hate to disappoint. Not gonna happen.

Four years together, and not much came out about her personal life, even thoughts about anything other than its relationship to therapy. Yeah, here and there, she'd offer a crumb or two.

Once in a discussion about a date, she spilled something.

"Lisa introduced me to a Middle Eastern restaurant. Believe it or not, other than hummus, I never experienced the different types of food."

"Oh?" Rachel's tone changed. "What did you eat?"

"Something called Kibbee, made with ground lamb, and let me tell you, Rachel, if you…"

"Raw or Cooked?"

"What?" Matt asked. "Cooked of course, why?"

Rachel's eyes crinkled with a smile. "Well, I'm Jordanian, and I ate that food growing up."

"Raw meat?" Matt asked.

"Yes," she said with a scant faraway look.

A moment later, she sat erect. "Anyway, tell me about the date."

And that ended that.

Now his nostrils couldn't avoid the sultry cologne coming from the stunner, Sapphire, carved in his peripheral vision.

Some kind of flowery scent? With vanilla?

Whatever. Try and ignore her.

Her stupid tapping?

Matt shifted his gaze down, observing jeans, sneakers, clogs, and one pair of pink suede, platform boots.

Tapping.

Otherwise, silence swallowed the room, like a teal-colored tidal wave. So much for Rachel's breezy wall color.

He could… Nope. Not going first. Would be easy for him. But tough. Volunteered too many times. Let someone else start.

Come on, Rachel.

He rubbed his eyes and peeked at her. Clasped hands, downward gaze also.

Thought you didn't like long silences, one of the other things you dripped out a while back. And talk about a short introduction. Couldn't you at least tell us a family estrangement existed in your background? You hinted that when I told you about Sophia.

A different approach with groups? Shared this vague piece of information with the others in their sessions?

Who knows?

Who cares?

She listened better than most and talked, when necessary, communicating with her hands.

The first time he walked into her office, he braced himself. With two strikes, would it be an out?

He found her through a friend. Even though Mom and Des practiced, didn't want them to know about his therapy. So, winged it again.

The characters he met earlier? Couldn't remember their names, but the experiences?

How could he forget.

A bearded man in his fifties, long braid, dressed in scrubs shook his hand, welcomed him into a small office, cluttered with papers and books on his desk. The saving grace? Lots of light from an enormous window.

The therapist shared his name, but nothing more until Matt said something.

In the first session, the man stared at him, tapping his foot.

"Not sure where to start," Matt said.

"Where would you like to start?" The man asked.

Matt shrugged, experiencing a subtle tightness in his chest.

The man continued staring and bobbing his head like a bobble head.

"Well, how long have you practiced?" Matt already knew but wanted something beyond stares and bobs.

"What do you imagine?"

For the next forty-five minutes, a ping-pong game unfolded. In between the torturous stillness, Matt asked something and got the same response. At the end, he made another appointment.

Give the guy a chance.

The second session?

Worse.

The man's air conditioning broke. Sauna, no. Steam room, yes. Matt's face dripped like a leaky faucet.

"Can you tell me anything besides throwing questions back at me."

The man nodded. "I'm studying at the Wooster Institute of Psychoanalysis." He removed his socks and shoes. "And to me, a comfortable and holding environment helps people heal."

Matt peeked at the man's feet and dripped more.

"What are your thoughts, Matt?"

"About what?"

"About my revelation."

Matt glanced at his IWatch and sprang up like a high jumper.

"Sorry, I just received a notification for an emergency meeting at work. Gotta run. I'll consider everything you shared. Thank you for your time."

Maybe someone younger and female might provide different results.

An initial evaluation with a woman in her early thirties proved more uncomfortable. She spoke more than a few words. Yay. Good sign. But after the first few minutes, she kept talking, telling him she hailed from California and believed in full transparency.

"Matt, I want total first-name basis and ask me anything. Curious about my personal and professional life, I'm an open book."

Matt tilted his head. "Not sure what else I need. You told me about your background and the reason you chose the field, so I think I'm good for now."

She blushed and twirled her hair. "What questions might you have about the packages I offer?"

"Packages?"

"Of course, didn't you study my website?"

"No. It said you're a licensed therapist, so I contacted you."

"My goodness, you missed a lot of information. I provide so much more than individual psychotherapy." She leaned close and twisted her hair more. "I'm also a dating coach, and I offer a Silver, Gold, and Platinum bundle."

"Thanks. I'll keep that in mind."

She pulled out her smartphone and lifted her eyes. "What's your phone number again?"

Matt texted it to her.

"Good. Just received it," and her thumbs pressed away.

His watch pinged.

"There. You'll love the other services. Just click the link, and I'll review them with you right now."

Okay, everything comes in threes, so one more time.

The first session with Rachel? Wary at first, but once he settled into her rhythm, he found a psychotherapy home. Sophia in looks and presentation.

No airs. Eyes changing, soft or dark, depending on the subject.

For him, most important? Attentive and engaging. Yeah, he imagined her as a second Sophia. Isn't there a theory regarding therapists, and mothers? He snickered for a moment and lifted his eyes.

Everyone kept their eyes down. He peered at Rachel. Pretty good for a woman of her age. Petite, dark bouncy curls, smoky eyes, and olive skin. Italian or Jewish? Nope, Jordanian.

Whatever.

Never focused on her appearance. That's all he needed, developing feelings for a therapist. Not going there. Never will.

A booming voice cracked the silence.

"Well, I'll start. I'm Jason Robinson. I'm twenty-eight and work as an investigative freelance reporter." Jason paused. "I'm here, well, I guess because I need a push to go forward with my life."

Man, what a big dude—bigger than him. Herculean but seemed cool like a gentle giant.

"I'm Shalene Marcus and..." she inhaled and fiddled with her rings. "I, um, went through a traumatic experience that made me..." she nodded, staring at her thumb as she twisted the ring on it. "Distrustful." She peered at Rachel. "More later except I'm twenty-seven and work in the digital marketing arena."

Pretty but tight expression. Nerves?

A swan popped into his head, as the redhead began. So willowy, she might blow over. He leaned forward, and almost fell over deciphering her muffled introduction.

"I'm Yardley Stein, twenty-seven, third-year law student, and I've, ah, if you can't tell, struggled with eating because of some things that happened, and," she blinked, "I hope I can talk more-depth." Her gaze remained remote.

Nerves for her, too. Yeah, you can't miss the eating disorder, but please speak up.

"I'm…" Matt's voice was drowned out by another.

"Sapphire Garcia, here."

Okay, go ahead.

He turned to scintillating eyes staring into the distance. "I joined, well…" She combed her fingers through her hair. "Cause I'm almost thirty, a therapist, and need to get my stuff together." She sighed. "Major, major trust issues." She smiled at Rachel.

No details came from the others, which worked fine for him. No plans to discuss the craziness of his relationship with Juliette or even Nic until he determined he could trust this crew.

Matt sat with his fingers interlocked in front of his legs. He looked around before he said. "My turn?"

"Nervous?" the stunner asked.

Matt smirked at her and shifted his eyes to Rachel. "A bit. Not used to sharing with strangers." He cracked his neck and took a breath.

"Matt Ryan here. A few months past thirty." He nodded to Sapphire. "I work in finance, and why am I involved in this group?" His eyes found Rachel's. "Rachel thought I'd be a good fit."

Everyone chuckled.

"But in all seriousness," he said, "I've experienced some betrayals."

He gulped. "I guess I, too, need to work things out." He paused and coughed. "For starters, my parents divorced, a while ago. Now, I'm closer to my father because of bumps in the road with my mother." Matt slouched back and glanced at a few members. "Love my mother, but things happened causing some distrust."

Matt hesitated and gazed out to the middle.

"I'm a twin. My sister, and my mother, like Rachel, are clinical social workers."

He paused and extended his legs out.

"Although I haven't seen a shrink, therapists have been part of my world since childhood, and I have a profound respect for the healing profession. Plus," Matt adjusted his posture, smiled, and raised his right finger. "I'm no therapist, but I try to contribute in my way."

He grinned. "That's all for the moment. Oh, except. Glad I'm here. Kind of."

Everyone laughed, nodding.

"You said the most," the Stunner said.

Matt rubbed the top of his legs. "Yeah, maybe because of the therapists in my life."

He noticed Jason cocking his head.

"Hey brother, anyone ever tell you that you look like the guy from *Game of Thrones*? What's his name?" Jason tapped his fist on his chin a few times.

"Jon Snow." Sapphire said, gaped at Matt, and sipped water.

"That's right."

"All the time." Matt's eyebrows lifted. He nodded, and his eyes swept the room.

A quick smatter of giggles fading into the walls.

Quietness settled in the room.

Here we go again. Feet shuffled. Tapping resumed.

A sudden bark came from the stunner. "Are we going to sit here, or are you going to give us guidance," she asked, "again?"

Matt peered at her. A little rough.

Rachel smiled and appeared unruffled.

"Sure. We can discuss something light or spend the remaining time exchanging more. What are your thoughts?"

Matt raised his hand. "Since I shared last and found the introduction not so bad," he looked around, "I'd be happy to talk more, unless someone else prefers another round."

Everyone shook their heads.

He fidgeted again and leaned forward. "As I mentioned, trust is a biggie, and I'd guess the same for you."

His eyes circled the room. Smiles submerged with nods.

"I don't trust anyone," Matt said and sat back.

Yardley raised her hand. "Also, forgiving oneself." She peered around the room and shrank into her seat.

A little louder for her. Good.

Rachel eyed the clock on a nearby end table. "We've about twenty minutes left. Are you prepared to start, my friend?

Matt nodded. "Yeah, I think so."

"How about first disclosing a little more about why you don't trust anyone?"

His cheeks became hot like someone lighting a match on each side. He said, "Whoa, let me wallow in shallow water before diving into the deep end."

"Okay, begin your story wherever you want."

Matt bent forward and clasped his hands. "I don't want anyone to think I'm a narcissist, but I've been told enough about my looks."

A snort.

Silence plowed into the room.

He looked around. Sapphire scrutinized him with arms folded.

The vibration became louder.

Matt tightened his lips and locked his inner fangs. He turned in slow motion toward her. "No way do I use them or take them for granted."

Sapphire lips curled up, and she turned her head.

Not getting involved in her bull. He pivoted toward the others and began his story.

"My last year in high school, it began. A transformation. I still couldn't see the big deal, but according to the ladies in school, I went from a skinny geek into…" He shook his head. "I don't know, whatever. I started lifting weights the summer before senior year, got contacts, and joined the rowing team." He put his head down for a moment. "None of these issues matter except lots of attention. Girls walked by and purred, 'Hey Jon Snow.' *Game of Thrones* started that year so, yeah, been told for a long time."

He looked up. Everyone's eyes on him. He wouldn't give the Stunner eye contact. So glad she didn't sit across from him.

"In senior year, an aggressive cheerleader grabbed my arm at the end of one of our rowing competitions. She licked her lips and took me into the car, and, well, I'll leave it at that. First time, if you know what I mean."

He looked at Jason who nodded with hands clasped over his mouth.

Easier than looking at the women.

"Now I tell you this because I trusted women. Cherished them, drilled into me by Mom and Des." His twin. His lips kicked up. "My sister got in my face. 'Don't you dare, Matt Ryan.' Not good for you or the girl so." He grinned. "I listened, and hookups never became my thing. Even in college, a gorgeous teaching assistant, oh man, she brushed up against me. Puckered her lips, but…"

"You could've pressed harassment charges."

Matt looked towards Yardley. Glad she spoke loud enough.

"I know, but I didn't want trouble. I figured between avoiding and ignoring her she'd leave me alone, and she did."

"Good," Yardley said.

"Yeah, so most of college, I rowed and focused on my studies. Math major."

"Hey brother, math? Good choice because it all comes down to the math. Right? From music and the rest of God's universe." Jason grinned. "Not to interrupt."

"No problem, and you're right about math." Matt chuckled.

"Yeah, well I'm a God man, and He's the All, man, a mathematical genius."

Wow, cool guy. First impressions correct about him. Didn't Gladwell talk about that in his book, *Blink*?

"Yeah, I never considered math in those terms. Good point."

"Please share more, brother."

"So, I had a couple of relationships, one somewhat intense, but nothing like what happened…during my second year in grad school."

Matt looked at Rachel. She lifted her eyebrows.

"Later for that one, but a bit more which brought me there." He leaned forward, lacing his fingers. "Anyway, my mother hosted one of her Salon events. Long story, but she hung out with a crowd following the divorce and claimed the Salon invited people from a variety of wellness disciplines. What did they discuss? Who knows? Mom claimed," he used air quotes, "*diverse topics* like long ago when eminent people gathered at the home of women in high society."

"Sounds like you don't believe her."

Matt shifted his gaze to Shalene, fixated on her rings.

Wow, a first for her. Quite direct.

"I hate to doubt my mother, but based on what happened you'd understand."

Matt paused. His eyes focused on Rachel again. "Well, that wraps things up for now. Just coming attractions."

"Thank you, Matt, for leading the way." Rachel said. "You okay?"

Matt nodded with a smile and thumbs up.

"Wonderful." She beamed and shifted her gaze to the others. "Glad you showed up and look forward to seeing all of you next week."

Matt stood first. No way am I walking near that spitfire. I'm out of here.

He saluted everyone except Sapphire. "Nice meeting you. See ya."

The Stunner's voice trailed behind. "Until next time."

Chapter Two

Rachel shut the door and rested against it. She rubbed her eyes. Please come back.

Fatigue spread its tentacles, and her body slid down along the door. Not a surprise with a first and intense session.

Better get going. She pushed up, plodded toward the coat rack, and examined her alpaca sweater jacket and cloche hat. She stroked the silky wool on her outer covering. Glad I prepared for one of winter's surprise showings, a glittery splash. Too much snow this year. Should be over, but like life, you never know.

Before shutting off her lamps, she sat for a moment and reflected on the first session. Matt left in a rush. Can you blame him? Sapphire jumped on him like a cat clawing an enemy's face.

That Sapphire. She assumed every good-looking guy was a bad boy, but she pegged Matt wrong. Rachel knew Matt well. He'd rebuff Sapphire's jabs like someone brushing off a speck of dust.

Rachel wagged her head. She loved Sapphire, but her sharp edges sliced into anyone perceived as threatening. With her history, made sense.

When Sapphire complained about not making enough progress, Rachel questioned if she could do more for her.

"No. You're not responsible." She shook her head. "It's up to me. Besides," she said with sparkling eyes, "until I resolve my issues, we'll remain together."

When Rachel first suggested the group, Sapphire balked, but Rachel's promise about keeping it safe, helped her come around.

"I know, Rach. The next step, sharing with others, but still lots of…you know." Sapphire punched the center of her chest.

"My dear Sapphire, I understand. No guarantees, but first, this crowd won't judge you. Take my word for it. Second, I believe this experience might put much of this to rest."

Sapphire got up and hugged her. "Trust you with my life, Rach."

Does she still? Could have done a better job navigating tonight. Will try harder next time. If they return? Oh my God, I hope so.

And using the word visible? Where did that come from? Did she ever say that to any of them?

Uh-uh, and not a coincidence.

Invisible remained a theme in her own therapy.

Let me sit longer. Eyelids falling.

Leah. Born in the womb together. Different coloring. Different temperaments. Leah lighter with straight hair, but same eyes, topaz color. Lashes fanning to their brows. Sisters, in flesh, no doubt. But soul sisters? No. Rachel once heard her father, Eddie, complain to their mother, Myriam, about Leah's behavior. His pacing, back, and forth.

"What did we do wrong?" he asked her.

Myriam said something and sniffled.

"I know. I know," Eddie said, moving closer to his wife.

Rachel scurried away. Their conversation embedded in her mind.

Leah often screamed at Rachel. "They favor you."

Their seventeenth birthday. Consequential.

Tabouli, hummus, seasoned rice. Papa rushed from the patio and placed grilled lamb kebobs and charred vegetables on the antique dining table.

Umm. Her mouth watered.

"Okay, Papa, you say grace and serve the food, and I'll share our special story." Myriam winked.

"Sure, I do all the work." Eddie grinned.

Myriam threw him a kiss.

"I love that story, Mama," Rachel said.

"I'm sick of hearing it," Leah scowled.

"Well, I'm not sick of telling it." Myriam's tone became solemn. "Time for grace." She put her hand out. Eddie and Leah joined. Rachel squeezed her mother's and did the same with her father's bigger, callused one.

Myriam nodded to Eddie.

"Bless us, our beloved Creator, from your splendid home. Not only for this food but for your gifts of love, family, safety, and health. Myriam and I cannot thank you enough for showering us with our jewels, Rachel and Leah. Amen."

"Amen," Rachel, Leah, and Myriam said in unison.

Myriam stood, took everyone's plate, and served the skewers of kebobs, rice, and tabouli. She wiggled her eyebrows at Rachel and Leah. "Papa grilled just right. Medium rare."

"Eat while it's warm," Eddie said and chomped on a piece of lamb. "Myriam, whenever you're ready for the story."

"How come you said Rachel's name first, Papa?"

Her mother frowned while she spooned the last of the rice.

Her father's eyes stayed on his food, and he sliced another piece of lamb, scraping the plate.

He clasped his hands together and stared at his dish. "Leah, my jewel, I didn't notice."

"Please, Leah. Not tonight." Myriam's topaz eyes darkened.

Leah slammed back into her chair and plunged her fork into a kebob.

Eddie waved his hand forward. "Mama, we're waiting."

Myriam moved her plate and leaned forward with laced hands.

"After Papa and I married, we wanted a family, and within a short time, I became pregnant. And soon, better news, the doctor informed us more than one."

Myriam beamed, and Rachel clapped. "So cool Mama. Tell the rest. The best part."

"Me and Papa heard both heartbeats. Fast but distinct and," Myriam's eyes locked on Eddie's, "Papa teared up, grabbed the doctor, and smacked a kiss on his cheek, and said—you finish Eddie."

Her father wiped his eyes. "See. I still get choked up." He took his napkin, blew his nose, and turned to his daughters. "So, I said, *Thank God and Thank you.* I don't think he knew what to do." Eddie banged on the table and roared. Rachel took his arm, laughing so hard, her belly ached.

Now Rachel blinked and yawned. A couple more minutes.

She shut her eyes. The scene changed.

The next day, Rachel walked by her sister's room and tugged on her new sweater.

"Hey."

Rachel turned around. "What?"

"When did you get that?"

"I don't remember."

Leah's eyes closed midway, walked toward her sister, and jabbed her finger into Rachel's chest. "Did Mama buy an extra present for you?"

"What? Noooo."

"I don't believe you. Cause she always does more for you!" said Leah, trembling.

Rachel pursed her lips and kept walking. Footsteps stomped behind her.

Bam.

Rachel tripped and fell. "What are you doing, Leah?"

She stood up, and Leah slapped Rachel's face, catching a section of her nose.

"Ow!" Blood splattered over her hands and clothes.

"What a baby! I didn't hit you hard. Who knew you'd bleed so easily?"

Rachel grabbed tissues from a box nearby. "You're a witch, an ugly, ugly witch! Do you hear me?" She packed the tissues under her nose. "I'm sick of your jealousy."

Leah dropped her hands and slouched against the wall.

Rachel glared at her and snatched more tissues.

She noticed Leah slumped over, tears rolling down her face, and heaving.

"I can't believe you called me ugly," Leah said.

"What'd you expect? Look at what you did?" Rachel dabbed her sweater with one hand and held tissues beneath her nostrils with the other.

"You called me u-u-u-gly," Leah stuttered and appeared dazed.

Rachel wiped her nose. "My God, you sound like *I'm* the one who hit *you*."

"You called me u-u-u-gly."

"Oh, shut up. Everyone says things like that."

"No, no, you called me u-u-u-gly." Leah blinked and stared at Rachel. "I'll never forgive you for this." She staggered toward her bedroom and closed the door, whimpering.

Rachel's eyes fluttered, and her coat dropped to the floor. She shook her head. Time to go home. She reached for her coat, stood, and put her hat over her fluffy curls. She trudged toward one of her Tiffany lamps and shut off the light. Before moving to the other, she scrutinized the gooseneck floor lamps. Long, elegant bases, crowned with glorious, sea-blue, stained-glass shades. Ah, the view you have of each member. If only you could talk, what would be your observations?

And how about toward me?

What words would drop?

Let me guess. Lady, you need to keep working on your issues. You're helping these young people escape the confines, holding them back, but how long will you stay behind your own prison walls?

Rachel headed into the night. Snow dotted the trees and branches. A sparkling, but fleeting exhibit. Gone tomorrow. And speaking of tomorrow, thank God, she'd continue extricating herself from the pull of the muddied past.

Rachel and Alexandra–March 25th

With mascara applied to lush lashes, Rachel studied her reflection. Unusual, enormous eyes dominated her round face and shifted attention away from her bumpy, Middle Eastern nose. Sam loved her nose and used to kiss the tip. "Perfecto."

Rachel's eyes brimmed as she summoned the image from long ago.

Sam.

Gone five years. Arms wrapped around her. He offered comfort when she became the target of Leah's icy behavior. His eyes clouded anytime she said, "Leah's maltreatment. Exclusive for me."

The opening of her mind's vault last night prevented Rachel from shutting the door. For the rest of the evening, her twin's matching topaz eyes trickled into her thoughts and dreams.

Stop. Finish getting ready for Alexandra.

Wear something other than jeans, and watch what happens, Lady Therapist.

She colored her lips with glossy plum lipstick, fluffed her loose coils, damp from a quick shower, and looked in the mirror again.

With her hands on her hips, Rachel glanced at her toweled image.

Not bad for fifty-five. She studied the wrinkles in her muscular but older arms and shook her head.

So, what? Who else will see them except the pooches?

She trudged over to the opened, louvered closet doors and glided her fingers across flowing silk and cotton dresses. Rachel chose two and arranged them on her wrought-iron framed bed.

Which one? She pointed her finger at both.

With clients, Rachel put herself together and donned chic business attire, even in virtual sessions. "Yes, I dress the same way when we meet in the flesh," she said to each client who struggled. "Rise, take a shower, and get out of your pajamas or sweats. You'll feel better." She nodded her head up and down. "Well, at least in that area, I practice what I preach."

The aqua dress shouted, "Wear me!"

Finishing touches? Large hoops dangling between her curls.

Ready. She sauntered out to her living room, which revealed a whimsical and daring side to her. Since losing Sam, she decorated with more colors, bolder ones.

Why not?

Rachel imagined him, laughing as he rolled his eyes saying, "That's ma wife."

The camelback, rose-colored couch, splayed with leopard-print pillows offset by striped vintage chairs, invited a grin from her. Yup. Sam would get a kick out of this.

She adjusted her glass coffee table as she slogged barefoot on her lush oriental rug.

Zsa Zsa and Gabor, her white toy poodles, pitter-pattered right behind her. Rachel plopped on the chair sitting in front of the antique desk. Her laptop remained open, anticipating her to power up. She pressed the button, and the Zoom invite appeared from Alexandra. Her seasoned therapist no longer saw people live, so virtual therapy did the trick.

Two additional minutes. Time for the vault door to fling open. She blinked.

Swish, swish. The windshield wipers screeched across the front window. The rain pounded. Rachel couldn't tell what blinded her more, the torrential waterworks outside or the flood of tears streaming down her face. Her father? Gone. Just like that?

Rachel gripped the steering wheel, sped down the Mass Turnpike, and crisscrossed along the flooded highway toward the medical center. Her car screeched in front of the valet station, and she threw her keys at the attendant, rushing into the hospital.

She ran down the corridor, pushing through medical personnel dressed in colorful scrubs, stomping around in their clogs, waving their arms, pointing in different directions. Amidst the beeping machines and voices from beyond the curtains. Rachel tracked down her mother's location and took the elevator to the Intensive Care Unit. An exhausted-looking, overweight, middle-aged woman, sitting at the nurse's station pointed where her mother arrived from surgery. Rachel dashed, entered the room, and found Leah with clenched hands and tears trickling down her face. She nodded to Rachel.

"What did the doctors say?" Rachel asked.

Leah grimaced, and without looking at Rachel, she trembled. "Not good."

"What happened?"

"Not sure. But on the way home from the movies, they hit a tree."

"What?"

"Mama mentioned heart, heart, so they think Papa suffered a heart attack."

Leah's eyes locked on her mother.

Rachel watched her mother breathe before glancing at her sister, whose eyes didn't waver from their mother. The *lub-dub* from the heart monitor dominated the room.

Rachel asked Leah about her life and her son, and *good*, or *fine*, bounced back. She gave up and slept until her sister rose and mumbled about checking on her husband and son.

A moment later, Myriam's eyes opened. Rachel grabbed her mother's smooth olive hand and caressed the long, elegant fingers. She brought them to her lips and pressed hard on her mother's skin, breathing in the familiar musky scent.

Myriam shuddered, and the monitors started flashing. Medical professionals hurried into the room, shouted, and pushed Rachel out the door. More yelling.

Her insides cracked. To ward off crumbling, she paced back and forth. Hands clasped behind her.

Stay positive. Remember what you tell your clients.

Rachel continued walking when she noticed Leah rushing toward her.

"What happened?"

Rachel sat on a bench and slumped. "I held her hand, and I think," she said with a sob, "she died. They're trying to bring her back."

Leah approached the door and almost collided with the doctor emerging from the room. With downcast eyes, he said, "I'm so sorry. We did everything." He wagged his head before murmuring about what happened.

Rachel's words were lodged in her throat. She sought her sister's eyes, but Leah's stunned expression remained unreachable to her.

"They were only fifty-two." Rachel said.

Leah nodded, not giving Rachel eye contact.

For a moment, Rachel lowered her head, with a boulder shattering her heart.

"You got to see Mama last?"

Rachel looked up, unable to see through the pool of water marring her vision. "What?"

"You heard me!"

"I'm shocked you're doing this. Our parents just died, and you're…" Rachel shook her head in disbelief.

"I'm leaving," Leah said in a strangled voice. "Call me tomorrow," she departed wailing and stomping out of the ICU.

Rachel sat, hung her head, and sobbed. When a nurse approached her and asked if she needed anything, she thanked her and said no.

After a few minutes, she stood up, grabbed her jacket, and exited the hospital. While waiting for her car, she wiped her tears and said out loud. "Thirty years old and alone now."

Rachel gripped the desk and returned to the present. She scrunched her eyes and glanced to the side of her computer where a small mirror lay face down. She picked it up and stared at her watery reflection.

No more.

She jerked her head and shoved the memory back inside, wiping her eyes to block the tears. Save this pain for Alexandra, will you.

She took a breath. Get ready for showtime.

"Alexandra is a godsend," she said and wiggled her eyes at her dogs. "You two prepared for a therapy session?"

Zsa Zsa and Gabor cocked their heads.

With a chuckle, she clicked the link, and Alexandra's face appeared on the screen.

Rachel smiled at her Octogenarian therapist, who appeared ageless. Her beautiful silver coils were arranged in a loose bun with wisps framing her elegant olive-skinned face. Her chocolate eyes, encompassed by elegant, curved brows, sparkled as she peered at Rachel.

"Hello, Rachel."

"Glad I'm here!"

"Well, I always look forward to our meetings, and, of course, I'm pleased your loyal followers are joining us."

Rachel stole a glance at her beloved dogs. "Yes, I believe a treat for them as well."

"How are you?"

"Well, shaky."

"How so?"

"Things got stirred up last night, and guess who showed up?"

"Ah. Tell me more."

"Last night, my group came together for the introductory session."

"How did things turn out?"

"I'm not sure."

Alexandra inclined her head.

"You know me. Never good enough," Rachel said. "I think I could've done a better job."

Alexandra moved her head side to side. "Rachel, after being with you for all this time, I don't doubt you did the best you could."

"Well," Rachel said, "my client, Sapphire. I've mentioned her, the one with the most glorious eyes."

Alexandra nodded.

"She got sarcastic with Matt, and I should've said something more supportive."

Alexandra lifted her eyes. "Sometimes saying less is best. Besides, they trust you, which is why they came."

"Yeah, the session raised the old issues with Leah. I don't have to explain to you, but I will. Could I have done something different?" Rachel dipped her head, with her topaz eyes watering.

Alexandra leaned closer. "Rachel, we've examined this over and over, and you've done everything."

Rachel stared back and swallowed. "I understand, but sometimes certain memories come back. Last night's session beckoned them."

Alexandra arched her eyebrows, nodded, and more strands slipped from her bun.

"I thought about the incident after our seventeenth birthday." Rachel's elbows on her desk, chin in her hands. "Things got worse as you know. We saw each other less even though I commuted to college. She worked eighty hours a week and climbed the corporate ladder. Even after eloping with wealthy but wimpy Jonathan, money, professional success, and a beautiful baby boy?" She scowled. "Not enough for her."

"Rachel, you know this, but it bears repeating. For some, no matter how much someone acquires, it's never enough. They remain insatiable. Leah viewed you as the favorite child, and she never worked it through."

Rachel's eyes pooled again. "When I went to social work school and found you, she snickered at me in a rare phone call. I suggested everyone could benefit from therapy including her, and she said, 'Oh Rachel, now you think you're Mrs. Sigmund Freud. Mind your own business,' and hung up on me."

"Rachel, without sounding condescending, no matter how much therapy has become mainstream over the last few decades, some people still view it as a stigma."

Rachel laced her hands together. "I know, and even though she suffered from postpartum depression, she refused, claiming her situation as a sign for one child only."

"My dear, listen to your words."

Rachel stared at Alexandra. "But I think back to when I grabbed my mother's hand in the hospital room. Should I have called Leah?"

"What if your mother passed while you looked for Leah?" Alexandra leaned closer to her screen. "Would you've wanted to miss that special, last moment with her?"

Rachel blinked, moving her head back and forth.

"Would Leah have thought of you if the opposite happened?"

"No." Tears cascading down her face.

Alexandra waved a tissue at her.

Rachel laughed, taking one herself and dabbing her eyes. "Thank you! This helps."

"Of course, and Rachel, how fortunate for your clients to have such a remarkable therapist."

Rachel beamed. "Oh, my goodness, you made my morning, Alexandra. Like I say over and over, I wouldn't be the person I am without you."

Alexandra shook her head. "I'm uncertain about that."

Rachel paused. "Okay, a few other things." Rachel described the last week in greater detail. Just prior to the session concluding, Alexandra's raised her eyebrows again. "Any more thoughts about our other discussion?"

Rachel tilted her head. "Not sure I'm ready."

"Do you mind me asking?"

"No, keep the question coming. Someday, I might surprise you.

At the end of the session, Rachel powered down her computer and dwelled on Alexandra's ultimate question. Whenever she considered the possibility, a familiar splinter surfaced, puncturing her heart.

Not yet.

She turned around, catching her dogs looking at her. "Okay, you two."

She went over, holding each of them, petting their white curls, warm bellies, and planting a red kiss on their heads. "For now, you're it!"

Chapter Three

Matt—March 26th

The intense, rich aroma of dry-aged steak wafted around Matt as he sipped on his San Pellegrino at one of the premier steakhouses in the Boston area. His stomach gurgled, *Feed me,* but being disciplined, he'd wait for his date.

Hold tight, bud. An in-bone, New York strip coming your way. Your tastebuds will be satisfied soon enough.

The world-class franchise never disappointed Matt with its elegant ambience, stellar service, and delectable steaks.

Buzzing, clatter of dishes, and footsteps passed by him. Matt's eyes circled the room. All kinds of couples and families immersed in each other and their food.

A couple of women strolled by and smiled with that knowing look. One beauty turned around and rolled her tongue in her cheek as she mauled him with her eyes.

Matt nodded and shifted his gaze.

Within a few seconds, he glanced back and saw her seated across from a male companion. Eyes grabbed Matt's for another moment.

Not my thing.

He brushed away a piece of lint from his navy jacket, and his gaze moved down to his crisp white shirt and pressed jeans.

Yup. Casual, chic, and impeccable. His sister's words.

Whatever. Matt smirked when he thought of his twin.

He glanced at his watch.

The name of the game for him? Early.

Matt didn't apply the same standards to others but expected their arrival within five or ten minutes of the agreed time. A watchful server approached him, in his crisp uniform of black trousers, white shirt, and black bow tie.

"Sir, can I offer you anything at the moment?"

"Thank you, but I'll wait a little longer."

He drank his sparkling water, and his mind wandered.

The group.

I hope Rachel can pull this off because I'm not convinced.

That Sapphire, exotic, but so what? Talk about nerve.

Don't worry honey. What's that saying about beauty?

The host led a young woman to his table. Matt stood up and greeted her.

The tall, slender woman, dressed in a tight, sleeveless black dress, didn't disappoint in looks. Long platinum hair, big chocolate eyes, and a toothy smile.

"Well, uh, Jenna, or Jena," Matt said and offered his hand. "Nice to meet you!"

"Gina spelled Jena," she said with a giggle and sat down, "Everyone gets confused."

Jena batted her eyelashes. "I'm so glad to meet you! Your sister wanted this so bad to happen."

"Yeah, I know."

The server appeared.

"Um, Jena, what would you care to drink?"

"How about a pomegranate Cosmo with a lime twist?"

The server bowed and left.

Jena, twenty-eight, worked in advertising. She'd been an acquaintance of Desiree, his sister, and begged Des several times for an introduction to her brother, Desiree pleaded with Matt. "Puleeze. Once."

Des promised her brother that Jena could be fun and thoughtful, but not vacuous, which Matt avoided at all costs.

After a couple of nudges, he called Jena.

"So, Jena, what do you do for fun?"

Four martinis later, in between servings of calamari, hearts of palm salad, strip steak, and mashed potatoes, Jena babbled about her exercise routine, rock-climbing, work drama, heartbreaks, and longing for a successful husband and a family.

Jena batted her eyelashes in between bites and gulps.

Botox, artificial lashes, tattooed eyebrows, and round, high, breasts—implants, he guessed—soon became obvious as she slurred her speech.

He didn't care about beauty enhancements since he knew women struggled in a world of internet, cosmetic-induced treatments, but from head to toe before thirty?

Out of nowhere, an image of a face with crystal blue eyes appeared. Matt's eyes widened, and he bent closer.

Focus on Jenny. Wait a minute—*Jena.*

When the server cleared the table, Matt suggested coffee.

"Oh, Matt, how 'bout ma place," Jena said, "Ware I got café, tea, a Moi." She howled. Matt noticed a few diners glance at them.

Jena clapped her hand over her mouth, dropped her stained napkin, and as she grabbed it, she tumbled, rescued by a watchful server.

"Sorrrrwe."

With glassy eyes, she gawked at Matt. "Wah ya say, hansom?"

Matt's eyebrows lifted. "How about we get a taxi, so you can return home safe and sound?"

"Ohm, you wonna come over and play?"

Matt paused.

She blinked her eyelash extensions, giggling.

He studied her.

Her eyes locked onto his. "I think ya wanna. Can see it in your babe blueees."

He hesitated and blinked back at her.

Nah. Man, you crazy? You never go home on a first date. Plus, she's drunk. And don't offer her a ride home.

Matt smiled. "Thank you, but not tonight. I've an early breakfast with family."

"'Kay," Jenna said, bobbing her head with such enthusiasm the table shook.

Matt helped her out of her seat and made sure she took her purse and jacket. He kept a strong link on her arm, as she almost tripped on her stilettos.

They stepped outside, and he requested the valet get a cab for her. Snow dusted the ground again this late March evening, and Matt couldn't wait to hop into his sturdy Jeep Wrangler.

When the taxi driver arrived, Jena pouted. "Come on, I wanna know more about you!"

"Nice meeting you, Jena, but like I said, an early morning call, and I think you need sleep."

Matt paid the driver, and as the taxi drove away, he jostled his head and dragged his hand through his hair.

Boy, she likes her alcohol. How well does Des know her? He chuckled and imagined his sister's answer to his command.

"No more introductions."

Yup, she'd ignore him.

Des wanted the best for him. More than once, she said, "A corrective experience will help you work through the past for good."

His response would be a question? "Am I hearing the words of a therapist?"

"No, you're hearing the words of a beloved sister who you pushed around nine months in the womb. Now my turn."

"Des, I love you, but no thanks. I'm working on it, and I'll venture out again when the time's right for me."

Matt's Jeep came around the corner. The valet eased open the door, and moving into the driver's seat, he reflected on the encounter. That woman couldn't have been a better reminder of why he avoided dates with unknowns.

If she hadn't become intoxicated and had asked one question

about him, he might've considered another date, but with her behavior, no way.

Also, he made the right decision about not driving her home. These days, too much happening between men and women. Even bringing her to the door could cause problems.

Yes, he kept his rule of no drinking on first dates, which he limited anyway, but that didn't prevent false accusations from occurring.

Yup, stay the course, buddy.

The snow became heavier, unyielding, and stubborn about resisting ushering in spring's greenery. Matt turned on the wipers, swishing and squeaking, back and forth.

Winter, honey, enough. Time for sister spring.

Mesmerized by the swirling snow, Matt found Sapphire squirming into his mind again.

"I wonder what her deal is?" he said out loud, which he often did in his car. "She's a therapist? God, some therapist." Matt swayed his head from side to side. "How does she treat attractive men who request her for therapy?"

Matt turned his heated seats on high and blasted the hot air. Okay buddy, give her a chance. He hovered over the steering wheel. Ignore her bites. She's a hurting pup, like you. Right? She's in therapy, like you. Again, right? At least, she admitted she has problems.

The plows and sand trucks moved along Route Nine. He slowed, hearing the gravel beneath his tires as he made his way home to Brookline. In a short time, cars stopped, and flashing signals showed an accident ahead.

Would he ever trust a woman again?

Sure, he could have a casual dalliance. But not his thing. Women threw themselves at him. Even tonight, signals came his way, but he wanted more than feeding his male urges. Man, you are who you are. The problem? When he fell, he fell hard.

His heart bruised like a black and blue mark.

Don't go there, man.

He moved his gear into park and turned on some music. Patient by nature, he'd make the best of the situation. Matt turned on his iTunes, and skipping a few songs, he found one that met his musical palate for the evening, by Kat Edmonson, "When You Wish Upon a Star."

He began humming the jazzy melody, and his mind wandered to a golden face with lots of hair and dazzling sapphires. He inhaled and envisioned the woman who would join him on this therapeutic journey over the following nine weeks. Matt tried recalling the scene with Jena, but Sapphire replaced her.

Matt shifted his car into drive as the vehicles advanced again. What do you know about her? Nothing, except her rudeness. He drew another long breath and became annoyed that she rented space in his mind. Just because she works as a therapist, doesn't mean she's performed enough self-examination.

Matt changed the song since Ms. Edmonson's sexy voice drew his attention to Sapphire. Let's try Santana—and blasted "Europa" from his speakers.

The dazzling blue gems dominated again. Go away, lady. He rubbed his face with one hand.

The snow swirled around him. The car ahead of him braked, snapping Matt out of his hypnotic state. He grasped his steering wheel, cut a hard right, and slammed his brakes. His body remained rigid like a rock. "Focus, man, focus." Matt's breathing slowed down, and the harness around his body released.

He bobbed his head. No more thoughts about that siren, uh-uh, and enough sexy music, changing the song.

When Matt reached his condo, he took the elevator and stumbled into his residence, exhausted. Without turning on one light, he threw off his clothes and fell onto the bed. Sleep arrived almost the moment he laid his head on the pillow, but not before another fleeting visit from an exquisite set of sapphire eyes with a flowery scent accompanying them.

What's he going to do for the next nine weeks? Been with beautiful women. Keep being nasty to me, and that'll take care of things.

But what if she shows a soft side? What happens then? Umm, he mumbled. His eyelids became heavy, and his mind unlocked night's door, allowing entry of forbidden treats with golden arms around him.

Chapter Four

Session Two—March 31st—Sapphire

Sapphire shut her eyes and inhaled the eucalyptus and spearmint spray. Rachel introduced the spritz at their initial session, and she became hooked on the aroma, smothering her home and office with it.

With each slow inhale, Sapphire's chest loosened like a corset being untied. The first arrival, unusual for her, Sapphire planned on going next after what occurred this past Sunday.

Who thought such behavior would take place in church?

Sapphire entered the cathedral at ten past twelve for the noon-time Mass on Sunday and swept into the pew. While pulling out a missal, she looked up and saw a twenty-something young man with thick glasses, leering at her and rolling his tongue over his lips.

Sapphire averted her eyes, thinking his action meant nothing, yet she sensed eyes on her again. She peeked at him, and he ogled her, licking his lips in a more pronounced fashion.

An old tightness entwined her. She rose, bolted to the rear of the church, and voiced her displeasure to a few ushers about the incident. One, an older man with a stained T-shirt and grubby jeans, gestured and said, "I dunno. Leave me out of it."

Another man, more sympathetic, dropped his mouth in alarm. "I think there's something wrong with him."

He suggested she contact the pastor. She thanked him and noticed the strange man turn around, searching for her.

Forty-five minutes later, when Mass ended, she hurried down the stairs, steadying herself on the railing. She picked up the pace and walked to her condominium nearby. Fire coursed through her veins.

No way. Not dealing with this.

The next day, she stirred, looked out the floor-to-ceiling window in her Newton home, and clapped her hands. The crocuses peeked through the soil.

Ah, spring. Yay!

Four seasons. What a treat! You New Englanders, born and raised here, stop complaining about the weather.

No clients until later today. This morning, exercise and errands, but first, the priest.

She made a strong pot of coffee, her favorite, French Roast. While it percolated, she engulfed the dark-bean aroma until it reached a gurgling finale. The coffee pot's beeping interrupted Sapphire's habit of twirling hair strands at the nape of her neck.

She pinched her arm. Don't you dare return to that! The fuzz means growth.

Instead, she poured a cup of the simmering brew, sat, shut her eyes, and gulped. "Ah."

Sapphire glanced at her device. "No more avoiding," and she tapped the parish number into her phone but froze before touching the call symbol. Self-deprecating messages tried to stifle her.

What if he doesn't believe me?

What if he does, but minimizes the situation?

"Oh, come on, and why would you make this up? Huh? Push call!" Sapphire said almost shouting.

The priest answered on the first ring. After she explained what had occurred, his voice broke, agreeing no one should deal with this, never mind in a house of worship. He couldn't recall the family, but he'd keep his eyes and ears open.

When Sapphire ended the call, she got up, raised her arms, and danced as if she floated toward the clouds. There, you took charge right away, just like you encourage your clients to do.

Now, while waiting for the start of the session, Sapphire relaxed, immersing in the eucalyptus and spearmint scent, until she heard brisk footsteps. The door opened, and Matt entered the suite, carrying a jacket over his shoulder.

She caught his eye, and he gave her a quick wave. "How ya doing?"

She said, "Good," with a grin, but his eyes left her as he pulled out his phone, sat down, halting any further conversation.

Sapphire bristled from the snub and said no more. She peeked at him for a few seconds and examined his dark hair and wide shoulders. He wore business attire, tailored black trousers with his jacket behind the back of the chair. His open white shirt revealed thick chest hair. When his eyes lifted, catching her staring at him, Sapphire's cheeks blazed, and she averted her gaze.

"I didn't have time to change my clothes."

Sapphire glanced at him again as his eyes fixed back on his phone. "What? Oh, I didn't notice."

Matt didn't look at her.

"By the way, Matt, if I can refer to you as Matt?" Sapphire asked.

"Sure can."

"I apologize for my sarcasm last week."

Matt crossed one leg on top of the other, keeping his eyes on his phone. "No problem."

With a frown, Sapphire dug her fingers through her hair and let her head fall back. "Sometimes I bite. I'm working on my overreactions."

Matt's eyes didn't shift from his phone.

Except for a mild vibration and his fidgeting, an eerie stillness crept into the room.

Sapphire almost said something else, but the discomfort shattered with four sets of feet walking behind one another, entering the office with quick hellos and nods.

Jason, Shalene, and Yardley took the remaining seats, and Rachel settled in her office chair.

She gazed at Sapphire with raised eyebrows. Sapphire understood she saw her early arrival as a good sign.

Rachel glanced about the room, with dancing eyes. "Pleased to see all of you."

"Did ya think we wouldn't show up?" Jason asked, flashing his pearly teeth.

"I'm glad to see you did," Rachel declared, with a spark of mischief in her eyes.

"I, for one, wouldn't do that to you," Matt said and looked at his phone before tucking it in his pocket. He raised his head, and his dark blue eyes connected with Sapphire's before focusing on Rachel.

The others joined him.

"Well, good," Rachel said. "Does anyone have thoughts they want to share about our last session?"

No one responded, keeping their eyes steady on hers.

"Sounds like no, so," Rachel examined Matt. "Matt, you began your story last week. Ready to continue?"

"Of course," Matt said, eyebrows knitted together. "I'm ready…"

"I ought to go next!"

Everyone turned to a determined voice.

Sapphire focused her eyes on Rachel.

Rachel said, "I see. Well, of course, if that works for you, Matt."

"Sure."

"Thank you," Sapphire said, almost shouting, trying to catch Matt's eye.

"No problem," Matt said, not looking at her.

"On Sunday, some weirdo gave me strange looks, leering ones in church, of all places, and… well, it affects someone like me more than usual."

"Uh, I can't imagine that not bothering anyone, Sapphire, especially a woman," Shalene said.

"Yeah, but worse once you hear my situation."

"Are you okay?" Jason asked, his eyebrows knitting together.

"Yes, thanks. I'm better because I jumped into action, but still, it raised issues from the past, which I planned on discussing but not this soon."

Matt tilted his head upwards with his deep blue eyes fixed on hers. "No woman should be subjected to crude behavior. Never, but especially in church."

Everyone muttered in agreement.

"Please tell us your story," Yardley said.

Rachel nudged her chin toward Sapphire. "Whenever you're ready, dear Sapphire."

Sapphire ruffled her hair and took a deep inhale. "Okay, here goes. I'll start from the beginning because it's important for everyone to understand that stuff happens no matter what kind of protection you have."

Sapphire sipped from her coffee cup and nodded. "I grew up in Miami, and we lived on the ocean. I know. I can hear laughter right now." She smiled.

Glad that Matt's in my peripheral vision.

"Our house burst with love, and that makes a home, doesn't it?" she asked, hands on her coffee cup. She looked at Rachel then the others—except Matt. Each of them nodded with a smile.

Rachel's right. They seem caring.

"Our house had beautiful architecture, Mediterranean Revival, I think, with a warm, gorgeous inside. I focus on the house, smaller than others in our socioeconomic bracket, because it evokes so many positive memories." Sapphire smiled. "My parents didn't discuss finances, so for a long time, I didn't know the extent of their wealth."

Her gaze passed Rachel.

"And they, in turn, didn't know their parents had money." She laughed. "My abuelos, both sides, escaped Castro's Cuba. They arrived in our great country with nothing but the clothes they wore."

She peered at everyone. "I love our country."

"Me too," the others responded.

Phew. You never know.

"They started businesses, invested, and bought real estate."

Sapphire placed her cup down on her portable mug warmer and kept her eyes down. "My parents instilled in me and my sister, one sib, the importance of hard work and family. All of us, grandparents, aunts, uncles, and cousins, so close."

Sapphire's eyes pooled. She took a tissue and dabbed the drops. "Right now, feeling the family love." Her eyes circled the room, seeing concern on the other members' faces. "Please. I'm fine. Just thinking about my grandparents' and their despair about Cuba. They hoped the recent uprise would create a liberated Cuba, but it didn't." Sapphire took her cup again and sipped the coffee. "Glad I have a warmer because I love it even at night." She gripped the cup.

"It doesn't keep you awake?" Yardley asked, in almost a whisper.

Sapphire shook her head.

"Sorry to interrupt." She slunk into her chair.

"No, please. Helps me collect my thoughts," Sapphire said.

A fleeting moment of silence. Sapphire winked at Yardley.

"I'm telling you I lived a charmed life for much of my childhood. Our parents referred to us as *Hermosa* or *Bella*. Mama convinced Papa about using the name, Sapphire."

"Your eyes, right?" Shalene asked, with a glimpse of her dimple.

Sapphire nodded. Without looking at Matt, she said, "I, too, never took God's gifts for granted." She grinned. "Take my word for it, my parents wouldn't allow it."

Her hair fell over part of her face, but she could see the others smile.

Wow. They seem like a warm bunch. Rachel's right.

"So, I share this part of my life because no matter how much privilege and love surrounded me, it didn't prevent what happened."

A black, slithery eel swirled around her chest. She closed her eyes, inhaling deep breaths of the aroma.

"My dear Sapphire, how do you feel about continuing?"

Sapphire

Sapphire nodded. "I must finish this, but first…" she gulped her coffee. An elixir for her.

"Ah." She smiled through tears.

She slapped her thighs a few times.

"I started dancing at five years old, but tap became my one and only." Sapphire shut her eyes. "I practiced in our basement and watched videos of great tap dancers including Savion Glover." She opened her eyes wide and gripped her coffee cup. "Although I don't remember, Mama and Papa told me later they watched me in my shiny, black tap shoes, trying to follow James Cagney, tapping in *Yankee Doodle Dandy*." Her gaze became far away. "My younger sister chose gymnastics instead of dance. They loved me and Maria so much."

Sapphire's eyes skimmed the room. Everyone's gaze fixed on her, and from what she could see out of the corner of her eye, even Matt's.

Not looking at him after he snubbed me.

"When I turned fifteen, I celebrated my Quinceañera."

"Sorry to interrupt, Sapphire but your Quincea…what?" Jason asked with a broad grin.

"No problem. Quinceañera glorifies a young woman's fifteenth birthday in the Spanish and Latin American culture. I'd say it falls somewhere in between a debutante from blueblood families to sweet sixteen parties of long ago. You're the Queen of the Ball. Everyone dresses to the nines, and…" Sapphire's insides became like a glass of bubbling champagne as she laughed, hugging herself. "What a blast."

"I bet you looked beautiful," Yardley said, with a whisper.

"I guess, but I remember it being the happiest day of my life." Sapphire's eyes shifted to the floor. "One of the few going forward."

An ominous silence shrouded the room. The vibration became louder, and Sapphire's gaze stayed down. "I'm okay. Just preparing myself to get the rest out."

She blinked a few times. "Now the going gets rough."

She caught Rachel about to say something, and she waved her hand. "I'm fine."

"A year earlier, I began attending an elite dance school, specializing in tap. An ex-Broadway dancer, Hugo, founded it, and because of his reputation, every parent wanted him teaching their children." She sneered. "Little did they know."

A cold draft breezed through her.

She pulled her sweater tighter. "One night, my mother ran late. Hugo did his usual complimenting of my abilities, but then something shifted."

Sapphire folded her arms. "The man, you know the one at church, his expression reminded me of Hugo's." She began rocking. "Hugo rolled his tongue over his lips and started kissing me, whispering *Bella, Bella*."

Tears streamed down her face, and she cast her eyes around the room. The others crouched over their seats.

"It felt bad but good at the same time," she said, her voice cracking.

"My dear Sapphire…"

She put her hand up but didn't look at Rachel. "I need to keep going."

"After that night of kissing and hugging, Hugo told me no one must know. Our secret for our *special* relationship," Sapphire said, her throat raspy like sandpaper rubbed against it. She opened her pocketbook and found bottled water. "Time to switch from coffee," she said swallowing a mouthful.

"Things progressed. Touching me everywhere. One night, he— he…" She scrunched her eyes and tightened her hands with knuckles like polished stones.

"Sapphire?" Rachel asked.

"No. Almost there."

Just say it. This crowd seems safe. What's worse than what happened. Huh?

"…raped me." She exhaled and rocked. "I cried, but he hugged me, reassuring me it would get better," Sapphire said, with a forced laugh. "Soon, I became confused. With him, I blocked out negative thoughts. But when alone, I started viewing myself as dirty. A soul covered in soot. No one must know. My parents would be ashamed."

Sapphire glanced at everyone. "So, I never told anyone about the abuse except Rachel."

A sigh came from Matt.

Sapphire could see in her side vision that he looked straight ahead. "My mom told me about the horror of these things. How did you get away from this horrible situation?" he asked, in a growling voice.

Sounds protective, but not looking at him.

"It took a while. About eighteen months. My life revolved around academics and dance, including private lessons, code for Hugo. No one suspected. I didn't understand the damage until I took a summer psychology course before senior year."

Sapphire took a deep breath, inhaling the delicious scent. "I started losing weight. My mother scrutinized me for a couple of weeks. I avoided her until she grabbed my arm and got into my face, choking up. I told her my dance classes interrupted my studies. *Quit,* she yelled, *nothing should interfere with your health.*" Her mouth quivered. "My parents didn't know I feigned sickness and canceled the last two private and group dance classes. Too frightened to tell them or Hugo I wanted out."

"What happened?" Jason asked, knuckles bulging from a rock-solid fist.

"He texted me with *I love you* and heart emojis." Sapphire paused and took another gulp of water. "He became more threatening, calling me names. After Mama said quit, I told him never bother me again, and blocked him."

"Good." Jason slapped his fist into his other hand. "I'm not a violent man, but boy, this guy would test that. Someone close to me suffered sexual abuse. I'm so sorry this happened to you."

"Thank you, Jason."

Murmurs from the rest of them.

"Did he try calling you?" Shalene asked.

"No. I think he roared like a ferocious animal but cowered when confronted."

"What did you do after?" Yardley asked, her saucer eyes welled up.

"I focused on school and already applied early decision to a small college in western Massachusetts. When I got there, I felt like I arrived home. Loved and missed family, but I needed the change. Met lots of great people. Partied for the first semester, but after too many mornings of fuzzy memories, I said, no more. The next three and a half years, total school, falling in love with everything psychology, and joining committees related to my passion."

"Psychology?" Shalene asked, with a half-smile.

"You got it. Besides school and my circle of nerdy friends, nothing. I dulled my appearance. No makeup, and I wore geeky glasses, and various baseball caps. Walking between classes, I'd put on earbuds and listen to podcasts about psychology. When people saw me, my demeanor screamed boring, but I didn't care. Believe it or not, I felt okay because I felt safe."

"Any romantic relationships?" Matt asked.

Wonder why he asked that? Don't get defensive, Sapph.

Sapphire shook her head without turning to him. "The year between college and graduate school, one relationship, a narcissist at best. After, I dated here and there, but for the most part, no. Men, off limits." Her eyes found Rachel's. "I *used* to say off limits without a time frame, but Rachel helped me change my position to off limits for now."

Sapphire's eyes welled staring into Rachel's. "I don't know what I would've done without you."

"I'm a guide, nothing more," Rachel said, her eyes now glistening. "My dear, courageous you did the work."

Sapphire's tears rolled onto her clothes until a strong hand passed her a tissue.

Even buffed nails on him.

A comfortable hush entered.

Sapphire scanned the room. Jason and Yardley wiped tears from their faces. Shalene twisted her rings.

Not turning my head, but boy, he moves his legs a lot. Guess when you're that tall, not easy finding a comfortable position. Don't focus on him. Claims he's not a narcissist, we'll see.

"My dear Sapphire, how are you doing after so much sharing?"

Sapphire inclined her head back and forth. "Not sure, but I put it all out there. I guess I needed to." Her eyes grasped Rachel's, then drifted down for a moment. "Even though I'm a therapist, not sure but…" She let out a long sigh before she said, "Relief, maybe?" Sapphire folded her arms again. "I think this letting it all out shifted something positively."

"Besides relationships with men, do you have any other thoughts about how the trauma affected you?" Rachel asked.

Sapphire shook her head, "Aside from my family and my small but loyal circle of friends, trust remains an issue." She glanced at the others before her gaze landed back on Rachel. "I love being a therapist, and it's easy for me to hide. Why? Because we focus on our clients. But that's it." Sapphire clawed her hands. "The residual effects of the abuse? An unmovable infection grating on my soul."

"You're not alone with a negative self-image, Sapphire, but Hon, you already know this up here." Shalene pointed to the side of her head. "You're not the infected one," Shalene said.

"No, Ma'am, you're not on both accounts," Jason said.

Yardley gulped, nodding in agreement.

Matt crossed his leg over his ankle and leaned in. "I guess that's why we're all here. We carry burdens tough to unload."

"I'll say it again. What a creep. No, a deviant!" Jason pounded his chair. "Sorry," as he put his fist to his mouth.

Sapphire smiled. "No apology, please. It helps me."

"Would you ever consider telling your parents?" Yardley asked in a hushed tone.

"Never." Sapphire shook her head hard with eyes on Rachel. "I know them. They'd blame themselves. Not doing that to my parents. Rachel and I've discussed this, and she agrees with me."

Rachel nodded.

"Did you ever see him again?" Matt asked.

Sapphire shuddered without turning to Matt. "I'll tell more another time."

"Hon, how did you get through it?" Shalene shook her head.

"Therapy, family love, and…" Sapphire put her hands in a prayer position and shifted her gaze to the ceiling.

"Are you talking about God?" Matt asked, leaning forward.

"Why?" Sapphire pivoted to Matt. "You have a problem with that?"

Matt lifted his head, wide-eyed, raising one palm. "Uh, just asking."

Sapphire glared at him.

Matt peeked at his watch and sprung up. "Need to leave a few minutes early. Thanks, Rachel. See everyone next week." With that, he jogged out of the office.

Sapphire lifted her chin like a warrior getting ready for another battle.

For a few moments, an uncomfortable silence stole the room.

"Sapphire, my dear, I think you might've misunderstood Matt." Rachel's eyes searched hers.

Sapphire fixed her eyes on Rachel. "Are you kidding? I don't think so."

"Well, we'll see, but I urge you to consider the issue his question raised for you."

Sapphire nodded.

Later that night, Sapphire sank back in her cast iron tub, trying to melt her glacial fortress.

You won't heal if you keep getting defensive.

She splashed the bubbles and glanced around the refurbished bathroom. A gift from her parents. A terracotta tiled floor, pedestal sink, and pastel painted walls, reminiscent of her warm Miami home.

Her fingers moved to the back of her head before halting midair.

No more twisting. You want a bald spot? She slapped her dominant hand. Obey.

She lowered deeper.

Wow, so much relief from sharing.

That guy, Matt. Let up on him Sapph.

Seeing Hugo again? A normal question.

Asking about God? Nothing wrong with that question.

Maybe, you're attr…

Don't even think about it.

Sapphire closed her eyes, breathing in the aroma from the candle. She tried to empty her mind and meditate, but dark blue eyes remained front and center.

Chapter Five

Rachel and Alexandra—April 1st

Rachel stared back at her therapist.

With laced fingers, Alexandra flashed a smile. "How did things go this week?"

Rachel bit her lip. "Well, so-so."

"Tell me more."

"First the good. Something happened to Sapphire, and she shared her sexual abuse. The first time beyond our sessions."

"So—good?"

"Yes. She'd call me if she experienced negativity or distrust, but she didn't."

"Big leap for her."

"Yes, but…" Rachel shook her head. "Fiery Sapphire emerged and misinterpreted Matt again. I think I should've intervened."

"How?"

"I don't know."

"How could you? Are you a mind reader?"

"No, but she hurled daggers at him because he asked for clarification about God."

"Could there be an attraction?"

"Yes. But Matt's discipline shows itself in every part of his life, including when he goes on dates, and Sapphire's trauma makes her relationship adverse. So, I think nothing will trickle into the session. I just hope he comes back."

"It doesn't sound like he'll drop out."

"No, he's a loyal guy, and he promised he'd ride the storm even if things became uncomfortable." Rachel grimaced. "But you never know."

"Rachel, it sounds like he trusts you, so try to stay centered. It takes courage to run a group which I've never desired to do."

Rachel blinked at her long-term therapist.

An enigma.

Who are you, Alexandra? You've revealed so little over the years.

Single and with a few siblings. Belief in God, I think. Other than that? Not much.

High boundaries?

Higher than hers.

Do you even like me? Hope so. Think so.

My clients? They know I adore them.

Alexandra tilted her head.

"What else is happening?"

"Not much, but as usual, I thought about what Sam might say. We often conferred about cases."

"Ah, Sam. What might he think about your life now?"

Rachel paused for a moment.

She never forgot the day they met.

Both were there for a conference on the therapeutic relationship. With all the newfound fads, Rachel remained steadfast in the belief in its importance.

A large crowd of therapists. I guess others agree.

"How do we maintain its significance during these times of quick, quick, and…"

Clang.

Rachel with other heads turned to a man with black fluffy hair, streaked with grey, bending over to retrieve his thermos and notebook.

When he sat up, he placed oversized glasses back on his nose, locked eyes with Rachel, and smiled, his face getting redder.

"Mister?" the presenter asked.

He nodded. "Placo, but you can call me Sam."

"You were asking?"

"Um, let me think." He scratched his head for a moment. "Ah, well." He cleared his throat. "We'll use my ADD as an excuse."

Rachel laughed along with the rest of the group.

He snapped his fingers. "So, yes, about so-called quick results…"

He found her eyes again and smirked, shaking his head, and at lunch, they wandered toward the same table.

"Are you married, Rachel?" he asked, removing his glasses.

"Not yet," Rachel said, drawn to his large chocolate eyes. "You?"

"Nah. Long-term relationship, but neither of us ever discussed marriage. She left me for someone else a couple of years ago."

"That must have been difficult."

"You'd think, but not. Like letting air out of a tight balloon instead, which alarmed me. I guess we, being therapists," he said with a glint in his eye, "know that may have been diagnostic for avoiding a troubled marriage."

Six months later, they faced each other, and when the priest said "…all the days of your life," Rachel's watery eyes blurred grasping Sam's melted chocolate ones.

Create a child right away? "Yes," they said in unison as they held hands and stood in their new house, an old but cozy Cape. "A loving nest for our most important creation," Rachel said, turning to her newlywed.

"Let's try right away," Sam said, wiggling his eyebrows.

And at the end of their pleasurable moments together, Sam grabbed her face with his powerful hands, big brown eyes searching every feature, finishing with a kiss on her nose. "My favorite. Not perfect, but beautiful."

Six months later, infertility treatments. For two years, the quick pinch of the needle, preparing her eggs for retrieval, became a welcome, but one too many times.

"Guess we should accept it," Rachel said when the insurance company denied further coverage.

Sam's powerful arms wrapped around her, his chin rubbed against wet cheeks, and tears mingled with hers.

Adoption? Chances of a baby? Not at their age.

"God led us to a profession of nurturing others, so we'll put our energies there," Rachel said.

The next twelve years?

Shared a practice together, traveled, and alternated dinner parties with like-minded friends. Sam donned a Chef's hat and apron, and stir-fried one of their favorites, sausage, pepper, and mushrooms, evoking tantalizing smells.

"What do you think, love?" Sam laid a morsel on Rachel's tongue.

"Umm." Rachel said, while chewing.

"Come on, you two. Don't keep it all for yourself," said a few voices from the other room.

"Where are you, Rachel?" Alexandra waved her hand.

Rachel's eyes pooled. She lifted her finger and closed her eyes as drops drizzled like a soft gentle rain.

A lump.

After returning from Mass on a day when black and grey swirled around them, Sam winced while changing his clothes.

"Let me look."

Sam waved her off as he rubbed the protrusion interrupting his smooth skin. "Been here for a few days."

"What?" Rachel placed her hand on her stomach as it heaved like a roller coaster.

Sam put his arms around her and planted a kiss on her head. "Don't worry. I'm sure it's nothing. I'll call the doctor tomorrow."

On Monday, Sam sent a picture of the glaring lump to his doctor. Within a few hours, Rachel drove with him to Mass General Hospital. The physician saw them and ordered a CAT Scan stat.

A cancerous mass.

The oncologist recommended surgery for the removal of the osteosarcoma.

Chemotherapy followed.

Rachel opened her eyes and dabbed her cheeks. "Alexandra, I still see myself cringing as Sam's body withered. His beautiful black hair, gone. His skin became parched and thin. I held him and every bone popped out."

She shook her head.

"I know Rachel. Words can't assuage the pain. I've shared with you what I heard long ago that time doesn't heal wounds but the intervening events."

Rachel nodded. "I remember the morning. A glorious sunrise splashed the sky." Rachel's eyes found Alexandra's again. "Silver, rose, peach. I held him and kissed him. And cupped his face between my palms. He smiled and…" Rachel's face fell into her hands, and she sobbed.

"I understand, dear Rachel. No matter the circumstances, saying goodbye to a loved one? Never easy."

Rachel wiped more tears. "The Hospice Nurse couldn't have been kinder. She hugged me before she placed the stethoscope on Sam's chest." Rachel gulped. "I see her nod, and my insides ripped into itsy-bitsy pieces."

She lifted her eyes to Alexandra. "I guess I needed to revisit this."

"Of course. Each time one goes back, as you know, it brings you to another place."

"I loved the Mass. The trumpet player blew into his horn, and the chorus sang like angels, *Ave Maria, On Eagles' Wings*, and *Let There Be Peace on Earth*. Sam's favorites. Leah's absence didn't matter at the time but returning to an empty house did."

Rachel glanced at the keyboard before looking into Alexandra's soft brown eyes.

"I remember walking around dazed, and Janine and Bridge checking on me every day. They pushed me. *Get dressed, Rach. Do what you tell your clients.* So I did, and one day I peeked in the mirror and saw limp curls, bloodshot eyes, and sunken cheeks."

Alexandra nodded her head, and her eyes appeared even softer.

"I slapped my face and called the girls and yelled, *I'm back.*" Rachel giggled through her tears.

Alexandra's eyes sparkled. "And what did they say?"

"Ya gotta live girl. Sam wants that for you."

"And."

"Well, I've tried. I got right back to work. After being gone a month, my clients asked very little." Rachel lifted her eyebrows. "Fine with me."

"How else have you embraced living?"

"You know already. Zsa Zsa and Gabor."

Woof.

Rachel swiveled her chair. "Come here." Both poodles scampered toward her, and she stroked their heads, pink tongues dangling.

She turned back to Alexandra.

"Besides your beloved pooches?"

"I bought a condo and decorated it." She moved her chair away and swept her arm around.

"Lovely and personifies you."

Rachel's heart bounced. "Yes. I'm happy in my place."

"So, Rachel, something tells me you're ready for something else. Am I wrong?"

Rachel blinked, closed her eyes, and took a deep inhale. "No."

Alexandra nodded. "Ah. A change of heart?"

"Maybe, this much." Rachel squinted one eye and held up her thumb and index finger with a tiny space. "But if you're suggesting another relationship…" Rachel inhaled and laced her fingers. "Not sure about that. How could I ever trust someone other than Sam regarding the Leah-Damian problem?"

"You haven't tried, so how do you know?"

"I can't imagine."

"I understand, but you won't know unless you try, right?"

Rachel raised her eyebrows and sighed. "How do you even dip

a toe into the jungle world of dating? Those apps? Unh-unh. I've explored them." Rachel wagged her head. "Talk about unrealistic, and from what my clients share, full of dishonest people."

"I know. It's a crapshoot, luck of the draw, but that's not the only way."

"I'm aware of that, but it doesn't matter, because I'm not there yet. Maybe a new activity."

A twinkle of mischief captured Alexandra's eyes. "Okay, how about doing something sensual for yourself?"

"Like what?"

"Well, since you have a Middle Eastern background, how about belly dancing?"

"That's a thought." Rachel grinned. "Maybe, I'll check out some classes. If nothing else, it might make me feel sexy." Rachel laughed louder as she shut her eyes, shook her hair, and gestured with air-finger cymbals.

She opened her eyes. "I already feel sexy again."

Later that night, she and her best friends and colleagues, Bridget and Janine, came together for their weekly Friday gathering—food and a movie. Tired of restaurants, they alternated homes, cost-sharing takeout. Tonight, Italian at Rachel's.

After Janine brought over the take-out orders from their favorite hole in the wall, they sat around Rachel's round pedestal table with a rattan base in her colorful kitchen, drank Chianti, and munched on Focaccia bread blotted with tomato slices, olives, and oregano. Bridget, a six-foot lean Amazon, and Janine, a fiery red-haired, Rubenesque woman, concentrated on Rachel's update about signing up for belly dancing as they munched on their food.

Rachel halted mid-sentence as she observed her friends glancing at each other.

"Okay, ladies. What's that look?"

Bridget wiped her hands and leaned onto the table. "Uh, Rach, are you kidding! After five years you want something sexy, but you're avoiding men?"

Rachel glared at her, then Janine, who turned to Bridget and back to Rachel. "Ah, sorry, my friend, you aren't practicing what you preach!"

"What are you talking about?"

"Oh please," Janine's eyes narrowed. "You tell us about your stunning client who refuses to get past her past, and duh."

"It's different for me."

"Yeah?" Bridget folded her arms. "Tell us how so?"

Rachel raised her finger as she uncovered the main dishes. "Let's eat before we get into it."

As they plowed into their main meals, Rachel stared at them. "Look, I'm a woman of a certain age who lost her husband, the only man who got the situation with Leah."

Bridget wiped her mouth, put her fork down, and blinked at Rachel. She turned to Janine and said, "You want to remind her, or should I?"

"You're a therapist, for heaven's sakes. You know dysfunction lies everywhere," Janine said and took a bite. "Speaking of heaven, I've just died and went there. Ladies, this pesto is divine. Want to try some?" Both shook their heads, "Okay, but Rachel, do you think some guy in his fifties or sixties will judge you once they hear the story about your jealous sister, and her nasty son?"

"Well, Sam understood because," Rachel shrugged, "you know, other therapists do."

"Ok Rach, let's put on our therapy hats, which we try to avoid when we're together." Bridget said.

Janine sipped her wine. "Yeah, no, can't do."

They laughed.

"Let's be serious, Rachel." Bridget blinked. "What do you say to your client, Gems, as you call her when she says she can't ever trust another man?"

"Well, first, Bridget, I never experienced sexual abuse, thank God, so not the same thing, but sure, I remind her the past doesn't have to define the future."

"My point." Bridget's eyes bored into hers. "So, what about you?"

"Ya know, Rachel, other than my therapist, you, and Bridget, no one knows my history, of not letting it stand in the way of searching for love. Even though I don't have the best scorecard," Janine made a fist with one of her hands, shaking it, "I'm not giving up."

"Not the same, Janine."

Bridget pointed her fork at her. "What did Sam say before he died?"

Rachel ate a few more bites. "Alright, I get your point, but what do you suggest?"

Janine's eyes twinkled. "Remember how much you talked about you and Sam reading about Tango by Moonlight and said to each other, *Let's do it?*"

"That's a pretty sensual dance," Rachel said.

"Yeah, and?" Bridget folded her hands, turning to Janine.

They stared at her.

"Listen Rach, you can be sensual and even sexy, without getting physical with some stranger," Bridget said, "and don't you think Alexandra's idea of belly dancing pointed to that?"

"She didn't suggest partnering with someone."

"Okay," Janine said, "but we are. She's your therapist, not your friend. We can be more direct."

Janine raised her voice. "Start living, friend. Sam's gone. Yes. He lives in another place, a better one, but you're not there yet."

The friends glanced at each other. "We've been discussing this," Bridget said.

"Thanks a lot," Rachel said.

"Oh, come on," Janine responded, "like we're cutting you down? Don't you trust us?"

Rachel sighed. "Of course, I do."

"Good," Bridget said. She opened her hobo and picked through her bag. "Here, I printed this out. The Tango Society of Boston holds classes every Wednesday. That shouldn't interfere with your group, right?"

"No, Thursdays for the group."

"Good," Janine said. "Why not try a lesson say, next week?"

Rachel cocked an eyebrow. "We'll see."

Bridget frowned, and Janine shook her head.

Rachel's eyes narrowed. "What's the problem? I didn't say no."

Chapter Six

Rachel—April 6th

Five days later, Rachel opened the solid wooden door to a large dance studio. She gave a silent prayer, shrugged, and entered a wide-open space with hardwood floors and metal folding chairs laid out against the wall. A few paintings by Argentine artists hung on bright red walls. Latin music strummed in the background, with a classical guitar center in charge of the song. Chatter all around.

Her heart soared as she became immersed in the vibe.

No one knew about tonight's venture.

After her friends pressed her, Rachel read over the pamphlet Bridget printed out for her, and the next day she sat at her computer. With slow precision, Rachel moved her hands over the keyboard and typed the *Tango Society of Boston*. With her mouse rolling over the website, she clicked on the link to classes and events.

After a half hour, Rachel powered off her laptop, sat for a few minutes, and considered what to do. She glanced at her dogs and asked, "What are your thoughts, you two? Is it time?" The dogs cocked their heads in unison.

Rachel laughed. "Okay, maybe Wednesday we'll try it."

Now, Rachel walked over to a long-haired, younger gentleman—well, at least younger than she, who took registration.

"Hi, my name is Rachel Karem. I signed up a few days ago."

He scrolled his index finger down the list. "There you are. Welcome Rachel!" He smiled. "I'm David. Your first time?"

"Yes. I took a couple of lessons years ago by watching YouTube, but don't tell anyone." She put her hands around her mouth. "I'm a novice."

David's eyes shined.

"You've arrived at the right place. The teacher hails from Argentina, and he'll repeat the basics as he does every week. In the second hour, the advanced students learn a few more intricate steps. You're welcome to stay and watch."

He lifted his eyebrows. "And if you feel daring, maybe catch a partner and dance."

Rachel beamed. "I think I'll watch before diving in."

"Look around our space and introduce yourself to others. They're a congenial crowd. The lesson starts soon."

"Will do. Thanks so much!"

Rachel's eyes circled the room. A diverse group of people, men, women, young, older, dressed in black or colorful attire chatted, swirled with a partner, or practiced their steps, black shoes shuffling or stomping on the floor.

A few people approached her and introduced themselves.

Lara, a seventy-ish-looking woman with long gray hair, loose clothing, and musky perfume said she had been coming for years, but loved revisiting the basics.

Another woman, Claudia, in her thirties, shared with Rachel she attended for one month and became addicted to Tango. Her eyes crinkled, and she touched the red rose on silky black hair, swayed in an orange and black wide-skirt dress. Someone yelled her name, and she spun around like a whirling butterfly.

Nice people so far, and so many grey heads. Yay. The zipper around Rachel's chest unfastened.

"Buenas noches." A voice weaved through the crowd.

The instructor, Guillermo, a tall, dashing man of about forty-five or fifty, with thick black hair streaked with silver, clapped his hands and waved for everyone to come closer.

"Let us begin," He said with an inviting Spanish accent.

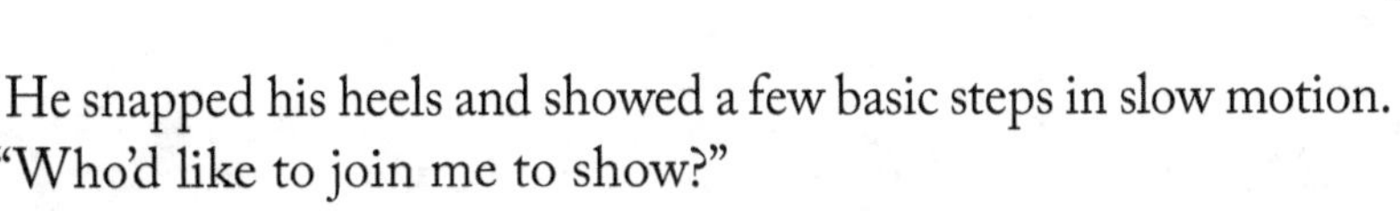

He snapped his heels and showed a few basic steps in slow motion. "Who'd like to join me to show?"

Hands shot up.

"Okay, hermosa," pointing to a middle-aged woman. "Come."

The average-sized woman wearing her hair in a chignon, sauntered over to Guillermo and placed her hands in his. Over the next thirty minutes, Rachel watched the couple move their feet, ruling the floor.

Every few minutes, Guillermo stopped. "See what I'm doing." He'd point his toe, and again shift it to show his students. Next, his partner would do the same, floating along the wooden planks as she performed the dance steps.

Rachel became so entranced by their actions she didn't notice more people, entering the studio until she heard a low throaty voice say, "What a surprise!"

"Shhh!" A few voices echoed.

She turned around to see a long-haired woman whispering and grabbing onto a tall man.

Before pivoting back to the lesson, she peeked at the man and woman. The statuesque woman, about her age with ash blonde, silvery tresses, whispered to a lanky man of about the same age. He looked around while the woman conversed and tugged on his arm.

Although the man's silver mane, longer than most for his age, stood out, his eyes captured her attention. An ocean of wonder. At first glance she thought grayish-blue, but when he shifted, the light reflected the blue-green of the Caribbean Sea.

Not wanting to stare, Rachel focused again on Guillermo's deep voice and nimble gestures. He clapped, asking if anyone knew the easiest way to follow Tango. When no one responded, he turned around and raised his arms. "Take the word Tango and form an acronym. T for slow—lead steps forward with left foot, and the follow mirrors by stepping back with the right. A pause, where the lead moves ahead again with their left foot, a smaller step."

"Entiendes?"

"Yes."

"Muy bien." Guillermos showed the N, where he took a small step forward again with the left in preparation to step to the side with the right. Next, for G, he leaped to the right, bringing his right foot alongside the left.

He paused, lowering his eyelids, and circling around. "Ah, now the O, the final and very sultry step." Guillermo closed his lips and gave a one-sided smile. "Here goes." He dragged his left foot towards the right. "Ahhh." He clapped and gestured with open arms and palms up. "That's it. Then back to T."

"Now let me show. Please, another hermosa volunteer."

Claudia stepped forward, bubbling over. Guillermo dazzled her with a wide smile. "See how Tango infuses us in a short time? Come, come my dear."

Claudia took Guillermo's hand and followed his lead.

Rachel concentrated on the student and teacher, with the lead using one foot, and the follower mirroring.

Wow. Mesmerizing. And that O step.

Guillermo dragged his left foot towards the right. Claudia followed with perfect precision.

After a few repetitions, Guillermo bowed to Claudia. "Thank you!" Guillermo clapped and gestured for others to direct their applause to a blushing Claudia. "Let us stop for our intermission." He bowed again.

Claudia emerged out of the crowd and approached Rachel, gushing. "Isn't he wonderful?"

"Yes, he is, but so are you!"

Claudia's eyelashes fluttered. "Thank you! I try."

They grinned in unison.

"Rachel, are you staying for the advanced and practice lesson?"

"For a short time."

Claudia said, "Great," and waved after someone called her name.

Rachel glanced at her watch. Should I?

Okay, Janine and Bridget. I kept my promise.

I even might return. But what about now? She looked around. People chatted and twirled with laughter swelling the room.

She inspected her attire. Purple skirt and top, black kitten heels, not Tango shoes, but they'll do.

Okay, a little longer. What do I have to lose; my famous words to others? Rachel strode to the refreshment table and reached for some bottled water. As she turned around, she bumped into a body that stretched over her for a soda. Her eyes looked up into the face of the silver-haired gentleman from earlier.

"I'm so sorry. I didn't see you behind me."

The silver-haired man studied her before responding.

"Not a problem. I should've alerted you."

Rachel gazed at him. He remained deadpan as he spoke, then did an about-face and walked away with no interest in engaging in further conversation.

Well, so much for that.

Not only did he not apologize for invading her personal space, but he didn't even introduce himself.

Good-looking and knows it. No thanks.

Bad boys. Everyone who liked, loved, or lusted after one—including her, long, long ago—suffered heartbreak. They could be ancient and still have that attitude. Besides, she came to dance, not find love, and the man seemed taken by the statuesque woman.

Rachel stood with a few others, and watched Guillermo provide instructions to the advanced dancers.

"Now I dare you, beginners. Find a partner and join the other dancers in a less trafficked area," Guillermo said with a twinkle in his eye.

I'll stay for a bit longer.

Rachel focused on their feet. Eyes glued to the intricate movements.

Maybe someday she would master the art of Tango dance.

A determined yawn insisted on emerging which she suppressed when someone tapped her on the back.

She twisted and came face-to-face with the silver-haired man.

"Excuse me, I apologize for being so abrupt earlier. When I'm in unfamiliar surroundings, I get nervous, so I forget to introduce myself."

Rachel peeked at the half-smiling man. "And you are?"

"Oh, see! I did it again. Michael here, and pleased to make your acquaintance."

"I'm Rachel, and I'm pleased to meet you as well."

"Would you like to give the dance a try, Rachel?"

"I'm not sure. I feel like I might stumble."

"Well, we can stumble together. How about it?"

Rachel nodded.

Michael stretched out his hand, and she placed hers in his. They moved to a quieter section of the room, and he took the lead, beginning with the basic T step, moving his left foot forward, and Rachel following with her right foot coming front.

"Rachel, you follow well, but let's do it again. I forgot to put my heel down first."

"Of course, I think we'll repeat this a great deal."

The couple proceeded with the basic T, moving to A, and they practiced the basic two parts for a few minutes.

"What do you say, Rachel? Should we go for the N, which is my role?"

Rachel nodded, peering down at her feet.

They returned to the beginning and then onto G and O in a methodical movement.

Rachel became comfortable in the firm grip of immense hands. When she glanced at them, a luscious tingling awakened from its long slumber.

No!

With a quick shift, she focused on the dance again.

Lights began flashing, signaling the program's end. Rachel looked up at her partner and caught him staring at her with her hands still in his.

Flashes of glitter electrified her limbs, and she jerked away from his grasp.

"Um, well, Michael. Nice meeting you and…" She tried holding her voice steady. "I enjoyed us partnering together."

"Will you be here next week?"

"I hope so."

"Good, let us…"

The woman talking to Michael earlier, appeared out of nowhere, tapping him on the shoulder.

In a throaty voice, eying Rachel up and down, she asked, "Hey handsome, who's the lucky lady who took you for your first… dance?"

Rachel's heart froze.

"Justine, let me introduce you to Rachel." Michael kept his eyes on Rachel and folded his arms as Justine moved to link hers with his.

"Hello Justine, nice to meet you."

Justine nodded with a smirk, sizing her up and down. "You as well!"

She turned to Michael and said something in his ear.

"Thanks again, Michael," Rachel said, moving away from the couple. Before getting her coat, she turned toward them and saw Michael backing away from Justine.

Get yourself out. You see. It's the usual with handsome men of a certain age. They're up for grabs, especially by aggressive women. Not my thing.

Rachel waved goodbye to a few people without stopping.

Came for dancing, not dating. Look what happened when you gave it a second thought.

No way.

She stepped outside into the early April evening and took a deep breath. The crisp air delivered a fresh and streaming relief from her disappointment about what had occurred.

Rachel

Rachel reflected more on the evening's events and ignored the chatter from passersby, until a voice from behind barged into her thoughts.

"Hold up there, Rachel."

She turned to see Michael hurrying toward her and stopped as he caught up.

"Sorry about the interruption," Michael said.

"No problem."

"I disagree, but more about that another time." He stopped and stared at her. "If you plan on attending next week, I'd love to partner with you again."

"Maybe." Rachel turned, hypnotized by his eyes. "I just don't want to interfere with..."

"You aren't," Michael said.

Rachel nodded. "Then, I'd like that. We'll stumble our way to better."

"Good." His eyes lingered on hers for a moment, before looking toward the row of vehicles. "Let me walk you to your car."

"Unnecessary, thank you."

"At this late hour, it is."

They strolled in silence, hearing others behind them.

"Well, here's my car."

"Very good. Until next week, Rachel."

With that, he turned around, heading toward his car.

"Michael!"

He wheeled around.

"Yes?"

"Has anyone ever told you that your eyes are spectacular?"

He stared at her.

"Oh, yes, a few times."

This time, Michael rewarded Rachel with a dazzling smile.

"Until next week, Rachel."

Michael bowed to her and reversed direction again, walking away.

Rachel realized she could've offered him a ride to his car, but on second thought, she understood one couldn't be too lackadaisical, no matter how nice someone seemed. If she partnered with him another time, shouldn't she learn his last name? My God, you never know where a mass killer or misogynist might lure their prey.

Yes, she'd inquire more next time.

Wait a minute. Not a date, honey.

Yes, intriguing. Yes, attractive, but his nervousness might be code word for arrogance.

Rachel saw his figure disappear into the darkness of night.

She shivered before her internal furnace emitted heat that rose within.

Newsflash—hot flash. She shook her head, turned on her ignition, and rolled down the window of her Volvo SUV. Her hands glided over the leather seat. Expensive, but one of the safest. Rachel pressed her keyless gear into drive.

Yes, safety. A necessity in all areas including relationships, and trust creates safety.

After what happened with Leah and following Sam's death, therapy stitched most of the wound, but poison still oozed out.

Embarrassment about her family situation never departed for too long.

But what more could she do?

How could she explain the messy situation to another?

Her close friends reminded her that many people experienced these kinds of betrayals, but she couldn't wrap her head around Leah's venom and her influence on Damian.

Her friends were therapists, and for them, little if no family. So, of course, they understood. But others?

How come you don't have a family?

Don't you have any brothers and sisters?

How about cousins?

She heard the questions, even if implicit.

No, in her life, she wouldn't risk judgment about something out of her control. Bridget shared an article written by a therapist for an online website for older people that confirmed the phenomenon.

Parental alienation was the worst, but others existed also.

Sam, her greatest ally, said, "Her loss, Lovie. She doesn't deserve you." He'd squish her in his arms.

She drove outbound along the Charles, and topaz eyes revisited. Younger ones.

Her nephew.

How she wanted a relationship with him.

That day she opened the cream-colored envelope.

Her fingers skimmed along the embossed font, and she shut her eyes as she detected a flowery scent, bringing the envelope close to her nose.

She read the invitation, and her eyes became dewy.

Damian invited her to his photography exhibit in Manhattan. OMG!

Bridget wouldn't leave her husband, so she and Janine would make a weekend out of it.

She often read about his rising star. Many likened him to the late Herb Ritts and Annie Leibovitz. After years of ignoring her outreach, Damian, now well-known, acknowledged her. Maybe, she hoped, just maybe, a chance for a better relationship.

A month later, she and Janine drove to New York. They taxied from their midtown hotel to the show. As they entered, people crowded the fancy gallery. Rachel, black curls cascading down her back, dressed in a red cocktail dress and matching Christian Louboutin stilettos, navigated her way through the throngs with Janine, her dress smothered in electric blue, behind her.

Rachel's practice introduced her to a variety of people, so she didn't feel the least out of place. She caught sight of her nephew, his matching topaz eyes, standing erect, smiling, and conversing with an older couple.

How many years since she saw him?

There he stood, tall and muscular, brownish hair like his mother's, long and pulled back in a ponytail. His monochromatic beige attire from open collar to jacket, trousers, and shoes uttered expensive, chic, and unique. A close shaved beard stressed his brilliant smile and chiseled looks. When he looked up, Damian stared for a moment at Rachel. She saw the flicker of something in his eyes, shrouding it with a wide grin. He approached Rachel, kissing her on both cheeks.

"Auntie," he said in a smooth voice. "I'm so glad you came."

He stretched out his arms. "You've changed little."

"Well, I'll take that as a compliment, but you, my handsome nephew, look magnificent. Doesn't he, Janine?"

"Yes, he does," Janine said, tugging lips upward.

With a pasted smile and lingering glance at her, Damian turned to Janine. "Thank you for coming. And you are?"

"Janine, one of your aunt's best friends."

"Please to make your acquaintance." Damian extended his hand to Janine, shaking it as he looked around. "I need to greet a few other guests. Help yourselves to hors d'oeuvres and drinks." He saluted them. "I'll be back."

Damian made an about face, moving through the crowds. Rachel saw hands reaching out to her nephew as he kissed and hugged his admirers. Before she turned to Janine, a familiar voice called out.

The memory dissolved. Rachel shook her coils and rubbed her eyes.

You can't erase permanent ink, but you can paint over it, right?

She arrived at her condo.

Save it for Alexandra, will you?

She'd attend another lesson, but not without protecting her heart. Stories of betrayals from lovely clients echoed and heightened her own. How could anyone question her caution about dating?

Keep the door ajar, but with only a sliver of an opening.

The sands of time emptied into the lower chamber of her hourglass, and she didn't know what might arise before God determined the final trickle.

The possibility of love in the latter half?

Don't bet on it.

Woof. Woof. "Coming, my loves."

Rachel turned the key into the arched oak door to her condo. Paws padded the other side. She blinked, and her hands pressed against the smooth wood before opening the door. She tried not giving a second thought to the evening, but a silver-haired visual stuck in her mind.

Chapter Seven

"Whooweee." With hands on his hips, Jason shook his head. "One week, and the return of grey, drab, empty." Jason sniffed. "And stale."

Not for long. Jason's eyes circled the church basement. Slab walls, cement floor, colorless stacked chairs. Let's change the scene, right now.

A splash of brightness swallows the bleakness, a repeated mantra from Harry. He shared the mantra with the boys at the first meeting as they cast their eyes around the room.

Since then? "Hey, Mr. J. Love the spruced-up look."

He took out his iPhone, turned on his Bluetooth speaker, and adjusted the settings.

Time for some tunes. He rubbed his hands together and pressed the side of his phone.

Let's bring sunshine into our other senses.

For the next sixty minutes, Jason hummed to the range of songs. He swayed around the space, taped colorful posters on the bland walls, and stood back pleased with the application of splashed stickers and positive quotes.

The pastor gave Jason permission to add anything he wanted but warned him: "Don't leave valuables behind."

On weekends, in the church's conference room, he clicked away on his laptop with three cups of Espresso Con Panna, in a tall thermos by his side. Every few minutes, he sipped on the strong coffee as he explored quotes from his favorite authors, including Frederick Douglass and Napoleon Hill.

The hours ticked away.

Time to go home and put all of this on paper.

Late into the evening, Jason pressed hard on thin pens and wrote letters with a steady, precise swirl, wiggling his fingers in between.

The pastor complimented the dazzling posters. "Jason, my brother, you do calligraphy?"

Jason chuckled. "No sir, but," as he stroked his chin, "maybe I'll consider learning."

"Looks like you don't need lessons, but you could show the young men how to write."

"Sir, I'll add that to their learning needs."

Sometimes he'd devote an entire Saturday and part of Sunday toward his commitment.

Jamil, Abdul, Jared, and the rest of them. Love those guys. So glad they like the Toastmaster techniques that embroidered the lessons.

Maybe it would help them stay on the right track.

And glad I told them about TM's impact on prisoners and reports showing the decrease in the recidivism rate.

One week, Mikey came to the lesson and said, "Went to see my cousin and told him about Toastmasters. And Mr. J., you know what he said? *I'll check it out.*"

Jason grinned. "Good job Mikey. Let's keep spreading the love and lessons."

So glad he discovered Toastmasters. The best kept secret.

He arranged the fresh signs. The one or two he didn't hand to his students remained undamaged from the past week.

No monetary value, but maybe someone read the large affirmations staring back and reflected on their life.

Could the quotes inspire them to fulfill a dream?

Hope so. Would it prompt even one person to consider a different path?

He applied extra layers of tape on the largest piece of cardboard and stuck it on the portable podium he purchased on Facebook Marketplace. He backed up and gazed at the Napoleon Hill quote: *Whatever the mind can conceive and believe, it can achieve.* The most popular. Every week, he recreated another and gave it away to someone who didn't have one.

"Remember? Review it every day."

The eager recipient of the week bobbed their head. "Promise."

Sometimes, he'd question the advice he doled out to others.

Dude, are you practicing what you preach? How come you're not living?

When Rachel pushed him, a familiar crunching in his chest unfurled like a rabid animal gnashing its teeth. "Can't right now. Too risky." He'd display his pearly whites. "Trying to figure that out with you, but don't worry, Ms. Rachel, I'm having a ball with my second job, while still loving my first."

His calling? An independent investigative journalist.

In grad school, he discovered *Investor's Business Daily. Ten Secrets of Success.* None of the other secrets mattered without number ten, being honest and dependable. Couldn't be anything else. Yup. Harry's moral compass echoed through him.

Because of this, sources trusted him and shared valuable information.

Yeah, I'd go to jail before giving them away.

Most of the time, he worked from his home office. In between researching or inputting information on his computer, he'd click the invite for a Zoom call and lean close to the screen talking to someone reliable. Sometimes the source typed words into the chat that Jason alone could decipher.

Other times, he flew to locations and met people in a coffee shop, hotel lobby, or a park. They'd either be waiting or strolling toward him, often disguised by wearing sunglasses, or donning a baseball cap, while displaying a nondescript expression. If Jason knew the person, he'd pat them on the shoulder. "Looks like the perfect face for poker."

The rest of the time, Jason dedicated his energies to boys ranging from ages fourteen to twenty. He developed a program for young men around presentation and public speaking, which he learned from Toastmasters. He ruled against a formal club.

Nope. Commit to one month at a time. Hope for more.

Twelve of them attended no less than three times a month. If they missed, they'd show up for the alternate class and often bring along a friend.

In every class, the young men sat in rows of four. They'd fidget, shuffle their feet, and wait as Jason passed out a sheet of paper with the rules displayed in large print.

"Okay, guys. Let's recite them together."

Most read at a very elementary level.

If I have my way, not for long.

Six months ago, he introduced a third day. An in-depth story-telling class. Jason pointed to the three or four books stacked on his table and asked, "Which one do you want me to read tonight?"

He'd walk around, flipping the pages in the book, and raise or lower the pitch of his voice depending on the sentence. With the book in one hand, Jason swept an arm in front of the group, often stopping, putting one hand on his thigh, and widening or narrowing his eyes. Each boy gaped at him. Sometimes, he'd scrunch down and lean into one of the young men as they looked back wide-eyed.

While in Toastmasters lessons, his inflection remained more subdued except at the end for Table Topics, the extemporaneous part. Jason began the tale, turning and twisting, gripping his hands or spreading his arms out. Mid-story, he'd gaze at his engrossed students.

"Okay, Tobias, or J.M., or Abdul, your turn." In the first two or three meetings, each of them boggled their sentences, "Um, um, I dunno… Oh, come on, Mr. J."

Jason folded his arms, shaking his head.

A hesitant hand rose, and one boy would stand, grimacing.

"Okay, so, um, the dude, Malcolm, went for a ride…"

The story would continue until Jason asked, "Who wants to finish it?"

After several months, hands would fly up. "I will," or "Come on, Mr. J., my turn," and moaned at the end of the session. Each of them stayed, asking questions as Jason pulled a few of the posters from the wall. He'd hand them a new one as they walked out together and peppered him with questions.

"Hey, Mr. J, you married? Got a girlfriend?"

"Nope, not at the moment."

"Why not?"

"Well, I'm pretty busy with working and hanging out with you guys."

"What ya do for fun?

"Binge watch some good shows."

"Me too, Mr. J."

They'd ask all kinds of questions, which he often turned around to focus on them.

Jason smirked, thinking about the crew about to enter the basement.

He never knew how many would show. We'll see.

Tomorrow night's group session popped into his mind.

What would it bring?

He nodded his head, secured the last sign on the wall, and pushed the cooler full of icy sodas toward the front.

Whew, Sapphire. What a spitfire. Talk about jumping down Matt's throat. Glad it's not me. Who could blame her. Sexual abuse. Did it contribute to the fire? Her story made him think about Lola. Set him ablaze.

Gotta talk about it. And Harry, of course. His heart panged. Slow brother, slow.

Would the others play a video of their entire story?

Doubt it unless something triggered them.

The redhead, Yardley. Quivering animal. Boy, she needs food. And how about a voice? Couldn't make out her words. What's her story?

And the sister, Shalene?

Average height, slender, a cross between Whitney Houston and Kerry Washington. But super serious. What's up with her?

Callie's face flashed. Her sparkling smile.

Sugar, not as sweet as you. No way. Yeah, I'm biased. Yeah, I know what you'd say. Everyone's got a different sass to them. Yeah, yeah, yeah, but not going there. I don't even know if she's got a honey. Has said little yet.

Harry's face replaced Callie's.

Yeah, I can hear you echoing Callie. Rachel tells me all the time.

She's cool. You'd like her. She wants good for me, but like she said, up to me.

Footsteps and loud voices trickled into the entryway as a door slammed.

Ten of the boys arrived, laughing and sauntering toward Jason, fist bumping.

"Hey, brother!" Jason flipped the cooler open. "Help yourselves guys."

Each grabbed a soda, uncorked it, and slurped the drink. "Thanks, Mr. J."

They came a long way.

The first time they arrived, suspicious and surly expressions jotted their faces. They showed up because someone, a parent, grandparent, or sibling, heard the pastor announce it.

They needed role models, so he spoke to them as if they were his peers.

In the earlier meetings, they wore pants down around their butts and ripped T-shirts. Their eyes roved up and down his attire of sneakers, jeans, and a tailored shirt.

At the end of the second lesson, one or two said, "Hey Mr. J., like your style," or "Um, I'm gonna copy you."

Within a short time, three of them entered the meetings with ironed shirts tucked into belted jeans.

"Oooh, Tito. Copying, Mr. J.?"

All of them now appeared with buttoned-downs and pressed jeans.

"A few more minutes, guys." Jason passed out the week's agenda when four others entered.

He looked up, and his chest tightened as if a python wrapped itself around him. Abdul limped toward him with purple protruding around a black and blue eye and an arm in a sling.

"Mr. J., sorry I'm late."

"Hey, no problem, brother," Jason said, maintaining a stoic presence. "What happened?"

"Someone picked on my sister, so, ya know. But I'm okay, Mr. J. Don't ya worry. Glad I'm here." Abdul took the soda offered by Jason, and with the can in his hand, made an air fist bump to the others.

Jason passed the agendas to the first in each row. They gave one to the person next to them.

"Caleb. You're assigned tonight. Ready brother?"

Caleb cracked a grin and stomped to the podium. He fist-bumped Jason and clipped the wireless mic on his lapel. "Okay you guys, bow your heads." Each young man closed his eyes and put their hands together.

"Thank you, Lord, for allowing us to be together tonight." Caleb glanced at Jason, who nodded with dancing eyes. "Amen."

"Amen," the others said.

Caleb glimpsed his notes and then raised his chin and put his shoulders back just as Jason taught them.

"Good evening, everyone." Caleb looked at Jason again with a sheepish smirk.

Jason's lips kicked up and gestured to the others with open arms.

"Good evening," the participants said in unison.

Jason focused on Caleb, but when he glanced at Abdul, the snake tightened its grip.

Breathe, brother, breathe. And face it, you got triggered. Not different than Sapphire. Can't wait.

He turned his attention to the earnest students sitting in front of him.

Chapter Eight

Session Three—April 7th—Jason

Jason strolled toward the building.

What do I share?

So much. Too much.

Rachel's voice rang like a whisper from the mythical goddess Echo. "You've got a choice. Stay invisible or discover the healing power of new relationships."

Last night? Did that prompt him to move forward tonight?

Yeah, his experiences differed from the others. No one came close to relating. Maybe Shalene but not quite.

He preferred not to focus on people's skin color.

The verse from the book of Samuel remained sealed in his mind forever:

"Man looks at the outward appearance, but the Lord looks at the heart."

Harry's instructions adhered to him like superglue. Keep an open mind with people from all kinds of backgrounds.

His schooling and line of work gave him that opportunity, so having a white therapist didn't matter. From what he heard, therapists entered the profession because of pain or dealing with differences. No matter what her background entailed, she got him.

Yet, with years of therapy, he couldn't trust and move beyond the past. His losses made him suspicious about getting close to anyone. Those who heard his story understood, but how could he continue this way? So, with some resignation, he agreed to try the group.

Now, Jason entered the office with a wide smile.

Pretend, brother.

Matt and Sapphire sat across from one another scrolling their phones, and a heavy silence plugged the room.

Great, just what I need, but hey, focus on you.

"Hey," Matt said, glancing at Jason.

"Brother." He fist-bumped Matt.

"And Sapphire, how ya doing?" Jason asked.

Sapphire sat in the same Peel seat she chose for the last two sessions. She nodded. "Better and better, thanks." Sapphire's hair fell over her face. "I didn't think I'd share so much."

Jason leaned toward Sapphire. "Yeah, took guts. Not sure I'm that courageous."

"Take my word for it. You are, and I'm not so gutsy. Hadn't planned on divulging this so soon, but…" A faraway look appeared in Sapphire's eyes.

"Yeah. I get it." Jason began shifting back and forth in one of the Peel chairs. "Hey, Matt, I know you wanted to go next?"

Matt stored his phone in his pocket and shook his head. "Not in any hurry. Why?"

"Yeah, well, something happened last night while I ran my class that, ah, brought things back."

"Hey, no problem, man. To reiterate, no urgency here. Tell you the truth, I'm okay with waiting."

Jason chuckled and lowered his head for a moment. "Yeah, I get it. I think I ought to, ah, ya know," he waved his hand around, "talk. So, thanks."

Matt grinned and nodded. "Sure. By the way, what's the class you're running?"

Sapphire's head rose.

Jason leaned forward, addressing both while neither looked at one another.

"Well, I've been fortunate in my life." Jason tilted his head. "And not so fortunate, of course, otherwise none of us would be here, right?"

Matt and Sapphire bobbed their heads.

"So, to deal with both, I thought about giving back to the Black community and run some meetings for teen boys, based on Toastmasters. You familiar with that organization?"

Both nodded.

Jason lifted his eyebrows. "Glad to hear. I haven't met many who are."

"Why are you not including girls?" Sapphire asked.

"Yeah, I thought about it, but with hormones raging at that age," Jason shook his head, "I thought, let someone else handle the young ladies." He sat back. "Fewer distractions, the better. I mean, competition and maybe fighting over a girl's attention or the other way around."

Sapphire responded with a vigorous nod. "Got it! Adolescent girls have their own issues. You're smart to keep it to the boys."

"Thanks!"

"Sounds great, Jason." Matt stretched out his long legs, leaning back. "I've thought about doing something similar. So, thanks, man. Fuel for thought."

"Yeah, it's cool, brother. Let me know if you want some help."

"Will do."

Clicking heels approached the room. Matt raised his eyes at Jason. "Rachel makes her presence known."

"Yup, she's got her own walk. I don't know how she manages in those high heels."

Rachel rushed through the door, huffing. "Hi everyone, sorry for my late entrance."

Matt glanced at his watch. "You're not late."

Rachel settled in her seat. "Ah, I know, but I prefer to beat all of you here."

More chatter. Yardley and Shalene strolled in together.

"Whew, we just made it," Shalene said.

"Hi!" Yardley said, in an almost inaudible tone.

Everyone smiled back with hellos.

Rachel clapped her hands and beamed. "I'm most pleased to see you this week. How's everyone doing?"

The members nodded, with a few, "Good."

"Sapphire, do you have any thoughts after last week?"

Sapphire cocked her head. "Not only do I feel better but…" She hesitated, putting her chin on her fist. "My healing reached another level."

She gazed at Rachel. "Three clients thanked me for a fabulous session. One of my adolescent girls told me I seemed happier than usual, and one young adult woman asked if I fell in love." She laughed. "Yes, even in a week, something shifted."

Sapphire halted for a moment with a downward stare and looked up again. "I'm optimistic about becoming more relaxed and less rigid with my clients and, I guess, life." She turned to each member. "So, thanks for making it safe, listening, and helping me become a better therapist."

Jason clapped, and the others joined him. "Ride on, Sapphire."

Sapphire's eyes sparkled at him and the rest of the group, and she returned her gaze to Rachel. "Maybe I'll become a fabulous therapist like you."

Rachel's eyes glistened. "My dear Sapphire, I'm so pleased and…" Her voice choked. "You'll be better than me."

"Not sure about that, but thank you."

Rachel put her hands together. She shifted to Matt. "And now, my friend. You left in a hurry last week. Anything you want to say?"

"All good."

"I believe you allowed Sapphire to take your place last week." Rachel looked at Sapphire, who glanced at Matt.

"Thank you, Matt." Sapphire said.

"No problem." Matt's eyes remained on Rachel. "But since I'm in no hurry, I'm giving up my place to our friend here, Jason." Matt nodded in his direction. "I think he needs tonight more than me."

Jason smiled and offered Matt a salute.

Matt smirked. "Like I said, no problem, man, and not urgent for me."

Rachel peered at Matt. "As long as that works for you?"

Matt gave a thumbs up.

"Alright then." Rachel put her hand out to Jason. "Jason, my friend, you have the floor."

Jason scanned the room. "Gonna test your knowledge about current trends. So here goes. What's one of the most dangerous cities in America for black people?"

He waited for a moment.

"Chicago?" asked Shalene, with her half-smile.

Jason shook his head with a no.

"Washington, D.C.?" Matt asked, sitting forward with hands laced.

Once more, Jason shook his head.

Yardley put her hands up.

"You've got me," Sapphire said.

"A place you wouldn't imagine." Jason said, eyes circling the room. "Omaha—where I lived until my last year in middle school."

Matt scratched his head. "Never would have thought of it."

The women shook their heads.

"Yeah." Jason smiled at Rachel. "Neither did our friend here."

"I learn something every day from spectacular people like you."

"Aww. You give me too much credit." Jason swallowed back broken words. Yeah, this lady's got his back.

He cleared his throat.

"Besides Sapphire, any of you know anything about childhood sexual abuse trauma?" The others mumbled a yes.

Where do I begin? He glanced at Rachel. Eyes inviting comfort like being wrapped in a soft, sable blanket.

"Okay. I'm going to start with Lola, my mother. My mom died around my sixth birthday, and for a few years, Harry, my dad, and the grandies, my dad's parents, repeated, *Mama became sick and went to Heaven.*"

He rubbed his head. "Every so often, a memory came back. A

needle in a dangling arm. If I raised the issue with Harry or the Grandies, they'd shush me. By the time I reached ten, they cloaked it in more sophisticated words. *Mama suffered from a complicated disease.*

"I became curious about my mother, and Dad shared snippets with more coming out later." Jason's eyes pooled as his father's features materialized. "He didn't want to overwhelm me."

Jason leaned forward. "Buckle up. Here's some of the story shared by Dad."

He closed his eyes and pressed the start button on the Way-Back machine.

"Dad left high school and joined the military and returned four years later to Omaha. Dad met Mom a few weeks later." He nodded and chuckled. "Dad told me how it happened. *Son, I saw her working in a coffee shop, and I was smitten.* Not until later did I find out about my mom's past. Biracial. Never knew her parents and grew up in foster care. Harry—*Dad*—I interchange…"

Jason opened his eyes, took a tissue from the box, and dabbed his forehead. "I sweat easy."

"Not alone, man." Matt smirked.

"Thanks Bro. Think our size and the subject matter contribute." He grinned at Matt.

I could become friends with that guy once the group ends.

"So, Dad hinted that Mama and he got married." He squinted one eye. "Think my mom may have become pregnant. Not sure. Just a hunch. If we talked about Mom, Dad would say, *Marriage first. Children next. Understand?* He reminded me it doesn't bode well for people coming from an unstable background."

"I think it's best from any background," Sapphire said with her hands gripped on her coffee.

Yardley and Matt nodded.

"Couldn't agree more," Shalene said without smiling. "You should hear my parents on the topic. Yowzah."

"Yow…what?" Jason asked with a chortle.

Shalene covered her mouth. "Sorry."

"No, Ms. Shalene. Need something sweet to offset the bitterness. 'Preciate it."

Shalene twisted her rings, gave Jason a half-smile, and her dimple bloomed. "I use the word, I don't know, for emphasis. Know what I mean?"

"Gotcha." Jason winked at her. His eyes lingered for a couple of seconds and shifted downward.

First pretty thing since…

A loud slurp.

Jason looked up. Sapphire's eyes shut. He could see her swallow as she held the cup.

Glad for that slight interruption.

"Back to my story. Oh…" Jason raised his index finger. "One thing. Jump in any time with questions or comments." He peeked at Shalene. "Even a *yowzah* helps lighten the mood."

She kept her eyes on her fingers, but he could see a smile caress her mouth.

He flashed one back at her.

Okay, Callie, sugar, she's got potential. Yeah, pretty. Different from you, but pretty.

"A little more about Harry." Jason leaned forward. "Dad stressed to me the importance of good grades. He said, *I want a better life for you.* He worked as a self-employed handyman, got his G.E.D., and took college courses at night. I stayed with grandparents many nights."

Jason stopped, and with his hand rubbing his chin, allowed several seconds to pass.

Silence colored the room again.

The buzzing from the heater made its presence known.

"You okay to continue?" Rachel asked.

He nodded.

"Good. Now, before you do, I'm wondering what made you so determined to go next?"

"Something happened last night that triggered me. A young kid came into my lesson, injured from a beating, so I knew it was time to talk about my stuff." Jason felt the familiar coil snake around his chest and paused. "Give me a moment." He glanced at Rachel.

Her familiar response, warm eyes, almost welling up. Her expression comforted him.

This lady has my back.

Jason looked up. "I accepted my family's explanation about my mother until I reached middle school."

Click, click, click.

Jason's eyes shifted.

Sapphire's nails snapped against her coffee cup, and she gazed outward.

"Guilty." Jason knitted his eyebrows and leaned toward her with a grin.

She bristled like a cornered porcupine. "Oh my God. Sorry." She put down her coffee cup and gripped her hands. "I'm eliminating a bad habit." She shook her head. "And replacing it with another, not as bad."

"No problem, Ms. Sapphire. Need the distractions in between all this sharing."

She bobbed her head, and some tresses slipped over half her face.

Jason shifted in his seat. "Started attending St. Michael's at age eleven. Dad and the Grandies, my grandparents," Jason swallowed but refused the waterworks' entry, "worried about the rough crowd entering public middle school, so Dad, Harry, worked extra hours, and he and the Grandies paid for my tuition. I knew other kids attending, so I gave him no resistance. Also, I loved learning, and Dad emphasized all the books I would read."

"So, I'm not the only nerd in the room?" Sapphire asked.

"No Ma'am. I'm a proud member of the Nerd Club." Jason grinned.

"I'm nerdy, too," Yardley said in a wispy voice.

"Should I say me too?" Shalene pulled the ring on her baby finger.

"Right along with you." Matt raised his hand.

"We may have more in common than what brought us here." Jason grinned.

A few giggles and yeses bounced back at him.

"Rachel, you plan this?" Jason gave her an exaggerated frown.

"What can I say, my friend? Sometimes coincidences don't exist." Rachel's eyes crinkled into a smile.

Jason hesitated and nodded. "So, I go to this posh school and see lots of two-parent families. Dad warned me this might happen but reminded me of the love in our home, so I'd jibe about him and the Grandies. At some point, a couple of friends asked about my mother. I told them she died of an illness. Then something strange happened."

Jason sighed and blinked.

"A few blurry memories came forward. One of Lola, caramel arms around me, reading, and whispering, *You the best boy in the whole wide world.* Another I couldn't make out except seeing a body on a couch. I put it aside as best I could, and being a kid, focused on sports and grades. But a couple of years later, something else popped into my mind. The more I concentrated the clearer it became. I started remembering my six-year-old self and my confusion back then."

He closed his eyes.

"Mama laid on the couch, eyes black and blue, wet stuff came out of the side of her mouth, and something stuck out of her arm. *Wake up, Mama.* Paco and Niko, my secret friends, said *Shh,* and we played even as sudden rain slapped the roof loud and hard. They whispered. *Be a big boy. Mama and Papa showed you the angels are bowling.*"

Jason opened his eyes and noticed everyone leaning forward. "No idea how much time passed. Imaginary friends came in handy."

His gaze descended to the floor. "I remember talking to them and directing my toys. I didn't look up until I heard Dad's usual singing and can't remember seeing his face because he grabbed me and kept me inside his coat. One hand moved and pressed buttons on the phone. *Emergency*, and with his voice over my ear, he said, *Mama's very sick. Doctors are coming.* The memory faded, but it shook me. Everything started making sense. I raised the topic with Harry and asked for the truth. His answer? *Not yet.*"

Jason steepled his hands together and glanced at Rachel.

She nodded and raised her eyebrows.

He bobbed his head. "Taking a pause." He swallowed and looked below to the side of his chair, "There it is," grabbed and uncorked the bottle, and gulped half the sixteen ounces of water.

"Ah. Needed that." And he placed the bottle by his side.

Jason rubbed his hands and sighed. "One day, I'd had it. My friends kept asking, *What disease did your mother have?* I approached Harry a few times and said, *Come on. Fourteen next month. Ya gotta tell me more.* He'd look back and say, *Soon.* The third time worked. Dad, hands on hips, turned to the window, then back to me. *Okay, tomorrow's Saturday. Let's talk about it at breakfast.*"

Jason nodded and glanced at the others. "We went every week. Dad made it a fun ritual."

"You can hear his love." Sapphire nudged the hair half covering half her face.

Jason's eyes misted. "Yeah, my dad did his best." He shifted in his seat and kneaded his eyes with his fingers.

Stillness tiptoed into the room again.

Jason blinked a few times as he collected his thoughts.

"So, there we are in the diner. Harry, my dad, brawny but exhausted, sipped on his steaming coffee while I slurped on a vanilla milkshake. We chit-chatted about sports until the food arrived. Harry put his cup down and pointed to my meal. *Eat.* He began cutting his food, and in between bites, he shared the truth about Lola."

Jason paused, shut his eyes, and massaged his head.

"You, sure you're okay to continue, my friend?" Rachel's eyes probed his.

Jason opened his eyes. "Yes, Ma'am. I'll repeat what our friend, Sapphire said. Need to get this out."

Jason examined the others, faces scrunched up and gawking at him. "Don't y'all worry about me."

"Dad went slow, and I recall his story word-for-word. *Your mom refused to share much about her childhood. From what she knew, protective services received a report about a three-year-old on the street with cigarette burns on her arms. That would be her. The sexual abuse started a few years later. Around the time you turned six, she started screaming in her sleep.* Harry looked at me. *Your mother trusted no one. In the morning, I wrapped my arms around her and promised I'd protect her. Lola, your mother, nodded, but if I brought up therapy, she'd walk away.*"

Jason paused again, looking out. "I can see dad's face right now, clear as a shiny window, studying my face. *You okay, son?* And I said, *Yes.*"

He sat up and slapped his thighs. "The truth? Didn't have much bonding with my mother." Jason peered at Rachel. "You know, Ms. Rachel. I still feel bad about that."

Rachel shook her head at him.

Yeah, I know that message. No, Jason. You don't deserve guilt. She left far too soon for a stronger attachment to her.

Jason clasped his hands. "Dad shared more. *She wanted to erase something that couldn't be erased. So she numbed through alcohol and drugs. My heart broke for her, but I couldn't let it interfere with work.*"

Jason halted and folded his arms.

"Dad's eyes teared up, and he said, *But more than work, you came first and still do.* I remember grabbing Dad's hand, and he chuckled. *Don't you worry about me, son. I do the worrying.*"

Jason's eyes became dewy. He blinked hard and kept his eyes on the floor. Don't want Rachel fretting.

"No money came from Dad, so he couldn't figure out how Mom paid for her habit. Engagement and wedding rings disappeared. Dad confronted Mom, but she denied it."

Jason sighed and scanned the room. "I knew none of this, but as I said, my grandparents came into the picture more often."

Jason stooped and picked up his water for a few long gulps and held onto the bottle.

"I asked dad about the night with the needle, and he nodded. *Your mom got assaulted by her dealer and almost died. The first responders arrived on time. Although Narcan saved her, I realized I enabled her.* Dad rubbed his eyes. *Told her to get into a program, or you and I would move out. Next day, she promised.*"

Jason stopped for a moment as he glanced at the other members.

"Dad's eyes teared up. *I had high hopes, son, and I remember humming and bolting up the stairs.* For the next part, I remember his eyes bored into mine. *I hope I'm doing the right thing, but you deserve the truth.* Dad swallowed, sipped the last of his coffee, and sighed. *I got into the apartment, and your mother didn't respond. I saw a note and knew.*"

Jason stared at the floor. "I kind of remember a weird sensation. Dad stared at his empty cup and tapped on it. I waited, and he lifted his eyes. *Son, your mom asked for forgiveness and wrote about how much she loved you. And…* Dad fiddled with his cup again. *No easy way to say this. She hung herself.* Dad wiped his eyes again and roamed every inch of my face. I grabbed his hand and squeezed it. *I'm okay, Dad. Glad you told me the truth.* He squeezed it back. *I hope so, son. Other than love, no precise formula for parenting.* He paid the bill, and we trotted out together arm-in-arm."

Jason's eyes brimmed with tears and drops trickled down his cheeks.

The tissue box found its way to him.

"Thanks," he grabbed a few tissues. Without turning or looking at anyone, he raised his index finger and paused.

Rachel's eyes joined his. He nodded. She gets me and my signs of being okay.

"On the way out, Dad asked me if he said too much, but I told him I kind of put two and two together. I hugged him and thanked him for giving me the truth and taking good care of me."

Jason looked up through foggy eyes. "It didn't register how much until a few years later." He placed his head in his hands, sobbed, and tasted the saltwater drizzling down his face.

Matt

Nothing but muffled cries captured the room.

Man, not sure what to do.

Don't want to insult him.

Jason bolted up a few seconds later. "Hey y'all, I'm mighty fine right now. Better than I thought." Jason's booming voice cracked. "Don't you worry about me."

Whew. No action needed.

Matt nodded and observed Jason whisk several tissues from the box and blow his nose.

Jason smirked at Rachel. "This therapy thing works and look," he crushed the tissues in his hand, "I'm gonna buy a case of these for you."

Rachel passed the basket to him and shook her head. "Not necessary, my friend." She pointed to the narrow closet where she kept her supplies. "I store them by the cartons."

Good, we need some humor.

"Where's the *y'all* from?" Shalene asked.

Glad you asked. Sounds southern.

"We left the Midwest at some point and moved to North Carolina, so I embraced the southern charm." Jason grinned.

Aha. Thought so.

"Jason, could you share a bit about how this affected your decision to become part of this group?" Rachel's eyes glittered like a polished brown zircon.

Nic loved brown zircon and growled at me if I associated it with cubic zirconia.

Jason put his hand on his head, nodding. "Well, let me say this. After my mother died, everything blurred. Between my dad and grandparents, I became occupied, boxed my memories of her and shove them into the attic of my mind."

He paused. "You don't know what you don't know until, you know, if that makes any sense?" He scanned the room, noticing everyone shaking their heads.

"At the end of middle school, I let images of her come through the door, if you know what I mean, but my dad and grandparents swathed me in protection and love, so I accepted what happened." Jason glanced at Rachel. "But I never thought about more losses. Young people don't. And for the next few years, Dad and the grandies kept me believing it wouldn't happen."

"Yes." Rachel nodded.

"But more losses happened, and trust in everything and everyone, including God—gone. Why bother to connect when everyone ends up leaving?" He ceased for a second, clasping his hands toward his mouth.

"Enough for now." Jason tapped his thigh a couple of times. "Except," he glanced at Sapphire, "your story helped me understand even more about what my mother went through."

Keep your eyes on Rachel, man.

"Thanks, Jason, but," Sapphire shook her head, "unlike your mother, I came from a loving family which prevented my situation from being far worse." Sapphire combed her hand through her locks. "Hugo's abuse caused PTSD for me, but I don't know… Like I said, something clicked."

Sapphire spoke with an unfocused stare. "And I'm more confident about my path toward healing."

Even in his periphery, he caught her glorious eyes on Rachel, spawning a grin. "Can you believe I'm saying this?"

Maybe she'll be less edgy.

"I can." The corners of Rachel's mouth tilted up before her soft eyes shifted back to Jason. "Anything else, my friend?"

Jason shook his head. "No, ma'am."

Rachel swiveled her chair to the other members of the group.

Each appeared lost in their thoughts. "We've a short time left, so if someone feels comfortable beginning, please do." Rachel glided her eyes to him. "You know, my friend, twice you yielded to others. How about you share more of your story?"

Matt nodded. "As long as the ladies are okay with it?" He ignored Sapphire and peeked at Shalene and Yardley.

Shalene bobbed, and an elusive smile swept across her face, while Yardley's green eyes expanded with hands gesturing yes.

"Well, compared to Jason, I feel like my story pales." Matt lifted his eyes towards him.

Jason waved him off. "Brother, you don't have to suffer loss from death—not to experience pain. Besides, I thought my situation couldn't compare to what happened to Sapphire."

Not looking at her.

"Thanks, man." Matt twisted his neck around. "Alright. So, remember I mentioned a consequential night?"

His eyes skimmed the room, skipping over Sapphire. Everyone nodded.

"Yeah, well let me give you some background. My mother became involved in these Salon gatherings after my dad left her for Mandy."

Matt paused for a moment, and he gazed out.

"Sorry, just thinking about the divorce. My mother suffered two betrayals, not one."

He glanced at Rachel. Her soft eyes soothed him. He nodded.

"So, what do I mean? Well, neither of my parents suffered in the looks department. And, no offense ladies, but sometimes women disregard a man's marital status."

"What do you mean?" Sapphire's tone was brittle, like chalk.

"Getting to it," Matt said without looking at her.

"Women pursued my dad left and right, which Des and I became aware of as teens. One day, Mom overheard us whispering our concerns, and she barged into the conversation. *My loves, please don't agonize. If I see a woman mauling your dad with her eyes, I narrow mine, and they back off. Besides Dad and I are devoted to one another.*

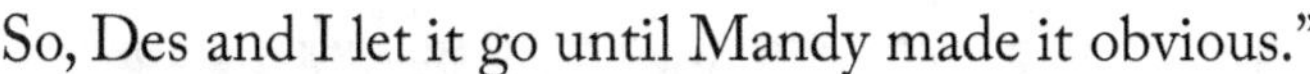

So, Des and I let it go until Mandy made it obvious."

"And Mandy is?" Sapphire asked.

Less uptight tone.

"Sorry. Now my father's wife but was Mom's best friend."

"Whowee." Jason shook his head.

"Two betrayals." Yardley's voice dwindled like evaporation.

Jeeze. Looks like a skittish fawn. Needs reassurance. Hope she can carry it off in the courtroom.

"You got it, Yardley."

"Tough stuff," Jason said.

"Yeah. Des confided in me on break in sophomore year. *Hey, Twinnie.* A special name for each other. *Watch the way Mandy whispers to Dad and glides her fingers on her arm.*"

Matt grinned thinking about his sister.

"She insisted we broach the subject with our mother, but that didn't go well."

Matt took a breath.

"Mom brushed it off. *You two, are too protective. Mandy loves me, and just enjoys flirting with your dad. And your father and I are fine.* So, Des and I put it aside."

His heart hopped like a frog.

Whoa. Hitting me more than I thought.

"Things got strange in my junior year in college. Des and I came home on winter break, and Quentin, my dad, seemed different. He stared out the window more than we recalled, and if we approached him, he'd shove his phone in his pocket."

Matt crossed his legs and flashed a smile at everyone. "You'd love Des. She keeps me honest. And picks up on things such as catching Dad with a separate phone."

He rubbed his lips. "She asked me if I noticed his alternate device, and I said, *No.* She laughed and swatted at me. *Typical guy.*"

He peered at Yardley and Shalene. "My sister told me I didn't notice important things and could be blind to women's follies. You think she might be right?"

They nodded, and Sapphire shouted in an exasperated tone. "Yes."

Okay, so she and Des agree.

"The therapist speaks." Matt wouldn't shift his gaze to her. He stretched his legs out again. "I promised Des I'd pay attention, and my perceptive sister? Right again. I noticed Dad's…" Matt shook his head, paused for a moment, and looked up again. "No other way to say it; shifty behavior."

Fingernails clicked, clicked, and clicked.

There she goes again. Not looking at her. So she can bite my head off again? Uh-uh.

Matt bent his legs and dropped his laced fingers between them. "Didn't want to address it with my mother. Predicted to Des what would happen, and it did."

Tap, tap, tap. What's up with her? If these are good habits, what's the bad one?

Matt lifted his eyebrows. "There we were, sitting in our kitchen." He glanced at Rachel. "A beauty for anyone even if you don't cook." He laughed. "Stone countertops, hardwood floors, walnut cabinets, and lots of light."

"Sounds like the one my parents created."

Turn to her, man.

"Central place for everyone." Matt glanced at Sapphire, and his heart flipped like an acrobat.

God, I can't look at her again. He rolled his shoulders back.

"There's my mother and I eating a Caesar salad, and I said, *Um Mom, Des and I are concerned about Dad, and I don't know, Mandy's behavior toward him.* My mother bolted out of her chair, and her eyes hurled daggers at me. *What are you talking about?* I didn't know how to respond. She threw her napkin down. *Your father and I are fine*, and she got in my face. *How dare you and your sister suggest anything inappropriate between them.* And she stomped out of the kitchen."

Matt stretched his legs out and folded his arms. "You can imagine what happened." His eyes roamed the room, and he caught everyone nodding. "The next year, Des and I came home for winter break, and Dad and Mom called us into the great room to announce their divorce."

He coughed and pitched forward. "Dad showed little emotion, but my mother—God, she couldn't stop crying." Matt paused and squeezed his eyebrows together.

Keep control bud. No watery show here.

Quiet stole the room again.

He gazed out and focused on one of the Tiffany lamps. "My mother caught me staring down my father, and as usual, she came to his defense. *Matthew, don't. Do you understand? We're divorcing each other, not you.* Dad kind of mumbled in agreement."

Matt found Rachel's eyes.

She knows the story.

Matt looked at the others except Sapphire and put his arms out. "And you know what happened? My mother, wearing her quintessential therapy hat, asked Des and I, *What are your thoughts?* I remember my mouth dropped in disbelief, and I stood up, and walked out. I heard Des say something like, *I'll talk to him.*"

Matt blinked.

"Des and I did talk. She took the high road and reminded me this shouldn't be a surprise."

Matt stopped again, opened his mouth, but the letters wouldn't form into words, so he sat.

"Matt, my friend, what would you like to do?"

He glanced into the comfort of Rachel's eyes.

"Just figuring out how to verbalize the rest of this. As Jason said, need to get this out."

No way am I voicing the stunner's name.

"For the next few days, my mother stumbled around the house with a wild-eyed expression. She canceled her clients, remained in bed, and wouldn't open the door when Des and I knocked."

"You must have been worried," Yardley said without whispering.

Matt cracked a smile. "Yeah, we were, but by the next week, the rinsed dishes in the sink and folded clothes in the laundry basket, reassured my sister and I that Mom would heal."

"How about your father and his betrayal?" Sapphire sneered.

Not pivoting to her. Keep your eyes on Rachel.

"Yeah, I, ah, kept my distance from him for about a month."

Matt leaned forward with hands between his legs again. "But my mother insisted I stay connected to my dad, and if you want to know the truth, I missed him, so we reconnected."

"What did he say about it?" Shalene tilted her head as she twisted one of her rings.

Matt lifted his eyebrows. "We never discussed it. Even when he told us he planned on remarrying, Des and I agreed that we'd be cordial but spend as much time as possible with Dad alone."

"Did he marry Mandy?" Jason cocked his eyebrow.

Matt nodded. "Yup."

"Ouch."

"I know, but we did our best to put it aside, and my mother pretended she'd be fine."

Matt paused for a moment. "Found out later, my mother carried more pain than she let on, and the long weekend which I'll talk more about another time, made me realize how much the divorce affected her."

"How about you?" Rachel asked.

Matt's body braced for a moment. "I don't worry about me. I can take care of myself?"

"Really now? Then why are you here?" Sapphire's tone scratched like a worn-down pencil on paper.

For a couple of seconds, words bulged in his throat and couldn't squeeze out.

An uncomfortable silence thundered through the room.

Come on, man. Open your mouth and control your response.

He turned his head and stared into the depths of Sapphire's eyes, crystal blue facets.

No honey. I don't care how gorgeous you are. Unlike the song, not going *crystal blue persuasion* on me.

"Same reason you're here, Sapphire. But I don't jab people for not sharing everything the way you see fit. Okay?" Matt's eyes locked onto Sapphire's until she turned away.

"Hold on, y'all. I think we're here for the same reason." Jason peered at everyone before his gaze reached Rachel's. "I'd say we're wounded animals. Wouldn't y'all agree?"

"Amen!" Shalene's rubbed her fingers.

"Of course," Yardley said. "My goodness." She shook her head with her luminous eyes widening. "I think we need to recognize all of us have needs, and Matt, don't you think the divorce did more to you than you admit?"

Matt maintained his gaze on Sapphire, who wouldn't give him eye contact. "Yes, I'm here because I've got major trust issues, but you haven't heard all the contributing factors. And, yes, again, the divorce affected me and caused pain, but when you hear the rest, it might make some sense to you."

Sapphire's fixed stare on the floor remained unwavering.

Patience, Matt. Patience.

He turned his attention to Yardley. "So, let me finish before being interrupted. I don't focus on their divorce too much. Lots of parents get divorced." He glanced at his watch. "By the way, ladies, no offense, but some of you misinterpret men's aloofness," Matt stood, putting his jacket on, and pivoting to Sapphire who looked up, "as cockiness, when it might be something else." He pulled his shoulders back. "Night everyone. Thanks, Rach."

CHAPTER NINE

Rachel and Alexandra—April 8th

Alexandra, oh my God.

The session couldn't arrive fast enough.

She rose early and took Zsa Zsa and Gabor for a vigorous walk, breathing in the early crisp air of spring.

They trotted past one of the resident's gardens.

Yes, they're the ones with a display of daffodils every year. Soon glorious yellow and white creations from God will blanket that garden, followed by the ephemeral but spectacular tulips.

"Hello." She waved to an older gentleman who jogged by her. She saw him on their usual route at their usual time.

"Hi," his strained breath, huffing and puffing.

She suppressed a laugh. At first, she thought he smiled, but realized he grimaced instead as he trudged along the road.

Thirty minutes later, Rachel jumped on the Stair-master for a fifteen-minute sprint followed by weight-bearing exercises with her favorite YouTube exercise guru. With five-pound weights, she flexed slow steady movements, then up and out. Rachel's face dripped with sweat, and she glided her fingers along one of her biceps.

A woman of a certain age. More crinkles, wrinkles, and flab, but look what happens if you keep at it.

She flexed her arm and touched underneath. Triceps, not so easy, but not bad for an older gal.

"Change requires practice and repetition, to achieve results," she said to most of her clients. They'd blink when she displayed a flexing of her arm. "See, over and over."

She remembered showing Alexandra, who returned a rare laugh.

Yes, Alexandra, seated before her now, silver coils loose, gazed back with her usual serene appearance. Over the years, Rachel couldn't figure out what she thought.

Does she even like me? Well, if nothing else, she respects me, I guess.

When Sam passed, she provided sessions twice a week, and her dark eyes reflected the sorrow Rachel experienced.

Alexandra trained in the old method of psychodynamic psychotherapy—speaking less and listening far more.

Rachel trained the same way, but over time she became more expressive with her clients. Sometimes they'd giggle together, or she flexed her muscles, clapped, raised a fist to cheer for them, or gave them a powerful embrace.

"Everyone returned to the group," Rachel said and summarized what happened. Alexandra's eyebrows knitted together which comforted Rachel.

She pays attention to me.

"Matt gave it back to Sapphire, and Jason intervened. He reminded everyone why they were there. Even Shalene and Yardley, the least verbal so far, affirmed what Jason said. Yay!"

"Rachel, it appears something is happening, and you're contributing to it." Alexandra cocked her head.

Rachel pulled back and swayed. "I don't know. Sometimes I think I should say more, but…" She bit her lip and her eyes roved over the keyboard.

Alexandra shook her head, bringing her hands together in prayer fashion. "What? What more could you've said? You continue to put too much on you. We've been over this time and time again."

"I can't help it. I always feel there's more I could've done, no matter the situation."

"What are you referring to this time?"

"You know. It keeps going back to everything *Leah*."

Alexandra's eyes softened. "What got raised for you?"

"Well, the situation with Damian. Could I have created something different with him?"

"What do you think?"

Rachel's eyes lifted. "I don't know. My mind returns to that night in the gallery wondering what made him do what he did?"

"His mother's reach extends beyond, as you've stated."

"I know." Rachel paused and allowed her thoughts to go back three years.

A sucker punch to the chest described her response when she received the news.

No one told her about Leah's cancer.

How could Leah not contact her?

They were not only sisters but twins. In the womb together and arriving in the world within a few minutes from one another.

Their estrangement became an obese entity.

Several years passed without much contact.

Leah's last act of rage came a few months after Sam died. She surprised Rachel and stormed into her condominium on a late afternoon before the Christmas season. She brought the note Rachel sent her nephew, inviting him to the Holiday Boston Pops' concert, and dangled it in her face.

"How dare you?" Leah said, crimson with contorted features. "Stay away from my son."

"I thought he might enjoy the concert since he loved the arts." Rachel's voice quivered.

"You go through me. Do you understand?" Leah pointed her finger into Rachel's chest.

Rachel recoiled, pushed her sister's hand away, and trembled as she walked backward.

"That's it, Leah. I've had it. Get out. Right now!"

Leah stomped toward the door and twisted the knob, but she

halted and swirled around with topaz eyes smoking. "You've been so jealous of me."

"What?"

"Oh, don't give me that *what*. You couldn't have children of your own, so you tried to make Damian yours."

"Leah, I wanted to be his aunt, not his mother. You couldn't stand it. You're the jealous one."

With nostrils flaring, Leah swung the invitation, tore the paper into little pieces of paper, and dripped them onto the floor.

"I will have no contact with you again. Stay away from my son. He has no relationship with you. Nor will he." She flung the door open and clacked down the path.

Rachel waited.

Leah's car door banged, and her car backed out of the driveway like a growling wolf and sped away.

Rachel didn't miss her sister's rants, but she couldn't deny the tearing of her heart. Deep down, she accepted the plight of their relationship, mangled beyond repair, but the news of Leah's death crushed her.

She sat in the back pew of the cathedral and watched throngs of people mesmerized by the priest's gesticulating and singing praise for Leah and her contributions. Her sister revealed a different persona with other family members and friends, and now, a couple of her cousins stood in line to offer a few words during the eulogy. Rachel looked toward the ceiling.

Leah, now in the splendor of God's home, do you have a different perspective?

The two cousins, the only ones alive or in the area, widened their eyes and turned their heads.

"Ouch." Her body shook like a trapped animal. Before they walked out with the casket, Rachel didn't wait for the final procession and slipped out of the church, with tears streaming down her face.

She hovered outside, lowered her eyelids for a moment, and

engulfed herself in the final hymn, "On Eagle's Wings." At the end of the last stanza, she trekked away from the church and said, "I love you, Leah! I never wanted our relationship to unfold the way it did. I'm throwing you a hug and a kiss. Say hi to Mom and Dad."

Now Rachel blinked and took a gulp of her hot coffee.

"Sorry! I returned to the day of Leah's funeral, thinking about the devastation I experienced. I'll never get over it."

"Rachel, I'll borrow a page from you. All of us have wounds, but we hope they become laparoscopic scars. Don't you say that to your clients?"

"I know, and I need to talk more about that day in New York with Damian, but I want to discuss my visit to the Tango Society." She caught Alexandra's lifted eyebrows. "Yes, that's right. Not solo dancing, but Tango. Surprised?"

Alexandra leaned forward with merry eyes. "Well, you went beyond sensual dancing for yourself. How did that transpire?"

Rachel talked about her friends' encouragement to take a dance class that involved a partner, and she described the class and encounter with Michael.

A relaxed smile crossed Alexandra's face as she sighed with eyes probing Rachel's. "Tell me more."

Rachel shared the events, including the statuesque woman, Justine, a sly viper, attempting to keep Michael in her grip.

"Women like Justine make me want to surrender. I know you understand. They use their wiles to fool men, and the male rarely sees it." Rachel shuddered.

"Well, Rachel, first, how do you know this man won't see it? Second, do you think so little of yourself, not to throw your hat in the ring?" Alexandra then leaned in closer. "And last, do you want to remain invisible?" Before Rachel could answer, Alexandra raised her eyebrows. "I believe you challenge your clients with the same question. Correct?"

Chapter Ten

Shalene—April 12th

Shalene's eyes darted back and forth as she made her way to the cafe. She counted her steps, 1002, 1003, 1004…, and Shalene reminded herself how far she'd come working with Rachel. *Thank God, for Rachel, my mother and God, of course.*

She remembered the day. The nightmares, night sweats, and her inability to venture from her home prompted her mother to visit. The microphone buzzed and awakened Shalene from the first decent sleep in days. She plopped her feet on the hardwood floor, pushed herself up, and staggered toward the intercom.

"Yes."

"It's your mother. Who else would arrive this early?"

Shalene rubbed her eyes and pressed the button to let her mother enter.

Seconds later, a loud knock came from outside.

Shalene opened the door with the chain lock still attached and peered out.

Her mother glared. "For heaven's sake, please unlock this door."

Lena Marcus, who resembled Lena Horne, entered Shalene's condo and perused the living room. "Glad to see you still keep things tidy." In her elegant red power suit, she sat on the love seat with perfect posture and studied her daughter.

"Mother, why did you come here?"

"Listen, girl. I've had it. I'll sit here until you call that therapist."

Lena opened her clutch bag, took out a business card, and shoved it toward Shalene. "Take this and dial her number right now."

Shalene grabbed the card from her mother, who never said, *girl*, and studied the words and photo. "You want me to see a white woman, after what I've been through?"

"All the more reason!" Lena shook her index finger at her daughter. "You demonize every white woman. How can you? Look at all our friends?"

Lena stood up, moved next to Shalene, and grabbed her hand. "Remember, God doesn't see color. You forgot. Good and bad cuts across all humans. Understand?"

Shalene sat, held her mother's hand, and gripped the card with the other. "Okay." Shalene took her iPhone, pressed the numbers, and as she pushed the call symbol, she rewarded her mother with her dimple, making way for a smile.

"My beautiful daughter, I want you to live. Yes, you've suffered, but time to remedy it."

"I know, Mother. I love you too."

She smiled, thinking about Lena and the encounter that changed everything.

For the last year, she made gains and left home beyond visiting her parents. She went out to friends' houses for one-on-one gatherings, and a few months ago, she began working from the library twice in one week. Once again, she returned to her safe haven, the library, her one-time stomping ground. The first time? Not easy. She stood in the foyer and gripped a nearby desk to ground herself. She took deep breaths, and her eyes circled the wooden shelves holding God's creativity. All those stories. Inspired by the hand of God. Neverending books lined the walls and stared back at her, colorful rows saying, *Welcome back.*

Shalene worked in a reserved room with no one around, and she expanded from two to three times a week. She'd leave the room for quick visits to the restroom. Soon, she went beyond that safe, isolated haven and waded into the romance section of the library.

She'd bend down, and her hand glided over several authors until she found her favorite, Beverly Jenkins. She'd pull it from its place, look at the back cover, and turn the pages.

Yes, I want to own this one. Going online. She'd pull out her phone and take a picture. With delicacy, she'd hold the book as if it were a Fabergé egg and return the treasure to its rightful position.

Sacred. My view of books.

If no one came into her personal domain, she'd linger, rove over the reading nooks and study areas, and observe a few individuals on couches or bean chairs, reading or studying without looking up.

Do they feel safe in the world? Will I ever again?

If voices came within earshot of her, she'd scurry back to the solitary room.

For the last two weeks, Shalene took a breath and sat at a computer in the open space. The first day experimenting with this endeavor, she trembled and offered a sliver of a smile to the librarian sitting at the reception desk. With kind eyes, the receptionist studied the appointment schedule and told her she didn't see a reservation for her. Shalene swallowed, and her dimple emerged with a wider smile accompanying it.

"Thank you, but I think I'm going to sit in the open area."

A splash of pleasure sprayed her for making this leap, but Shalene kept her head down and stared at the computer. Her ringed fingers began clicking on it, and she became so immersed in her work, voices, footsteps, and rustling faded into the background.

One day, she stretched her arms out, and realizing what she just did, grinned. Yes, Rachel would be pleased, she thought, doing something without thinking. The old Shalene is back, or maybe a newer, better version instead?

She saw a teenager roaming around. He appeared confused, but she paid little attention and returned her eyes to her computer.

Bang.

The teenager tripped and fell against her chair. Shalene shook and pulled her wooden chair closer to the desk as she composed herself. Her eyes widened, and terror dashed through her until the boy's words tumbled over like falling building blocks.

"So sorry, Ma'am. I mean Miss."

She turned around and saw the boy who shivered like a trapped chipmunk.

Shalene forced her lips to tilt upward. "Thank you. Please don't worry. I'm fine."

The cherry-faced boy breathed a sigh of relief. "Okay." And scampered away.

Shalene closed her eyes tight and crammed back a memory trying to escape.

No way. She gripped the table. Calm down. She focused on her work again.

See? You can get through it.

Now, Shalene walked to the café and lifted her head, turning right and left.

Whew. No sign of her.

Stop.

Keep listening to Rachel's voice.

You're like a magnificent warrior queen. You've received battle wounds, but you not only survived, but will thrive. Your presence says it all.

Shalene stopped for a moment and pumped her fist in the air. Yes.

She pulled her arm down right away and turned her head to see if anyone saw her.

So, what if they did?

With shoulders back, she lifted her head and relaxed the grip on her laptop case.

Wow, they say that starfish pose doesn't make a difference, but it does for me.

She entered the café and scoped out the environment. The early hour brought throngs of people, but at 10:00 A.M. only a few customers sat at tables. An older group of veterans, distinguished by their caps, sipped on their coffee, chatted, and laughed. Otherwise, some lone rangers concentrated on their drinks, snacks, and laptops in front of them.

No one looked up.

Fine with me.

After purchasing coffee and a scone, she found a booth and opened her laptop. *So far, so good.*

Shalene concentrated on the screen and got back to work. She didn't notice the time until her stomach growled.

Time to eat.

She went to the café's website and tapped hot pastrami sandwich with dark rye bread on the order form, and as she waited, she continued to click away on the keyboard.

While typing, a server's hand placed the sandwich and Diet Coke next to her. With her chin in her hand, she looked up to thank her. The sun burst splashed across the window like Mardi Gras Coreopsis flowers and impaired her vision except for the outline resembling a familiar woman. A jolt surged through Shalene as she did a double take, paralyzing her for a moment. The server appeared to notice and cocked her head, with a frown. Shalene sat back in her seat, and with a forced smile, told her everything looked delicious. When the server departed, Shalene leaned back and slouched in her seat as the coil around her chest released its grip.

Listen, you. Breathe. Not going to heal if you see every tall, young blonde-haired woman as a brute.

She bit into her sandwich, closed her eyes, and chewed. *Umm,* she said almost out loud. Her body quieted from the storm, and she overcame the temptation to leave. Each day she came further but needed regular practice and risk-taking to hush the demons of the past.

Pleased with her ability to overcome the desire to run, Shalene consumed the entire sandwich. She munched on the pickle in between bites. *Why not,* she thought, staring down at her lithe body? *Celebrate! Now, take the leap for the next group meeting.*

Yes, she'd request to start her story, unless Yardley insisted, but she didn't seem aggressive or fiery like that Sapphire.

Whew!

Poor Matt, but he handled her well. But still, would he return? How much can someone take? He looked like he could handle himself. She hoped he'd return because, for a rich, white dude, he seemed okay. At one time, she wouldn't have thought twice about the color of anyone's skin, but after what happened…

Time to explain the events that occurred long ago.

That sunny day popped into her mind, and a shadow loomed over her.

Don't go there, Shalene.

Rachel's right. The more you practice positive messaging, the more the past will return to where it belongs. The running video in her mind, which decreased since working with Rachel will freeze and become a picture in a photo album, which she will close without a second thought.

Yes, time to make that happen. Know Rachel will help. And speaking of Rachel, what's up with her?

Chapter Eleven

Rachel—April 13th

Rachel twirled around in a wide purple party dress with black stockings and brand-new Tango shoes.

Get in the mood.

She stared into her oval mirror with hands on hips and began stepping side to side. "Olé," with dancing eyes and arms in the air. She turned and snapped her fingers at two bouncing pooches with lolling tongues. A bolt of energy shot through her body and left an inner radiance like embers in a furnace.

Now, Rachel almost skipped toward the studio, lost in thoughts Alexandra planted in her mind. Her therapist asked those two questions, the second one, so out of character for her, and Rachel couldn't stop threading them through her mind.

Did she see Sam as the one and only man who might show kindness and openness? She laughed, maybe… for a moment, maybe not, which her cloistered heart refused to accept, until…

No!

Could someone puncture her armor? Might it be… Don't go there, Rachel. She shook her head and plucked even an etching of such a possibility invading her thoughts.

The second question. Did she consider herself not good enough to throw her hat in the ring? Did she want to stay invisible? Maybe her unconscious mind provided clues. She told the group members she wanted more visibility for them, but what about her?

Yes, but not competing for a man, never mind with a cougar like Justine.

Not wrestling with a big cat. Not afraid but not her style. If a man couldn't see through such behavior, he deserved her.

Justine? The claws came out. Not a meow but a growl.

Did her bold behavior remind her of someone?

She didn't want to compare her dead sister to Justine, but… could that be the reason for her placating someone whose eyes ripped her to shreds?

Something to discuss with Alexandra because dating hadn't even been on a dot on her horizon.

At least in her conscious awareness. Could her willingness mean she'd reconsider taking a risk?

Since Sam died five years ago, she focused on work, friends, and, of course, her pooches, Zsa Zsa and Gabor. Before she left, Rachel squatted down, embraced her dogs, and avoided the warm moisture from the tongues reaching for her face.

Not right now, sweeties, but later, promise, as she rubbed their curly white hair and warm bellies.

You two are sunshine even through stormy times. What would I do without you, Janine, and Bridget, and…?

Work. Yes. Work

Rachel stood and spoke to her dogs. "You join me sometimes in the office and online. We are privileged. Confidantes and helpers." Zsa Zsa got on her hind legs and wagged her paws. "Yes." Rachel laughed, patted her head and moved to Gabor. "Yes, you help too. You have healing abilities." She retrieved her purple bolero jacket and danced toward the door. "We need to cut back in a few years, and maybe, we'll move some place warmer with people who share our values and faith."

Now Rachel peeked at her watch and slowed her walk toward the studio. A fog swirled around like a gossamer veil. Even with the fickle weather, she loved New England, but a warmer climate would be better for her as she aged.

Maybe a relationship with someone in Massachusetts isn't in God's plans.

Over the last year, her besties pressured her, but the idea of dating sliced through her resistance like a dull blade.

Okay. They're right. What do I have to lose by meeting someone for coffee?

Not telling anyone, not even Alexandra.

One night before going to sleep, she crept into her living room and surveyed her surroundings.

Rachel, ah, no one can see you.

She opened the door of her laptop and booted up the internet. Two baby elephants with curled connected trunks came alive. She typed on her keyboard, and as if reaching for the forbidden fruit, her hesitant hand rotated the mouse to the first website.

Click.

Hera. The dating community for women choosing first. She registered with a unique pseudonym. Next, she explored others that her older clients referenced, *Flame* and *Connect,* and signed up for them.

I'm having more fun creating *nom de plumes* if nothing else. Another site, *Soar,* piqued her interest based on the chatter about its professionalism.

Alright. With a seven-day trial for each, why not start tonight?

An hour later? *Aargh.* Men with bulging bellies and unkempt long beards or inauthentic photos emerged under her requested categories. Other than a few differences, the apps replicated each other.

Delete, delete, delete.

Wait a minute, what about the traditional site, *Synchronicity.*

How could you forget, Rachel? Maybe because it's past midnight and you're exhausted?

She began typing answers to a questionnaire required by the organization, and one quarter through, she froze. Uh-uh, not my thing. Too weird. She clicked off the website and slammed her laptop shut.

What did you expect? Based on your clients' experiences, you know the territory. Treacherous. Stories about being catfished, ghosted, and the new one, fizzled, and both sexes lied about their ages.

Rachel gave women a pass. Why? Because most males preferred younger females. The men could be seventy but wanted a woman no older than fifty. Rachel recalled one client a haggard, sixty-year-old widower insistent on dating someone at least fifteen years younger than him. She suggested he consider someone within ten years of his age. He refused.

If a woman looked in the mirror, an overweight version stared back. No matter what angle she examined, an unattractive body persisted, magnified by menopause.

Men? Some shared the same anxieties even at a younger age, but for others, Brad Pitt or George Clooney returned their gaze.

And some things haven't budged much in five thousand years.

No way am I going out on a date this way, and in the twenty-first century, it seems the only way. Anytime she allowed a seed to sow about dating, the weeds of the online world sprouted and strangled any further thoughts.

She snapped out of her daydreams and entered the studio. Chatter, background Latino music, and a swishing of colorful clothes infused the room. The contagious energy spread to Rachel and excitement billowed through her body.

Wow, what fun.

Rachel pushed back her hair and fluffed her curls as she sauntered into the room.

Head high, shoulders back. Yes, Mama, I will, almost laughing.

Would Michael attend, or did he only talk the talk? If he tried to engage her, she'd need to get his last name. His face visited her a few times in the last week, but she scribbled over it if any other details materialized. Don't be too optimistic.

Familiar faces appeared, and decorative hands waved to her. Rachel's eyes swept the room, and in a corner of the studio she saw

Michael talking to the same stunning woman, Justine. Rachel's heart plummeted like a falling star, and she turned on her heel and mingled with the vibrant crowd.

She approached Claudia who bubbled over, grabbed her arm, and drew her into conversation with a couple of others.

A moment later, a deep voice interrupted and tapped her on the shoulder.

"Hello, partner."

Rachel turned around and found herself drowning in the blue-green eyes that captivated her a week earlier.

"Oh, hello!"

"You ready for another night of stumbling," Michael's eyes lifted, "with the hope toward improvement?"

"I thought you might be taken this evening," Rachel uttered with a gleam in her eye.

"No, I don't renege on a commitment." His eyes fastened on hers. "Justine inquired if I would like to practice with her, but I said thanks, I have another partner."

Michael gave her a brilliant smile as Rachel blushed and turned away for a moment. His hand went under her elbow. "Let's get a beverage."

He signaled for her to go ahead of him. They wove through the crowds. Rachel smiled and said hello as they made their way to the table of drinks. Rachel beheld the brilliant hues circulating the room, and she placed her hand on her skirt.

Glad I didn't skimp on the color.

They reached the table full of bottled water and other light drinks, and Michael extended his arm over others and retrieved a couple of bottles. He took her hand and led her to the black stacking chairs against the wall as they waited for the lesson to begin.

"Michael, I never got your last name."

"Parnell, like the Irish leader of the nineteenth century."

Rachel tilted her head. "Hmmm, I love Irish history, but I never heard of him."

"I wouldn't have, either, but I discovered I'm an indirect descendant of his. He was a popular and charismatic leader in Ireland, but he got himself in trouble because he took up residency with a married woman whom he ended up wedding. But you know how that worked back then, and I suppose even now."

"I do, very well, being in the helping profession."

"In what sector of the profession do you help others?"

"I guess I didn't tell you, but I'm a clinical social worker; psychotherapist."

"No, I don't believe you did. Are you in private practice?"

"I am. It sounds like you have some familiarity."

Michael grinned. "I've done some therapy myself over the years."

"Wow. Impressive. Many men resist it. Did you find it helpful?"

"I did. I sought help during two challenging times in my life. Once, while a medical resident in ophthalmology. At the time I engaged in an intense relationship with another resident, but sad for her, she became addicted to amphetamines."

"I understand." Rachel nodded. "I've heard that isn't uncommon for some professionals to use drugs to stay alert. Did you see much of that?"

"Well, yes and no. It's tempting to consider, but I avoided it. My girlfriend did not." Michael sighed, looking straight ahead. "We loved each other very much, but she loved the drugs more. I did everything to help her, but to no avail." He turned to her with a hint of a smile. "The therapy helped me see I couldn't want her recovery more than she did, so I ended the relationship."

"I often say the same thing to my clients. Despite how much I hope for something better for them, I can't hope for it more than they do."

His eyes crinkled with a smile. "Sage advice from the Maestra."

A flush spread across Rachel's face. "Um, thank you, but I wouldn't go that far."

"Don't minimize it. You can educate someone how to commit to memory and become adept in medicine, but it takes an extraordinary person to assist in the healing of the heart, soul, and mind." Michael's eyes lingered on her for a moment.

"How lovely of you to verbalize it like that, Michael. Nice to know we help heal others in different ways."

Michael nodded.

At that moment, Guillermo entered, emanating effervescence, and clapped three times, paused, and repeated the gesture.

"Good evening, my friends. Here we are together for another lesson in the magnificent dance of the Tango. Are you ready?"

A few voices called out, *Yes*.

"I can't hear you. Are you ready?"

Everyone yelled louder, *Yes!*

"Let us begin with the lesson."

Guillermo invited a volunteer to join him. A thin, older woman with bleached blonde hair swayed her hips toward him. She placed her hands in Guillermo. They demonstrated the basics, and at the end, he bowed and gestured toward the woman which signaled an applause.

"Now my amigos, we move to newer steps. Pay close attention."

"Muy bien." He clapped his hands again, and he and the woman twisted, turned, and swept along the shiny hardwood floor. The woman's wide skirt swooshed. Her leg over his in one move.

Guillermo stopped and invited the guests to practice.

"Are you ready for a new adventure, partner?" Michael's eyes locked onto hers for a moment.

"I am, sir." Rachel studied his hands as she placed hers into his. A tingle jotted through her like a bolt of lightning.

Ooh. Don't let that happen. Concentrate on the moves.

But her antennae couldn't ignore Michael's body close to hers.

For the next hour, Rachel fumbled with Michael as they conquered the intricate patterns of the Tango. Rachel caught Michael's eyes on her each time her gaze traveled above his chest.

At the end of the practice, they strolled over to a quieter part of the studio.

Michael stood a foot taller than Rachel. His eyes roamed up and down, and a warmth crawled up her face.

"I didn't realize how petite you were."

"Yes, I'm vertically challenged."

"Well, it doesn't detract from your vivacious presence." Michael laughed.

"Ah. Thank you for the compliment."

"The truth." His eyes clasped hers for a moment.

Too intense. She chirped a laugh and played with her skirt. "My mother lectured me that good things come in small packages. It took years for me to accept her reminders."

"Your mother offered words of wisdom."

Rachel grinned. "Yes, sometimes. I loved her very much, but at times, her issues of being overprotective could be overwhelming."

"I'm sure, but who doesn't have issues? You wouldn't have a business if the world existed with perfect humans."

Someone turned up the music, and Michael stretched out his arm. "Shall we try again?"

"Yes, Dr. Michael." Rachel's eyes sparkled.

She put her hands in his, and for the next hour, Rachel remained quiet, focused on the dance steps, and stifled pushy thoughts about how well they fit. The Latino vibe enveloped her, and it unshackled a creative spirit restrained for too long.

She tipped her head back at one point, and Michael leaned into her and brought her closer to him.

Everything inside crackled like fireworks.

Savor this.

The hour ended, and Rachel found Michael studying her before he bowed. "It's been an honor to dance with someone as deft as you."

Rachel beamed. "The pleasure was all mine."

"You know there's a Milonga this Saturday where we get to dress in festive clothing."

"Yes, I heard about it."

"Would you consider attending and giving me the privilege of being my dance partner for the night, Rachel?" Michael's eyes explored hers. "By the way, I never caught your last name."

"Yes, I'd love to dance with you at my first Milonga, and Karem's my last name."

"Karem? What's the ethnicity of that name?"

"Jordanian."

"Ah, I wouldn't have guessed. I pegged you as Italian."

"Many people do. Karem, I understand, means generous."

"How fitting for someone in the helping profession. Well, Rachel Karem. I look forward to seeing you on Saturday evening." Michael gazed at her for a few seconds. "Oh, let's exchange numbers in case something happens. It's rare I get called, but if there's an unexpected trauma for eye surgery, I could receive a call for consultation, which might be quick or not."

Michael pulled out his wallet and handed Rachel a card showing his credentials and work number.

"Do you have a card, Ms. Rachel?"

Rachel took his business card and brushed her fingers across his until he released his hand. Without looking at him, she stroked the raised font on the card. "I like yours. Let me give you mine." Rachel dug into her pocketbook, found her card holder, and plucked out a card.

"Here you go, Dr. Michael."

Michael's eyes crinkled.

"Touché."

Michael examined the card and looked at her. "Again, I'm impressed."

"Likewise."

The couple walked away from the studio, and Rachel reached her car.

"Until Saturday evening, Dr. Michael."

"Yes, Ms. Rachel. I'm looking forward to it." Michael bowed again, walked backward for a few steps, and turned around. He strolled along further, then looked back at her with a wave and brilliant smile.

Rachel opened the car door, laughed, and fluttered her fingers.

"Ah." She gripped the steering wheel and stomped up and down on the floor of her car. "Oh my God."

She laughed. A warm glow infused her body, and Rachel associated a color with it. Rosy-peach sprinkled with gold like a summer cocktail. She turned on the ignition and began the trek home. Could Alexandra be right? Could Michael unbolt the tight clamp surrounding her heart? Would she take a risk?

She swatted at a negative message trying to burrow into her happiness.

Turn on the radio.

"Siri, play 1979."

Rachel twisted one of her curls around her index finger and hummed to the oldie but goodie.

Dr. Michael Parnell, we shall see what God plans for me. Or… Okay, Rachel, say it.

Us?

Chapter Twelve

Session Four—April 14th—Shalene

They waited.

A snapping tension reverberated through the room, and the empty seat protruded like a glaring blemish.

Matt always arrived early, but not tonight. Five minutes passed.

Shalene peered at Rachel, who appeared more fatigued than her usual energetic self.

She knew little about Rachel, nor did she wish to intrude. Every so often, Rachel shared that she engaged in her own therapy to deal with issues. She told Shalene that every therapist should examine themselves and know what it's like to sit on the other side.

At one point, Rachel's widowhood slipped out. Other than hints about loss and estrangement, no self-disclosure.

She didn't need to know more. Rachel created a safe environment for her. The first white woman she'd trusted in a long time.

Since the incident, Shalene remained a serious and skittish version of her natural animated self. So far, she spoke few words in these sessions. Except for Rachel, she stayed cautious about sharing with people different from her. Now, Jason didn't seem bothered by the others. Of course, he hadn't endured what she did.

Wait, a minute. How did she know?

She imagined her mother grabbing her shoulders and asking, "Yes, how do you know?"

Shalene looked down at her hands. Although she inherited

her mother's beautiful tapering fingers with long nail beds, her manicures showed a penchant for clear gloss only.

The manicurist couldn't persuade her with the variety of colors—*poppy red, peachy peony, tantalizing blue.* Not for me. Don't want to detract from my rings.

She loved her rings, with eight adorning her fingers, and at times, like this evening, extra rings on each thumb for good luck.

Tonight might be the night she started—after Matt.

Rachel glanced at her clock.

"We'll give Matt a few more minutes before starting."

"I hope he returns," Yardley said in her usual subdued voice. "He seems like a nice man."

Everyone nodded. Sapphire kept her eyes downcast but bobbed her head.

"I'm confident he'll appear," Rachel said. "We'll give him a few more minutes.

A car door slammed, and footsteps clomped and hurried into the building. The doorknob turned. Matt, tie undone, entered the office and sat in his usual chair.

"Sorry everyone. A meeting went overtime." Matt looked at Rachel. "I should've texted you."

"No problem. Just glad you're here."

Matt looked down at his sleeves, undid the cuff links, and rolled up his shirt. He grinned at Rachel. "Hey, you know me. I promised I'd never bail, no matter what occurred."

He gave Sapphire a fleeting glance and turned back to Rachel. "I think, uh, since I walked in late, I'd like to defer to someone else rather than get more into my story."

Rachel shook her head. "Okay, well, Shalene and Yardley, you've not shared anything yet. Would one of you like to begin?"

Yardley crouched her head and extended her hand to Shalene. "Please go ahead."

"You sure?" Shalene asked.

Yardley's eyes widened. "Absolutely."

Shalene examined her hands again. Her eyes sought Rachel, who returned with an enthusiastic nod. That's all Shalene needed. Her eyes widened as she scanned the room.

"Okay, everyone. Here goes."

Shalene splayed her fingers. "I grew up in one of the nicest suburbs in Boston. My parents met in law school. Dad came from, as he states it, *humble beginnings*, but didn't feel poor because his mom said they were rich in love."

Shalene looked up with a half-smile, and the others smiled back. "My Dad joked with my mom because she came from a family both rich in love and," she rubbed her fingers, "*cha-ching*, adding that they were privileged but not spoiled."

Nods and tilts.

"My brother, Steve, and I lived a cool but sheltered life. We went to private schools and excelled in academics and sports. Our parents wanted us to have the best and to protect us from racial prejudice, which we experienced if we left our safe places of school, home, and church."

"What happened the times you did?" Sapphire asked.

"Ooh, you don't know my mother, Lena. She'd stare them down, and they'd slink away like a fox." Shalene smirked. "No one messes with my mother."

"She sounds formidable. What kind of law does she practice?" Matt leaned forward and laced his hands.

"Guess?" Shalene held back the frothy mirth within her.

"I know. Litigation." Yardley's thin smile widened.

"You got it." Shalene's released her laugh. "My parents enforced richness with love in our home. We grew up watching them debate on national and world issues. My mother gestured with her hands to get her point across while my father walked around with his hands in his pockets nodding."

"That's great, Shalene. Terrific role models." Jason tapped his hands on his chin. "Harry, Dad, did his best under the circumstances." His gaze shifted from her to the floor.

"Thank you, Jason. I'm most fortunate, but your dad did well, considering what he and you endured." Shalene twisted her thumb ring and peered at him.

He nodded but kept his eyes on the floor.

"I hope I didn't say anything offensive?" Shalene gulped as she studied him.

Jason waved her off. "Nothing to do with you, Ms. Shalene. Please keep going." He folded his arms and nodded.

"My parents never sugarcoated the history of slavery, but they emphasized to us that it existed throughout the world, and our great country strove to correct things."

Sapphire bobbed her head. "Got it, Shalene. Like I told everyone, my grandparents on both sides escaped Castro's Cuba, and I can visualize their response right now."

"Some of our discussions centered around the ethos of the great MLK's teachings, and my parents, people of faith, dedicated themselves to our church community."

"They sound fabulous, Shalene." Matt fidgeted with his pockets and stretched his legs out.

Shalene twisted her ring on her right index finger. "They're cool. After Sunday dinners, we'd go to the living room, and my father would open the Bible, flip the pages, and read a random verse. You should hear his voice. Lots of people said he sounded like the old actor Richard Burton. Not sure who he is."

"Sounds familiar." Matt raised a finger. "I think my parents mentioned him. Rach, you've heard of him, right?"

"Well, as a woman of a certain age…" Rachel's eyes sparkled like smoky topaz stones. "Yes, Sir Richard Burton's acting became legendary with his marvelous voice."

Shalene nodded. "My father. Amazing. Anyway, he'd ask us our thoughts about the verse, and Stevie and I would push each other. *You go. No. You go first.*"

Shalene stopped, allowed her thoughts to drift, and she touched each ring on the other hand.

Stillness skidded into the room.

Someone shuffled their feet, and Shalene glanced at Rachel. "Sorry. Just thinking."

"No problem, my dear." Rachel's eyes probed hers. "You okay to continue?"

Shalene's dimple blossomed. "I am." Her eyes circled the room. "Everything seemed great. My brother graduated from high school and left for college in Florida. Two years later, there I am sitting at graduation. Flashbulbs, videos, parties, and college out west."

"Why out west?" Jason's eyebrows knitted together.

"I don't know. Warmer and bigger." Shalene offered him a half-smile. "Now, I wonder if things would have been better if…" Shalene wandered. "Never mind. Anyway, my parents took me to college, and things seemed perfect. Roommate, perfect—a nerd like us." Shalene put her hand over her mouth to tame her laugh.

Jason clapped. Matt raised his thumb, and Sapphire and Yardley giggled.

"And classes, perfect. By the way, I majored in marketing. And the perfect word for freshman year?" She giggled again.

"Perfect?" Sapphire bent forward, slapped her thigh, and stomped her feet with the others joining in laughter.

"Laughter has healing components." Rachel shook her head and dabbed her eyes. "Look at you." Her hand swept the room.

Shalene waited. This group seems good. Rachel said I'd fit in, and I think I do.

"Ms. Shalene, look what you unleashed." Jason kneaded his eyes. "I know you've got more to share which won't be such fun, but boy, Ms. Rachel's right, laughter should be bottled as an antibiotic."

"Thanks, Jason. I think I needed that as I get to the rest. So…" Shalene blinked. "Our university offered Greek life. Lots of sororities to choose from, and I rushed a few and got chosen by my favorite. Guess what I did?"

She glanced at everyone, and their heads shook.

"A cartwheel." Shalene put her hands over her mouth.

"Ms. Shalene, you're full of surprises." Jason's eyes locked on hers.

Shalene's heart darted like a squirrel. Yowzah. He's a cutie.

"Okay. Time to get serious. I joined this one because it seemed diverse, but I found out later, not the case."

"What do you mean?" Yardley pitched forward.

"Getting to it." Shalene gulped. "Freshman year, we lived in our dorms. I attended meetings, and the group seemed focused on service. Summer came. Went home and did an internship as an influencer with an internet company. Sophomore year, I moved into the sorority house, and that's about the time things changed."

Shalene put her hands on her thighs and tapped them. "A new president wanted us to change the focus and promote feminism. We'd sit at meetings, and she'd raise her fist about women's oppression. Most of us stayed quiet, but you know the drill. A few vocal people clapped and shouted, *Yeah*."

She played with her rings again and studied her pinky finger. "Look, as a woman—a black woman—I'm all for pushing equal rights, but it's all we talked about, so what did I do? Stopped going to meetings."

"I don't blame you." Sapphire's hair fell over her face as she tapped her foot louder than usual. "Sounds like a form of bullying. Conform. Otherwise…"

Shalene flashed Sapphire a sideway smile. "You know where this is leading."

Sapphire nodded with an unfocused stare.

Shalene let out a deep exhale. "My absence didn't go unnoticed. One night, a couple of sisters stood in front of my room and blocked my entrance. *Why aren't you supporting us?* My stomach roiled, but I did my best to sound confident about my right to attend or not. They gave me a dirty look but left me alone."

"I can't stand bullies," Sapphire hissed and wrapped her arms around herself.

"Never happened to me, but I agree." Matt shifted in his seat.

Jason and Yardley nodded.

"A few weeks later, a couple of sisters joined me in the cafeteria. They told me how turned off they were about the sorority's direction. They planned on leaving unless it changed course. I reached for their hands, and we pledged to support each other. But I didn't feel so strong. Every time I entered the house, my stomach did jumping jacks, and I started losing sleep. So, what did I do? Arrived home late and left early."

"Must have been tough for you." Yardley tilted her head.

Yowzah. She's even speaking more.

"Yes, but I spent hours at the library and started volunteering with a wonderful organization, The Golden Rule Club. Anyone heard of it?" Shalene's eyes swept the room.

Everyone shook their heads.

"Well, let me tell you. The best experience of my life. It saved me." Her eyes shined. "The coolest club. Serviced the downtrodden, and at my first meeting, I said, *Girl, you arrived home.*" Her lone dimple emerged.

"All kinds of shapes and colors of people attended the gathering. Black, brown, white, conventional clothing, goth, lots of tattoos and piercings, and people dressed like me. You know. Kind of boring." She giggled. "Except for my rings."

"You don't look boring to me." Sapphire grimaced. "Not with all of those gorgeous rings on gorgeous you."

"Thank you." Shalene peeked at her. "You made my night." She shifted her eyes and examined her rings. "I guess what I mean is that everyone had a unique style, and most important? We wanted to help others."

"What did your sorority sisters say about your absences?" Matt lifted his eyes and crossed his legs.

"Getting to it." Shalene lifted her finger and took a deep breath, warding off anxiety slithering into her body. She closed her eyes.

"My dear, are you okay?"

Shalene opened her eyes and anchored onto Rachel's. "Yes. Just remembering what happened next." She blinked a few times. "One spring day, while in the ladies' room, I'm washing my hands, humming a cool song, and look up in the mirror and notice a senior sister, hands on her hips, glaring at me. I shut the faucet, turned, and kind of froze." Shalene's eyes roved over her hand. "I see it now like yesterday. She started lecturing me about my loyalty to *the cause*. I listened and ignored my wet hands. Drip, drip. Too afraid to even go for a paper towel. Just stood there and nodded."

She halted and shut her eyes again. "I'm okay. Just breathing in the delicious scent."

Take a deep breath, Shalene.

"So, after the sister stomped out of the ladies' room, I decided it was time to resign. But funny thing, I'd start the email, and…" She shook her head. "Something stopped me from finishing it." Shalene swallowed and her gaze became unfocused. "No matter. I don't think it would have stopped what came next."

Shalene looked up at the other members and fanned her fingers.

"This is where it gets… You know."

"Anything we can do for you, Shalene?" Jason pushed his eyebrows together.

She shook her head. "Just have to go for it."

Shalene glanced at Rachel.

"You're doing great, Shalene, but you know if you wish to stop, just give the signal."

Shalene's one dimple sprang, and she offered Rachel a hint of a smile. "Like everybody else, once you get going, you want to keep the momentum."

Her lips formed an "O," and words careened from her throat.

"By the spring, I was spending more time with The Golden Rule Club." Her smile exploded from within her. "Lots of fun, which helped me not to think about the sorority. Needed to resign. But my fingers hovered midway around the keyboard anytime I tried. Too much. Okay, after exams." She put her palms together and clapped her fingers a few times. She glanced above everyone's head at the sea-green walls and swallowed.

Her eyes found their way back to Rachel and then to the floor. "Okay." She played with a couple of rings. "One day in late spring, I joined a few of my peers for Club Day."

She glanced at the others who stared back and pitched forward. "I know." A forced laugh ripped from her. "I kept you waiting, so I won't delay anymore."

"No hurries, Ms. Shalene." Jason's eyes skimmed the other members. "I think I can speak for all of us. You take your time."

Nods and yeses emerged.

Shalene mouthed thank you. "I still experience the day. Not a cloud in the sky. Sun rays that warmed the soul. Green grass that ushered in the smell of spring. I remember all of it."

She stopped, focused on each member, and cleared her throat. "My heart jumped for joy. Helping people. My family's modus operandi. Have you felt that way when helping others?"

"All the time, Ms. Shalene." Jason rubbed his head.

What a cutie pie.

"I do it for a living." Sapphire's eyes sparkled. "Nothing more rewarding."

Beautiful and just as nice—except toward Matt.

"Shalene, you and Jason, got me thinking. I do, but need to do more." Matt nodded at her.

Ignored Sapphire. Understandable.

"My parents ingrained it in us." Yardley gave a sliver of a smile.

Yowzah. Expressing more and more.

Shalene glanced at the orchids in the office. Phalaenopsis. Mesmerizing. Following her first visit with Rachel, she went out and purchased a few. So haughty, and elegant, and for some reason, reassuring. A metaphor for resilience. If their petals died, they returned for another bloom. Maybe another.

"So that day I passed out pamphlets about our club, and later in the morning, a few women, black and white, arranged a booth near ours. They kept shouting at by-passers about their message of no hate." Shalene's voice choked, and she placed a hand over her mouth. "Now, it seems so hypocritical. They pumped their fists in the air and swept their arms. A couple of the more aggressive women asked, *What's your problem?* if people ignored them. I wouldn't look at them."

Shalene shut her eyes and twisted her rings more. "So, I'm getting this out. We got ready to leave, and I caught Isla, a woman, a Viking incarnate, snarling at me. I remember my heart pounded like someone punched my chest." Shalene's eyes welled up. "She called out my name, and I couldn't move. She came too close and towered over me. *Where've you been? You're not joining our gatherings to stop the hate? Think you're too good for your sisters, Shalene?* I backed away from her and held my head high, even though I shook. *Isla, I don't know what you're talking about, but I'm about to leave.*"

Shalene gulped, grabbed the sides of her chair, and her eyes clasped onto Rachel's.

"My dear Shalene…" Rachel's face searched hers.

"Just needed your face for comfort." Shalene blinked. "I want to keep going, but I'm staying steady on you."

"Whatever works my dear."

"I forced myself to turn around, and footsteps ran behind me. Claws dug into my shoulder, and I tried shifting. *Bam.*" Shalene swallowed and didn't take her eyes off Rachel.

"I felt my face almost spin around, and I fell. *Traitor.* A clump of my hair fell in front of me, and fists hit me until someone pulled her off."

"Oh my God," Sapphire blurted out. Matt's large hand extended in front of her, and she held it for a minute. Her eyes moved to his for a moment. "Thank you for that." His eyebrows drew together, and he placed another hand over hers. "Anytime."

Shalene nodded, released her hand from his, and sought Rachel's face again.

"I tried to stand, but swayed and everything around me swam. Someone caught me as I fell, and everything kind of blurred. The shape of friends and police, I think, blaring sounds from sirens became louder. Strong hands lifted me onto a gurney, and after strapping me down, a needle pinched my skin. Whispers of, *Everything will be fine.* Then, nothing."

Shalene's eyes shifted from Rachel to the others.

Jason's arms were folded.

Matt's eyebrows stayed drawn together.

Yardley's hands gripped together with knuckles protruding.

"If Isla were here right now, I'd get in her face." Sapphire's eyes narrowed.

Shalene nodded. "The next thing I remember was a far-away sound, and a drum pounding in my head. Everything seemed too loud. I tried lifting my arm. Too heavy, and my mother's voice said something."

Shalene's eyes clasped onto Rachel's again. "*What's she doing here,* I thought, but then, fell asleep."

Shalene looked down and lifted her feet. "My poor parents." She shook her head. "So upset and worried. Believe it or not, no broken bones, but lots of internal bleeding and emergency surgery because of an injury close to my femoral artery. My mother couldn't stop crying, and my dad, well, did his best to stay composed and take over. I still hear his voice. *Shalene, the D.A. plans on pressing charges against the young woman, but they won't tell me more, since her father is a big-named donor. No matter what happens, you're coming home.*"

"Ms. Shalene, I don't mean to interrupt, but I can't believe what you endured." Jason pounded his fists on top of one another. "You think it was racism?"

"I considered it, but she hung out with black women." Shalene smiled at Jason and shifted her gaze. "But that didn't stop me from hating white women—until I met Rachel."

Rachel's eyes glistened.

"More about that later."

"Thank God, you're alive." Sapphire scowled. "But I have a question."

Shalene smirked at the fiery woman. "Sure. Love your passion, Sapphire."

"Thank you. Can't help it." Sapphire's tresses fell in her face. "I want to know what this Isla looked like."

"I don't know. Blondish hair but sparse and big boned. Like I said, she reminded me of a Viking woman without braids." Shalene studied Sapphire. "Why?"

"You're beautiful, slender, and elegant, and I bet the lug envied you."

"You think? Because Rachel also posed that to me a while back."

Sapphire nodded and jutted her chin at Rachel. "Therapists understand envy and jealousy. Right, Rachel?"

"Yes." Rachel tilted her head. "As I told you Shalene, it could be; and now you hear another therapist hypothesizing the same thing."

Shalene nodded. "Okay. Thanks. Not sure how it will help, but maybe." She grinned.

"What happened next, Shalene?" Yardley asked.

Shalene offered Yardley a half-smile. "Things got better." She turned her gaze to her rings again. "I returned home with my parents and spent the summer recuperating. Lots of nightmares about Isla and what happened. My mother wanted me to see a therapist, and I refused but did accept a doctor's prescription for medication. That fall I attended community college and then transferred to a Black Christian college in the South."

"Why no therapist?" Matt rolled his hand. "Resistant like the rest of … well, I'll speak for myself."

"Not alone, Matt." Jason roared.

Yardley shook her head.

"Not sure." Shalene's gaze became unfocused. "Fear or just hoping to put it all past me. I don't know."

"Well, as the only therapist here besides," Sapphire put her hand out to Rachel. "Of course." Her half-covered face turned to Shalene. "I guess it doesn't matter. You're here now."

"Thank you so much, Sapphire." Shalene blinked and pivoted her head. "But I think Matt posed a good question even if I don't know the answer."

Matt put his hands on his belly and bowed.

"What would you like to do next, my dear?" Rachel's head cocked.

"I'm going to finish this." Shalene nodded and took a deep breath. "I get to this small school and immersed myself in my studies. I joined a Golden Rule chapter, and for the next three years, studies, volunteering and hanging out with a small circle of friends. After graduation, I moved back to the Boston area, and for a while, things seemed good. Started a job with a digital marketing company and with my parents' help, purchased a small condo in Boston. I even stopped the meds. The past seemed like a faded photo, at least until…" Shalene stopped, made a fist, and placed it on the center of her chest. "Well, until what happened next."

Shalene's eyes grabbed onto Rachel's again. "Who thought the world could shrink so much? One morning in March at the bakery where I bought coffee every morning, crowds of people waited in line." She shifted her gaze to her rings then back to Rachel. "I handed my favorite server a tip, turned around, and Isla's face leered at me."

"Are you kidding?" Jason grimaced.

Shalene glanced at him; his herculean arms folded as he shook his head.

"No." She sighed and returned her gaze to the floor. "Her eyes bulged at me. I said, *What are you doing here?* and she said, all full of herself, *I now work in Boston.* I tried to move past her, but she blocked me and told me the D.A. dropped the charges and expunged everything from her record. I pushed past her but heard her laugh. *Maybe we'll see each other again.*"

"Oh my God. The world is too small," Sapphire scoffed as she combed her hair away from her face.

Shalene nodded, and her hands found her lap. "For the next week, I called in sick. Sleep…" She looked up for a moment. "Bad. Isla's face came at me, like a gigantic lizard."

"She sounds like a lizard," Sapphire chirped and then covered her mouth. "Sorry."

Shalene blinked at Sapphire. "Don't be. It helps." Shalene's eyes found the floor again, and she grabbed the sides of the chair. "I took Benadryl, and then something happened."

She glanced at Rachel. "The pandemic. A horrible thing, but it rescued me. I worked from home, able to avoid friends and family, but…" She tapped her knuckles. "My mom." Shalene shook her head with a half-smile. "A few months after everything began, my mother insisted I visit them. She knew and said, *Girl, no more excuses about therapy.* For a while I stomped my feet and said, *No way*, until a few years ago."

Now Shalene glanced at the group. "That's about the time I agreed to meet Rachel." Her eyes pooled, and through her blurred vision, solemn looks returned.

Tears trickled down her face. Jason swallowed, handing her a tissue, and everyone shook their heads.

"I didn't believe I'd trust another white woman again." Shalene's eyes flickered, revealing her dimple. "But I did, and I do." She turned her gaze to Rachel.

Jason leaned forward. "Hey Shalene, I get it. Something horrible happened to me." He sighed, "Which I'll get to, but I stayed away from people. All people and even God almighty."

Members nodded.

She saw Rachel peek at her watch before soft eyes locked onto Shalene's. "Thank you for going so deep. Like everyone else, you're most courageous, dear Shalene. How are you doing?"

Shalene's gaze went outward. Then she looked up. "Not sure, but I think okay."

Rachel's eyes searched Shalene's. "We have a couple of minutes left, my dear. Any further thoughts about any of this?"

"Right now, I feel kind of…" Shalene paused. "I guess…*free*?" But I'll let you know next week." She grinned at Rachel and the others.

"Okay, everyone…"

"See everybody next week." Matt bolted up and glanced at her. "Hey, thanks Shalene. You're one brave lady." His gaze rove over the room before settling on Rachel.

His deadpan expression shifted to a dazzling smile. "Thanks, Rach." And with a salute to her, he pivoted his massive body and leaped out the door.

Chapter Thirteen

Rachel and Alexandra—April 15th

Rachel arrived early for her Zoom appointment and waited for Alexandra's permission for entry. With her chin in her hands, Rachel studied the screen, still amazed at what technology could do. The pandemic created pain for many, but she benefited from the power of virtual therapy. Yeah, not groups, but individuals. Why not?

The signal for admission appeared, with an elegant Alexandra smiling at her. Her white locks were woven into a loose braid.

"Hi, Alexandra. How was your week?"

Alexandra leaned closer with hands clasped. "Very well. Thank you for asking, and now tell me about you and yours.

Her usual response.

Nothing new.

Are you any different, Rachel? Noooo.

"Let me start first with the group dynamics that unfolded."

Rachel paused after expressing her concerns about Matt.

"I don't think his abrupt departure related to Shalene's story. She talked about her PTSD and agoraphobia without labeling it. Not Matt's situation."

"What are your thoughts?"

"The only thing I can think of is the buildup of stories. Everyone's trust issues are emerging. Sapphire with men, and Jason's around loss. He's not finished with his story. Now Shalene with white women." Rachel shook her head. "I'm not sure." She gazed outward past Alexandra for a moment. "I guess we'll find out next week. I hope." Her eye contact returned to her therapist.

"What do you mean?"

"Oh, you know me. I continue worrying. Am I saying enough? Am I providing the right amount of support? Have I missed something going on with Matt?" Rachel grinned. "The endless plight of a therapist—never good enough."

Alexandra studied her. "I'll say this again and again. Why do your clients keep showing up if you're not good enough? And from what you've shared about Matt, he sounds like he'd tell you."

Rachel paused before giving a tentative nod. "You're right. Thanks for the reminder."

Alexandra remained quiet. Rachel became familiar with her more subdued style long ago. Not hers. She couldn't stand a lengthy silence or pause. No problem, she never attended a session without something to discuss.

Rachel stared back at Alexandra. "Now on to the Tango lesson and Michael. You're right. I've every right to throw my hat in the ring, and I kept that in mind Wednesday night."

Alexandra's eyes asked for more.

Rachel shared about her exchange with Michael and the ever-present Justine hovering around.

"They have some connection, but I know nothing about it or much about him."

"Well, you'll find out, won't you?"

"Maybe, but I'm still not convinced that he's different from some men out there."

"Again, how will you know unless you learn more about him, and…" Alexandra leaned in, a silver coil of her loose braid fell out, "what do you imagine could be the worst thing possible?

"He's a narcissist or a sociopath who kills women."

Alexandra frowned. "Anything's possible, but?"

Rachel sighed. "Well, I guess I don't really believe that, otherwise, I wouldn't meet him at the Milonga this Saturday."

Alexandra's eyes lifted. "Aha."

"Yes, he asked if I'd be his partner for the monthly event. We get all spruced up." Rachel's eyes sparkled. "Now that, I'm dying to do. I love dressing up, as you know."

"I do."

"No matter what happens, I can wear my beautiful red dress, black stockings, and extra makeup."

Alexandra offered a mischievous look. "Who knows, maybe more?"

Rachel shook her head. "I don't know. I guess I'm no different from my clients. Trust remains major for me."

Alexandra nodded.

"But the good news?" Rachel's head rose like a watered flower. "For the first time in years, I've pushed myself to get past the past."

"Yes." Alexandra's eyes shone. "And do you think running the group helped you?"

"You know. It might have." Rachel paused. "Even if this connection with Michael goes further, not sure it will," her hands went up, "it'll take time for me to trust him. He's going to ask about family. You know that."

Alexandra put her hands out.

"You, Janine, and Bridget think my situation is no big deal, but since all of us are therapists, we get it. The average Joe or Josephine doesn't."

"What makes you so certain?"

"Oh, come on. We hear about people who've no clue about family estrangement. Yes, they understand dysfunction, but how many times have we heard, *Family first, no matter what?*" Rachel inclined her head forward. "Even for murder, look at the Bulgers."

"Yes, I suppose you're right, but I'm not convinced most people are so oblivious to not understand certain situations arise, not in one's control."

"I know you're gone for a few weeks." Rachel gulped. "And I'll miss you, but when you come back, I'd like to discuss Damian again."

Alexandra's eyes softened. "Yes, we'll have much to catch up on, and of course, we can talk about your nephew."

Rachel nodded. For the next few minutes, she spoke about random issues and wished Alexandra a wonderful trip. When the session ended, Rachel powered off her computer and turned around toward her living area. The leopard pillows and red sofa exuded a more daring and creative streak.

Damian!

He showed his majestic eye in early adolescence. On the rare occasion, she saw him, Damian's long fingers grabbed a camera. *Click, flash*. Laughter from people whose photos he snapped. Leah sent them to Rachel via iPhone. Rachel tapped on the attachments and hoped some, even one, might be of her. Never. After a while, fewer invitations arrived, and soon no pictures followed.

Sitting in the new townhouse she purchased following Sam's death, Rachel sat at her kitchen table, flipping through swatches of colors and fabrics. She'd walk around her living room with a large pad and sketch her ideas on paper. She wanted to share her creativity with Damian, but God forbid, and at the time, she often closed her eyes.

A casket flipped open, and Leah popped up like a piece of bread from a toaster. Her finger wagged in Rachel's face. "Stay away from Damian."

Now Rachel shook her head, and the dogs scampered around her as she stared out the window and opened the vault again.

Jonathan marched toward her. She saw the other guests turn, watching him take long, steady strides. His balding head lost more hair, and his usual pallid face appeared beet-red.

"Rachel, what are you doing here?" He kept his voice low.

"Jonathan, nice to see you too," Rachel said without a smile.

"Yes, hello," Jonathan said.

"Damian invited me. Didn't you know?"

"No, I didn't." His face came closer to hers. Rachel could see his labored breathing.

Damian emerged from the crowd and sauntered over to them. Jonathan glared at him.

"What are you doing?"

Damian, with a drink in one hand, looked at his other hand before responding. He grimaced. "I didn't think I needed to check with you about my showing, Father."

Jonathan heaved. "How could you?" He shook his head. "Rachel and, um…," he glanced at Janine.

"I'm Janine."

Jonathan gave a brisk nod and turned to Rachel. "For your well-being, I think you should leave."

Rachel shifted her gaze to Damian. His eyes glazed over before he gave her a fixed smile. "Auntie, Father's concern might be overblown, but it's up to you whether you listen to him."

Jonathan threw his arms up. "Rachel, this exhibit might upset you, so…," He scowled at his son before laying softer eyes on Rachel. "I think there's enough pain right now so, well, don't say I didn't warn you." Jonathan wandered toward some people calling his name.

Someone grabbed Damian's arm, and he excused himself from Rachel and Janine.

An invisible fist to the chest caused a pang. Rachel lowered her eyes, dreading the undeniable truth about Damian's intentions. She peeked at Janine, who lingered close and studied her friend.

"Rach, something's not right. You feel it too, don't you?"

Rachel lowered her eyes again and nodded.

"Maybe we should go, but I'll do whatever you want."

Rachel surveyed the room and noticed a few people gesturing at photographs that she couldn't see from her position. Some strolled by her, whispering, and shaking their heads.

Rachel licked her lips. "I need to see this through."

They moved toward the photos. More people gawked at Rachel. She heard a couple of them. "Isn't that the sister? Must be. Other than the hair, spitting image of his mother."

Her phone rang with the familiar ringtone and picture.
Saved by the call. Better not to go down that path right now.
Later. Maybe this time it won't hurt as much.

Chapter Fourteen

Rachel and Michael—La Milonga—April 16th

Saturday evening arrived, and Michael texted her, telling her so far, so good for tonight. This time, Rachel couldn't ignore the thrill pulsing through her veins and sent a positive emoji to confirm.

She looked in her full-length, wooden-framed oval mirror at her attire and giggled.

Wow. *Soy la Senora Karem.* The reflected image wore a red dress with black touches. The dress cinched at her waist with a full skirt ready for twirling. She touched the clipped crimson rose secured above her ear with the hair pulled from that side of her face to highlight the ornament.

Rachel gazed down her legs, cloaked in black sheer stockings with black dancing shoes covering her feet. Her smokey topaz eyes carried extra brown-taupe eye shadow, kohl eyeliner, and lots of mascara. She nodded at her image, dipped back for a moment, and smiled. She then stood up—head high and shoulders back.

There. How's that, Justine? You're not going to intimidate me.

Rachel, remember what you tell the people you try to help.

In the office, she often showed a stance of confidence with her clients. She'd rise out of her seat, put a book on her head, and walk in her high heels with slow precision. When she stopped, she'd invite her more insecure, usually female, clients to try it. They'd take the book from her, exaggerate a slow stride, and

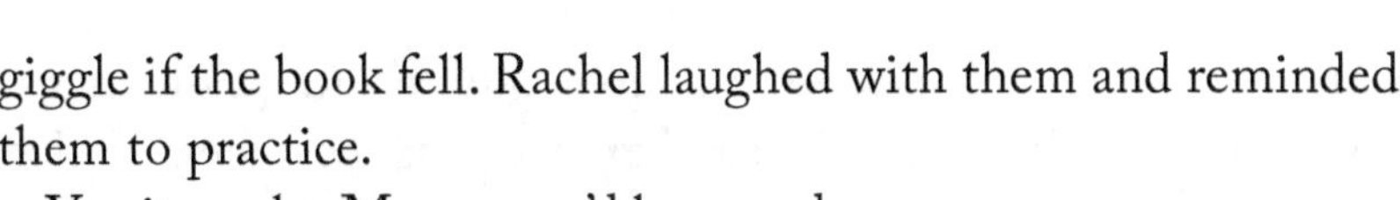

giggle if the book fell. Rachel laughed with them and reminded them to practice.

Yes, it works. Mama, you'd be proud.

She took one more glimpse of herself, put her hands above her head, and snapped her fingers.

"Olé!"

Now Rachel strolled to the studio and spotted Michael coming toward her. His eyes shined, and he took her hands and examined her from head to toe.

"You look stunning."

Rachel's eyes roamed over her partner. "You look pretty fabulous yourself." She examined his attire—a white, open-collared shirt with an expensive-looking black jacket and trousers, sharp black shoes peeking out. His silver mane displayed a recent trim with length in the back.

His unusual eyes sparkled. "Shall we head in?" He reached for her arm and tucked it under his, and they entered the studio. Rachel sizzled like an electric current.

The music and chatter synchronized with colorful clothing. Women twirled in their wide dresses, and men bowed to them.

She turned to Michael, and his eyes locked onto hers. "Again, you look ravishing. I pale in comparison." He bowed and took her hand to kiss it without shifting his gaze.

Rachel's cheeks blazed, and she shifted her eyes. "I can't wait to start."

"Yes, I'm looking forward to dancing with you this evening." Michael glanced at her feet. "Have you been practicing those basic steps?"

"A little, doctor, but if you want to know the truth, I haven't ventured out to something this elaborate in a very long time, so I'm a bit nervous."

Michael cocked his head, about to say something until loud clapping interrupted.

Guillermo bounded on the dance floor in a black costume,

entwined with silver and jewels, matching his ebony hair threaded with gray strands. As usual, he radiated and dazzled the crowd as he provided a few announcements.

With a big smile and in his melodic Spanish accent, he said. "Be courteous, my amigos. Newer people stay on the outskirts of the dance floor." With his hands behind his back, Guillermo roamed the room. "But remember, all of us were once beginners. Be polite to newbies."

The lights dimmed. Guillermo clapped his hands and waved everyone forward.

Rachel peeked at Michael, and he took her arm, leading her away from the advanced dancers. "Señora, are you ready?" Michael turned his palm out, and Rachel placed her hand in his. "I think so."

My hand in his. So, so sensual…. Rachel?

They positioned their arms, and music filled the studio. For the next ninety minutes, Rachel concentrated on Michael's movements and focused on the basic steps. With laughs and fumbles, she followed him and tried ignoring the powerful hands that guided her.

We fit well together—as dance partners, that is.

Lights flashed. Intermission. Michael grabbed her hand and led her to a seat. Sensations of scintillating colors blended and flowed through her. Michael removed his jacket and touched Rachel's chin. "Going to get some bottled water for both of us. I'll be back." She smiled. "Meet you back here," and pointed to the restroom. He walked over to the refreshment table, and Rachel sauntered into the women's room. Everyone chatted away as they waited in line, and some women eyed Rachel, scrutinizing her outfit. She saw Claudia, who gave her a hug. "What fun, huh Rachel?"

Claudia walked away, and as Rachel gazed in the mirror before leaving the ladies' room, she caught a stunning woman about her age, studying her from the other side. Rachel waved, recognizing the woman—Justine, Michael's acquaintance. Justine cocked an eyebrow, smirked, turned her head, and swayed out of the ladies' room, fluffing her silver tresses behind her.

The snub felt like a slap across the face. Rachel glanced at herself in the mirror one more time, puckered her lips, and forced her rubbery legs to move. She went out to the studio and saw Justine chatting to Michael, touching his arm, and flipping her long, glorious locks away from her. Michael's eyes darted back and forth as he held two bottles of water. Rachel caught his eye, and he nodded to Justine before striding toward her. Rachel shifted her eyes to Michael but caught Justine's fixed stare on her.

"Here you are." Michael offered her a bottle. "Drink up because I'm looking forward to a vigorous second half. How about you?"

Rachel blinked before nodding.

Michael leaned into her. "Did I say something wrong?"

Rachel gazed into the glorious ocean eyes that took on a gray appearance. "Well, I have to ask you a question."

"Yes?" Michael's face came closer.

"Is Justine an ex of yours?"

Michael bristled at the question. "Why do you ask?"

"Well, she seems strange around me."

Michael took a sip of water. "I'd rather not discuss Justine." He shook his head. "Somehow she ended up here." He studied Rachel. "I honestly don't know how; except she knew I planned on learning a new type of dance."

"Well, it's obvious she's drawn to you."

"Well, I'm not drawn to her." Michael looked out to the crowd. Rachel followed his gaze and saw Justine talking to a younger man. "I thought she got the message."

"Michael, I never asked you, and I know we're just dance partners, but are you…?"

"Are you dating others or in a relationship? Is that your question?" He frowned at Rachel.

She nodded, unsmiling. What did he expect?

"The answer is no. You don't know me, but I wouldn't be here engaging with you if I was."

Rachel swallowed. "Okay, but you'd be surprised how many

people wander around pretending they are who they say they are."

"I suppose, but that isn't me." His eyes softened. "I've been divorced for quite some time."

Rachel gulped some water, and Michael took the bottle from her and placed it on a nearby table. He reached for her hand again, and they moved to the dance floor. Michael asked without turning, "What about you? Divorced? Never married?"

Rachel said, "No, I'm widowed." She slipped her hand out of his.

She sensed Michael's eyes on her. "I'm so sorry." They stopped at the edge of the dance floor, hearing the program about to resume. "When did your husband die?"

"A little over five years ago." Rachel stared out at the crowd.

She heard the music begin and turned to Michael.

Rachel extended her hand again, and Michael bowed and took her hand. His sea-changing eyes hypnotized her as he guided her to the dance floor. "I hope to become proficient enough to do the sacada those graceful dancers have mastered."

For the next two hours, Rachel's heart hummed as she swayed with Michael. They took a couple of quick water breaks but continued, exhausted, until the music slowed down and the emcee returned.

The affable Guillermo ended the evening by telling everyone how pleased he was to see so many enthusiastic Tango dancers. "I hope to see many of you next month. Adios, for now, my amigos."

Everyone applauded and returned the Spanish goodbye with the same zest.

Michael's hand twisted with hers as he led her to their chairs and retrieved her accessories. As he placed the jacket on Rachel's shoulders, his fingers brushed her neck and singed every cell in her body. With the rest of the jubilant crowd, they strode out of the building toward Rachel's car. Michael took Rachel's hand again, and during the stroll Rachel savored the silence until they reached the driver's side of her car.

She leaned against it with her hands, and Michael came close to her. "I had an amazing time with you, Rachel, and look forward to seeing you again."

"Yes, the same for me."

Michael stood back for a moment and shifted his gaze until his eyes bore into Rachel's. "I don't know if I'm being too hasty, but would you like to go out for dinner with me sometime?"

Rachel's heart jumped. "Well, I…" Her mouth froze.

"I'm sorry, I shouldn't presume…"

"No, no," Rachel's said, almost yelling as the words tumbled out. "I mean, yes! I mean—I'd like that."

Michael chuckled. "I know what you mean." His eyes caressed hers. "Good." He tapped the roof of the car before moving away. "I'll be in touch." Michael walked backwards again, waving to Rachel. She watched him until he turned, a bright silvery light moving into the night.

Chapter Fifteen

Yardley—April 20th

The amount of food seemed too much as Yardley measured.

Would she gain too much weight?

The doctor said no.

The nutritionist said no.

Even Rachel said no.

So, it's no. But how do they know?

Did they care if she became heavy?

Trust them, they insisted. She sighed. What choice did she have? Daniel refused to see her unless she stuck to the program. Would they get back together? Yardley couldn't imagine not.

Almost six months.

God, it felt longer. Texts became more frequent, and Daniel agreed to monthly FaceTime meetings, but a no each time she suggested meeting before mid-June.

She poured the Ensure into a large glass and gulped half of it. Lots of calories, but… well, it tasted good. She'd never admit that to anyone. Maybe she should have half, but Daniel's face loomed with a finger shaking. "Don't you dare."

Alright, before I go to bed. Promise.

Yardley sat down and stared at the potato with a small slice of butter, ginger chicken, and broccoli with cheese. She inspected everything on her plate and picked up her fork and knife to cut her food.

Okay, I'm following the nutritionist's plan for the fourth week. It's been pretty good. Again, Yardley took a whiff but tried not to focus on the pungent aroma, never mind the taste.

She shut her eyes, took a bite, and for a moment, a piece of potato sat on her tongue.

Ooh! So good.

She chewed quicker than she wanted, but almost couldn't help it. Her fork plunged into another piece, a big one.

Stop.

Don't get carried away.

Slow it down.

She took a deep breath.

Then her fork dug into a juicy piece of chicken.

Hmmm. She shut her eyes again, munched, and swallowed.

Another piece of chicken, and she did the same thing.

Yardley's eyes swept her elegant but immaculate studio apartment. She scrutinized the Tiffany lamp—tall, almost haughty. Rachel's lamps captivated her so much that she bought one for herself. She observed her beautiful divider, happy to get a six-panel one of teal with almond blossoms, keeping the bed area separate. Teal, her favorite. Rachel also seemed to like that color.

Rachel.

So glad she discovered her with Mom's help. She couldn't imagine finding a better match. She recalled that first day, and due to her reluctance to attend therapy she refused to say much. Rachel made it easy and talked about things that might interest Yardley. Soon, Rachel's warmth melted Yardley's frosty protection, and her one-word, two-word answers strung into full sentences and catapulted from her throat.

Yardley smiled and nibbled on more of her food. She tried to concentrate on the intuitive eating idea, and so far, so good. She halted for a moment to feel her hip bone. Yup. Still there. Good.

She continued eating. She planned on leaving a fourth of her food on the plate, but this time she ignored that voice.

The hunger seemed more pronounced tonight. *Intuitive eating, intuitive eating*, she repeated. Then she shut her eyes again and said the mantra suggested to her by Rachel.

I need my body to live.
My body takes care of me.
I owe it to my body to nurture and nourish it.

There, right again, Rachel. Like Rachel said many times. Replace the old messages of being bad or fat with a mantra. Rachel told her that she learned the mantra from her mentors, and she suggested Yardley modify it. Once they determined the right words for Yardley, Rachel suggested she write it down, look in the mirror, and repeat it out loud every morning and night.

Yardley ate every crumb from her plate. She wiped her mouth and paused. Wow, she couldn't hear the old voice.

Guess what? I'm going to have some of that Halo ice cream. Only three hundred calories in a whole pint. She went to her freezer, pulled out the delicious chocolate-chip cookie dough, her favorite, and scooped half into a bowl. She licked the spoon, and before sitting down, her thoughts went back to therapy.

Rachel stuck by her through three relapses and saw her while she attended intensive outpatient treatment programs. After Daniel told her he needed a break, the reality of losing him trumped her obsession with eating or not eating. She agreed with Rachel to do anything and everything to get better.

Six months now. Yay, but not out of the woods yet.

Every so often, creeping thoughts about Ashley emerged, tempting her to withhold. Everyone thought Yardley's eating disorder originated because of her survivor's guilt, but only Rachel knew the truth. Even with her, she hesitated sharing. A clamp tightened around Yardley's chest every time she ventured back to those thoughts. Better, but still there. At least, she opened her mouth now. One time, her lips cemented together when food appeared in front of her.

Everyone said it became her way of punishing herself.

Yes.

But they didn't know the truth.

Nor would they.

Rachel thought the group might benefit her. She'd hear others give voice to secrets that might prompt her to do the same.

What's the point?

You know, so why share it with others? Rachel nodded but told her of the power of telling others. A corrective experience—to see you aren't alone.

Yardley's head shook so hard it felt like she might fall over.

No.

Other than you, who would understand the extent of my guilt?

Rachel leaned closer. Yardley stared at the topaz jewels in her face, changing with each word she stated. Dark, then light, brown, then olive green. Could those eyes convince her?

Yardley blinked. She focused on Rachel's voice. Rachel claimed that she'd be surprised. Even though their stories might differ, others carried similar feelings. Guilt, shame, distrust.

Now Yardley moved her attention back to the eyes, peering at the unusual eyelashes that fluttered at her.

Wow, are those real? Or does she apply those new, fluffy lashes which are the rage?

She couldn't ask but thought of her own heavily mascaraed lashes, covering the red. Who wants red eyelashes, especially with green eyes. If anyone asked, she'd retort, *I'm Jewish. Do you think I want a Christmas-like appearance?*

She saw Rachel cock her head.

No, I won't ask about the lashes.

She then offered a slight nod. Rachel asked if that meant yes, and in Yardley's usual style, a yes whispered from her vocal cords.

Rachel clapped and produced a faint smile from Yardley.

Wow, she's so animated.

Would I have been more without Ashley's influence?

When she posed this question to Rachel a few weeks before

agreeing to the group, Rachel reminded her we're all works-in-progress and said, *Who knows what could happen in your next chapter. Wait and see.* She then winked at Yardley.

So positive.

It made Yardley eager to please Rachel, the one reason she agreed to join the group. She also trusted her with her life. When she agreed to meet with her, a few of her Jewish friends questioned her choice. Why a Shiksa when there are so many Jewish therapists? Yardley tilted her head, concurring, but she had already arranged the appointment. *So,* one of her closest pals said. *Just cancel. Find someone who understands the customs of Judaism.*

She considered her advice. When she presented her friend's suggestion to Daniel, he balked. His brow furrowed, raising his arm with an, *Are you kidding? You think all my teachers are Jewish? Do you think most of my patients will be? You like how she sounded?"* A soft, *Yes,* emerged from Yardley's throat. He almost shouted, *Try her!*

Yardley ran it by her parents and told them Daniel's opinion. They joined him, reminding her of the importance of tolerance, part of their great heritage.

After surrendering her monosyllabic voice halfway through the first session, Yardley challenged Rachel. Her eyes danced, recalling the conversation like it had occurred yesterday.

"I'm Jewish, you know."

"Yes, I wondered from your name."

"Have you worked with Jewish clients?"

"Many. In fact, some of my closest friends and colleagues are Jewish."

Yardley couldn't resist her mouth turning up.

"And guess what else, my dear? I often tell my friends, *You were Chosen. We were saved. We're all going to the same place wherever that might be.*"

A thrill spread through her body.

This woman, Rachel, did something to her.

What?

Well, she would figure it out, but right this moment, she's okay in my book. She couldn't wait to tell Daniel and her parents.

Now, she sat at the table eating her ice cream. She came a long way. She knew Daniel didn't trust it yet, but he would. Wait until she told him about the group.

She couldn't tell how helpful it was, but the good news? No triggers to prompt her to withhold food, but she'd pay close attention. No gaining too much weight.

Some days she'd stare at an obese, disgruntled figure returning her look. Other days, the real Yardley smiled back, and those positive times were increasing. The nasty figure showed up less and less. When that unhealthy woman appeared, Yardley became determined to withhold food, but then, Daniel's image materialized in living color. That forced her to push through on those bad days.

Even this last year in law school couldn't override Daniel.

Wow, the power of love. The greatest virtue in her eyes, no matter what the ancients said.

She considered the members of the group; all spoke before her. Matt seemed nice enough, but he hasn't finished his story. Tomorrow night, she'd tell him to go ahead. No hurry for her to share what happened.

Yardley paused and reflected. Why wait? She nodded. It helped her hear the others first. Their stories made it safer for her to disclose hers.

That man, Matt, seemed tolerant of Sapphire and her attacks. She endured abuse, awful, but don't vent your anger on others. Maybe Matt could convince her that not every successful man was a jerk. Or, she might just have the courage to say something to Sapphire, using Daniel as an example. Not perfect. But almost and so good to her.

Yardley sighed again before taking another spoonful of Halo.

Daniel! He'd be so proud of her right now. Not ready to do this in front of him, but soon. She must, or she'd lose him.

How about Jason?

What a doll.

So even keeled and pleasant. She knew he had more sadness to discuss but seemed not to take it out on others, unlike Sapphire.

Shalene, horrible what happened.

Even though Shalene didn't think it was racist, she could understand her aversion to white women. Boy, she hoped Shalene came to recognize not every white girl acted like that bully.

Well, she must've. Otherwise, she wouldn't have seen Rachel if that were the case.

She'd wait for Matt. Maybe next week she'll tell her story. Would she divulge those dark, buried thoughts sitting at the bottom of her mind's chest of memories? She shook her head. She just didn't know.

Yardley glanced at the leftover Ensure before opening the freezer. She placed the nutritional shake in the refrigerator.

I'll drink the rest of it tomorrow morning.

Ice cream, it is.

She took the pint of ice cream and scooped the rest in her bowl. After finishing it, her tongue lapped up drippings from the spoon, and she stared at the bowl. Her eyes narrowed, looking around to assure herself no one could see her.

Ridiculous.

Just go for it. Yardley then picked up the bowl and indulged her taste buds, with her tongue slithering along the surface.

Umm, a forbidden delight of the most impolite.

Umm again.

Would the nasty witch appear tomorrow, calling her fat?

Right now? *Umm.*

What would happen if she shared her terrible secret? The deep, deep one? What then?

Chapter Sixteen

Session Five—April 21st—Matt

Matt removed his tie and unbuttoned his two top shirt buttons. He preferred a neat, impeccable appearance, but after going for hours with precise attire, time to lighten up. After opening the door, he found everyone had arrived before him. What a surprise. The rest of the crew might be eager to get going, but not him.

He caught Sapphire's eyes immediately. "How ya doing?" He turned his head before she responded.

He nodded to Shalene, whose dimple surfaced, and to Yardley, who whispered, *Hello.*

God, will she ever speak louder? Did her eating disorder affect her voice? He'd find out. Correction. They'd all find out.

Jason put his fist out. "Hey, brother."

"Hey, man." Matt returned the fist bump.

"How's everyone doing tonight?" Matt asked.

Shalene smiled, Yardley shrugged, and Sapphire responded with, "Good," while she glanced at her phone.

"I'm okay. Thanks for asking. You?" Jason smirked.

Matt nodded. Glad someone could talk. These gals need to lighten up.

Rachel walked through, hurrying as usual.

"Well, it's our fifth meeting. Almost halfway done. Any thoughts about this?"

Everyone shook their heads. Jason smiled. Shalene's dimple disappeared. Yardley sunk into her seat, and Sapphire's gaze looked outward.

What a crew.

Matt looked at Rachel. How did she deal with them one-on-one? Ah, probably different in that scenario.

"Okay, so it looks like Matt began a brief part of his story, and Yardley hasn't started. So, my friends, what do you think?" Rachel asked.

"I think I want to wait," Yardley said in a whisper.

God, am I the only one having trouble hearing her? Do I need a hearing test?

"I didn't hear ya, Ms. Yardley." Jason nodded, dazzling her with a smile.

Okay, I'm not alone.

Yardley cleared her throat. "I'd like to defer to Matt."

"Are you sure, Yardley?" Rachel's eyes probed hers.

Yardley nodded with a wisp of a smile.

"Matt, are you ready to continue?"

Matt nodded. "I am."

Rachel gestured with her hands.

Matt leaned forward, not looking at anyone. "Before I get into my story, I want to correct a couple of issues." He then gazed at Rachel.

"One. I'm not anti-God. I attend church here and there." He kept his eyes on Rachel, who nodded.

"Two. I know women deal with lots of things that men don't think twice about. My sister and mother never let me forget, but…" He raised his right index finger. "Not all men are jerks, and…" He pivoted to Sapphire. "Some men are used as well. Not as bad as what you went through, but not without damage." He turned to Rachel again.

Rachel scanned the room. "Anyone want to respond?"

Sapphire kept her eyes downcast, her golden mane covering half her face, and shook her head. Shalene looked at Matt, nodding.

"I understand, Matt," Yardley offered, wide-eyed. Matt rewarded her with a sparkling smile.

"Brother, I get it." Jason nodded.

"Thanks." Matt rolled his head around, shrugged his shoulders, and sighed. "Alright, now I'm going to tell you about Juliette."

Flick, flick, flick.

Boy, she can't stop herself.

Matt turned to Sapphire as she snapped on her cup.

"Sorry," she said, without giving him eye contact. Her hair fell over her face as she placed the cup on the floor.

Not responding to her, he shifted his seat, and his eyes remained on Rachel for a moment. He nodded.

"So, more about my mother's divorce. I worried about her, you know?" Matt's gaze found the floor. "I came home a lot on weekends to check on her. I think the betrayal did a number on her. Every so often, I'd find her on the computer in the kitchen, studying the dating websites. *Synchronicity, Soar,* and *Connect.* Have any of you heard of them?"

"Oh yeah." Shalene's dimple emerged.

"No, I haven't because…well, I'll tell you another time." Jason waved his hand.

"How about you two?" Matt spun in the direction of Yardley.

"Heard, but not much."

"How about you?" He pivoted to Sapphire.

"Of course. I'm a therapist. I guess you forgot with all the therapists in your life."

Sarcasm. No smile.

Matt swung his head around and found Rachel's soft eyes again.

Man, just look at Rach. Don't look at the stunner.

"My mom would look up and smile. She's got beautiful dark blues and…"

"Like you." Yardley gifted him a dash of a smile.

"Hey, thank you, Yardley." Matt glanced at her and reciprocated the smile. "I've been told we look alike. Anyway, Mom often checked in about…" Matt laughed and used air quotations. "My feelings."

"Of course! That's what therapists do."

He pivoted again to Sapphire. Her one exotic eye stared back at him.

Looks like she even tried to smile.

He nodded and returned his gaze to Rachel.

"So, where was I? Oh yeah. Every time, she asked. I'd stand and kiss the top of her head. I'd say, *Mom, I want you to find love again. You deserve it.*"

Matt laced his fingers and dropped them between his legs as his gaze became unfocused.

"But man." He shook his head. "For the next two years.… Oh, forgot to mention. Following graduation, Des and I moved home to work and prepare for graduate school, so while living there, we met some of Mom's dates."

Matt rubbed his face with one hand. "Oh, man." He shook his head, leaned back, and stretched his legs out. "Des and I, well, we knew she could do better. Some seemed nice enough but weird." He looked up. "Mike Bradford or Brady, an accountant, seemed okay at first, he stumbled over his words with a constant *um* in a monotone voice." Matt peered at Jason. "He could have used your Toastmasters class."

"Sounds like it, brother." Jason grimaced.

Matt smirked. "A few others showed up at the door, but one *bad boy* as you ladies call them, stayed longer. Des called him a slimeball. Every time the slick, gray-haired creep came to the house, he'd wink at us like we were fourteen. Thank God, and I mean that, my mother started seeing less of him, but she began to change more."

Matt leaned forward, and with his hands clasped between his legs, he stared into the distance.

"Her transformation became obvious. On weekends, she wore short dresses and heels this high." Matt displayed his hands with a space of about four inches. "And she went out into the city…"

Matt shook his head. "I guess. Who knows?" Matt sat up straight and lifted his eyebrows. "Hey, I love my mother, but like I said to my sister, *Nothing we can do about it. Let her get it out of her system.*"

Matt combed his fingers through his hair and sniffed. "So, now that night. Thought I'd surprise my mother with a visit," he chuckled, "but it didn't go the way I expected. She looked shocked as I entered the house. I said, *Wow, Mom. Don't get too excited.* She gave me a shaky smile and wrung her hands. Said for a long time, she'd planned on hosting one of her mysterious Salon events at our house and didn't expect me and Des to just show up. I didn't appreciate the reception but promised I'd get a bite to eat and stay in my room, even though the crowd would enter through her office on the other side of the house." His right eye twitched, and he began rubbing it. "So, there I am, a few hours later, into a good book, and I realized I was still hungry, so I decided to go into the kitchen for more food. I got down there and started rummaging through the refrigerator. Out of nowhere, I sensed someone in the room."

His chest tightened as if a jagged knife tore through him, and he wrapped his arms around him.

Man, just get through this.

"I turned around, and this gorgeous woman stood in front of me."

See not so bad, man.

"Slender, medium height, golden skin, dark hair, and green eyes fringed by dark thick eyebrows. Her age?" He tilted his head side-to-side. "Difficult to tell. Early-to-mid-thirties. She, uh…" Matt bobbed his head. "Displayed an unusual flair. I can see her now. High-neck purple dress, stilettos, and get this." He smirked at Rachel who kept nodding at him. "A feathered derby hat. Very different."

"Hoowee, sounds like quite the getup," Jason hooted with a clap.

"Yup. She made her presence known." Matt nodded with his gaze becoming unfocused again. "We did the intros, and I asked her if she lost her way. Big house and all that, and she cocked her head." Matt coughed. "I can remember most of the conversation.

No, just curious about Sophia's handsome son. So, I asked what she wanted to know, and…" Matt grunted. "I should have known, but get this. She walked back and forth, hands behind her back, with eyes roving up and down."

"Gosh, she treated you like an object," Yardley said.

Matt lifted his eyebrows. "Yup. Just the beginning, but I was oblivious. She informed me that she needed to see me for herself, and then she looked around and said, *Your mother will kill me, but you're a big boy and can decide for yourself, so take my card and call me when you're home again.* And then she winked and tiptoed toward the stairs from where she came."

Matt paused.

"You okay continuing my friend?" Rachel's soft eyes blinked at his.

"I am." Matt nodded.

"Juliette Poleco. Therapist and Relationship Coach, specializing in adults from all lifestyles." Matt's eyes found the floor. "Even her business card stood out. A perfect square with a curvy, purple font spelling her name." He shook his head.

"A *relationship* coach?" Sapphire scoffed as she leaned forward.

Don't look at her.

"Yup." Matt stared straight ahead.

"What does that even mean?" Sapphire's rough voice sounded like a pepper grinder.

"Who knows?" Matt threw his head back and exhaled. "There's much I didn't know." His gaze returned to Rachel, and he nodded. "I couldn't stop thinking about her, so the next day I sent her an email, suggesting we get together. She wrote back, *How about next Saturday?* Then, she gave me her cell number and asked for mine."

Matt kept his eyes on Rachel. "She mesmerized me from day one."

"Brother sounds like you got stung. I'm guessing by a poisonous bee." Jason nudged with eyebrows knitted together.

"Yup. A Queen." Matt glanced at Jason and snickered. "Which I'm getting to but wanted to mention what happened the next day. I asked my mother about the lady with the derby hat. Boy, not a good idea. My mother's face turned white. *Why? How did you meet Juliette?* Whoa. So, I minimized the encounter which, in truth, was nothing much anyway."

Matt scrunched his face and wrapped his arms around himself again. "I wanted to know how they met, and she gave a vague response. Something about a wellness gathering, and though Juliette was younger and childless, they shared similarities."

Matt released his arms and shook his head. "My mother changed the subject. At the time, I thought, *just as well.* I returned to school that week, and me being me, became focused on my papers."

He looked around. Wait until they hear the rest.

Matt rubbed his face with his palms and shook his head. "We texted that Thursday, and…" Matt chuckled. "She said, *I recommend you not share our get together with your mother.* That alone should have been a clue. Like I discuss my romantic relationships with my mother? Not."

"She acted like you were a little boy who needed lessons," Shalene said.

Matt's eyes caught her downward lips. "Yeah. You got it, which I found out the hard way." He worked his jaw in a tight circle. "And funny thing. That Friday night, on the way home, I thought about Juliette's age. Nine years older than me. For a moment I wondered, *Good idea?* And then her beautiful face showed up. *Nah, no biggie. Twenty-first century after all.*"

Now Matt looked up. All eyes on him.

"So, we went on a date, and…" Matt paused. "Well, I didn't think what happened would."

Matt put his hands behind his head and stretched his legs out. His eyes found their way to the top of one of Rachel's Tiffanies. "My mother planned a weekend trip with her therapy friends, so I knew it would be easy to prepare for my date without a litany of questions."

Matt's gaze moved outward as he folded his arms and smirked.

Therapists. What a different breed.

He shook his head.

"Hey Brother, you want to share what's going on with you?"

"Just thinking about therapists." He continued shaking his head. "Good people, but they speak a different language."

A giggle.

The stunner. Glad she laughed but still not looking at her.

"Yeah. For as long as I can remember, my mother talked about *the process*, whatever that meant. Every time she said it my sister and father laughed, and then my sister becomes a therapist." He shook his head again with a half-smile. "They're all around me."

The stunner laughed louder, and he saw Rachel smile at her.

"Anyway. I'm digressing, but now you have a flavor of my household growing up." Matt nodded. He pulled his legs in and laced his fingers again. "The first night stands out. I wore my best jeans, a purple shirt, and dark blazer."

Matt raised his eyebrows at Rachel. "Just had a haircut. Wanted to look my best and make the evening memorable." He lowered his head. "Ladies, uh, I admit I'm a bit of an old-fashion romantic." He glanced at Shalene then Yardley.

Not looking at the other one.

"I brought a single rose. Lavender." He put his head down for a moment and then lifted it. "Does anyone know its symbolism?"

Nos echoed around the room.

"Wonder and awe."

"Good to know." Jason nodded.

"Why awe for the first date?" Yardley lifted her eyes.

"Well, red symbolizes love. Yellow wisdom. Coral desire. White purity, and pink gratitude, so I chose lavender."

"Well, you did your research." Sapphire's tone scratched.

Matt kept his eyes on Rachel. "Yup. Tried. Anyway, I arrived at 5:30. In time for the 5:40 sunset, and she's waiting all decked out in a teal-colored dress with her black hair splayed over her shoulders." Matt widened his eyes. "As I told Rachel, quite the siren."

"She lured you to…" Shalene peeked at Matt with her hands grabbing the chair. "Sounds like something… not so—"

"Yup. She did." Matt's jaw tightened like an unmovable lock.

"Sorry." Shalene said. "I can see I upset you."

"Not you, Shalene, and I apologize for cutting you off." Matt forced his lips upward.

Shalene's eyes softened like silk.

"It still bugs me I could be so stupid. I was thinking with the wrong org… Sorry, ladies." Matt's jaw relaxed, but steam flooded his chest. "Let me get to this. So, we enjoyed cocktails. She insisted drinks on her, and dinner, I insisted on me. The beginning of a three-month, intense passionate relationship."

Matt folded his arms, and his eyes circled the group before landing on Rachel's. He twisted his mouth. "I fell hard, and she claimed the same." He lowered his gaze. "She requested I not share our relationship with anyone until… well, I don't remember, but at the time, I agreed to anything she wanted. We were together every weekend. Her home or a beautiful hotel."

He paused and brought his hands close to his mouth.

"How are you doing my friend?" Rachel's eyes probed his.

Matt nodded and swallowed. "I'm okay, Rach. Just thinking, but as usual, thanks for asking." The corners of his lips struggled to tilt upward again.

"I bared my soul to her, but what did I learn about Juliette?" His gaze became unfocused again. "Not much. Sure, she told me she came from privilege but kept her family of origin at arm's length. Divorced and heartbroken. Promised she'd share more someday. And how did she meet my mother? Again, elusive. Her middle name."

"Hoowee. Like a sketch without color or details inside the lines." Jason nodded.

"Man, a great metaphor for Juliette."

Matt kept his eyes steady, clasping his mammoth hands to his chin. "Yeah, New Year's Eve, a memorable one. That's when Pandora's box opened wide."

Matt rolled his shoulders around. "I started getting itchy about revealing more to family and friends. She'd arch one of her gorgeous brows, pucker her plump lips, and purred, *Not just yet, darling. Soon. I promise.* I'd nod as if I were an obedient, wag-tailing puppy," Matt grunted. "Just didn't have my tongue rolling out." He inhaled. "Christmas, like Thanksgiving, she left for retreats planned long before we met." Matt caught Yardley's head bobbing. "So she said." His eyes shifted to Rachel's. "She texted me from the mysterious retreat gathering and said she'd introduce me to friends at their annual New Year's Eve Masquerade Ball, so I, uh, couldn't have been happier. Couldn't wait."

Yup. Juliette? A drug for me. The withdrawal felt physical.

"Christmas came and went. Juliette got back in time for the party and demanded we meet there. That irritated me, but I chastised myself out loud. *Relax, no biggie, a strong woman asserting her independence.*"

"Why so tolerant?" Sapphire asked in a less abrasive voice.

Look at Rachel.

"Not sure. Been figuring that out with Rach." He winked at Rachel.

He licked his lips and shifted his seat. "I arrived at this huge estate, got checked in, and walked into the foyer. All dressed up in my black Tux and wearing a black satin mask reserved for me. Someone put their arms around my waist, and I grabbed the hands. Soft and familiar. Juliette's. Of course, she looked gorgeous. A scarlet halter gown and matching mask glittered with gold. She took my hand, and we passed people dressed to the nines. Red, gold, and black colors all around us."

"Quite the party, brother."

"Yeah, man." Matt glanced at Jason before staring ahead. "Lots of expensive champagne, caviar, and other cool appetizers. We start dancing and kissing, and then it happened."

Red coals seared his chest. He sighed. "I can still see it. Clear as a flawless diamond."

Matt blinked as he tried to dampen the heat.

"Matt?"

"I'm okay, Rach. Still angry at myself for being so, ah, gullible." Rachel shook her head.

"I know. All of us miss, but…" Matt exhaled. "So, this older man came over to Juliette and said, *I assume he's the boy toy you described on our holiday together?* And I felt like my heart went over a cliff."

"Oh my God." Yardley's voice rose a few octaves.

"That's what I thought." Matt said, with his eyes glued to the floor. "Juliette ignored my response and tried introducing me to this guy, Oliver, who snickered at me." Matt's voice growled. "I just did an about face and stomped down the hall. I heard Juliette follow me and hiss. *Grow up Matt. I made it clear we weren't serious.*" Matt sighed as he shook his head. "I remember saying, *Don't gaslight me Juliette. I thought we had a good thing going. So much for love and monogamy, which you agreed on.* She said she didn't and something about the power of denial, but here's the clincher. She said, *Even if I promised such a commitment, I'm allowed to change my mind.*"

"Where's the quote from Jesus about wolves in sheep's clothing?" Shalene grimaced.

"Book of Matthew," Jason said.

"I thought things couldn't have gotten worse. They did. On my way out I heard a familiar voice, and I turned to see my mother kissing a young man."

"Hoowee." Jason's mouth gaped open. "What a nightmare."

"I shouted, *Mom?!* She saw me and covered her mouth. Then she noticed Juliette and marched over to us. She screamed at her. *Are you dating my son?* I think someone yelled, *Catfight.* Juliette shouted back. *Not anymore. Besides you look like you have a boy toy of your own.* That was enough for me, and I left."

Matt saw Jason, Yardley, and Shalene.

Wow. They are cool. Their concern permeates like osmosis.

And the stunner. Nope. Not checking her expression.

"I'm fine. I blocked Juliette while I waited for my car, and I texted my mother and told her not to communicate right now."

Matt clasped his hands again and brought them close to his mouth.

Man, two betrayals. A boulder crashed into his heart and cracked it into pieces.

"I stopped at the family home, took what I brought, and drove back to school even though most people hadn't returned from winter break. Went to the gym for hours to get Juliette out of my system and let me tell you…" he glanced at everyone, including Sapphire, "the intense workouts did the trick. For the next few months—papers, exercise, and graduation, but I decided not to walk for the Master's. Didn't want an encounter with my mother and made excuses to Dad and Des. I attended Des' graduation ceremony but left early and told her we'd have a separate dinner. I pretended with my mother and gave her a hug. No matter what she did. I didn't want to embarrass her."

Matt's eyes darted around the room.

"I hear you, brother." Jason's eyes closed.

Yeah, poor guy. Probably wished he *had* a mother.

"What happened next?" Shalene asked.

"Dated here and there." Matt laced his hands and let them drop between his legs. "Let myself fall in love again but another story for another day. Found out more about Juliette. Her actual age? Forty."

He shook his head before shifting his gaze to Rachel. "After Des pushed me, I pursued therapy, landed here with Rachel a couple of years ago, and…" Matt fidgeted in his seat. "Still struggling with trust."

He turned to Sapphire, whose eyes remained downcast. "So, just to reiterate, even though I wasn't abused, I felt used by someone who I thought loved me."

Sapphire eyes softened and caught his. "I get it."

"You're right on, brother." Jason said. "You ladies, got to know we can have our hearts broken too." He glanced at the three women.

"We just might handle it different, like a battered warrior." Jason nodded. "Appearing stoic but broken inside."

Matt nodded. "Thanks, man. I couldn't have said it better."

"What about your mother?" Yardley asked in her usual wispy voice.

Matt chuckled. "She did her work, and… ah," he looked down. "We kind of worked it out, but…" He halted for an instant before leaning back and staring at the group. "Now that I'm talking, I think…" He interlocked his arms. "Yeah, there might be a need for another conversation with her."

His gaze moved to Rachel. "Anyway, therapy helped me understand my mother. Even though she's a therapist, she has flaws. How about that, Rachel? You agree? Don't therapists have their own issues?"

Chapter Seventeen

Rachel—April 23rd

All ten eyes observed her. Clients often hinted to therapists about their issues, but never posed it the way Matt did.

She could feel a warm, crimson tide spread across her face. Between her olive skin and dim lights, she doubted anyone could detect it. Without flinching, she grinned and threw the question back to Matt.

"What do you think?"

He laughed, and that ended that.

Now Rachel flitted around her living room to quell the crinkling in her chest. *What are you so nervous about? You researched this man left and right. He's not a mass killer, rapist, child abuser or wife beater. My God, you don't even work with that population, so stop it.*

Her dogs followed with tails wagging. She sat on the couch, crossing her legs, then uncrossing them and patting the cushion for Zsa Zsa and Gabor. They jumped up and let her glide her fingers through their curly coats.

So, she'll smell like a dog. So what?

She forgot to ask him if he liked dogs. If not, no thanks. *Hold on, honey, you're getting way ahead of yourself.*

The call came Tuesday. Michael left a voice mail, first telling her he couldn't attend the next couple of Thursdays. Her heart took a nosedive. Then he invited her to dinner on Saturday. Her heart reversed direction. Oh God, it's just dinner. Okay, admitting it to Janine and Bridget, it's a date, a real, old-fashioned date.

She planned on attending the Tango class anyway, but at the last minute, decided against it. Fatigue consumed her, so she stayed home. With a heavy blanket on her, she crunched on buttery popcorn and watched a modern-day Cinderella story on Hallmark.

Rachel glanced at the clock. Time to leave, glad that Michael texted her a few hours ago, asking if she'd meet him instead of him picking her up. Something arose at the hospital, and he knew they'd not make the reservation if he drove to pick her up.

Yes, better I have control of the situation.

Rachel retrieved her jacket, threw a kiss to the pooches, and drove to a popular restaurant in the heart of Boston.

Rachel now sat across from Michael, trying to contain the vibrations coursing through each particle of her body.

Slow down, lady.

"Since you listen to stories, I assume you want to hear mine—unless you want to go first?" Michael said, cocking his head.

Rachel took another sip of her wine. "Please, go first. I'm more comfortable listening." She shifted her seat. "I'm ready when you are."

"I come from a loving family. The oldest of three, we grew up on the North Shore. My father practiced as an eye doctor, so my brother and I followed. My sister, the youngest, took another route and became a pediatric oncologist." His eyes captured hers. "How am I doing, Madame Therapist?"

Rachel chuckled. "Mighty fine, doctor."

His gaze went outward. "My parents died, siblings live in New York, but we remain close and try to connect a few times a week. Anyway, life became more complicated."

Michael brought his wine to his lips while Rachel's heart sank fast.

Close family. How would he view hers?

"My wife, Ingrid, and I met in medical school, and we married after completing our residency. With school loans and so much time in school, we waited before we tried having kids, which we both wanted."

He paused for a second, then shifted in his seat. "We assumed it would be easy and," Michael leaned closer, blinking, "you don't know how much you want something until you discover it's not that simple. Yes, we couldn't get pregnant, so we had fertility treatments."

He took another sip of his wine and stared at Rachel. "Years. We were about to give up. Then, right after her thirty-seventh birthday, Ingrid became pregnant. Nine months later, our beautiful Roisin came into the world."

Rachel's eyes welled up.

"I'm sorry. Did I say something?" Michael asked.

They were interrupted by the servers placing their dishes in front of them.

Michael's eyes probed Rachel's.

"No, I'm fine. Please continue and tell me about your daughter's unusual name." Rachel didn't wish to re-open that wound. Too painful, even after all these years.

"Roisin, an ancient Irish name, means *Little Rose*. When I suggested it to Ingrid, she liked it. Our Little Rose." Michael looked outward, before bringing his eyes back to Rachel.

"Anyway, because of the stress of the treatments, the difficult pregnancy and Ingrid's age, we thought it best to have one child." Michael sighed. "It seemed right."

"And now?"

"Well, you can't go back in time but, I'll finish my story, and then," said Michael, "I'd love to hear more about yours."

Rachel cleared her throat. "Please, the focus is on you, not me right now."

Michael laughed. "A usual therapist response?"

Rachel smiled, turning her palm up for him to continue.

He peered at her for a moment. "For a long time, I thought it seemed the right choice for our family."

Rachel paused her fork, put her hands together.

"But Roisin might have done better with a sibling." Michael bit into his salmon dish.

"From the beginning, she seemed advanced for her age. Talking, walking, all the other developmental tasks early on."

"With two very intelligent parents, I'm sure she inherited much."

"Yes, thank you." A relaxed smile spread across Michael's face. "And trust me, Ingrid didn't let that slide. She insisted Roisin be exposed to everything, so she'd have the best opportunity to choose."

"Don't you think most parents want that for their children, and if they have the means, do what they can?"

"Yes, but I think Ingrid, well-intentioned, might've gone a bit overboard." Michael shook his head. "And I went along with it."

Rachel took another bite of her snapper. Wow, this guy seems hard on himself. Say something Rachel.

"I'm sure you did the best you could."

"I appreciate that, but there's more." He blinked, appearing to go inward.

Rachel's eyes drew together. "You feel okay about continuing?"

Michael chuckled. "Ah, the therapist comes out again."

"Sorry. I don't mean to act like one."

"Don't worry. I know it must be part of you." His gaze held still for a while. "Just teasing before I get to the more somber events."

Rachel's heart pounded. She knew from experience that some unpleasant revelation would emerge. She always hoped she'd be wrong, but often, her fine-tuned intuition ended up spot on.

"So, Roisin became a perfectionist. She played the piano, soccer, and excelled in school. We sent her to the best, including Athena, one of the most rigorous private schools in the country. When she turned twelve, she started cutting." He stared at Rachel. "I'm sure you're familiar."

"Yes, but I don't see adolescents, so I learn more from hearing adult histories or stories about their children or siblings."

"Clever enough to hide it from us, but one day, Ingrid saw her changing socks. The scabbed lashes intersected with open ones across her feet. Ingrid screamed and called me in a panic. Ingrid found a top-notch therapist who dealt with cutters."

"How did your daughter feel about that?"

Michael shook his head. "You know adolescents. Not well."

Rachel blinked, nodding.

"Anyway, she went. The cutting subsided. Ingrid stepped back from her Internal Medicine practice and watched our daughter with a third eye. Although I worked a great deal, I made it a point to go to important events. For the next few years, all seemed well."

Michael stopped and licked his lips. "From the outside, our beautiful, intelligent, gifted Roisin appeared to have it all."

The servers brought over coffee.

"But not so well." Michael poured cream into his coffee as Rachel peered at him, taking a sip from her coffee cup.

"College applications, and of course, where did Roisin want to go? Harvard, Yale, Princeton. Nothing else would do. We pushed her to apply to others—Brown and Williams. At first, she stamped her feet and refused, but someone must have convinced her because she came around."

What should I say? You're a therapist. Say something, but what?

Just listen. Think of him as a client or friend.

Michael looked down at his coffee and stirred it. "Even though she excelled in her testing, Roisin became inconsolable after receiving the news of being wait-listed by three of her favorites."

He steepled his hands to his mouth with an unfocused stare. "Although accepted by Brown, she became withdrawn. The day of graduation, old Roisin appeared, intense but smiling as she accepted her diploma with the highest of honors."

Michael stopped and sighed, laying his hands on the table. "To make a long story short, Ingrid found her hanging in the closet."

Rachel knew, but couldn't restrain herself, bringing her hand to her lips. Her eyes pooled with tears, and she grabbed Michael's hand, shaking her head.

Tear streamed down Michael's face. "My beautiful Roisin. Gone."

Rachel continued shaking her. "I don't even know what to say, except I'm so sorry."

Michael nodded. "Ingrid and I had already drifted apart, so when Roisin took her life, our relationship's life support went kaput."

"Not unusual," Rachel almost whispered.

"My brother and sister and their families rallied around me."

Michael stared at Rachel. "Like I said, they live a few hours from here, and took turns staying with me off and on for months. I'm blessed I have them."

Rachel nodded.

"In fact, having family means everything. I don't understand how people have cut-offs or allow anything to interfere with their connections. Don't you think there's something very wrong when that happens?"

"Sometimes, but like many things, it can be complicated." Rachel's insides crumbled as she did everything to keep a steady demeanor.

"I don't know." Michael grimaced. "I can't think of anything, but you're the professional in that arena."

Rachel forced a laugh. "It's not so black and white."

"Speaking of family, we never got to your story."

Chapter Eighteen

Session Six—April 28th—Yardley

In a bulky sweater covering her thin body, Yardley sat alone as she waited for the others. She rubbed her hands together, thinking about what to say. A tingle went up and down her spine. What would they think? They'd feel bad about Ashley, of course. Everyone did. How could she ever share the truth after that?

Besides, they'd watch her. Would they notice her filling out the sweater after last night's meal? *Ridiculous*, she could hear Daniel say.

Matt sauntered into the room with a slack tie and undone collar. Almost as handsome as her Daniel, but not quite. Anyway, not her type, not Jewish, and too movie-star looking. Maybe he and Sapphire should be together. Sapphire. Does she have an edge? Even though Matt seemed calm, she got under his skin. What a pair they would make. She cleared her throat, attempting to hold back her laughter.

"So, are you ready?" Matt asked, saluting hello to her.

"I guess," said Yardley.

"Not so hard once you begin. In fact, I'm glad you asked about my existing relationship with my mother."

Yardley gave him another half-smile.

"I, uh, need to call her and not just to say, *Hi, checking in*." Matt leaned forward. "Your question got me thinking that we need to have a deeper conversation, even though things have improved."

Yardley nodded, wide-eyed.

"I never gave her a break, no chance for her to explain. Oh, she tried, but I rebuffed her." Matt sighed. "Yeah, even though we see each other more, I'm ready to have that longer talk soon." Matt stopped, nodding. "I know she's waiting for me, so thanks."

Gosh, what did I say?

"Here's where Rachel's right. This group's offering something that, well, I didn't think it would, at least for me. Bringing things to a new level." Matt's eyes gleamed. "Same thing could happen to you. Let me know if you need some help like you offered me."

"That's gracious of you to say, Matt. Thanks."

Sapphire arrived and didn't make eye contact with Matt, who drew out his phone.

"Your turn, right Yardley?" Sapphire's eyes sparkled.

Yardley nodded.

The others entered, including Rachel. After greeting everyone and checking in, Rachel glanced at Yardley.

"Okay, my dear, I believe you should go next."

Yardley nodded. She drank some water and straightened her shoulders.

"I'm getting into my Wonder Woman state as much as I can."

"Hon, you go, girl," Shalene spoke with a shine in her eye.

She raised her bottle as a toast to everyone.

"I'll try to speak louder, so here goes." Yardley laced her hands tight. "I was the youngest of two girls and grew up in the Big Apple. My mother, Ruth, and father, Asher, doctors, met and fell in love in medical school."

Yardley glanced at everyone. "I'm Jewish, as you know, and my great-grandparents survived the Holocaust. So, my parents enforced the importance of our traditions."

"Attempted genocide. Beyond hideous," Matt growled.

Yardley turned to Matt and studied the frown etched in the corner of his mouth.

What a sweet man.

"So, if you couldn't tell," Yardley uttered a soft laugh, "I'm shy.

Opposite of my sister. She was three years older than me, smarter than me, and people said she *lit up a room.*"

"Hey there, Ms. Yardley. First, you light up a room. You understand." Jason bobbed his head with his mouth becoming a straight line.

She saw the others bob with the same vigor.

"Thank you, Jason and everyone." Yardley rubbed her fingers. "We looked alike, but different. I did well in school. A's and B pluses, but like I said, she did better with all A's. We went to a private school." She shrank back a bit. "Super hard to get into, and boy, they pushed us."

Yardley blinked and strung her hands together tight.

"My sister received lots of attention. I was about thirteen, and things got bad. She hung out with a different crowd and started wearing lots of black eyeliner, extra mascara, and red lipstick, along with shorter skirts and tighter shirts."

Yardley stopped again. Her mouth bunched up.

"She started coming home late, and her grades went down. My parents tried to shield me, but one night I opened my bedroom door and peeked out after hearing my sister yell at my parents. My mother said, *Shh. You'll wake your sister.* Ashley ran by me to her room, and I shut the door."

Yardley glanced at Rachel and grabbed her soft eyes for support.

"A short time later, I heard my parents tell Ashley they arranged a time with a therapist. She stomped around the apartment and screamed, and my mother said, *Just one meeting, please.*"

Yardley swayed in her chair and looked at the ceiling. "I'll never forget that day. They came home, and my sister's face was beet red and wet. She flew again to her room and slammed the door. My mother looked at me, waved her hand, and asked me about my day. I don't know what happened, but I think no more therapy for Ashley."

Yardley wrapped her arms around herself and closed her eyes. "Tough stuff coming." She turned to Rachel whose eyes widened like glittering brown stones. "Please don't worry. I'm okay." She positioned herself as erect as possible on the soft chair. "In late May, my sister never came home. No one knew where she went. My mother paced around the apartment and kept texting and staring at her phone. I recall asking if I could do anything. She'd say, *No, no. Everything will be fine.* My Dad arrived home, and they whispered to one another. More phone calls to Ashley's friends and their parents. No Ashley. By 9:00, I became sleepy even though I worried about them, and they insisted I go to bed. I can still feel my body rolling around in the sheets, but sleep soon took the reins."

Yardley bent her fingers and pressed them together and studied her knuckles. Milky white opals on top of her hands.

She looked up at the other members.

They do seem caring. Just like Rachel said.

"The next morning I heard my mother crying. I tiptoed out of my bed and opened the door. My father had his arms around my mother. *Shh,* he said, *Ashley will walk through that door soon.* They saw me and told me to get a bite to eat. I shook my head. Sometime that morning, someone called and said someone else saw Ashley get into a dark limousine. Dad alerted the police, and Sunday they contacted the media. They canceled their commitments, and I stayed home from school. For the next week, my sister's face and videos appeared everywhere."

Yardley stopped for a moment, relaxed her body, and sank down into the chair.

"Dear Yardley, how are you doing?" Rachel's tone, coated with concern.

Yardley peeked at Rachel and forced a sliver of a smile. "Like everyone else, need to get this out." She blinked at Rachel and sighed. "Here's the worst. By Wednesday, the authorities asked my parents to travel to Vermont where someone found a body fitting Ashley's description under some brush."

Ashley peered at the other members and saw heads down shaking or staring back wide-eyed.

Her breath became shallow as she drowned in a tidal wave of the past. She shut her eyes again and inhaled the delicious scent. *Smells different. Kind of like orange or—lime? Need to ask Rachel. Keep breathing, Yardley.*

Ah, the aroma. *Umm.* Like a Classic Cosmo. Favorite drink. Only drink. She and Daniel clinking their glasses together.

"Hey, Ms. Yardley?"

Jason's voice roped her back to the present.

Her eyes fluttered and shifted to Jason with folded arms and knitted eyebrows.

"I'm not going to say are you okay, 'cause I know you're not, but anything we can do?"

Yardley shook her head and cleared her throat. "Thank you. Just took a bit of a break." She inhaled again. "My maternal grandparents had arrived a few days earlier from Florida. My parents left, and we waited and waited until later that night. My grandfather's cell rang, and I'll never forget…" Yardley's eyes filled, and her voice broke. "His face turned white, and he grabbed a chair to hold. He looked at us, and we knew."

"Oh my God." Sapphire pitched forward. "No words will justify…"

Matt, sitting next to her, offered his massive hand, and she slipped hers into the cocoon.

"The next couple of days—service, burial, and Shiva. I didn't returned to school that year and opted to do assignments from home. That summer, we traveled to Europe. A few days after we got back, my parents informed me they had an opportunity to relocate to the Boston area but wanted my input. I remember a light sensation lifting me like a balloon. I didn't want to go back to where it all began and told them. We hugged each other."

Yardley touched her face, and the tissue box made its way to her.

"Thank God, Ms. Rachel has those boxes," Jason said.

Everyone chuckled, and Yardley giggled as she dabbed her eyes.

"We came to Boston and moved to the Back Bay. I entered high school, a private, high-achieving one, and focused on studying. They had a philosophy that small classrooms cultivated free expression and greater learning, and it did. At least for me."

Yardley sat up erect again. "Here's the tricky part. I began having fun. But one day, while walking with my friends to Copley Place, I saw someone who looked like Ashley. I started hyperventilating, and my friends stopped. *You alright?* I took deep breaths and nodded. We kept going. None of them knew about Ashley, and if they did, no one mentioned anything. I didn't tell my parents about it, but I couldn't get the image out of my mind. So, what did I do? Studied more. I'd skip dinner and reassure my parents I'd eat later, but I didn't. I started going to bed without dinner."

Yardley slunk into her chair, and in almost a whisper she said, "I ignored my stomach and started enjoying this control over my food. A month later, my parents confronted me. *Do you think we wouldn't notice an eating disorder?* My mother demanded that I remove my clothing and place my bare feet on the bathroom scale. I did and can still see my mother covering her mouth and calling for my father. I watched the numbers on the scale tick down from 120 to 100 pounds and caught my father's red face and growling tone. I remember running to my room and saying almost out loud. *No. They can't make me eat.* I liked that light feeling, and it helped me not think about Ashley."

Yardley peeked again around the room.

Such nice people. So non-judgmental. But we'll see what they think later.

She took a deep breath again. "For the next week, my parents didn't say anything, but the following Sunday, my mother told me she arranged an initial session with a therapist." Yardley shook her head. "I remember doing what I'm doing now, shaking my head but with more vigor. My mother almost bared her teeth and said, *No discussion.* I begged her for one more chance. *Please, no therapy. I promise to do better.* But I never told her about the clumps of hair falling out, or my period stopping, or the fainting spells. She wouldn't budge, and the day before the appointment, I collapsed, landing overnight in the hospital, and entered an intense outpatient treatment program and individual therapy. Within two years, my eating disorder submerged, and life became filled with friends and fun. All good for a while." Yardley stopped and noticed her sweater soaked with tears.

Soundlessness saturated the room. Nothing stirred until someone sniffled.

Yardley turned her head.

Jason took a tissue and blew his nose. "Hey, Yardley. Don't mind me." He wiped his eyes. "Yeah, big guys like me are softies at heart, but speaking of heart, your story…" Jason shook his head. "Well, first, I'm so sorry about what happened to you and your family."

Yardley heard the others murmur in agreement.

"And didn't mean to interrupt, but it touched off…" Jason heaved.

She waved his apology away. "You didn't interrupt me." She gave Jason a half-smile. "I needed to pause."

Yardley stared outward and continued.

"Food became an ally rather than a foe—at least for a while. I'll summarize the rest to make this long story less lengthy. I graduated. College at Vassar. Fabulous time. Met Daniel, my love, studying medicine at B.U. in the middle of my senior year, while I came home one weekend. Accepted to law school. Another graduation. And then it started again…"

Yardley laced her hands together tight as a bow string. "I began thinking about Ashley. I don't know why except life seemed too good. Ashley's face became more vivid than ever. Luminous blue-green eyes with arched red brows, and her laugh…" Yardley bobbed her head. "I can hear it now. Food became enemy number-one, again, and I began slipping."

Yardley glanced at her knuckles again. "I made an appointment with Rachel—recommended by someone who knew someone."

She smirked at Rachel. "Lots of good therapy with more intensive treatment episodes. The bad thing? Daniel wanted a break from our relationship. We talk and text, but he wants me to work on me."

Ooh. I got most of it out. And they are so nice about it. Maybe the rest can come out.

"I still struggle with body image and weight." Yardley stared at her knuckles which looked as if they would pop out of her hands. "My parents don't know that it worsens when I see their sadness."

Yardley's face dropped to her hands, and sobs racked her body. Sapphire got up and hugged her.

After a few moments, Sapphire peered at Rachel. "The unfairness of life."

Rachel nodded.

Yardley pulled out a tissue and wiped her tears from her streaked face. She inhaled a deep breath and smiled first at Sapphire, then to the rest of the group.

"When they don't think I notice, I see my mother and father walk by Ashley's picture. They turn their heads and muffle a cry." She shook her head. "I don't think they'll ever get over the loss."

"What about you, Yardley?"

"Wh-What?" Yardley bristled, turning to Jason, then Rachel, and again to Jason. "It's complicated." She glanced at Rachel a final time. "I'm not ready to talk about that part." Yardley slunk into her chair.

"I'm sorry, Yardley. Did I offend you?" Jason asked, forehead creased in confusion.

She shook her head. "Nothing to do with you, Jason."

"Whew, last thing I want to do." Jason leaned forward. "I think your sister's death tore me up because," Jason's eyes searched Rachel's for reassurance, "of my situation that I haven't shared yet."

Yardley's eyes darted around the room. "I think I'm done for now, so…" She peeked at Jason, then Rachel.

"How are you doing, Yardley?" asked Rachel, her lips drawn together in a straight line.

Yardley sniffed and nodded. "I-I-I think I'm okay. Each bit I shared feels like shackles being removed, one at a time."

"Yes, Ma'am. Couldn't agree more," Jason said, gazing outward.

Jason

Okay. I'm up at bat. Need to get the rest out.

He sought Rachel's eyes, and as if in slow motion, she swiveled her chair to Jason.

"So, my friend, you think you're ready to remove those heavy bags off of you?" Rachel asked with measured words.

Jason nodded. "Yeah, okay, but first I need to talk about what made us leave Omaha."

He closed his eyes for a moment and then folded his arms. "So, I used to hear Harry and my grandparents talking about the city and if it was still the right place for us. One day, he informed me he and the Grandies made a momentous decision about leaving Omaha. He asked me what I thought. I remember not having an opinion except wanting to play sports. A lot of my friends planned on attending the public high school, and I knew Dad preferred it if I didn't. *Don't know if we can afford the private school, son, but not sure I want you in the public one.* Dad reassured me that no matter where we ended up, I could play."

Jason chuckled. "You know. That made me jump. I said, *Dad, wherever.* So, we decided on Raleigh, North Carolina. Family, ease of living, job opportunities, and superb schools made it a no-brainer.

He rubbed his chin. "The drive across country? One of the best memories of my life. Dad could sing. Rich bass voice. Hoowee. He'd belt out songs from Muddy Waters."

Jason looked around. "Y'all know Muddy?" The others nodded.

"We'd clap as Dad sang "Mannish Boy," and "I'm Your Hoochie Coochie Man." I'd close my eyes when he described the environment. Smoke-filled club with people dancing, men in shirts and ties, twirling around women with high heels and flashy dresses."

Jason clapped. "We took our time and stopped at various sites before landing in Raleigh. Lots of relatives. Balloons and enormous signs of welcome. Hugs from aunts, uncles, and cousins."

Jason stopped, with eyes downcast for a moment. "Things seemed fantastic for a very long time."

Jason looked up. "Raleigh brought so much good in our lives, but…" Jason sighed. "Nothing stays the same."

He clapped again. "But focusing on the good. Dad found us a new house, and I still see his tears as he showed me my new room. Just like yesterday." Jason shook his head. "And guess what? It didn't take long for me to plaster posters of my favorite basketball players."

Jason glanced at everyone grinning.

"I know. Typical teen boy."

"Yup. My brother did the same." Shalene's dimple blossomed again.

"Me? Basketball and Football." Matt said.

"I had a few of those posters too." Jason saluted Matt. "Anyway, I get to high school, and what a hoot. Basketball, classes, and guess again?" Jason leaned forward and each person's gaze.

"Girls." Sapphire's eyes danced with his.

"Yes, Ma'am, but one only. I developed a crush on a girl named Callie. Big brown eyes, caramel skin, and a smile that captured my soul." Jason stopped for a moment and sat back.

No puddles yet brother.

He took both palms and rubbed his face.

"Jason…" Rachel's tone swathed in worry.

His hands dropped to his lap. "Ms. Rachel, I know you're protective of all of us, but I'm battling through this."

Rachel nodded at him.

"Dad worked at Home Depot and started a handyman business on the side. In a short time, he quit Home Depot and hired a couple of helpers."

Jason sat back, and his gaze became unfocused. "My dad. What a guy. I see him now flashing his phone at me on graduation. He said, *Jason, you show those pearly whites and that diploma you earned.* So, I did."

Jason chortled, and he glanced around as others joined him.

"Yeah. Graduation couldn't have been more special. Me and Callie received awards for high honors, and we pointed to the sky with a thank you." Jason's gaze became unfocused again. "Yeah, we had a strong faith back then."

He caught Shalene studying his cross.

"Yeah. I believe in God stronger than ever, but it got interrupted along the way. Getting to why."

Jason laced his fingers again and paused for a moment.

"Things remained positive except for being separated from Callie and the family. She chose a college in the South, and I accepted one in the Northeast. Bummer, but the internet remedied that. Me and Harry FaceTimed a couple of times a week. I'd catch Harry, Dad, with tears. He'd see me gulp or some other worried expression and would say, *Now, son, don't you go worrying about me. I've got them*, and he'd turn to the Grandies in the background who would throw kisses at me."

"You can feel the love, Jason," Sapphire said.

Jason turned to her. "Yeah, Ms. Sapphire, I did." His eyes skimmed the others.

They know something's coming.

"Every night, I'd connect with Callie." He grunted and moved back and forth. "I'd place a place a hand towards her, and then I'd bring my device to my face, and..." Jason enunciated his words. "Kiss it." He looked up with a smile and caught everyone returning it. "She laughed. Brother and sisters, you could almost taste the sweetness coming from her throat. Like a gulp of Crème Brulé." He shut his eyes. "*Um, um*. Delicious."

He opened them quickly and looked outward. "We'd see each other as often as possible, and..." He inhaled. "Hoowee. I desired her. But we believed in waiting until marriage, so we'd kiss, hug, and explore each other's arms, hands, and neck." He stroked his chin. "You know what? We loved touching each other's faces. It elicited some hunger. I know this might be TMI, but..." Jason shook his head. "Anyone who thinks hooks-ups are fun…" Jason stopped. "They should think again, because they have no idea. Nothing like savoring the slow steady buildup. Even without sex, the experience I had with Callie, an elixir. Electric ripples that come with love and passion entwined."

Not looking at the ladies. Just Matt.

"Hope I didn't say too much."

"Hey man. No. I get it. Uh. Your description hits the mark."

"The way it should be." Sapphire sighed.

"Agree." Yardley and Shalene echoed one another.

His gaze moved toward the floor. "Graduation came and went. Summer at home with friends and family. More of Callie. In September, I entered Harvard Business School. I had a communications background and wanted to become an independent investigative reporter. I thought having a business degree from an Ivy couldn't hurt."

Jason halted for a moment and clamped onto Rachel's soft eyes. "You know, Ms. Rachel, this next part. Well, the toughest."

"You say as much or as little as you can my friend." Rachel's mouth a crinkled line.

Jason pounded his chest. "Battle scars about to hurt but going for it."

Jason furrowed his brow and scanned the room before his eyes found the floor again.

"The two years flew by. I couldn't wait for graduation and to get down…" he patted his knee, "and ask for her hand." He glimpsed Matt. "Already asked her father."

Jason tapped his chin with his laced hands. "Graduation, again. Not a cloud in the sky. God shined His light on me and my peers. So, I thought." He rested his elbows on his knees with his chin sitting on his laced hands. "I texted Dad and Callie but no response. Something flitted through my stomach like a pesky insect, but I told me, *Stop, brother.* Went up on stage and heard the applause from classmates but no flashing camera. No Harry in sight. No Callie in sight."

Jason shifted in his seat. "I thought, *Hmmm*. Grabbed hands, hugs, kisses. All of it, so emotional. You should have seen my wet face. Couldn't turn off the faucet, but as I sat down, the flitting became louder, like something stinging my stomach. Dad, Callie, Grandies, where are you?"

Jason paused for a moment with fists, tapped his cheeks, and lifted his eyes to Rachel.

"Yup, here goes."

"My intuition told me something was wrong. I see everyone hugging their relatives. And I, well, felt like a spectator. Now I can describe it as a creeping, ominous silence that encircled me and kept me separated from the background cacophony."

Jason froze.

"My friend."

"No, almost there."

He took a deep breath. Orange. Lime. Soothing.

"Someone patted my shoulder. The Dean. Her compassionate eyes caused my heart to throb. She suggested we go to her office where a chaplain, a subdued police officer, and a man who introduced himself as Detective So-and-So stood."

Jason rubbed his knees. "These, here, buckled, and I grabbed a chair to steady myself. The detective explained that a terrible car accident occurred leaving Logan Airport."

Jason put his palm up as he licked his lips. "Y'all please don't say anything until I'm done."

Feet shuffled, but other than that, silence darkened the room.

Good. No interruptions. Time for the thunder and lightning.

"Dad's rental car went out of control, killing him and three other passengers—Callie and my grandparents."

A few sounds. Whimpers? He wouldn't look at anyone. Couldn't. Keep going brother.

Jason tapped his chin again. "I shook, screamed, put my head in my hands. A voice, I don't know whose, muttered some sympathetic words. I just kept my head down. The chaplain asked me something." Jason paused. "I don't remember much except for shaking my head."

He inhaled again. "The next week? Went through the motions. Friends stayed and helped me pack and move. I remember the chaplain calling, and brother and sisters, I thought, *No thanks.*" He peeked at Shalene. "At the time? God? Yeah. Right. Was there even one?" He put his head down. "Flew back to North Carolina, buried Dad and Grandies, and attended the service for Callie. My cousins stayed at the house. We'd take walks, and I'd catch them studying me. I'd fake a smile and say, *I'll be okay—in time.* But I knew once I settled my dad's affairs, I'd leave." Jason pounded his chest. "The boulder seemed unmovable and unbreakable if I stayed past that."

Jason searched the room and found the safety of Rachel. "My new employers were cool and told me to take as much time as I needed. The next two months, I numbed. Partied, alcohol, women. Crossed out my beliefs with a semipermanent Magic Marker." Jason grunted again and stared at the floor. "Some mornings, I'd say to myself, *Jason, brother, flex your brain power. What was the name of the woman from the night before?*"

He bolted up and caught Matt's eye. "And then?" He snapped his fingers. "Too much. I had enough drinking and carousing, and someone—or some*thing*—said, *Stop.* And just like that I did. The house sold, and I came back to Boston and my faith."

Jason pulled on his cross and kissed it. "My return to God? Something clicked. I needed Him." He smirked at everyone. "And thank God for that. I believe He inspired me to help the young fellas. That calling saved my life." Jason turned his head to Rachel. "And God brought me to you."

Chapter Nineteen

Rachel—April 29th

Rachel sat across from Janine Saturday evening, while they munched on Mexican food.

Besides Friday nights, she and Janine got together more than once on the weekend since both were unattached. They navigated friend gatherings around Janine's dating schedule. Every so often, Bridget joined them when her husband attended a sporting event, but not tonight.

Last Sunday, they walked their canines in a nearby park filled with dogs galore on the glorious spring morning. Rachel's poodles frisked with Janine's lapping Golden Retriever and Bridget's drooling Newfie.

People walked by, smiling at the threesome. Rachel observed her friends.

What a sight they must be.

Six-foot Bridget walking Brutus, Rubenesque Janine being pulled by Daisy, and petite Rachel keeping up with Zsa Zsa and Gabor.

Both women halted anytime Rachel expressed doubt about Michael and only resumed their walk if the dogs yanked them or stood wagging their tails. All three would laugh at the unspoken, "Come on, Mommy."

Rachel's heart darted as she shared her attraction to Michael. "What's the problem?" They'd ask almost in unison.

"He gorgeous, which makes me insecure. And not my thing to wrestle with a cougar for the prize. You know. One with pointy claws who wants to devour me out of the way."

"You're not so shabby yourself and have no reasons for insecurity, and who is the cougar?" Bridget asked.

Rachel shook her head and frowned. "A major cougar, Justine."

"Um, Rachel, since when did you become a shrinking violet?" Janine's voice slathered in sarcasm.

Rachel nodded, as she bent down to tie her shoe.

The date ended abruptly because Michael received an emergency surgical call. She forgot ophthalmologists are eye surgeons. He paid the bill and waved off her hand as she thrusted ten-dollar bills into his. As they walked out together, Michael's hand went under her elbow, and sparks infused her body.

She stiffened. So glad he couldn't detect the *zing* reaching every cell.

Michael's shimmering eyes lingered on hers.

"Thank you, Michael."

"Thank You! What a lovely evening you gave me."

As the car pulled up, Michael paid the valet, grabbed the keys, and took Rachel's hand to lead her into the car.

He leaned in and gave her a quick peck on the cheek. "I'll be in touch." And he closed the door keeping his eyes on her.

She waved, and as she drove away, she glanced in her rearview mirror. He watched her as he waited for his car.

"Did he text you this morning?" Bridget winked at her twice.

She and Janine stopped as Rachel leaned down to her dogs, petting, and cooing them.

Now Rachel and Janine continued eating their tacos and burritos, along with chips and guacamole. They agreed tonight to make an exception for *no therapy talk* to discuss their cases and save relationship chatter for dessert. Rachel suggested Janine go first before she updated her on the group. Janine shared her story about a lovely fifty-year-old single woman who reminded her of them.

"She's a doll. You know, the one whose fiancé committed suicide twelve years ago. I tell her, *Don't give up,* and," Janine's eyes stayed steady on Rachel's while she dipped into the guacamole, "she's come a long way. And if I have any say, she won't give up."

"I know what you're trying to get across, and I haven't given up," Rachel said, biting into her taco. "*Umm.*" She stared right back at her friend. "Would I have considered venturing out and attending a Tango society, of all places?"

"No, but I know you. Remember what you said. *I just want to dance?*" Janine cut more of her food. "You meet what sounds like an interesting guy, and you're letting the past interfere." She lifted her eyes toward Rachel, and before inserting a piece of meat into her mouth, she said, "You get my point."

"I do, but let's talk about the group first, before I get into Michael."

"I'm all ears."

Rachel updated her friend about the last session.

"Jason seemed okay when he finished his story."

Janine nodded, taking a sip of her wine. "Were you worried about him?"

"Only at the beginning. At the end, he kissed his cross and said something connected him to the boys he mentored." Rachel smiled. "On the way out, he hugged me and repeated, *Thank God for you too.*"

"You and God, huh, Rachel? That's a lofty comparison."

Rachel laughed. "He didn't word it the way you're interpreting it."

"What else did he say?"

"Not much, but at the end, he let the group know he wasn't sure if the sharing helped close the wound, but he'd sit with it and tell everyone next week."

"No matter how long we've been in the profession, we can't always know how and why it works."

"Right, sometimes you just don't know, even after all these years."

Janine took a sip of her sangria, moved her plate, and with hands on top of each other, leaned closer to Rachel.

"Okay, unless you have more, I want to hear about Michael."

"Let's have some dessert first."

"Isn't *he* dessert?" Janine's eyes danced.

"Wow, you're on your game tonight. We'll have to tell Bridget what she's missed."

Rachel went to her freezer and scooped a cup of vanilla frozen yogurt for each of them.

"I know he texted you, Rachel, so what's next?"

"I'll tell you about my insecurities first," she said, licking her spoon. "Ready?"

"All ears." Janine sipped her sangria.

"Sunday, I paced around my condo and imagined Michael not calling, not texting, and not acknowledging me. What if I attended a Tango lesson and witnessed Michael twirling Justine around the room, taking a lock of her glorious silver hair, kissing her hand at the end, and giving me a curt hello? I shook my curls and told myself, *Stop. Ridiculous. Go to church.* So, I listened to me and went to a 5:30 evening Mass. At the end, a lightness spread throughout me, and I said to me, *What will be will be.*"

"Okay. That sounds good. And then what?"

"Monday I saw lots of people, and you know what it's like. Energy, fatigue, and his blue-green eyes entered the picture."

"Hey, honey, we're human."

"No, I know, and that night he texted me and apologized, saying he'd been tied up most of Sunday and Monday. He went on in his message and told me how much he enjoyed our dinner. Then, he asked me about my availability for lunch on Saturday."

"Why lunch?" Janine asked.

"He volunteers with other physicians to travel to rural areas to help children who might benefit from his services and had a flight late that afternoon."

Janine nodded with a wide grin. "Sounds like a nice guy to me."

"You and I both know people can give to the world, but that's not always diagnostic of who they are, one-on-one."

"True, but he sounds like he's been nice to you—one-on-one."

"We'll see."

"Guess what, Rachel?" Janine squinted with a hard smile.

"Here goes. What?" Rachel asked, cocking her head.

"You think this guy's going to see you as defective because of Leah and Damian. That's what I think."

Rachel gave a long exhale before taking a spoonful of yogurt. She stared at Janine. "Okay, what if I do?"

"You need to get over it. What have you been doing with Alexandra since you started seeing her weekly instead of once a month?"

"You know."

"And what have you accomplished?"

"She's the one who pushed me to consider more than all work and no play. Okay?"

"Good, but now that you have a possibility of something in the second half, you're just, I don't know, finding excuses to label this man."

"Not true," Rachel swallowed, "but you're right about the Damian matter." Rachel's eyes became glassy. "And you witnessed it."

"I did and will vouch that it's not your issue. Not that I needed to witness it."

Rachel placed her hand under her chin, nodding.

That night, the gallery had swelled with admirers of the young, successful photographer.

Damian this, Damian that, so handsome, so talented, his mother would be proud, trickled into Rachel's ears and obscured other sounds.

She and Janine pushed through the crowd of invitees, munching on appetizers that included shrimp and chicken satay on skewers, avocado on toast, and caviar as they sipped on wine. Rachel recognized a few models with their long hair, perfect faces, and emaciated bodies.

"I hope they're in therapy to deal with their E.D.s," Rachel said to Janine in a whispered tone. Photographers with their modern and expensive cameras, snapped pictures of affluent young men dressed in designer jeans, and open-collared shirts, and their older counterparts attired in pin-striped suits with silk cravats or tieless shirts.

"Quite the Chi-Chi crowd," Janine murmured in Rachel's ear.

Rachel grinned. Yup. Damian sure found his footing among Manhattan's elites. Not impressed by celebrities, but sometimes, she admitted, intrigued. Either way, look at Damian. A satisfied smile settled on her face. Her nephew. Could this invitation mean… Don't get ahead of yourself. Like you tell your clients, slow and steady. Proceed with caution.

They almost reached the beginning of the exhibit, *A Celebration of the Women in My Life*. Rachel squeezed Janine's hands. Is there a surprise here for me? She glanced over at Damian, holding court for a few middle-aged women, with unlined foreheads, extra high cheekbones, and bee-stung lips.

You go ladies. If you can afford the enhancements, why not? But, too bad. I can detect the injectables streaming through your face.

Rachel turned toward the photos, amazed by Damian's ability to take older pictures and transform them into a works of art. The modern camera fusing with his scrupulous eye. She shook her head.

Damian approached them, a slow nondescript smile emerging on his face.

The image of that night faded away, but Rachel's gaze remained outward.

"Where are you, Rachel?" Janine asked, waving her hand.

Rachel shook her head. "Lost in thought."

"Let me see—about what? Or, should I say, who?" Janine lapped the rest of the yogurt on her spoon, before leaning closer. "Damian, Damian, where art thou?"

Rachel frowned. "Of course."

"Again, you did nothing wrong. Do you hear me? Nothing."

Chapter Twenty

Rachel—May 1st

The sun rewarded everyone with a spectacular coming attraction of summer with the temperature reaching mid-seventies on a glorious New England day. Rachel observed people bustling around the Seaport area as she sat at an outside table waiting for Michael. She wore a straw-brimmed hat, a sleeveless dress with an accompanying shawl, and Stuart Weitzman sandals.

Laughter, chatter, fun. She closed her eyes, inviting the rays to massage her face and a mild sea breeze to journey through her hair. *Ahh!*

She couldn't decide what made her experience the spicy sensations surging through her body.

The weather or Michael?

Come on, silly. You can't deny it, and what would Alexandra say? Never mind Janine or Bridget? She almost laughed aloud.

Click! Clack! Her eyes opened to a server leading Michael to their table. He wore jeans and an open-collared white shirt, which complemented his gray hair and sea-color eyes.

His presence caused Rachel's heart to plump as he swept down with a quick kiss to her cheek before pulling out a chair.

Stop you!

Rachel inhaled sharply and straightened her posture.

"You look ravishing," Michael said, as his eyes roamed below her face.

Tingles crackled through Rachel.

"You're pretty handsome yourself," she said, taking a slow, steady sip of water to disguise what might be visible to him.

Listen, he can't see your insides. Just stay cool and be yourself.

"How've you been?"

"Busy. Just like you."

"Yes, I'm stretched these days," Michael said. "After the divorce, I immersed myself in more professional duties, including what I'm doing with this group of physicians. We volunteer our services twice a year to the underprivileged who might benefit from our expertise."

"That's generous of you."

"I hadn't planned on any relationships soon, so I thought, why not?" Michael blinked. "But sometimes things come into your path when you least expect them."

His eyes penetrated hers.

Rachel gave a half-laugh. Before she responded, the server came over for their requests.

Once they ordered their salads, Rachel asked Michael to share more about this week's venture.

"I'm flying out of Logan in a few hours and will be going to the Appalachian area, helping an understaffed medical group to service people with eye afflictions."

Rachel peppered Michael with questions about the population, its needs, including its impact on their mental health.

"Yes, many of these people have lost friends, relatives, and their own children from the Opioid and Fentanyl crisis exploding across the country," Michael said. "Of course, you understand how physical affliction affects mental health. Some of these people suffer depression, luring them toward alcohol and substance abuse."

Rachel nodded. "Must be difficult to deal with that even short-term. Does it affect your well-being?"

Michael frowned and studied her before responding. "Good question, but even though I lost my daughter, I'm able to compartmentalize and remind myself that helping others less fortunate is a great salve. Even with my daughter's suicide, I believe I've been given much. What's that quote referring to that?"

"To those whom much is given, much is expected?" Rachel asked.

"Where's it from?"

Rachel waited for a moment as the server delivered their salads. "The Book of Luke."

Michael nodded. "Are you a person of faith, Rachel?"

"I am. How about you?"

"I've always been a semi-practicing Catholic, typical church attendance on holy days, but after Roisin died, I couldn't bring myself near a church. A few years ago, I realized I missed believing in something greater, so I dipped my toe back into religious life," Michael said, reflecting on this before biting into his salad.

Rachel sighed. "It's understandable. Some of my clients who've suffered major losses experienced the same."

Michael's blue-green eyes shifted in color as he stared at her, which invited her to do the same. A gentle wind interrupted as it wrapped its cool ocean air around them.

Rachel broke the spell, pulling her shawl closer to her.

"Speaking of losses. You're a widow." Michael's eyes lifted. "A young one." Again, his eyes explored hers. "We've talked enough about me. Now it's your turn if that's alright."

Rachel gave a half-smile and put her hands together. "What would you be interested in?"

"Anything you'd like to share." Michael offered his hand. "I want to get to know you."

Rachel placed her hand on his, feeling his massive fingers as he massaged hers for a moment.

"Well, let me tell you about my childhood, which leads to my complex adulthood."

Michael nodded. He unclasped her hand, eating bites of his food in between, giving Rachel full attention.

Rachel talked about her background, telling Michael about her parents, both only children, who fell in love with each other and gave birth to her and Leah. She discussed their loving approach to raising their children, saying little about Leah's jealousy and shared the devastation of losing her parents, young and vibrant middle-aged people.

Rachel gulped before continuing her narrative. *How much should I share?*

"My sister died several years ago of cancer."

Michael grabbed her hand again. "My God! You've experienced so much loss." His eyes didn't waver from hers. "Did your sister have children? I'm sure they'd relish a close relationship with their aunt."

"One son, only. Damian. He's a successful photographer who lives in New York."

"You must be proud of him."

Rachel offered a pensive smile as Michael took another bite of his food. Her thoughts returned to that fateful day.

She stood with Janine, eager for Damian to reach them.

He slowed his steps as he approached them, with a smile but a flicker of something... else. *What?*

"Auntie, I hope you and Jenny…"

"Janine." Rachel's friend uttered with a stern tone.

"Ah, right—Janninee," Damian said.

Rachel glanced at her, but Janine's obvious scowl remained on Damian.

"Uh, so sorry. I met so many people this evening. As I was saying, I'm pleased you're enjoying the exhibit."

"I'd love to see some photos of Rachel since she's been a significant woman in your life," Janine said.

Almost in slow motion, Damian turned to Janine and sneered. "I don't know what my aunt shared with you, but you're incorrect. She's not, and hasn't been, a *significant* part of my life."

A dark stillness reverberated, with all other sounds becoming white noise.

"What?" Janine asked.

Damian's face revealed no emotion. "You heard me. My life incorporated wonderful and beautiful women, including my glorious mother, grandmother, and my mother's two cousins who couldn't be here."

Rachel's eyes became moist. "Damian, you don't know the other side of the story. I tried."

"Yeah. Right." Damian's eyes moved to Rachel. "That's not my understanding." Damian folded his arms. "I hope you're not accusing my dead and beloved mother of embellishing, or worse, lying."

Rachel blinked.

"Auntie and Jenny, I mean Jaannine, I invite you to observe the rest of the exhibit, but I must offer my adieu and mingle with others." Damian stepped away but pivoted back. "Oh, but if you're looking for any photos of you. They aren't there, like you weren't there for me, most of my life." With that, Damian turned away, clasping people's hands, returning hugs and kisses, as he blended into the crowd.

Janine's nostrils flared. "What would you prefer to do, honey? It's up to you, but I say, let's get out of here."

Rachel nodded, trying to recover from the open wedge in her heart. She held her head high, noticing some eyes on her and the whispered, "Isn't that the sister? You can see the resemblance. I wonder why the exhibit doesn't include her."

When they reached the door to depart, Rachel heard Jonathan's voice. She turned with droplets leaking from her eyes.

Jonathan sighed. "I'm sorry Rachel. I even encouraged him to place you in one or two of the photos, but he'd have none of it."

Rachel shook her head. "I appreciate that Jonathan, but my sister's unfair echo rings loud."

Jonathan shrugged with hands up.

"Goodbye Jonathan."

Rachel walked out the door with Janine scoffing. "What a wimp."

Rachel nodded. "That's been the problem right along. My sister bullied everyone to see it her way or else."

Michael's voice brought her back to the present.

"You look far away." Michael cocked his head.

Rachel returned her gaze to him. She couldn't go there. Not yet. Would he understand family alienation? Could he know about making someone invisible? No, she'd need to learn more about him before she shared the depths of her sorrow.

"Well, I see little of my nephew. He's quite busy, traveling places to photograph influential people." Rachel smiled. "But I always want good for him."

"I'm sure you do." Michael's eyes gleamed. "Well, I hope he doesn't forget about his aunt. So, what else can I learn about Rachel Karem?"

Rachel laughed. "You sound like a therapist."

Chapter Twenty-One

Session Seven—May 6th—Rachel

Rachel entered the suite to her office and reflected on her lunch with Michael. After teasing him about being like a therapist, she changed the subject back to him.

Whew.

He went along with it and told her more about the upcoming trip to help the underprivileged. He also shared that he'd once considered becoming a plastic surgeon to assist those with facial deformities. Instead, he chose ophthalmology. "The eyes won," he said with a chuckle.

He walked out with her and again insisted on paying the valet. His lips found her cheek and lingered with an extended kiss, creating waves of pleasure throughout every cell of her being. Her eyelashes fluttered as he helped her into the car. Michael bent down to touch her cheek with one last graze before telling her he'd text her soon.

Rachel began the ride home, holding onto the delicious sensations pulsating in her body like the vibrations from a glorious harp.

Oh, my goodness. Who knew such feelings could be awakened at this age?

Wait, a minute.

Are you kidding? Who are you kidding?

You tell your older female clients what?

Then you wonder about yourself?

Hypocrisy or denial?

Rachel shook her head. You're no different, honey. Remember that.

She opened the door to chatter. Jason held court. Everyone stopped as Rachel entered.

"Nice to see all of you engrossed in—something. It sounds like an interesting conversation."

"I wanted to share more about Toastmasters, the best-kept secret in the world, and how it's helping the young men I see every week," Jason said.

"Yes, you've embraced the philosophy, but I think it's also the influence of the singer and not just the song who contributes more than you realize," Rachel said with merry eyes. "If you get my drift."

Jason beamed. "Oh, Ms. Rachel, you're one of my best fans."

"Well deserved, my friend." Rachel grinned before looking at the others. "On that positive note, all of you've shared your stories, or at least most of them. Any thoughts about that?"

With the majestic Tiffanies emanating their gentle lights, a warm glow infused the room.

Yes, something's changing.

Jason stroked his chin while Yardley gazed at the floor. Shalene glanced at her hands. Matt cocked his head and fidgeted. Sapphire passed her hand through her long mane.

Jason raised his finger. "Anyone mind if I go?"

Everyone shook their heads.

"I thought about Yardley, and I just want to make sure I didn't offend." Jason's eyes tried to capture hers.

Yardley's head sprung up like a Jack-in-the-box. "What? No." She shook her head. "You did nothing. In fact, I thought about sharing more tonight." She peered at Rachel.

Rachel's eyebrows rose, nodding to Yardley. "My dear, if you're ready, please do."

"I think I am," Yardley said with a hint of a grin. She swallowed and looked around. "This is really hard, but I know I have to do it."

Sapphire leaned over and offered her hand. "Grab it if you need some support."

"Thanks, but I'm okay for now."

"Unless anyone else wants to say something first?" Rachel glanced at the others.

Everyone shook their heads.

"Please begin, dear Yardley," Rachel said.

Yardley took a deep breath and let it out. "Here's what no one knows but Rachel, not even Daniel."

Yardley shrunk a bit. Then sat up. "Here comes my Wonder Woman suit again."

"Good," Rachel cheered.

Yardley, inhaled deeply. "You changed it up, Rachel."

"I did. They ran out."

"Orange Sherbert. Getting ready for summer?" Shalene's dimple sprang. "Oops." She covered her mouth. "Sorry, Yardley."

Yardley scrunched her face. "Nooo. Like all of us, a little humor helps. But here goes."

She shook her head. "Every detail remains imprinted in my memory. The first time happened right after I turned twelve. I couldn't find my coat, so I borrowed Ashley's to go to a friend's. A few hours later, I walked through the door, and Ashley ran at me, grabbed my hair, slapped my face, and started swearing at me. I remember becoming wobbly, not just from being hit but from being assaulted by her mean words."

Yardley paused for a moment and squinted. "Like it occurred yesterday." She gulped and opened her eyes. "My parents weren't home, and I started crying. I remember Ashley's face inches from mine. She screamed, *Crybaby! Shut up. You better not tell Mom and Dad. I'll just say you lied. Baby.*"

Yardley sat up erect and laced her fingers. "Ashley always showed a bossy side to her, but I loved her so much and didn't care. To tell you the truth, because of my shyness, it helped that she took over things. And, yes, sometimes, she lashed out—but never like this."

She took a deep breath. "I sat down crying, and she yelled, *Take nothing of mine again. You hear me?* I whimpered, *Yes,* and peered at her. She reminded me of a fanged animal."

Her hands laced together tighter. "I thought she'd leave me alone, but she didn't. Even though she never hit me again, I became afraid. Sometimes, she threatened me and would say, *You better not or…* I avoided her at all costs, and I hid it from my parents."

She blinked.

"The next year, Ashley became moodier and unpredictable. She'd cry if I received more attention from our parents, but other times, things seemed okay. She'd praise me for excellent grades and dance performances. You just didn't know."

Yardley paused for a moment before continuing.

Rachel recalled the first time Yardley revealed to her about Ashley's bullying. She could feel a blaze stir within her, before returning to her more neutral stance.

Yardley asked Rachel if anything like this happened to her?

Rachel knew it took a great deal for Yardley to raise the question.

"My dear Yardley, not quite in the exact way, but similar."

Yardley's eyes blinked tears, and in a choked voice, thanked her.

Now Rachel witnessed a more trusting Yardley about to purge a poison that had held her captive for all these years.

"After that, things weren't the same." Yardley's eyes welled up.

Rachel's eyes softened as she saw Sapphire's hand reach out to Yardley, who touched it for a moment, before letting go.

"I'm okay," Yardley said to Sapphire.

Wow, who knew this group would unfold like this in such a short time. She thought she'd need to give Yardley some encouragement, but no. She's fine.

No need to intervene, Rachel. Just listen.

"I overheard my parents discuss their concerns about her changes with them and wondered about drugs, but after interrogating her and searching her room, they couldn't find anything. They even made her urinate in a cup. You know. They were doctors."

Yardley peeked again at Rachel. "We thought Borderline or Bipolar?"

"We'll never know my dear."

"I know." Yardley's voice dipped. "She stayed up and down with me until she died. Sometimes she'd stare at my clothes and start laughing, or she'd call me a weirdo. Other times, she'd study my hair or my face, poking fun at my French braid hairstyle or makeup application. Even though I never told my parents, sometimes they overheard her. *Ashley, enough! Give me your phone. You will not get it back until you write a letter of apology, and we approve it.* This happened a few times, and Ashley would always say, *I'll try harder.* She'd hug me and tell me she loved me."

Yardley slumped more and wrapped her arms around herself.

Rachel saw her as a healing sparrow risking another flight.

"Because I wished for peace, I accepted her apologies the first two times, but after that—I couldn't trust her. You know?"

Yardley's eyes scurried around the room, and she hung her head.

"My dear, how are you doing?"

Yardley raised her head after a moment and nodded.

Rachel looked at the other members. Each of them kept their eyes on Yardley. Sapphire glanced at Rachel. Heartbreak in her smile.

Yes, as a therapist, Sapphire understood.

"I started having dark thoughts at night and imagined blowing black dust on my sister to get her to stop."

Yardley peeked at everyone. Rachel nodded and watched Jason wink with both eyes.

"I was thirteen, and even though I knew I couldn't cause harm to her, I started having nightmares."

Yardley swallowed and kept her gaze on the floor. "I dreamt that Ashley left, and none of us cared. In one…" Yardley paused.

Rachel noticed tears flowing down onto Yardley's sweater. Someone passed the box of tissues to her, and Yardley took it, muffling a thank you, without looking up.

Yardley dabbed her eyes, wiped her nose, and kept her head

down. She sniffled. "A closed wooden coffin. People came up to us, my parents and I, chatting like—like Ashley's death made sense. Like it was a good thing."

Yardley lifted her head but maintained a downcast expression. "I woke from these nightmares, and with my thirteen-year-old mind, I reminded myself I didn't wish her dead, but looking back, I wanted an Ashley redo."

Let her be, Rachel. She needs to regurgitate this toxicity once and for all.

"I remember hoping that we didn't have to wait until we became grown-ups. My wish came through with Ashley hanging out with that wild crowd. I felt bad about my parents' angst, but Ashley became so preoccupied that she ignored me."

Yardley looked up with her wet face. "Those last few months made me less fearful, and my nightmares about her banishment waned."

She looked down and shuffled her feet. "Then it happened. Ashley not only disappeared but appeared in the coffin just as I dreamt." Her voice became less audible. "I couldn't relinquish my guilt, not just for surviving, but for wishing Ashley's disappearance. Not right away, and off and on. Magical thinking, I know. But each time I tried to disinfect it from my mind? Failure."

Yardley bolted up, laced hands, protruding knuckles. "Now I see my thought process. It became like a spider web. Weaving negative ideas and feelings and catching anything that might permeate my blame for the kidnapping and murder."

Rachel observed everyone pitching forward as they attempted to hear Yardley's tale. She'd put it on herself not to embarrass Yardley.

"My dear, I know this isn't easy, but I'd appreciate it if you could speak a tad louder."

Yardley's teeth peeked through her lips, and she cleared her throat. "My fault. All my fault. Because I didn't want my grades affected, my adolescent mind needed to direct those torturous threads twisting it." She blinked. "Cutting came to mind, but I knew my parents with their medicinal-focused minds would detect this right away."

Yardley tugged at her sweater. "Everyone can see what I did. Something subtle, chic, and powerful. Food intake. Focus on your studies, Yardley. Skip eating. Eat less. No vomiting, no overexercising, just withholding."

She let out a broken laugh. "I learned from others, once you get used to the hunger pangs, no problem. I also thought I could fool my parents with this method."

She shook her head hard. "No. It didn't work." Yardley's lips tilted upward. "Not with the Doctors Stein. No coddling, but Ashley's death made them more vigilant about my safety, and they didn't miss a beat."

Yardley looked up. "That's my story. I wanted to disappear because I thought I caused my sister's death. Now I know how distorted thoughts and guilt can torture us." She cocked her head at Rachel. "And I'm so grateful Rachel convinced me to join this group."

"Amen." Jason clapped. "Hey, Yardley, I know ya know this. We can have two feelings toward someone. Love and… well, not love."

Yardley gave Jason a half-smile and nodded.

"Yardley, as someone who's been manipulated and deals with victims of bullying, it's terrifying, even with someone as close to you as a sister." Sapphire's hand reached for hers again.

"I know."

"I'll second that," Shalene piped in.

Matt leaned forward with clasped hands. "How are you doing now?"

Yardley nodded. "Trying to put my finger on it." She paused and took a deep inhale. "Relief, I think."

"Good. That's how I felt each time I shared."

The rest of the group echoed a, "Yes."

Yardley looked at Rachel. "Since joining this group, my eating disorder has improved. More than I thought possible. Oh, the self-sabotaging lurks if I think I've eaten too much, but not as much, if that makes sense."

Rachel couldn't suppress the frothy enthusiasm bubbling in her body, and she bobbed her head. "Yes, Yardley, it makes perfect sense. You, my dear, are amazing—as are the rest of you."

Yardley sighed. "Hey, everyone? I think I'm going to share this with Daniel."

"You go, girl," Shalene said with a wide smile and prominent dimple.

"I'm scared, but I need to do it," Yardley said.

"You can do it, Yardley, and I'm looking forward to hearing how it goes." Sapphire's eyes sparkled as she squeezed Yardley's hand.

Matt nodded. "You got me thinking, Yardley. I need to do a few things too." He stretched his legs out, and his eyes shifted to everyone with a moment longer on Sapphire.

Jason's hands pressed together over his mouth, then he took his cross and studied it. "You know what?"

Everyone shifted their gaze to Jason as he stalled for a second. "I'm going to add a drop of courage and do something, too."

Rachel could no longer ignore the message emerging from the cavernous chamber in her mind. *You aren't the only one.*

Chapter Twenty-Two

Rachel—May 12th

Rachel missed last week's Tango class. Without Michael's presence, she imagined a lackluster palette coloring the scene. After everyone left the group session, her heart pounded as she opened her phone, studying texts and voicemails.

No Michael. Nothing. Nada.

Emptiness filled as optimism depleted. See. No guarantees. Should've gone last night.

She became determined not to surrender Tango. You didn't go to find a date but to dance. Remember that. Even if you hear from him, you go.

The next morning, crisp and invigorating like the scent of a mint spritz, Rachel returned from a walk with Zsa Zsa and Gabor and noticed someone at her door, writing a note, with a vase of flowers standing. Rachel yelled and jogged toward the young visitor. She held the dogs back as they waved their paws at the stranger. He laughed and told her no problem as he stooped to pet her four-legged friends. He reached for the vase, full of coral roses, and stood up.

"Looks like you have an admirer." The young delivery person's eyes crinkled with a smile.

Rachel's heart vibrated.

"I guess so. Please hold on." She unlocked her door to let the dogs into the house, hearing them scramble toward the water bowl.

She thanked the man, brought her flowers into the kitchen, and smiled as the pooches slurped from their water dishes. Eager to see who sent them, she removed her jacket and squinted her eyes for a moment.

Don't assume.

Before she touched the glorious stems, Rachel ripped open the accompanying card and read the message.

Dearest Rachel,

Forgive me for not contacting you. I've been deep into corrective eye surgeries, but you haven't been far from my thoughts. I'll be here longer than I expected but will text you soon.

Michael

Rachel started skipping around the kitchen as her heart soared toward heaven.

Thank you, God. I didn't want to hope, but I'm so glad.

She went to the flowers, caressing the silky petals. Coral. She knew the meaning. Passion. It matched the desire burning in her body.

Who knew these dormant sensations would awaken after long thought dead? Okay, Rachel, now you understand what your clients mean.

This sumptuous experience she had remained sacred and reserved only for one. After Sam, she assumed none.

Now? Maybe, Michael?

She located her Waterford, a flared-shaped, delicate beauty, and took her time cutting the stems, picking off some leaves, and arranging each rose into the elegant vase. Nothing less for the majestic display. Michael's image appeared. His glorious silver mane, sparkling sea-colored eyes, and bright smile almost knocked her down. Laughter surged from her throat as if he witnessed her performance.

Wait.

Craggy letters appeared and invaded her lightness.

The message?

Don't get ahead of yourself.

Okay, but for now, let me enjoy. Erase those words.

On Sunday, after church, Rachel walked towards her car and smiled as she looked at her phone. Although kept in silent mode during Mass, she saw the flash through the slit of her bag.

She looked up to the sky. A sign?

Michael informed her that their group would stay until Friday. The needs of the people they serviced went beyond their expectations. They worked around the clock with time for sleep and meals only. Exhausting, he stated, but rewarding. His last sentence? He hoped she enjoyed the flowers, and he'd be in touch with her mid-week.

Rachel put the phone on her chest, took a deep breath, and hummed.

No matter. She'd keep the promise to herself. Tango on Wednesday, here I come.

Now, the full moon shined bright and eerie as Rachel drove to Somerville. She often wondered about the reality of the moon's effect on mood and events but brushed aside such superstitions. For one moment, she imagined the moon larger than life.

Could this represent what the future holds?

A whisper of a thought. *No, no, no, stay in the present,* as she retreated from her car.

Rachel entered the bustling studio. It felt strange without Michael in attendance. You never know, maybe you should get used to it. She shook her head and walked to the sign-in line.

David managed the registration, checking people into the studio. She reached the desk, and the much younger man offered her a dazzling smile, shifting his head to see beyond her. "I haven't seen your partner in dance, and," clearing his throat, "um, maybe more than dance?" David winked at her.

"The good doctor is on assignment. I've no partner for tonight." Rachel's said with a tone swathed in play.

"I'd be honored if you'd give me the pleasure of partnering for the evening."

"The pleasure would be mine."

"Buenos Noches!" Guillermo clapped.

In almost unison, everyone repeated the Spanish greeting, and Guillermo, in his usual fashion, shared with the students his intention for this lesson.

Guillermo brought a partner to reveal an additional step, and with slow, perfect precision, he and his very experienced volunteer showed the students the next lesson.

David strolled next to Rachel and whispered how simple Guillermo made it seem.

She nodded.

After a few minutes, the participants were invited to practice the steps, and David clasped Rachel's hands. They took their time, becoming acquainted with each other's movements to the music. As they flowed together, David said, "Terrific job, Rachel."

Rachel laughed and wagged her head. "I'm not so sure."

"Yes, you are quite skilled," David responded to her doubt. "And don't tell anyone." David glanced around the room. "But I've danced with others, and a few are quite clumsy."

"I bet you say that to all your partners."

David grinned and denied the charge.

They continued dancing until a few minutes before intermission. David returned to the registration table to catch attendees who arrived late. Rachel headed for the water table and sat for a moment, fanning herself. She smiled. Not only fun, but a great workout and a delightful distraction from thoughts about Michael. Although he was a part of this episode so far, concentrating on the dance removed her from worries and insecurities.

Rachel sipped her water again before heading to the ladies' room. She knew the beeline would arrive in a few minutes, so she hurried. She entered the lounge and rushed into the stall before coming out to check on her makeup and hair.

She searched for her lipstick and paid little attention to who came and went. She examined herself in the mirror, puckered her lips, and caught Justine coming out of the stall and heading to the basin next to her. Justine displayed glamour. Beautiful silver hair flowed along her shoulders, and she carried her tall, trim figure with ease. From the corner of her eye, Rachel noticed Justine examining her.

"Well, well, look at adorable you!" Justine's perfect eyebrows knitted together.

"Thank you!"

"So, where's Michael?" Justine asked.

Rachel sputtered and struggled to find words.

"Let me guess." Justine brought her index finger to her head, creating a *Jeopardy* sound. "One of his jaunts, helping people in faraway locations?"

"Oh, what makes you think that?"

Justine arched her eyebrows and chuckled before ambling out of the ladies' room.

Rachel tried to contain the invasive vine of uncertainty.

No, almost shouting out loud. *Don't let this narcissist ruffle your feathers.* She pinched herself and pivoted. With head high and shoulders back, she walked out to the studio and melted into the throng.

The encounter with Justine reawakened toxic spikes puncturing her protective shield.

She waved with a plastic smile as she waited for David to return.

Now she surveyed the room. Her eyes roved over the crowd until they landed on Justine, conversing with an attractive man. She shifted her head a few times and peeked again at a slender and poised Justine.

Rachel's self-doubts re-emerged. She visualized herself as a second bloom and cringed.

Impossible for you to regain lushness of the first, no matter how hard you try. What could Michael see in her after being with an elegant swan like Justine?

She shuddered and tugged on the invasive weeds sprouting in her mind.

The exquisite figure may flaunt her feathers, but underneath? An empty vessel? Aren't most narcissists?

Enough! She shouted behind her wall of silence and smiled as if all was well.

"Here you are." David grinned as he approached Rachel. Guillermo clapped for everyone's attention. The music began, and David extended his arm to Rachel.

He bowed. "Señora, may I be graced with the pleasure again?"

Rachel curtsied with dancing eyes. "Si, mucho gusto!"

For the rest of the time, they danced, incorporating the extra steps. Although Rachel's mind wandered once or twice, for the next hour, she focused on her feet to avoid stepping on David's.

At the end of the practice lesson, Rachel thanked David but declined his invitation to remain for the second half, where the skilled dancers held center stage.

On her way out, she encountered Justine again.

"You know," Justine gazed at her, "woman to woman, I should advise you about the probable outcome of your relationship with Michael." She lifted her eyebrows. "I'm sure I wasn't the first, as you'll not be surprised."

Rachel gave a catlike smile. "Thank you, but I'm quite familiar with relationships." She waited for a second, and with wide eyes, she purred. "I don't know if you know I'm a therapist with a booming practice."

Justine's body stiffened. "Yes, I've heard. So?"

Rachel realized she hit a nerve. "I think I know better than the average person. Wouldn't you say?"

Justine's nostrils flared for a moment, but she flipped her hair and smirked. "I suppose, but I believe patterns unfold." She cocked an eyebrow. "Wouldn't you say?"

Rachel peered at her. "Yes, but sometimes a corrective experience alters that."

Justine's body tightened, and she put her hands on her hips.

Rachel moved to leave, then turned again. "Justine, it seems you haven't come to terms with the end of your?" Rachel tilted her head. "Whatever you and Michael had, maybe you should talk to someone, you know, like a therapist."

Justine raised her chin, tossed her hair back, and with exaggeration, swayed her body as she blended into the crowd.

Rachel left with her head high, but once she reached the inside of her car, tears fogged her vision. She sat, gripping the steering wheel as she tried to ignore Justine's clawing barbs.

Get going Rachel.

Could she have been that blind? Did she miss the true Michael? She'd known him for a limited time, yet her intuition invited her to consider giving him a chance. Therapists pride themselves as open specimens and instruments of hope, which she hadn't applied to herself until she met the dashing doctor.

Since Sam died, she remained determined to focus on everything other than love and avoided dates altogether. Now, as she unlocked the safe to her heart, doubts re-emerged. Should she slam the door again, bolt it, and throw away the key? Rachel heard Alexandra's voice. No, no, no again. Thank God for Alexandra, but a long wait for her return.

Rachel wiped the tears and stared at the phone.

No Michael.

He said he'd text mid-week.

Stop! Maybe he's busy.

But couldn't he make time?

Stop. Not all about you.

Maybe you're a narcissist. Oh, come on.

Maybe, maybe, maybe?

Maybe you should stop obsessing.

What would she say to her clients? Duh. She shut one eye and peeked at her phone again.

Chapter Twenty-Three

Jason—May 12th

The room's usual swollen grayness shriveled as Jason posted more of his signs with stickers and bold writing.

Cool. Looks like a rainbow.

Jason continued with exquisite care to find positive quotes he thought might inspire his young stewards. Some came from such luminaries as Napoleon Hill, Frederick Douglass, and Martin Luther King. Although he recycled a few, often he'd rub his hands together when discovering a new quote from many of the books he devoured.

Hah. Jason stood smiling as he inspected the colorful posters. Valiant words sitting atop stared him down, emphasizing resilience and hope. Yeah, I get it.

He arrived extra early to subdue the snake coiling around his chest. He wrote out what he planned to say, and after last night, it became a done deal.

The night before, Jason told the young men he wanted to discuss something important.

"Promising you guys a very cool story."

"What's it about, Mr. J?" Caleb asked.

Jason waved his fist. "Grit."

The ten in attendance listened, and one or two moaned.

"Hey Mr. J, why not tonight?" Tommy asked.

"Because there's a lot to cover."

"Jeeze, Mr. J., I dunno if I can make it."

"Why not, Clyde? What do ya do that's so important?"

Clyde, a young seventeen-year-old with the sleeves of his dress shirt rolled high to reveal arm tattoos down to his fingernails, shrugged.

"You can make it. Anyone else have an excuse?"

"I'll be here, Mr. J," said sixteen-year-old Jamil with a toothy smile.

Jason winked and nodded at the young man who always arrived with pressed trousers and a tailored shirt, once sharing with Jason, "My Mama wants me to look good, like you."

The others joined Jamil with, "Me too."

"Good."

"Hey Mr. J?" a recovering Abdul asked. "Can we bring friends?"

Jason raised his eyebrows. "Sure. You know I'm always open. Just text me ahead to tell me who the guest might be."

Another young man, Jacob, said, "Yeah, I've been informing a few people about our classes."

"Well, guys, you know. If they follow the rules. Right. No weapons, no disrespect, and can you guess what I'm going to say?"

"Attire." Jamil beamed. He bobbed his head. "The guys I told kinda looked at me like I was stupid, but then," Jamil pointed his index finger, "I said, them, I mean, *those* are the rules."

Jason tried to suppress his laughter. "And how did they take it?"

Jamil put his hands out. "They kinda said, *Whatever.*"

A few giggles emerged.

"You know these meetings are open with those conditions, and not asking for much when I say neat clothing. Right?"

"Right, Mr. J," a few mumbled.

"I'd say dressing like we do, ya know, put together, makes us feel better. Ya think?"

They bobbed their heads with a few mutterings in the affirmative.

"What if we get lots of people, Mr. J?" Clyde asked.

"Well, so far, we get about ten to fifteen of you regularly both nights, and it's been like that since the beginning." Jason tilted his head. "But if more people are interested, we'll have to figure out something else."

"That doesn't mean we'll stop this group with you, does it?" Jamil stared at Jason with a furrowed brow.

Jason widened his smile. "Jamil, my friend, nothing's going to stop us from meeting. All I'm saying is, if it gets too big, we'll have to have a cutoff."

"Whew." Jamil wiped his brow with his hand.

The others laughed with, "Yeah."

"We like this group, Mr. J, so the new people can come, but maybe belong to another group?" Abdul asked.

"That's right. But I consider it necessary to let them hear what I have to say. Not only do I think it'll help you guys to hear my story, but maybe help them, you know, stay away from things not good for them? What d'ya think?"

Each of them nodded.

Now they trickled into the room. Not just his usual, but several more appeared, dressed in khakis or blue jeans with button-down shirts. Jason asked the newcomers to get in line. He took his hands and patted each of them down to ensure no weapons on them. Unknown to his students, Jason always touched his chest, where his own gun sat in silence. You never knew. The reason for acquiring his LTC.

Jason invited the guests to take a water or soda he set up just prior. After they settled in, he counted. Twenty-five, including his fifteen regulars. Good.

Jason suggested one regular say the prayer. Jamil raised his hand, and Jason gave him a nod. Jamil closed his eyes and laced his fingers. Everyone followed.

"Thanks God, for connecting us with Mr. J. You and he help us, Lord." Jamil opened his eyes. "Amen." The others followed suit.

"Okay, you guys," Jason's eyes roamed the room. "First, I want you to understand how much I've learned from you regulars."

"Ya have?" Clyde asked, causing everyone to laugh.

Jason's eyes glimmered as he stared at Clyde and the others. "I have." He paused. "Now, I'm going to disclose something I haven't shared with many people."

His eyes started to pool.

No flowing river right now, brother.

"I'm in a group smaller than this with people like me and you who've struggled."

"Like a therapy group?" Tommy asked.

"Yup, that's exactly what it is."

"Ours is a sort of therapy group," Abdul said.

"Yeah, I guess you're right." Jason smiled. "Okay, so here's my story, and I'll tell you what I've learned, plus a really cool story."

Jason revealed what happened to him from the beating to the losses. He pulled out his hanky and wiped his eyes. So much for the dam preventing the water from flowing.

"Yeah, so you see guys, real men cry."

He continued and noticed two boys sniffling but remaining composed.

When he finished, he said, "I know I look like someone who's had it easy, but now you know, not the case."

All eyes remained on him. A few of the guests grimaced. Others, including the regulars, shuffled in their seats.

Except for a few stifled coughs, stillness invaded the room.

One guest, Oscar, raised his hand without smiling.

"Ah, so what helped you get through?"

Jason pointed upward. "The man upstairs, yet I kept Him out of my life for ages." Jason tugged at the cross hanging on the chain around his neck. "Now, I'll never leave home without Him."

A few nodded. Two guests kept their arms folded.

"I know you guys deal with some tough stuff, but I told you about this because no matter how together someone looks, you don't know what you don't know. Are you following me?"

More nodding.

"Before we wrap up, I need to tell you about the Golden Thirteen.

Jason scanned the group. "Anyone ever hear of them?"

Everyone shook their heads no.

"Neither did I until recently. So, these guys wanted to become officers in the Navy long ago when racism existed loud and clear."

"It's still there," another guest said.

"Yeah, but not like before. And in fact, there's more of a soft bigotry of low expectations, which keeps us down. So, listen up. No more interruptions until I finish. Okay?"

"K," a few of them said.

"Good," Jason said. "Back then, these guys weren't wanted, and the white powers-that-be gave them less time to study, so guess what they did?" Jason looked at his audience.

"Tried harder?" Jamil shouted out.

"You got it, Jamil. They huddled in a room together, you know, like teammates. And even though lights went out at a certain time, some took blankets and stuffed them over the windows and pulled out flashlights, opened their books, and studied for hours. They yawned and squinted but didn't stop, and ya know what happened?"

Each boy shook their head, waiting for Jason.

"They not only passed but outshone the white guys trying the same."

The boys became pensive.

"But not fair that they had to do that," Clyde said.

"Nope. Fairness didn't even come close, but that's the point." Jason gave everyone the up and down. "Life's not fair, but you've a choice. Be a victim or do what these guys did. Try over and over."

"Hey Mr. J, what happened?" Abdul asked.

"Well, because the Golden Squadron outperformed the white men, they were made to retake the test, and again, all sixteen succeeded. Unfortunately, only thirteen became commissioned."

"What's that mean?" One of the quieter guests asked.

"They could hold office," Jason said. "Now, why do I tell you this story?"

They became fidgety.

"Not to give up?" Oscar chirped.

"Right, and you guys, guess what?" Jason jutted his chin out.

"What?" They asked in muddled voices.

"I've not been practicing what I've said to you."

The young men shifted in their seats.

"Yeah." Jason nodded. "I've allowed myself to stay busy and avoid living life fully."

"But Mr. J, everyone in your life died," Jamil said.

"Thanks, Jamil," Jason said with a shine in his eye. "But no excuse, because I bet lots of you've lost people."

Quite a few of the young males nodded.

"Just like I expect of you, I need to demand of myself. Keep going, brother." Jason's eyes became dark. "And that's what I've been figuring out. Like this group, my group's helped me."

"So, what are you gonna do?" Tommy asked.

"I'm going to live."

"Mr. J, like, what's that mean?" Abdul asked.

Jason's features calmed. "Oh, I've got a few ideas." He then beamed. "And when it happens, you'll be the first to know, or..." Jason raised two fingers, "or..." he raised three fingers.

Chapter Twenty-Four

Session Eight—May 13th—Yardley

The crisp aroma stimulated her lungs as she took a deep breath. A cloak of minty green extended to her core. *Umm.* She imagined it flowing through her limbs to the tips of her fingers and toes. Rachel gave her this tool when she body-shamed herself.

Fat. No. Breathe.

Gross. Stop. Breathe.

Blubber. Shut up. Breathe.

She cracked open her eyes, and Rachel winked at her. She returned with a faint smile and peered at the others.

"Daniel now knows everything."

"Brava, Yardley, Brava." Matt applauded, and the others joined him.

Shalene sprang from her seat and gave a high five, with, "You go, girl."

Sapphire reached over with a hug.

Jason's eyes sparkled. "Okay, girl, spit it out."

With heat crawling up her cheeks, Yardley nodded and peered at Jason. "Thanks, Jason, for letting me go first. What a relief."

Jason saluted her. "My pleasure."

Yardley grinned. "Last week, after leaving here, I sat in my car, took out my phone, and texted Daniel about a secret that only my therapist knew until tonight. I sat tense. You know me."

A few winks and smiles spread across everyone's faces.

They do know me now.

"I laced my hands together, and three minutes to the second, no Daniel, so I turned the key into the ignition, about to drive away, and the strings of our favorite Tchaikovsky's piece, "The 1812 Overture," played on my device."

"Love that too." Shalene half-smiled. "My parents play it a lot."

"Yes, love hearing it during the Fourth of July celebrations." Yardley grinned back. "I turned the car off and studied the message. *Let's get together tomorrow night, for a special Shabbat Dinner for us.*"

Yardley scrunched her eyes, gripped her fists, waved her arms, and stomped. "Oh my God." She opened her eyes. "I texted back right then. *How about 6:30, my place?* And the text dots moved so I knew what to expect, and there it came. The violin message sound played again. *Can't wait,*" and Yardley raised her palms. "And you know what?"

Everyone leaned forward.

"He gave not one but," Yardley gestured with three fingers, "kiss emojis."

Yardley brought her hand to her heart. "My Daniel." She paused for a moment.

"Never saw you this animated, Yardley." Matt nodded. "The real Yardley, a new version, or both?"

"Both." Yardley glanced at Matt, and then everyone else.

"Well, Ms. Yardley, keep it up." Jason beamed at her.

"Yowzah. Bring it on." Shalene clapped.

"Yardley, I can't say much to add to what everyone just said, except, wow." Sapphire's eyes dazzled. "Look at you."

Yardley tapped her chest. "Now you're adding to my inner glow."

"Well deserved." Sapphire wiggled her eyebrows. "But come on. Tell us the rest of your story."

This group's fabulous. I hope we can become friends once the group ends.

"Alright. So, that Friday night, I swung the door open, and my Daniel stood, grinning, and trying to balance the wine, halal bread and dessert. My hand shook as I took the wine from him. We hurried to the kitchen, put everything down, and he embraced me hard. That warm glow I mentioned sitting right here." Yardley rubbed her chest again. "Our hug felt like being wrapped in a warm glow of love."

Yardley cocked her head at the others. "You know what I mean?"

They nodded in their usual ways.

"The he grabbed my chin and stared into my eyes. *Oh, how I've missed you.* So, of course, I started to cry and whispered, *Me too.* Then we held hands and walked to the table. He poured the wine, lit the candles, and we recited the Kiddush, the blessing of the wine."

Yardley's eyes pooled. "Wonder Woman needs some tissues." And the box made its way to her. She plucked one from the box. "We sat down and ate one of Daniel's favorites, ginger chicken, rice pilaf, and asparagus, which I prepared."

"You cook?" Sapphire asked.

"Yes, when I'm trying not to starve myself." She cracked a laugh. "Not funny, but you have to find humor. Anyway, we kept the conversation light. He discussed his residency, and I talked about my last year of law school."

"You walking, Ms. Yardley?"

The corners of Yardley's mouth tilted upward. "I think I am, Jason."

"Good. You earned it." Sapphire clapped.

"Yardley shared the smile with her before sweeping the room. "Besides, my parents and Daniel wouldn't let me do otherwise."

"So more about your story." Matt nudged his chin.

"First, Daniel watched me eat most of the meal, and he said, *Glad to see that,* and I said, *Trying.* While we had our black tea and angel food cake, Daniel became quiet as he nibbled on the cake and started to twirl his spoon around the tea. *I'm eager to hear about this secret.* And I told him my nervousness about it. He didn't like that."

Yardley paused for a moment. "I can't say I blamed him, but I started stammering, and he said, *I've been beyond patient with your problems, and I know losing Ashley's been a tragedy and terrible burden on you but*, and he shook his head. *I'm sorry, but I want to move forward with you, if I can.* And then his eyes glistened. *Please talk to me.* We stood, hugged again, and moved to the couch. He cupped my face, and then caressed one of my hands as his face pressed into mine."

"Sounds so romantic," Shalene said with a mischievous smile, dimple in full force.

Yardley gave her a vigorous nod. "I'm so lucky. He leaned back and placed his arm around me and said, *I'm sorry for being so sharp with you.* He took my hands and intertwined them with his and told me I needed to trust him, so I kissed his hand, held it, and unwrapped everything. His hand tightened as I talked about Ashley's bullying, and I started heaving when I plucked my most forbidden thought from the crevice of her mind. My wish for Ashley's death."

Yardley's face became wet, and she pulled another tissue from the nearby box. "While I sputtered my secret, Daniel tightened his arms around me. *You're shaking like a leaf in the wind.* His body felt like a protective shield. I kept crying. *Shh*, he said. *It wasn't your fault, my love. You're not responsible for her death.* I told him I shared with all of you, and he squeezed me. *Yes, it sounds like the group process sped up the therapy.*"

Yardley paused and blew her nose. "And asked him, *Are you sure you're not studying for psychiatry?* and we laughed. He winked at me and said, *Just some remnants from my psychiatry rotation, but no thanks. Interesting, but I prefer cardiology, you know, getting to the heart.*"

Yardley laughed as her gaze drifted outward. Daniel's smiling face popped in front of her.

"He sounds fabulous, Yardley." Sapphire looked at her with glistening eyes. "Gives the rest of us, or should I speak for myself, hope." She opened her water bottle, swallowed, and looked down.

"Sapphire, you and Shalene, will meet someone deserving of you." Yardley peeked at both.

"Um, Yardley, and...?" Matt waved and pointed at Jason and himself.

"Oh my," Yardley laughed. "Of course."

Jason wiped his brow. "Whew."

"Tell us the rest." Shalene tilted her head.

"Yes. Almost done." Yardley nodded, and her eyes found the floor again. "Classical music played in the background, but I don't remember much. Soon, my eyes became heavy. A pillow went under my head, a wool blanket spread across my body, and lips brushed my cheek. *I love you so much. Sleep soundly.* And I had the most peaceful sleep I've had in years."

Yardley blinked. "So, everyone. I did it."

"Hey girl, you rock." Shalene beamed.

"Yup, you did it," Jason said.

Matt nodded. "Again, brava."

Yardley lowered her eyes. "Oh, my gosh. Thank you," She murmured. "I wouldn't have succeeded without your help."

"Hey, Ms. Yardley," Jason said with teasing eyes, "no more lowering your voice. Hear me."

"I won't!" Yardley said louder than ever. "How's that?"

Everyone laughed.

"Love it," Jason said.

"What happened next?" Sapphire peeked through her tresses. "Was he still there when you woke up?"

"No, he left, and I didn't hear his early morning text."

"And what did he write?"

"Ah, Yardley, if you feel we're asking too many questions, say the word." Matt's eyes fixed on Yardley.

Rachel caught Sapphire frowning at Matt before she shifted to Yardley.

"Yes, Yardley, like Jon Snow said..."

"I'd prefer Matt."

"Like *Ma-at* said, if it's too much, say the word."

Wow. Those two. Side to side, like a tennis match.

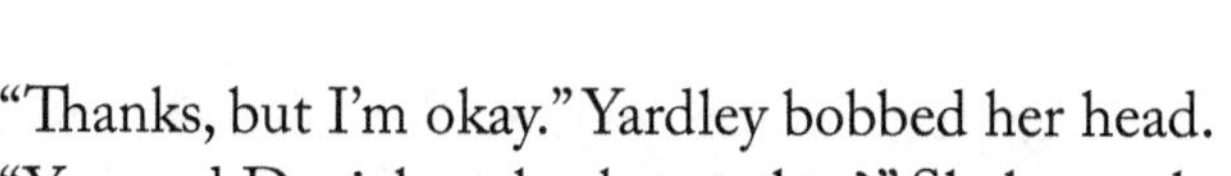

"Thanks, but I'm okay." Yardley bobbed her head.

"You and Daniel are back together?" Shalene asked.

"I think so. He's texted me every day, with love and emojis, but he's on a demanding rotation for the next few weeks so," she waved her head, "he doesn't have much time. I guess I'll have to trust that we're back together?" She shrugged.

"Sounds like it." Sapphire's eyes softened. "I'm excited to learn more." She cast her gaze around the room. "I'm sure I'm speaking for everyone here, even Jon Snow. I mean Matt." A smile jotted across her lips.

Matt focused his gaze on Yardley, but a smirk crept onto his face. "Yes, and," he glanced over at Sapphire, "for that, you can call me Jon Snow."

A flush of red tinted Sapphire's cheeks as she licked her lips, trying to smother another smile. She sunk into her chair and allowed her hair to cover part of her face.

"I just want you to tell you again that no way could I have told Daniel this without sharing here first." Yardley wiped away a tear rolling down her face.

"I think we're helping each other," Jason said. "To think, I dug my heels into the floor when Rachel suggested this."

Everyone nodded.

"Hey man, you weren't alone." Matt jutted his chin at Jason.

"You can say that again," Sapphire said before sipping some water.

Shalene waved. "Ah, me too."

"Me three." Yardley's eyes remained moist.

"Okay." Everyone turned to Rachel.

"I confess. I didn't know how it would go. Faith and hope in you and the process. How about that?" Rachel said.

Rachel

Tranquility blanketed the entire room. Each member seemed serene, like a still lake. No fidgeting from any of them. Rachel smiled as she dwelled on Michael for a bit. She'd received a text after returning home from Tango. The roller coaster speeding in her chest halted.

Ah. Maybe he's the real thing.

He arrived home late Thursday night and shared how he looked forward to seeing her. He asked if she'd give him the pleasure of accompanying him to the Boston Symphony Orchestra on Saturday evening. Without hesitation, she texted back, "Yes, thank you. I'd love to go." He then messaged her about the time he'd pick her up.

She snapped back to the present.

"Ms. Rachel, may I share something?" Jason's eyes lifted.

"Yes, of course."

"Let me tell you what I shared with the young fellas." Jason put his hand under his chin. "The night before, I teased them about an important revelation I planned on divulging, and guess what? Old and new attendees showed up the next night." Jason grunted and shifted back and forth. "I told them everything that happened to me and how it's held me back."

"What did they say?" Shalene peeked at him, fiddling with one of her rings.

"They wanted to know what I planned on doing next." Jason turned to Shalene and the others. "And I promised they'd be the second, but then I said the third to know."

"Who'd be the first?" Shalene's eyes explored Jason's.

"Since the group will be second, I can't share right now." Jason's eyes lingered on her longer than usual.

"Okay, being the second therapist here. How'd you feel after sharing?" Sapphire asked, sparkling gems dominated her face, glancing at Rachel. "I hope you don't mind."

Rachel wagged her head.

"You know. It felt like a turning point. Time to live. I know everyone who left…" Jason's eyes turned to the sky. "Would say…" Jason rubbed his chin and cocked his head.

"It's about time?" Sapphire asked.

Jason pointed to her. "You got it Ma'am." His gaze turned outward. "I can hear Callie whispering, 'It's okay, Jason. Live your life.'" He nodded with large chocolate eyes, shining.

Rachel's gaze swept the room again. Wow! Who would have thought Jason could break through the solid barrier protecting him from the outside world? And Yardley, what a surprise.

Jason's eyes looked up as he stared at Sapphire, then Shalene, and Matt.

"So, what about you? You've done lots of listening, which I appreciate, but kinda curious about what's new for you?"

Sapphire laced her fingers together and brought them close to her mouth. "Working on it."

Jason inclined his head toward her. "And?"

"I promise I'll share more next week, but I'll tell you something cool that's been happening since I came to this group."

"Please tell." Matt formed an impish smile.

Sapphire pivoted to him with a trace of a smile before scanning the group. "I started having this issue a while back, and but seeing Rachel helped it decrease." She cast her eyes on Rachel. "Do you get what I'm talking about?"

Rachel bobbed.

"Ready?" Sapphire asked.

Everyone nodded.

Sapphire bent her head and flipped her thick mane. The nape revealed roots of hair shorter than the rest sprouting like the buds of spring.

She twisted her head back and peered at the group with doubt. "I hope I didn't freak anyone out."

"No way." Matt said louder than usual, with a steady gaze. "That's courageous you shared and brava for your growth in more ways than one."

Sapphire dazzled him with her eyes. "You're too funny, but thanks."

Matt bowed his head without taking his eyes off hers.

"Also, you seem to like that word, *brava*."

"I do." He laughed.

"Hey, hon, you go, girl. Now I'll reveal something I've done," said Shalene.

"We're good to go when you are." Jason winked.

Shalene tugged the ring on her index finger. "You know I work from home, made easier by the pandemic."

Everyone echoed, "Yes."

"To tell you the truth, it made for a great excuse to feed my phobia."

The members leaned forward.

"I thought some of you figured it out, but other than my parents' home, I never left my place after the encounter with Isla." Shalene looked at Rachel. "You might say I experienced a version of agoraphobia."

She shifted to the group. "Did some of you guess it?"

"Not really." Sapphire offered a half-smile. "But it sounds like something's changed?"

"It has." Shalene splayed her fingers. "I've gone out more and more and even went into the office a few times."

"Brava, to you too Shalene." Matt clapped.

"Thank you!" Shalene grinned. Then she turned to Rachel. "Are you surprised?"

Rachel took a deep breath. "I don't know, but what I do know is how thrilled I am for you."

Shalene beamed. "I do have something else brewing in my mind, and I'm hoping to tackle it by next week."

"Can't wait to hear, Shalene," Yardley said. "You and everyone else have been so kind to me. I want good for all of you."

Shalene blinked a smile at Yardley.

"Aww, Yardley, real nice for you to say, and since we've only two sessions left, Matt? You're the man, bro. Wondering where you're at with everything?" Jason asked.

Matt nodded. "I'm getting together with my mother this weekend. Like I said before, I've kept her at arm's length each time

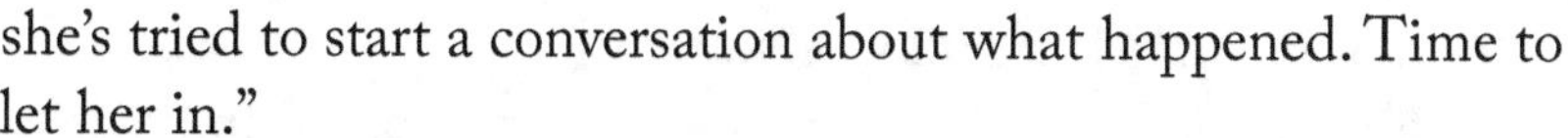

she's tried to start a conversation about what happened. Time to let her in."

"Bravo!" Sapphire applauded.

"Good one." Matt dipped his head toward her.

"Bravo to all of us." Sapphire leaned toward each member with a clap.

Rachel's eyes flooded with tears. Instead of embroidering words with excuses such as allergies or a cold, she allowed the streams down her cheeks.

"Hey, there Rachel, you upset?" Jason's eyebrows knitted together.

Rachel plucked a tissue from the nearby Kleenex box and dabbed her cheeks. "No, I'm just so overcome by your courage and ability to trust. You know what that means, don't you?"

No one responded.

"The group serves as a symbol. If you can take risks here, watch out world, here you come."

Everyone smiled. Water moistened their eyes.

Jason grabbed a tissue and shook his head. "Your waterworks are contagious."

Rachel sighed. "Okay, everyone. You've hinted about more divulgences, right?"

Everyone bobbed their heads.

"How do you feel about going longer next week, beyond our usual seventy-five minutes, if needed?"

"Sounds like a plan." Matt's gaze circled the room. "You agree?"

"Hear, hear," Jason said, with the others shouting a yay.

"Wonderful! So, my friends, until next week." Rachel raised herself out of her seat. "I'm looking forward to hearing more."

Everyone stood up.

Jason fist bumped Matt. "Hey, brother. Good luck with your mom."

"Thanks, man. She's okay. I've been a, well, I'll refrain from saying, but you get the picture."

"I do." Jason hesitated. "You're lucky to have a mom to make amends."

"I know, man." Matt nodded. "I know."

"And ladies, I can't wait to hear more from you." Jason bowed.

Shalene gave a thumbs up. Yardley threw a kiss, and Sapphire went over and hugged him.

"Hey, what about me?" An exaggerated pout spread across Matt's face.

"You need to earn it." Sapphire's eyes glimmered.

They hugged Rachel goodbye, and Sapphire waited for Matt. Rachel watched them walk side-by-side, laughing. Sapphire punched his arm on the way out.

Rachel observed Matt, almost falling, and saying, "Ouch." Her heart danced as Sapphire gave him another playful punch and heard giggles break out.

She left her door open and embraced the night's laughter, while she put on her red sweater coat, grabbed her purse and briefcase, and sauntered out to the car. She gazed at the stars as they offered quite a glittering performance this evening and inhaled the hyacinth aroma of the nearby shrub, blooming earlier than usual.

What a night. Who knew they'd show so much of themselves? She couldn't wait to share with her friends and Alexandra. She shook her head, and her mind meandered to her situation.

A pair of sea-blue eyes came into view.

A delicious flavor surged through her body.

Don't.

Why?

Because you don't know. Justine may be a narcissist, but that didn't account for everything. She shook her head. Okay, Rachel, you need to see for yourself. Is this guy the real thing or a fraud and a womanizer? Just because he had stellar reviews as a professional, doesn't mean it transferred to his personal life. You've heard too many stories about people like him, who revealed a darker, more nefarious side.

Stop!

Take a risk, like you encourage everyone else to do. You'll find out soon enough.

Chapter Twenty-Five

Rachel felt her core expand and soar like an eagle. Music created that sensation, but tonight, everything became heightened by the company and ambience surrounding her. Aware of his glances, Rachel couldn't ignore the muscular shoulders hidden beneath his shirt, touching her bare skin. She peeked a few times. If he caught her, his eyes blinked back, and her heart jumped. She gave him a quick smile before returning her gaze to the orchestra.

Oh, my goodness. This man's ability to conjure up buried delights couldn't be overstated.

Michael purchased annual season tickets in the orchestra section of Symphony Hall. Rachel cast her eyes around the magnificent grand center. The original concert stage floor built in 1900 suffered from wear and tear, so in 2006, they restructured it, but used the same materials from the earlier era, so as not to disrupt the acoustics. What a sight to see. Rachel's eyes roved toward the walls where casts of Greek and Roman statues lined the upper levels.

Her focus returned to the players, observing the violinists as they took their bows across the strings. Her eyes moved to the pianist, waltzing his fingers along the keys, then to the other sections of winds, horns, and brass. The conductor navigated all of this, like an artist creating a masterpiece from a mottled palette.

My God, what beauty you've allotted us humans!

She shut her eyes. Majestic and shimmering like silver, gold, and platinum performing in perfect harmony.

Michael leaned close to her and said, "Glorious. Fusing together as one."

Rachel turned and captured his eyes. "You read my thoughts." She settled back in her seat, bewitched by Michael and the surrounding magic. Ah, the real thing, her earlier doubts shrinking.

Soon, the orchestra stopped for intermission. After giving an applause, everyone rose and moved into the refreshment area. Michael rested his hand under Rachel's elbow, waiting for the crowd to advance.

"Have I told you how stunning you look?" Michael examined Rachel from head to toe.

Rachel looked down at her coral pleated dress, a wide belt cinching her waist. "Thank you. You did earlier, but I appreciate the encore." She laughed and flipped her hair to disguise the crimson, she knew, stretched across her cheeks.

"And how do you walk in those shoes? They're beautiful, but I'm amazed how women do it." Michael stared at her bone-colored Jimmy Choo heels.

"Linking arms with you makes it easy." Rachel's topaz eyes drowned in the depths of his.

Michael's eyes gripped hers for a moment before the crowd pushed them towards the door.

When they reached the lobby area, Rachel turned to Michael. "I'll make a quick dash to the ladies' lounge."

He squeezed her hand. "Of course. I'll get us something to drink while you do what all ladies do."

"Please, just sparkling water. Anything stronger and I might fall asleep."

"I understand. Hurry back."

Rachel flashed a smile before heading to the lounge. Not too long of a line. She hurried along. After coming out of the stall, she washed her hands and studied herself in the mirror.

"Well, well, well, we keep running into each other." A throaty voice said.

Rachel lifted her gaze to see Justine approaching her in a long-sleeved, silver beaded dress that hugged her body and silver stilettos to match. The dress reached to her lower calves with a slit on the side.

Rachel's eyes lowered to the expensive high heels before Justine wiggled herself in between Rachel and another woman. Without glancing at Rachel, she said, "Yes, isn't this a stunning dress? I bought it at Saks." She then ran her tongue over the edges of her teeth and smiled at herself. Rachel said hello before trying to move past her.

"Oh, no you don't." Justine's tall frame stood in front of her, eyes flickering.

"Excuse me?" Rachel frowned.

Justine bent closer to Rachel with a chiseled smile. "If you think this little jaunt with Michael means anything, you're mistaken."

Rachel tried to go around her, but Justine grabbed her arm, bared her teeth, and pretended to kiss her. She hissed, "He and I spent many passionate times together. Take my word for it. He'll be mine again in no time. See you outside." Justine let go of her arm, pivoted, and swayed her hips out of the lounge.

Rachel's breathing grew shallow. She closed her eyelids for a moment and inhaled deeply, attempting to stop the pounding of her heart. She gripped the edge of the counter, looked in the mirror, and steadied herself.

You can do this.

Ignore that witch.

Rachel pinched her cheeks, raised her chin, and smiled at women passing her in the lounge. She drifted out to the lobby, pushing through the crowd, and bobbed her head, searching for Michael. Then she froze. Justine and an older gentleman stood next to Michael. Although Justine attempted to engage him in conversation, Michael held two beverages, staring straight ahead as he scoped the crowd. Rachel headed toward him, and when he saw her, he grinned and raised a glass.

Justine spun around, and for a moment, Rachel would have sworn she saw fangs before Justine gritted her teeth into a smile.

Rachel approached them.

No matter how short you are, stand tall, you.

She took the glass from Michael, without looking up at him.

"Oh Michael, I just saw your adorable therapist friend in the ladies' room." Her eyes bore into Rachel's. "So sorry, but what's your name?"

"Her name is Rachel, Justine. *Rachel.*" Michael glowered at Justine. "You know that."

"Oh, of course. How could I forget?" Justine chortled. "Michael and I were reminiscing about our dates here at Symphony Hall."

Michael sighed. "I think it's time for us…" Michael wrapped his fingers around Rachel's arm.

"Before you leave, how rude of me. Rachel, I'd like to introduce you to my brother, Barry," Justine said.

"Nice to meet you, Barry," Rachel said in a stumbling voice.

Barry, a heavier male version of his silver-haired sister, darted his eyes, and smirked. "You, too."

The lights blinked.

"We really must go back inside. Are you ready?" Michael asked Rachel.

She nodded with a frozen smile.

"Enjoy the show…" Michael said. Before he could finish his sentence, Justine kissed his cheek, and said, "I look forward to talking to you soon." Michael scowled, but she had already pivoted, strolling away with her brother in tow.

Rachel's heart plunged. She sauntered in front of Michael and couldn't see his face. He grasped her elbow, but she kept her eyes on the people in front of her. When they reached their seats, Michael turned to her.

"It's not what it seems. I'll explain later." He grabbed her hand, lacing his fingers with hers.

Rachel nodded without looking at him. Although she enjoyed

the pitter-patter his touch evoked, it didn't assuage her emotions from the residual of Justine's venomous sting.

She concentrated on the musical enchantment trying to penetrate her ears, but she couldn't. The splinters in her heart awakened. Rachel shifted her eyes to the long, powerful legs of the man sitting next to her. She didn't know what to think about this situation with Justine.

How involved had they been? Did it matter if their relationship ended? Nothing to do with her, but what if…?

Don't go there. Yes, go there.

Could she be a pawn for Michael to dangle in front of Justine, trying to create tension? Jealousy?

What are you doing, Rachel? Too many toxic stories over the years. Stop.

She took a deep inhale.

"Everything okay with you?" Michael's mouth grazed her hair.

She nodded with a forced smile and mouthed, "Fine," without shifting her eyes from the stage.

Rachel's eyes became heavy. Stay awake. She widened her eyes. But soon she drifted again, and her head bobbed, finding its way onto Michael's shoulder.

"So sorry." She glanced at him.

"Don't worry." His eyes caressed her.

Rachel gave another quick smile before focusing on the musical ensemble a few rows ahead. For the next several minutes, she clasped her hands tight until the orchestra maintained bragging rights; their virtuosic prowess in a fast and furious finale.

The audience came to its feet with applause and loud bravos. The conductor departed the stage but returned for another bow. He left again, but the clapping didn't cease. When the conductor came out for a third bow, he waved his hand for his musicians to stand. They didn't budge from their seats. Rachel lifted her eyebrows. Without being asked, Michael said, "A tribute to the conductor." Rachel nodded and kept her eyes straight ahead.

The clapping faded, and the crowd gathered their belongings and lined up to leave. Michael took Rachel's jacket, and without making eye contact, she thanked him and pivoted toward the aisle, advancing with her row.

"Would like to wear your jacket now or later?" Michael asked behind her.

Rachel continued walking straight ahead. "I'm all set for now."

The throngs of people became noisier. Rachel took in those around her. Men and women about her age and older.

"Looks like we fit right in." Michael chuckled.

"Yes," Rachel said, again not turning around.

They reached the lobby, and Rachel accepted Michael's help. With her head down, she placed her arms into the jacket sleeves. Michael's powerful fingers grazed her neck as he untangled the curls, refusing to budge from their position.

"There." Michael pulled on a coil.

"Thanks," Rachel said with a wooden laugh.

They moved outside. An unexpected night breeze upset the earlier warmth. Rachel tugged her jacket tighter.

"Would you like my jacket over your shoulders?" Michael asked.

"No, I'm fine. I just think I'm more fatigued than I realized," Rachel said, without turning to him. "I think I need to make it an early night."

Who is this man?

Rachel

"Rachel, I'd like to…" Michael stopped mid-sentence, as he caught a cab pulling in front of them. The driver came out to open the door, and, with Rachel first, the couple climbed into the back of the vehicle. Before Michael directed the driver, he asked if she was sure about going home. Rachel brought her hand to her mouth and yawned. Michael gave the driver Rachel's address.

Michael's arm looped around Rachel's as they settled in their seat. Her heart ached, feeling Michael's sinewy body next to hers. Rachel gripped her fist. *No. I won't. I can't.*

"Full transparency. I want to explain Justine to you," Michael said.

Rachel closed her eyes for a moment. "You don't owe me any explanation."

Fingers brushing across her cheek caused Rachel to open her eyes.

Michael's hand frolicked to her chin, prompting her to look at him.

Without smiling, his eyes bore into hers. "Rachel, I need you to understand."

She fluttered her eyelashes. "Right now, I'm too tired to understand anything, and besides—I know little about you."

"What do you mean?"

"How do I know you're not a player?" Rachel said.

Michael released his hand and slapped it against his knee. He shook his head and looked straight ahead. "And why would I want to tell you the truth, if I were a player?"

"How do I know your truth is *the* truth?" Rachel asked, with a forced laugh.

Michael sighed. "Look, I know you hear many stories, but not all men are jerks."

"I know that, and yes, I hear painful relationship issues, but that's not all of it."

"Then what is it?" Michael asked.

Rachel peeked at his sea-blue eyes as they simmered in the dark.

"I have a complicated background, which causes trust issues."

"I'm sorry if something happened in your life, but I don't play those games."

"Oh, you assume a man betrayed me, but that's not it."

"I assume nothing, Rachel. In fact, you're the only one doing the assuming."

A whip of tension cracked through the now-stale air.

A familiar rollercoaster flew through Rachel's chest. She heard

Michael take a loud inhale through his nose, with a longer exhale through his mouth.

She closed her eyes again and tried to halt tears tipping onto her cheeks.

Michael grasped her hand. "Listen to me."

Rachel looked up, her eyes locking his, and nodded.

"I want you to understand what happened and where things are at now."

Rachel swallowed. "Okay."

"I met Justine on one of the dating apps for people over forty-five, and we enjoyed a nice first date, discussing our similar interests."

Michael paused. "Justine seemed intriguing, a former model who now owned a boutique women's clothing store in Boston."

He patted her hand. "Divorced for two years, with one adult son living in the South, she wanted to date again. Nothing out of the ordinary for the twenty-first century, which I don't have to tell you right?"

She bobbed her head without shifting toward him.

"By the second date, Justine, insisted she cook for me. At first, I refused. I didn't want to rush this and wanted to keep meeting in public, so she raised the idea of exploring dance opportunities. Ballroom, swing—Tango."

Rachel peeked to see Michael tilt his head side-to-side. "What a good idea. So I thought at the time. I had wanted to try it anyway, so I told Justine I'd get information on all three."

Michael laughed with a brittle edge. "Also, I shared with Justine my love for music, a variety of genres, and she claimed the same. She disclosed that she too subscribed to Boston Symphony."

Michael paused for a moment, frowning, and squeezing Rachel's hand. "Who knew?"

He released her hand and paused. Out of the corner of her eye, she noticed him examining his hands. A moment later, he spoke again, drawing Rachel's eyes to his.

"I hadn't been involved in an intimate relationship in some time."

Rachel expected the next revelation.

"Without sounding arrogant, I've been approached by many women over the years, but I never cheated on my wife, even at the end." His eyes took on a faraway look. "After the divorce, a number of women propositioned me, but casual relationships have never been my thing."

He looked at Rachel again, with a half-smile. "Still aren't."

His eyes returned to his hands, stretching out his long, powerful fingers before letting them go limp. He blinked and sighed. "But Justine knows how to use her sensuality and," he shook his head, "lack of subtlety, an appropriate description for her, in case you didn't notice."

Rachel nodded and smirked without looking at Michael.

"After four or five dates, I accepted her invitation to cook for me and," he folded his arms and said, "we became intimate. The relationship took on an intensity, but a brief one."

"Why are you telling me this?" Rachel frowned.

Michael turned to her, with eyes dark like a night ocean. "Because I want you to understand the brevity of it. It's important to me. That's why." His eyes remained steady on hers. "And since meeting you, short time that it's been, I—" He stopped for a moment, and her heart beat like a drum. "I've experienced something different, something real. I feel—" His eyes softened. "You make me feel alive." He brushed his hand across her cheek, causing her a mix of tingling and sadness.

Her eyes closed, and she allowed the caress to imprint on her soul.

"So, what do you think?"

She opened her eyes and fluttered her lashes again. "I don't know."

She heard a sigh, and he dropped his hand.

"Right now, I'm so tired. I can't think about any of this." Rachel leaned back, shut her eyes, and rested one hand on the seat.

She felt Michael's hand move on top of hers. An unsettling silence infused the cab.

The cab slowed, and Rachel opened her eyes. "Right here."

The cab drove into the driveway.

"Let me walk you to the door." Michael said.

"Unnecessary."

"I insist."

Rachel opened the door. She heard Michael tell the driver he'd be right back.

She walked in front of Michael and opened her clutch to take out her keys. She almost tripped. Michael caught her arm.

She turned her gaze toward him. "Thank you."

His face came close to hers. "You didn't answer my question."

Rachel blinked at him, trying to hold back the stream about to flow.

His face moved close. He hugged her.

"I want you to believe me, and I want to understand what makes you so distrustful." He removed himself from the embrace and took her chin.

She gave him a quivering smile.

Michael's eyes locked on hers again.

"I have an idea," Michael said with a smile shadowing his mouth.

Chapter Twenty-Six

Deep within the Berkshire Mountains in the northwest corner of Massachusetts, lay a hidden gem, a renowned art museum, the Sterling and Francine Clark Art Institute. Although unfamiliar to the masses, locals from surrounding communities and even some New Yorkers visited this marvel and immersed themselves in its delights. Developed in collaboration with Williamstown, Sterling Clark, heir to the Singer Sewing Machine fortune, chose this bucolic town to build a refuge for his private art collection.

Sapphire gazed at the Renoir painting of a Japanese dog, marveling at the Impressionist's ability to capture the delightful Tama's personality. She leaned forward and scrutinized the artist's strokes.

What a masterpiece.

She stepped back from the painting and noticed her breathing become deep, waiting for this overdue encounter. Not too crowded, but enough people walked the halls to provide a cushion of security.

She loved the Clark Museum, though she had not visited it for many years, and she recognized her connection to this jewel— her visits often happened when she needed to submerge in peace, inspiration, and strength. Now as she stood in front of the Renoir, confidence permeated every cell in her body. Yes, the day of reckoning.

She left Newton around 9:30 Saturday morning, preparing a Thermos of coffee before embarking on the three-hour trip.

In between sips of java, Sapphire snapped her fingers and belted out her favorite tunes. When the one lane road along Route 2 became two, a man drove beside her, honked his horn, and gave her a soft salute. She waved, but turned her head back to the front windshield, changing from music to inspiring podcasts.

The rolling hills in the western part of the state reminded her of the release of air from an over-inflated tire, the reason temporary residents sought this area as their home away from home. Those living in the hustling, bustling eastern part of the state appreciated all the offerings in this quiet but cultured mountain haven. During the summer interim, locals witnessed their arrival to second homes in fully packed vehicles—Range Rovers, Jeep Cherokees, and other high-end SUVS. Invariably they would step out of their vehicles, shut their eyes, and inhale the mountain freshness.

The shop owners and restaurants welcomed these wealthy patrons, whose *cha-ching* provided respite from sparse winter months and put their businesses back on a paying basis. Although Sapphire came from a similar background to summer visitors, she preferred the locals. During her college years, she chatted with the small business owners, breakfasting, lunching, or dining at local eateries. When unable to buy from their brick-and-mortar businesses, she'd go to their websites and make her purchases.

Yup, I'm more like them, thanks Mom and Dad.

Yesterday, Sapphire texted Rachel to tell her the plan. Rachel messaged her back within a short time.

```
You are most courageous, my dear
Sapphire. Please know I'm here if you
need me.
```

Sapphire smiled.

She tapped her heart.

I adore her. What would I do without her. Should I go back for individual sessions? Not sure.

Hah, lucky Rachel if I do.

Sapphire paced back and forth. Others sauntered by, studying the unique art works the museum contained.

His delay didn't alarm her since he always ran ten to fifteen minutes behind—at least he did in the past.

A month ago, she read about his visiting professorship at her alma mater. Her heart rammed into her throat, but she steadied herself.

Time to confront.

Sapphire picked the museum because of its proximity to the college. A safe place. Many professors and students strolled through its halls on weekends.

He wouldn't dare mar his reputation by making a spectacle of himself here.

Yes, no better place for this encounter.

With her back turned, the familiar, smooth footsteps made their way to her. She spun around and saw him. A standout. After all these years, his vitality didn't diminish. Salt and pepper hair enhanced his dark looks, and visitors stared at him as he approached her. Dressed in an expensive gray blazer, black turtleneck, designer jeans and Fendi loafers, Hugo smiled and trotted over with open arms.

"Bella," he said, with a dazzling show of white teeth.

Sapphire put her hands up. "Hello Hugo, I've a cold, so I don't want to spread my germs."

Hugo's head pulled back. "Are you sure you don't have Covid?"

"I tested. No Covid. In fact, I'm on the mend, but I'm just being cautious."

"Good." He nodded. His eyes mauled her from head to toe. "Bella, you're looking good."

Sapphire stared back, hoping the flips in her stomach would settle down. "Thank you, Hugo," she said with fierceness surging through her body.

Hugo tilted his head. "Something's different about you?"

"I hope so," Sapphire said with a gleam in her eye. "I'm no longer a teeenaaggerrr."

"I can see that," Hugo said, his eyes caressing her body.

Hugo seemed to ignore her dig.

She turned toward one painting. "You missed my point."

Hugo bent close to her, and she recoiled.

"What *is* your point, Bella?"

Sapphire stepped back and stared straight at him, nodding. "You know what I mean."

Hugo cocked his head and through gritted teeth said, "No, I don't. Please, tell me what you mean."

An uncomfortable silence engulfed them. Sapphire's fire ignited. No stopping now.

"Hugo." Someone tapped him on the shoulder.

Hugo spun around with an automatic smile plastering his face. "Paul, what a pleasant surprise."

Sapphire studied the diminutive man. Appearing around seventy-five years old, Paul, with a beret on top of his streaked, shoulder-length gray hair, round spectacles, and oversized sweater and jeans, reminded Sapphire of a certain type of professor.

All that's missing is the pipe. She suppressed a laugh bubbling in her throat.

"And who might this be?" Paul asked.

"Ah, allow me to introduce one of my most talented dance students from Miami whom I mentored long ago." Hugo spread his arms out. "She found herself in the area and contacted me. Sapphire, it's with great pleasure I introduce you to Paul, one of the esteemed professors who teaches acting at the college."

"Nice to meet you." Sapphire nodded. She recognized the professor, but never took classes with him.

"Yes, I'd extend my hand to you, but one can't be too cautious in these post-Covid times."

"I couldn't agree more."

"So, what brings you to the area, Sapphire?"

"I attended college here many years ago, and I read Hugo would lecture here this semester, so," she looked at Hugo, flashed her widest smile, and in an exaggerated voice, "I thought, wow. Wouldn't it be great to catch up?'"

Hugo gritted his teeth again, only discernible to Sapphire. "Yes." His eyes stayed for a moment on Sapphire before shifting his gaze to Paul. "Yes, I couldn't have been happier to hear from her."

"Well, I don't want to interrupt your visit." Paul looked down the aisle. "I can never get enough of the treasures here, so I'll bid you goodbye. Enjoy your get together. Nice to meet you, um..." Paul stalled for a moment.

"Sapphire." She offered an even wider smile.

"Ah, yes, forgive me. Words escape me these days. Sapphire." Paul shuffled along, studying the artwork in his path.

Hugo turned to Sapphire and offered his arm.

Sapphire shook her head. "Remember, I have a cold?"

"Oh, yes, of course."

Sapphire walked next to him and stopped in front of another Renoir painting. "I love Renoir. What a treat to have so many of his paintings housed here, wouldn't you agree?"

She turned to Hugo.

His eyes, crackling with sparks, bore into hers. "Yes," he said with control. "But I want to hear more about your point before Paul's interruption."

Sapphire's flames wouldn't abate. With slow enunciation, she said. "You know what I mean." She kept her eyes on him before putting her hands behind her back and sauntering to another painting. "I suggest you keep walking with me." She pivoted towards a glowering Hugo. "You don't want to make a scene, now do you?"

Hugo shifted his facial expression and tilted his head. "Whatever are you talking about?" A catlike smile emerged. "Forgive me. I'm just eager to hear what you have to say."

"You abused me, Hugo." Sapphire's voice remained low and steady.

His nostrils flared. He looked around again. "You were old enough to know..."

"No," Sapphire cut him off. "I was fifteen."

Hugo clicked his teeth. "No resistance came from you." He leaned closer to Sapphire. "And You seemed to enjoy everything I taught you."

Sapphire jolted, and her eyes welled up.

"Besides, you seem fine to me."

"Listen, I've been in therapy trying to overcome the effects of your abuse."

Hugo flinched.

"That's correct. *Abuse.* The reason I asked to meet with you."

"I don't have time for this stroll down memory lane. What do you want, Sapphire?"

"What do I want?"

Hugo folded his arms. He glanced around the room before inclining closer to her with an impassive face. "If you think I'm willing to apologize for something consensual between an older man and his student," his eyes latched onto hers, "I won't."

Sapphire stood with shoulders back and tried preventing the release of tears behind the dam. "What I want is for you to never contact me again." Sapphire raised her right finger. "And if I ever hear you've taken advantage of someone else, I'll come forth."

Hugo sniffed. "Don't worry, Bella, before my wife, you were my one and only student." His eyes moved again up and down her body. "No one could replace you."

Sapphire shook her head, and ice dampened her fire.

Hugo's deadened eyes lifted as if she became invisible. He glanced around the room and waved at a few people. Without looking at Sapphire, he said, "Nice of you to drive all this way. Goodbye, Sapphire." He called out to someone and walked toward a group of people.

Sapphire gulped, steadied herself, and headed toward the museum exit. When she reached her car, she turned on the ignition to find soothing, classical music. Tears streamed down her face. Relief mixed with a sense of closure. Before driving away, she sent a quick text and shared that she confronted Hugo.

Her phone signaled a response right away.

> You, okay? Need to talk?

Sapphire texted back.

> Thanks, but I'm okay. Will tell more when I see you.

She took her time driving home, listening to Chopin and Tchaikovsky, and arrived early for the 4:15 Mass. She immersed herself in the surroundings of the chapel, studied wooden plaques with stations of the cross, and reflected on her life. During the service, Sapphire concentrated on the sermon, given by her favorite priest. He stood at the podium and joked with the audience interspersed with thoughts on the day's gospel.

Sapphire experienced rays of lightness spreading through her body. She stayed for the entire last hymn, with her missal open, swaying, and singing aloud with the rest of the congregation, "Let There Be Peace on Earth." At the end, she closed her booklet, gazed up to the balcony, and clapped her hands at the chorus.

She walked out still singing and saying hello to other congregants until she noticed a familiar but unexpected visitor. For a couple of seconds, she became immobilized, and mouthed the words, "What are you doing here?"

With a pounding heart, she stepped forward.

Chapter Twenty-Seven

Shalene—May 18th

Shalene's eyes swept the foyer and landed on the grand staircase dominating the interior. She never lost interest, immersing herself in the building's beauty. Nothing but nothing matched the majesty of the Boston Public Library. The marble interior alone reminded Shalene of a palace entryway. Besides books, the bibliophile's refuge offered other treasures and architectural dreams.

She waited a long time to take this plunge, so she dressed to conquer, being of the opinion sometimes you are what you wear. With her hair swept into a chignon, she touched the long earrings dangling from her ears, and her hand brushed across her short-sleeved, silver cocktail dress with a matching shawl. Her three-inch Stuart Weitzman sandals stretched her five-foot frame into something longer, taller.

There. Take that.

She smiled and knew her dimple would grace her face, as she practiced in the mirror, pretending to speak to her nemesis.

Yes, tonight she'd face Isla.

For months, Shalene avoided the Boston women's professional group she joined five years ago. Every time the annual membership renewal arrived, she'd hesitate, but in the end, she'd click **yes** to sign up again.

Would she ever attend?

One of these days, she promised herself. Yet, even during the pandemic, with every meeting taking place on Zoom, she avoided it. No way. Even if she hid behind the camera, she wouldn't subject herself to Isla.

Now? Well, now's the time.

The final meeting of the year, outside in the courtyard with weather permitting.

It did. What a glorious spring evening!

Even before Jason gave the challenge, she became determined to take this next step. No more deleting the Evite to attend a monthly meeting. The group helped her feel stronger, less uptight.

The only way to conquer the bigger-than-life Isla? Meet her.

When she received this month's Evite, she scrutinized it. The reception at the Boston Public Library? Must go. All libraries worked for the bookaholic Shalene. That does it. She banged the key. Confirmed, then lifted her hand like a balloon was tied to her finger.

Yes! There. Pretend you're David, and she's Goliath.

She closed one eye and motioned with her hands an imaginary sling shot.

Yowzah. David's confidence.

Like Rachel said, practice.

Isla became President-Elect for this women's organization, and the agenda showed she'd be introduced by the outgoing President. Shalene intended to approach her, say hello, and pour water on this fear, once and for all.

Pleased that she arrived early, Shalene's eyes moved upward one more time toward the arched, vaulted ceilings.

I could stay here forever. Now, all I need is a crown, with a stack of books.

"Hey, Shalene. I smell delicious you from the door. Yummy."

Shalene turned to see one of her friends and colleagues, Tina, bustling toward her while groups of other women entered the magical setting. Two of the three or four other black women who worked for the digital marketing committee, she and Tina became fast friends.

"Hey, Hon. Yeah, I drenched myself in the latest Aerin fragrance from Estée Lauder." Shalene hugged her, before taking her hands and studying her friend, whose medium cornrow braids cascaded down her back. "Stunning you, as usual." Shalene touched one of her braids, taking in her short red sleeveless dress and matching stilettos.

"Thank ya, much, you too, and glad you agreed to attend." Tina's eyes danced. "Girl, I've missed you at these events. You're my partner in..." Tina put a finger to her mouth "...um, mischief?" They broke out in laughter. For the first time in a long time, Shalene's heart lifted, light and floating, like a fluffy, rosy cloud.

"Just too much going on, but I'm here now." Shalene fist-bumped her friend. "And glad you convinced me."

With more women joining them, Shalene's gaze circled the foyer one more time. Voices chanted, "*Ooh, ahh,*" and Shalene joined and said to Tina, "Takes my breath away."

"Yup, but going outside and indulging in a tasty cocktail will take my breath away more," Tina said.

"Nonalcoholic for me, but I'll make a toast, anyway."

"How come you don't drink, Shaleneeee?"

"Tried it and didn't like the way it made me feel."

"You ever get tipsy?"

"Like I said, not my thing. Let's go outside."

Tina and Shalene traipsed toward the courtyard and stood for a moment under one arch between pillars before heading toward the ornate fountain.

Shalene plodded closer to the pool and studied the lovely statue overlooking it. She pivoted back to Tina and waved to the others.

"Let's go register." Tina took her arm and led her through the throngs, saying, "Excuse moi," as she cranked her neck and put her hand on the side of her mouth. "I thought it sounded cooler in French."

Shalene smirked at her bold friend.

They found themselves in line with a few others. When they reached the desk, one volunteer registered Shalene. "I see this is your first time attending in-person. Nice to have you here."

"Thank you. Happy I made it."

"Well, is that Shalene?" A voice croaked from close by.

Shalene sealed her eyes for a moment.

Remember what Rachel said.

You practiced over and over, looking in the mirror and pointing to a tall blonde-braided, helmeted woman. *You don't scare me anymore, Isla, you big oaf.*

You've got this girl.

Shalene opened her eyes, holding her breath. She spun around and saw a big, overweight, pink-cheeked Isla approach her, with a large cocktail in her hand.

"So you finally decided to grace us with your presence," Isla said, examining Shalene up and down.

"Hello, Isla. Yes, about time I came," Shalene said, her voice steady.

"I see you kept your figure. How did you stay so thin during the pandemic?"

Shalene shrugged with buoyancy. "Kept a routine."

"I tried to do that, but *eat, drink, and be merry,* became my mantra, as you can see." She patted her stomach and hips, still studying Shalene. "So, what did you do in your," Isla continued gawking at her, "*rouuutiiine?*"

Shalene shook her head, observing a weak Isla, whose hair thinned as her body widened. "Nothing extraordinary. Just exercised and watched what I ate."

"Always the goody-two-shoes, Shalene," Isla sneered.

Shalene put out her hands. "What can I say, Isla?"

"Isla, please come over here." Isla pivoted to the voice calling her.

"Gotta go, Shalene." Isla eyeballed her up and down one more time. "Good to see you. Think I'll try what you did. If you can do it," she snickered, "so can I." With that, she twirled around and trotted in the other direction.

"What did that moose have to say to you?" Tina said, in a low voice.

Shalene covered her mouth, trying to suppress a laugh. "That's not like you, hon."

"I can't stand her. She's always looked down on me, and I know she does it to everyone, so not a race thing. Black, White, Brown, Asian. She sees herself as superior. How do ya know her?"

Shalene sighed, blinking her eyes. *Not going to disrupt my peace.* "We encountered each other long ago." She glimpsed at Isla, now engaged in conversation with the President. "Yup, she's the same, except not as…" Shalene hesitated, "svelte. That's a good word."

Tina smirked. "You are way too kind, girl. Look at her knock down those drinks. That'll put on the pounds."

Shalene giggled. "Yup, again. Sometimes the old verse, *you reap what you sow,* bears merit."

"More like you reap what you eat and drink from what I can see."

Shalene's dimple made a subtle appearance as she tried to suppress her smile. "We're being catty."

"Meow," Tina said with a grin. "Besides, she deserves it with her attitude."

The friends strolled together, stopping in front of a group of other women. "Look, Shalene came."

They turned toward them and clapped, with Shalene putting her finger to her lips. "*Shhh.*"

"Don't you shush us. Come over here and give us a hug."

Shalene's heart sang.

Way too long. I'm back.

Later that night, opening the door to her apartment, she put her hand in a fist and pounded it through the air.

Yes, you go, girl.

She threw down her purse, unbuckled her sandals while standing, spread her arms out, and skipped and danced around the room.

Can't believe I did it. Gosh, Rachel told me all this time that I gave Isla too much power. Look at her now. Pathetic.

Shalene put her hand to her mouth.
Tina's right. What a moose.
She continued to swirl around the room.
A handsome black man materialized in front of her.
Yup, Jason, I can't wait to tell you.
She stopped.
Hold on. Why am I so focused on him?
"Yowzah."

Chapter Twenty-Eight

Rachel and Alexandra—May 18th

The silver-haired coils fell, framing her darker than usual olive skin. Large chocolate eyes sparkled.

Wow. Alexandra appeared more animated than usual. Vacation must have done the trick.

"You look great Alexandra. May I ask where you went?"

"Yes, I spent almost three luxurious weeks in Aruba. And how are you?"

Rachel smiled. Ever the skilled therapist. She redirected without seeming rude. I learned from the best.

"I'm glad you enjoyed yourself, but," Rachel leaned in with an arm over arm, "I cannot express how pleased I am to see you. Lots has happened."

Alexandra beamed. "Well, I can't wait to hear. Wherever you want to begin."

Rachel shared everything that happened between Michael and her, including the blemish of Justine overriding the situation.

"I found out they had more of a relationship than he implied."

"And?"

"And what?"

"Rachel, we're talking about a sixty-something-year-old man, divorced, handsome, and successful. What did you expect from him?"

"I don't know, but cougar doesn't describe this woman, Justine. Her claws expand beyond the ordinary."

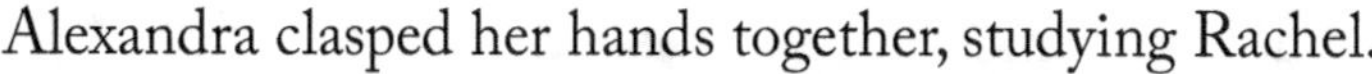

Alexandra clasped her hands together, studying Rachel. "What?"

"You've already surrendered."

"No, I didn't say that."

Alexandra lifted her eyebrows.

Rachel paused, returning to Saturday night.

A starry sheen dressed the sky, accenting Michael's silver locks. His eyes bore into hers. "What do you think about getting together next Saturday for a picnic in the Public Park? Hmmm?"

Rachel blinked, with heartbreak in her smile.

"What are you afraid of?"

She shrugged as her eyes glistened.

He took one arm and leaned against the door frame, using his other hand to brush her eyebrows, nose, cheeks, and, in slow motion, lips.

"I can't imagine what it could be."

Rachel shook her head.

Michael stood up. "Okay. I'm unable to attend the lesson this week, so I'll text you to confirm when and where in the Gardens. You take an Uber, and…" Michael folded his arms. "If all goes well, we'll go for a light dinner and I'll escort you home. How does that sound?"

Rachel nodded, and taking a deep breath she said. "Sounds good."

"I hope you can trust that I'm authentic. No lies, I promise." His head touched hers. "Justine's not important to me. Do you understand?" He pulled back again, eyes probing hers.

"Yes, I believe you."

"Good." He took one of her hands to his lips. "Time's marching on Rachel. Let's not waste it over the past."

Rachel laughed. "You sound like a therapist."

"Maybe I'll try my skills more if you can trust me and talk about your fear."

Rachel's eyes softened. "I might take you up on it."

Now Rachel searched Alexandra's face, waiting for her to respond.

"What do you think?"

"I'm thinking."

"How do you imagine he'll receive the information about my family's alienation?"

"I imagine he'll be more supportive about the matter than you are to you."

"Even though he made it clear he couldn't fathom how family members did it to one another?"

"Yes, Rachel, even with that. Once he hears your story, I know he'll understand the nuances this phenomenon brings to some families."

Rachel gulped. "I hope you're right, because if not, I'm done." Rachel leaned toward Alexandra. "Looking for love, even in the right places, was never a goal of mine."

"Not a conscious one."

Rachel cocked her head. "You believe my unconscious mind wanted more?"

Alexandra lifted her shoulders. "Who knows, but for whatever reason, God or the universe put him in your dancing path."

"Well, God may have, but sometimes not so pleasant characters interrupt our journeys."

Alexandra shook her head. "Really, Rachel? This man shows no evidence of being an unpleasant character."

"I know. I know."

Alexandra nodded. "Now that we agree that his nature, at least, isn't diabolical, what do you plan to do?"

"I guess I'll meet him."

"And will you tell him about Leah and Damian?"

"I'll try."

"What could go wrong?"

Rachel's eyes moistened. "Rejection."

"And when have you felt like that before?"

"Leah, my cousins, and…" Rachel took a tissue, dabbing her eyes. "You know, the most painful of all, Damian."

"That's the issue?"

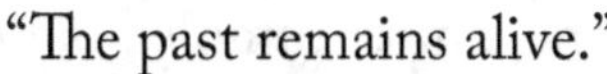

"The past remains alive."

"Rachel, I'd venture to say you're so worried about rejection that you'll reject instead of taking a risk, but," Alexandra cocked an eyebrow, "I remain convinced this man's here to stay if you let him. Do you hear me?" She moved her face closer. "Let's say your fears come true, and he judges you. As you tell your clients, then he's not worth it. But I don't believe that will happen."

"I'm not sure about your prediction, but yes, after Leah and Damian, what's the worst thing that could happen?"

"Let me ask you my usual. What else do you tell your clients about past and toxic relationships?"

Rachel's eyes glimmered. "A corrective experience offers healing and recovery."

"Anything else?"

"You've got me." Rachel laughed. "Love transcends?"

"Yes, and you know, Rachel, Michael sounds quite wise." Alexandra's eyebrows came together. "But he doesn't want to waste time, our most precious asset."

Rachel nodded.

"I suggest you remind yourself that an elastic band can be stretched so far."

Rachel's eyes moistened again. "I understand."

"And as Robert Browning wrote to Elizabeth, *Grow old along with me*, might apply here."

Rachel swallowed. "I don't want to get my hopes up, but sometimes I let myself daydream delicious thoughts."

"Good." Alexandra almost shouted. "Look at me."

Rachel almost recoiled from the unusual, stinging command. "Okay."

"Now I'm going to share something with you."

Rachel antennae went into high gear, waiting for a rare disclosure.

"I realize I reveal little about myself, but it's important."

"I'm listening."

"I just came back from one of the most romantic encounters in my entire life."

Rachel's mouth dropped open, and she almost tumbled out of her chair. "What?"

"I know." Alexandra chuckled. "You're shocked, but here goes. Marco, my husband of five years, tantalizes me over and over. We're in our eighties but live life as if half our age."

Rachel gasped. "You're married?"

Alexandra's head bounced up and down, gifting Rachel with an exquisite smile.

Rachel's brow furrowed. "How come you never told me?"

"I don't remember the reason I withheld this from you. Maybe because Sam died that same year. That would've been most insensitive. Also, it's never been my style to divulge, but now I thought, *What better time?*" Alexandra's eyes shined.

Rachel clasped her hands to her mouth, skin tingling with discomfort, trying not to appear too eager to hear more.

"I know." Alexandra's eyes widened. "You're shocked. The therapist with the highest boundaries shared something so personal. Maybe falling in love with my soulmate contributed to the change."

Rachel gawked. "Five years?"

"You're right." Alexander cocked her head, nodding. "I hadn't planned on disclosing this today, but as I listen to you, the real reason for my spontaneous eruption is because I wanted you to see the possibilities." She continued bobbing her head with her gaze outward before staring back at Rachel. "Yes, that's it. Now I hope it's never too late for love."

Rachel couldn't ignore the scarlet creeping into her cheeks.

"Am I making you uncomfortable?"

"I don't think so. Surprised, more like it."

"Yes, but I wanted you to know even at the ripe old age of eighty, a fire can ignite in ways often ignored by our youth-oriented society."

Rachel nodded, continuing to blink.

"We didn't meet until I turned seventy. I'd given up on the prospect of finding a partner at that late stage in my life, never mind passion." Alexandra shook her head, coils bouncing. "What a mistake, thinking like that."

Alexandra's eyes danced as her voice bubbled over in a way Rachel had never heard. "My dear Rachel, I share this because I want the best for you." Alexandra clapped her hands. "And I get a feeling this Michael may offer you *the other half of life for which the first was created*, paraphrasing the rest of the quote."

Rachel continued staring at Alexandra.

"Oh, dear, did I say too much?"

Rachel shook her head. "No."

"What's going on then?"

"I'm just so glad you told me something about yourself." She shook her head. "Wow! I knew so little about you." Rachel remained still for several seconds. What else to say? She hesitated, trying to quiet the whirl of messages twisting through her mind.

"Any other thoughts?" Alexandra inched forward, almost touching the screen, her face a landscape of worry.

Rachel's gaze became distant, and she blinked several times. A fluffy cloud sprang forth in her mind. And her eyes pooled, but words cemented in her throat.

"Oh, my." Alexandra's eyebrows arched, more than usual. "Please say something."

Tears rolled down Rachel's face as she looked at Alexandra. Shaking her head, she said, "I cannot tell you how happy I am for you." She swallowed. "Also, I think it's helped me in ways that I don't even realize yet." She cocked her head. "Thank you." She moved her hand to her lips and sent a kiss.

And then the unexpected happened.

Later that day, while in one of their favorite hangouts, Janine stopped, and her eyes became like saucers. In the shoulder-high aisle, packed full of romance novels, at one of the few independent bookstores still standing, Janine froze, holding a book in midair.

"Say that again."

Rachel put a hand over her mouth, trying to prevent laughter from spilling out. "Yeah, I know. So, there I am already shocked by her announcement, and she tells me that my guardedness worried her for years. Then she burst out crying."

Janine shook her head. "Even though I've cried with clients, I've done nothing like that."

"Me neither, but we haven't been in the field like her for fifty years."

"True. So, what did you say? I mean, did you feel you needed to take care of her?"

"No," Rachel said, with a sliver of sharpness to her voice. "Not at all. I told her I didn't think she even liked me, so it made me happy to hear she cared so much."

"Noooo." Janine's mouth gaped open. "Oh, my God. What did she say?" She turned her head to a middle-aged gentleman turning the pages of one romance. In a whispered tone, she said, "Let's move further down. You never know who could hear us, being in the profession."

"You're right." Rachel walked side-by-side with her friend.

Janine grazed her fingers along the books. "Nothing like a brick-and-mortar bookstore."

"Agree."

At the end of aisle, Janine said, "Okay, so what did Ms.—but now, *Mrs.* Alexandra say to that?"

"She looked…" Rachel paused. "I guess incredulous would be the proper word. She told me she couldn't believe I thought that way."

"Well, now you know she doesn't."

"I do, and now I know what I need to do."

Chapter Twenty-Nine

Something unusual swirled around the room. She couldn't quite put her finger on it.

Her heart tumbled earlier when she entered the office to see Sapphire and Matt studying their phones, disengaged from each other. In his usual style, Matt kept crossing, then uncrossing his legs, giving her a quick hello, while Sapphire, whose hair covered much of her face, nodded without smiling.

What a disappointment. So much progress between them, and now?

When Jason came in, Sapphire put her hand through her hair and waved with sparkling eyes.

Maybe I have it wrong. Jason and Sapphire? Who knows?

Right behind Jason, laughter emerged. Shalene and Yardley walked in together, with Shalene chatting about something. Yardley's wide eyes observed Shalene, gesturing with her hands more than Rachel had witnessed since meeting her.

Shalene bounced in her usual seat, and before Rachel began the meeting, she raised her hand.

"My dear Shalene, no need to raise your hand," said Rachel with a smile, "but go ahead."

"Wait until you hear what I did." Her ringed fingers covered her mouth. "Yowzah." A giggle followed.

Jason's eyebrows lifted. "I'm itching to hear." Jason eyed the others. "And I'm sure I speak for everyone else here."

"Jason, I took on your challenge."

Jason clapped. "I'll steal a page from my brother, Matt, here. Brava."

Matt tucked his phone in his pocket and leaned forward with a grin. "Sure. Hey Shalene, I'll join my friend." He applauded. "And when you're done, I've also got some things to share."

"As do I." Sapphire's gaze stayed on Rachel. "If possible, I'd like to go after Shalene."

Rachel looked at Matt. "You okay with that, my friend?"

Matt focused on Rachel. "Ladies before gents. No problem."

"Shalene, my dear, you have the floor."

Shalene stared at her ringed fingers before rubbing her hands together. "Okay, here goes."

She shared with the group about her encounter with Isla. She described how Rachel helped her develop some techniques to practice, and when she told them about *the blob*, everyone burst into laughter and clapped.

"Rachel, did you tell her to imagine a blob?" Jason folded his arms, exaggerating a frown.

"No sir, I did not," Rachel said, grinning and shaking her head. "Our dear ingenious Shalene came up with that visual all by her little old self."

Shalene bobbed her head. "Yes, and boy, did it help, along with other visuals. I dampened my fears enough to go, and by the end, a tidal wave washed them away." She clenched both hands, shaking. "I'm all done." Her dimple emerged as her eyes grabbed Rachel's. "A corrective experience, just like you said."

Rachel's eyes blinked, trying to contain the mist forming in her eyes. "I'm so pleased for you, Shalene. Liberation."

Shalene nodded before getting up and running toward Rachel. Her arms wrapped around Rachel.

"Thank you so much, Rachel."

"You did the work, my dear. Not me."

Shalene grabbed a tissue and blew her nose before scanning the room. "And thanks to all of you. No way would I have done this a couple of months ago."

"I heard you say *yowzah* before. What's up with that?" Jason squinted at Shalene.

"I resurrected my favorite word. I said it all the time before things went haywire."

Jason bobbed his head, winking at Shalene. "Good. We need those fun words."

Everyone else nodded in silence as a shroud of serenity blanketed the room.

Rachel shut her eyes for a moment, taking in the eucalyptus-spearmint aroma she'd spritzed earlier.

When she opened them, she observed everyone doing the same thing—except for Matt. He gave her a half-smile, which she returned with flashing eyebrows.

In a subtle voice, she said, "I hate to break the tranquility that's settled here, but it's time for us to continue." She peered at Sapphire. "Ready, my dear?"

Sapphire nodded with her eyes focused on her water bottle. Rachel studied the exotic woman, now sharing the culmination of what she needed to further her healing. She'd texted Sapphire that day to check on her. Sapphire returned one right away, writing *I'm good* status, but Rachel didn't know the details.

Sapphire's story began unraveling, and Rachel's eyes swept the room. Everyone seemed captivated by her tale. In between, Sapphire looked up at a few of the members, except for Matt. Maybe she sat next to him to prevent her from catching his attention, but it was weird that he, too, stared ahead.

Rachel remained intrigued by the sudden turnaround from the last session's playfulness between those two. Oh well, she'd find out.

When Sapphire finished, her glorious eyes captured Rachel's. "Thank you. I couldn't have done it without you." Rachel's eyes welled up again, as Sapphire made her way to Rachel.

"Oh, my dear, you're beyond courageous."

Sapphire stayed in her arms for a few moments, whispering *thank you* again.

When Sapphire released Rachel, she kissed her on the cheek and moved toward her chair with her fragrance trailing. Rachel observed her eyes snapping at each person with a mouthed *thank you*, quicker with Matt, as he gave her a curt nod.

What's up with those two?

"Wow, two magnificent warrior queens on display, with another who went before them," said Rachel, offering soft eyes to each woman.

Matt glanced at Jason. "Hey man, what do you say?" He began clapping.

Jason said, "Bro, I'm going to add something to sweeten the deal." He placed his fingers into his mouth and whistled.

Shalene stood up and took a bow.

"My goodness," Rachel said, laughing and bobbing her head at Shalene, "welcome to the real you."

"Sapphire, what about you, and Yardley too?" Jason asked.

Yardley giggled, shaking her head with rosier than usual cheeks.

Jason waved his hand to Sapphire. "Come on."

Sapphire shook her head, with an unfocused stare. "Not my style." She glanced at Jason with scintillating eyes. "But I appreciate your invitation."

Rachel studied the young woman for a moment. Not her way, but something else. Can't put my finger on it.

"Not to put you on the spot, Matt, but would you like to tell us what went on for you this past week?"

Matt nodded with a deadpan expression. "Yup. Lots to share." He scanned the room, without looking at Sapphire. "Ready everyone?"

Rachel studied the handsome young man. Over four years ago, he sauntered into her office for the first time, somber but polite. Not as massive as Jason, but almost. Handsome. A replica of Kit Harington, as everyone expressed, with a titanium shell surrounding him. During that initial meeting, Rachel tried to engage him, asking many open-ended questions. He answered but refused to elaborate. At the end of the session, she asked what he'd like to do about future visits. A slow, glorious smile made its way across his face. "If I may, I'd like to come back."

Going forward, Matt committed to regular sessions. He always arrived early and never complained when Rachel opened the door, grinning. "Five minutes?" He'd look up from his phone, waving his hand and mouthing, *no problem.*

Over the next year, he discussed Juliette, his mother, and the betrayal he experienced from both. Matt often leaned forward, stopping in-between his narrative. "Rachel, I don't know if I'll ever trust anyone again after what happened."

Rachel would study her splendid client. "My friend, you will. Believe me, you will."

"And my mother, oh she tries, and I've opened the door more than I thought," he'd shake his head, " but she needs to earn my trust back."

Rachel nodded. Being in the same profession, she came across Sophia once or twice at conferences. They said hello but never spoke to one another beyond that. Just as well, since she knew so much about Sophia, and Matt made it clear to his mother he'd never reveal his therapist's identity. "She knows better than to push me."

Then Nicole came along for Matt.

Would he talk about her here? She remembered the day. He came into the session, gushing. "She's the one, Rach." His deep blue eyes turned deep midnight. "I'm telling you. She's the corrective experience you always mention."

"Sounds lovely, my friend," Rachel said to him, but deep inside she worried. "I don't want to overstep my boundaries, but just, well, you know." Her eyebrows knitted together.

"I know, Rach." Matt smiled. "I appreciate your concern, but she's amazing." He leaned forward. "I know it's only been a few months, but she's the real thing."

Rachel nodded.

"Hey, my parents knew people who became engaged after a few months," his smile widened, "and they're still together." Then his eyes darkened, as he weighed his words. "Unlike my parents."

"Some people do luck out, but for others that is not the case. Because of your open heart," Rachel hesitated, "I'm protective of you, but please tell me if I'm overstepping my boundaries."

His eyes lit up. "No way, Rachel. I know you have my best interests at heart, and because I value your input, I want to bring Nic here."

"My friend, whatever works best for you."

"Rach, you're gonna love her."

Would he tell the group the total story about Nicole? Up to him. I hope you do, Matt. Unlike what happened with Nic, his disclosure might offer more healing and trust.

Now why can't I put my finger on the change in atmosphere?

Matt

He refused to look at her.

She appeared to do the same.

Just as well. No distractions tonight.

His eyes widened. Focus, man, focus. You've got to purge this. After talking to Sophia, relief, but need to discuss the bigger issue related to Nic.

"Okay, we'll start with Sophia, my mom, and then onto the second woman who broke my heart."

Matt glanced at Rachel. She nodded. "Whenever you're ready, my friend."

His eyes cast downward, and he paused for a moment. Quiet draped the room, which allowed him to concentrate on his words.

He looked up and caught Rachel's steady gaze. "Okay, the next rung."

Matt texted his mother last Friday, asking if she'd like his company for an early morning walk on Saturday. Within ten seconds, his phone pinged.

Yes, tell me where?

A three-heart emoji followed the question. Matt suggested they walk her normal route, the neighborhood surrounding his childhood home.

Matt arrived at 7:00 on a warm spring morning. The green lawn blanketed the front yard, displayed a splatter of tulips, daffodils, and pruned shrubs with the large country house behind it.

The warmth from earlier memories infused Matt, and when he got out of his Jeep, he saw his mother waving from the steps between one of many floor-to-ceiling windows. He walked toward her, his heart lurching upward.

Been unfair to her. Need to go forward.

The slender Sophia spread her arms out, but before Matt embraced her, he grabbed her hands and stood back.

"Hey Mom, looking good for an older woman."

Dressed in leggings, a T-shirt, and Hoka sneakers, Sophia's eyes danced. "My handsome son, you flatter me, but I'm nothing compared to you."

Matt's muscular arms wrapped around his mother. "Wow, Mom. You're too generous with your praise."

"Never enough, never enough."

Matt released his arms. "I'm glad we're doing this."

Sophia touched her son's cheek with glimmering eyes. "Before I start the waterworks, let's get moving." She put on her wrist weights, and mother and son started walking side-by-side. Matt listened to the familiar sounds of nearby lawnmowers and sneakers pounding by them.

"Mom, I'd like to do this more often."

Sophia didn't look at him, but tears streamed down her face. "Me too." He saw a slow smile lift on her profiled face.

"You wonder why I've kept you at arm's length?"

Sophia turned to him with pooled eyes, stopping to dab them

and blow her nose. "Yes," she said in a muffled voice. "And I understand." She glanced at him. "You had every right for your anger at my wayward path." A hollow laugh came from her. "I just didn't know if you'd ever let me in again."

Matt studied his mother, and her surprised outpour caused his heart to shatter. "I'm sorry for avoiding this for so long."

Sophia gulped, continuing to pump her wrist weights as they resumed walking.

"When you didn't respond to my letter last year, I thought," her voice broke again, "I need to accept this."

"Juliette, you, the whole Salon mystery just—I dunno," Matt shrugged, "I just couldn't…" He sighed. "I dunno."

"I'm glad you're here now." His mother peeked at him. "Maybe we can put the past where it belongs, but if I may, please let me elaborate on what I wrote."

"No need, Mom."

"But I need to do this."

Matt nodded.

"After the debacle with Juliette, I told her and everyone in that Salon group never to contact you or me again."

"Yeah, you wrote that."

"But I didn't share everything. Juliette showed up at my door and threatened me."

"What?" Matt stopped. "What do you mean?"

"Juliette never hid her lifestyle. I won't get into detail, but I never felt comfortable with the whole thing. She knew I became involved as a reaction to the divorce, and she threatened to tell colleagues about my participation."

"What?!"

"I'm a traditional therapist, as you know, and although I've seen people active in all kinds of lifestyles, it was never my thing."

Matt caught Sophia studying him.

"Even though I drowned myself in that crowd, which I found exciting at first, I never engaged in their *extracurricular* activities.

When I hosted the gathering, I made it clear—intellectual-type board games only—if people wanted to pair up, not in our house.”

"How about that young guy I saw you kissing at the New Year's Eve party?"

"We were making out." Sophia paused for a moment, looking straight ahead. "I guess I liked the attention." She shook her head. "The longing to feel young and desirable required feeding."

Matt nodded, trying to digest it all.

Sophia sighed. "I never had a problem with getting older, but after your dad left me, I couldn't get past it. Mandy and I were only a few years apart, but I looked for anything to help me understand."

"Not your fault, Mom. I love Dad, but he had his own issues, letting his narcissism get in the way."

Sophia kept her gaze forward. "I loved your father very much, but after that New Year's Eve crisis, the reality of the situation shook me to the core. The reality of losing one of my most precious assets put everything into perspective, and I contacted my old therapist right away." Sophia put her hand weight under her arm to wipe a cheek.

"I spent months crying and processing your father, the group, and most important," Sophia stopped, touching her son's arm, "the possibility of…" her voice now a quiver, "losing you."

Matt's eyes pooled. He swallowed. "Mom, I know my anger caused me to say those words, *never want to see you again*, but…" Matt shook his head, "I couldn't do it. You know the relationship hasn't been the same, but I never would have cut you off completely." He grinned at his mother. "I couldn't."

Sophia blinked.

"Besides, Mom, how could I go so long without hearing the word, *process*?"

"Oh you. Now that your sister joined the ranks of therapists, you'll get a double dose."

"Yeah, plus my therapist uses the word from time to time."

Sophia didn't respond to Matt, but he saw her lips lift.

"Yes. I'm still in therapy."

"I didn't ask."

"But you want to."

Sophia laughed. "How could I not be curious about the other woman, or should I say, the *other mother*."

Matt patted his mother's head. "Mom, I love my therapist, but you're not replaceable."

Sophia stopped again with misty eyes. "My son, thank you."

They resumed their walk.

"But let's talk about you again, Mom. Therapy? You still going?"

"Less now. Once every couple of weeks."

"You feel you've healed from the divorce?"

"More than I thought I could." His mother grinned at him.

"Something you want to tell me?"

Sophia turned her head to her son, with a glint in her eye. "I met someone."

Matt halted, his eyes lifting. "Really?"

"Yes, and he's not like the other characters."

Matt laughed. "Good. How?"

"Church, a widower."

Matt nodded. "Tell me more."

"You sound like me."

Matt chuckled. "Between you, Des, and my therapist, how could I not?"

"His wife died three years ago, and last year, he began attending the same Mass as I. We began volunteering at a fundraiser together, and our friendship unfolded."

"Hey, Mom. That's great."

"I told him about what happened."

"Wow, that took courage."

"I figured, at this point in my life, if he didn't accept me for who I am, better I know now."

"How did he take it?"

"Oh my God, he couldn't have been more supportive. He said,

Sophia, as St. Augustine stated, there's no saint without a past and no sinner without a future, and then he kissed me."

"Glad to hear, Mom. You deserve nothing less than great."

"I'd love for you to meet him."

"Sounds good."

Sophia's eyes squinted and lit with mischief. "And you, my remarkable son? I know I'm not supposed to ask, but I can't help myself."

"It's okay. You can ask a little now, but not too much."

"Tell me."

"Nothing to tell, but there might be soon."

"I hope so," Sophia raised her hands and bent her fingers into a claw, "and she better treat you well or else, hear me roar."

Matt smirked. "Spoken like a fierce lion protecting her cub."

"You betcha." Sophia laughed with a growl. "No more Juliettes ever again. By the way, whatever happened to that woman, Nicole?"

Matt

Matt's eyes flicked around the room without turning toward Sapphire. Shalene twisted her rings and stared at him. Jason rubbed his chin, and Yardley sat with unclenched hands, eyes blinking. He looked to Rachel. Her eyes opened before latching onto Matt's.

"That's all I got with Mom. What do you think, Madame Therapist?"

"My friend, what do you imagine I'm going to say?"

Matt nodded with a half-smile. "You'll ask my thoughts." He sighed long and heavy. "I think my relationship with my mother might become even stronger than I imagined."

"My friend, you said what I thought, except," Rachel said with a wistful smile, "not might, but *will*."

"Thank you."

A peaceful hush roamed the room.

"So, Matt, this, um, woman, Nic, you going to talk about her?" An intense voice interrupted.

Everyone's eyes shifted toward Sapphire—except Matt's.

Not going to look at her. Too much.

A moment of stillness invaded the room again as everyone waited for Matt.

He combed his hair with his fingers, and he nodded.

"Yup, time to talk about Nic. Here goes."

Two years ago, Matt attended a party. The pandemic was in full force, but he and all his friends ignored the dire warnings. All of them worked from home but got together for drinks or cards at each other's homes. On New Year's Eve, a coworker had a party. Because of the situation with Juliette, Matt vowed, *no more parties on that infamous date*, but his sister, Des, said her typical therapist mantra. "Go or come with me and my friends. You need a corrective experience."

Matt looked at Rachel and winked. "So, you know, I listened and went for this," Matt gestured with an air quote, "*corrective experience.*"

After valeting his car at his colleague Norio's North End Condominium in Boston, he arrived to find thirty to thirty-five people present. A couple of them wore masks. Their choice, but not his. Matt worked out regularly. Get sick? Took a risk like some others.

With an expensive bottle of wine in hand, Matt's stomach gurgled. He walked through the mid-sized condo, ready to dive into the homemade pasta dishes. Norio loved to cook, learning from his Italian-born grandmother, often bringing dishes to work. Matt entered the open, modern kitchen, where everyone congregated, serving themselves from platters of calamari, antipasto, spaghetti and meatballs, with dipping oils and bread everywhere on the quartz countertop. Matt couldn't wait to grab a plate. White cabinets and shiny hardwood floors provided a warm ambience sometimes missing in ultramodern homes. Dimmed lights flowed wall-to-wall, illuminating the other guests.

Matt caught Norio's eye, and the gregarious man turned toward him and waved him over.

"Nice place you have here," Matt said, studying the craftsmanship of the kitchen.

"Thanks, glad you made it," A smiling Norio said. "Man, I forget how tall you are. How tall are you?"

"Six feet, four inches."

"Hey, I'm no slouch at an inch under six feet, but would love to have those extra inches."

Matt patted his friend's back. "You're fine just the way you are. Besides, the ladies seem to love you."

Norio laughed. "My beard and Sicilian looks." He wiggled his eyebrows. "Tall, dark, and handsome."

"Are you talking about you again, Norio?" A voice purred in the background. Matt twirled around and found himself in front of a tall, model-like brunette with big brown eyes, dark skin, and hair falling down to her waist.

"Matt, meet my sister, Rapunzel. I mean Nic—for Nicole."

Nicole punched her brother's arm before turning her gaze to Matt.

Matt's eyes locked with hers, mesmerized by the dark goddess standing in front of him.

Her eyes roamed over his body before she put her hand out. "Pleased to make your acquaintance, Matt."

Matt stood, taking his hand out of his pocket. "Sorry, nice to meet you, uh, Nic." He lifted his hand. "Nicole?"

"Nic or Nicole, but never Nikki, Cole or Colie."

Matt's eyes danced with hers. "Got it."

For the rest of the evening, Matt and Nicole huddled in a corner, eating, chatting, and *almost* touching. Matt noticed the smooth dark skin, silky brown hair with streaks of copper which he wanted to touch. He couldn't get enough of her musky scent. At midnight, their lips brushed each other's, with Nic hinting at more to come.

For the next few months, they spent every waking hour together. Her place, his place, dinner, Netflix, and occasionally, with friends. Alone or with others, they couldn't keep their hands off each other, working from home as much as possible. Nicole's job as an aide to a local politician, required her to fly to the D.C. office every few weeks, always returning within a day or two. Matt couldn't stand it, and FaceTimed her in the morning and again in the evening.

By the fourth month, Matt met Nicole's parents and promised her she'd meet his soon.

Because of his relationship with his mother, Matt wanted to wait. He shared much about the situation with Nic but spared her the details about Juliette. Something told him to hold back.

By the fifth month, Matt noticed a change. Nic stayed for longer periods in Washington, sometimes for a week at a time. When she returned to Boston, she displayed an uncharacteristic moodiness, and more often, she snapped at Matt for the slightest of littlest issues. She claimed exhaustion. Affection halted altogether. She expressed no interest in celebrating their six-month anniversary. Matt could no longer ignore the obvious. A gray fog dulled his usual optimism. He detected a sudden shift in Norio's attitude. A flicker in Norio's eyes confirmed his suspicions when he mentioned Nic.

That final weekend, Matt planned on confronting Nic about the relationship. She beat him to it, telling him she needed a break. Matt said, no way to a break, but an end. Nic didn't seem very upset, confirming Matt's suspicions about a possible third party.

Their exchange remained vivid in his mind.

"Okay, Nic, I think you owe it to me. The truth. Another guy?

Nic's lower lip quivered.

"Come on, Nic."

"Matt, you're a beautiful person, and I don't want to hurt you, but if you insist."

Matt sneered. "I'm a beautiful person. Yeah, right. Not beautiful enough. Spare me the platitudes, Nic. Spill it. Who's the guy?"

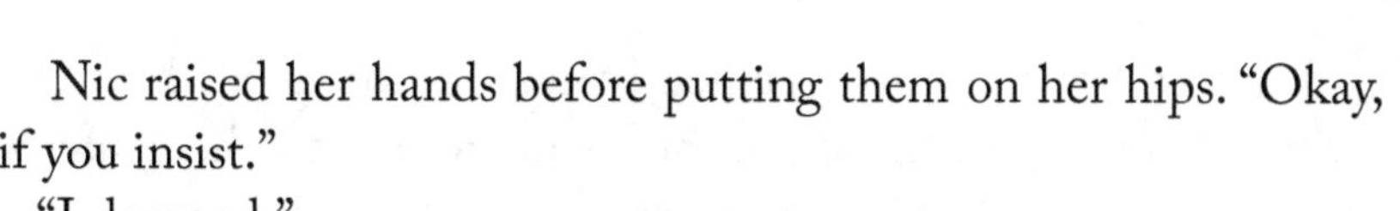

Nic raised her hands before putting them on her hips. "Okay, if you insist."

"I demand."

Nic's hands remained on her hips and moved closer. "Excuse me. You demand?"

"Look, forget the verbiage. Just give me the courtesy of telling me I'm not crazy."

Nic's eyes softened. "You're not crazy. I met a politician, and we fell head over heels in love with each other."

Matt bobbed his head. "Who?"

"I can't tell you because he's leaving his wife, and until the divorce, we need to keep it quiet."

Matt lifted his eyebrows. "So, you think this guy will leave his wife?"

"He will."

"Okay, I guess this is it."

"I'm sorry Matt."

"I'm not sorry, Nic. Thought we had a good thing. Guess not."

Matt almost contacted Rachel to see if she could see him sooner, but he decided he'd wait until the end of the week. A mending heart shattered again, but he was not suicidal or homicidal. Why give Rachel concern? He'd deal with it.

Nic never met Rachel. She dismissed the proposition when he suggested it.

"And why do you think that's a good idea?"

"I just think you'd love one another."

"Matt, that's weird. I can see meeting your mother, but your therapist?"

Matt shook his head, giving her a goofy smile. "Just thought it'd be cool. That's all."

It never worked out. Just as well since the relationship didn't either.

When Matt shared the situation with Rachel, she shook her head and reminded him he sensed something wrong.

He told her this time seemed worse, and he needed to heal. Didn't know if he'd trust another woman. Juliette, he came to understand, but Nic? Everything seemed so perfect.

Rachel prompted his memory with the famous derivative of Bible verses. *This too shall pass.* Matt found comfort in the verse, but not enough to consider serious dating again. In the last two years, he went out on a handful of dates, but the women, like Jena, didn't pass muster for him.

Beautiful? All of them.

Accomplished? Most of them.

Interesting? A few of them.

Deep and authentic? None of them, at least not for him.

His friends and family expressed exasperation when he declined, going out beyond a second or third date. When they asked what he was looking for, his answer was always, *Don't know. I guess I'll know it when I see it.*

Matt looked up. "That's it, and boy," he nodded with an unfocused gaze, "good to get it out."

His body felt like water released from a dam. No more tension. No more holding back. *Ah.* He closed his eyes for a moment, focusing on the rhythm of his body, like gentle waves rising and falling.

"Matt?"

Matt opened his eyes to Rachel's voice.

He blinked. "Sorry." His eyes reached everyone except Sapphire.

"I tried to steer clear of disrupting your tranquil state, but just checking in."

Matt sighed and nodded. "Like everyone else, feeling good."

"Did you ever see her again?"

The others' eyes moved to Sapphire.

Without turning to her, Matt said, "Yup. I did."

Matt leaned forward with his fingers laced, nodding.

Four months after the breakup, he stirred in the early hours of the morning. Matt glanced at the clock: 5:00 A.M. Time to get going. About to put his feet on the floor, he heard the buzzer. Who would show up this early? He looked at his Ring app. There stood Nicole, pacing back and forth. He threw on his workout clothes and went down to let her in.

Nicole stood in front of him, tears streaming down her face.

"I've missed you," she said, grabbing his face to kiss him.

Matt leaned back, unsmiling, but invited her into his home.

She sat down on the leather couch in the sparse but comfortable living room.

"Coffee?"

"Please, you know how I take it," she said, her voice smokey.

Matt turned, noticing her seductive eyes. Tears evaporated. So much for mourning the loss of me.

He brought coffee for both, and she patted the couch for him to sit. Matt shook his head and sat across from her, suggesting she tell him the reason for the early morning visit.

"I know you're a rise and shine guy, so I wanted to catch you before you left for the fitness center."

"Please get to the point."

Nicole untied her wool coat revealing a gorgeous white suit, which enhanced her dark complexion.

"I know you love me in white."

"Nicole, just tell me why you're here."

Nicole shared the story of her breakup from the politician and how it devastated her. "I should never have let you go."

"No, you shouldn't have. But you did. It's over, Nicole."

She moved closer to him. "Haven't you missed me?"

Matt licked his lips. "In the beginning, but I've moved forward."

"Have you met someone?"

"None of your business."

"Touchy, aren't we?"

"You broke my heart, Nicole. But after lots of self-examination, I concluded I don't want someone who can discard me with so little thought. I was going to ask you to marry me."

"Don't you believe in second chances?"

"Not second place."

"Oh, Matt. Level-headed Matt. So controlled."

Matt stood. "Let me walk you out."

Nicole narrowed her eyes, pounded the cup down, spilling coffee all over, and grabbed her coat. "I can walk myself out. Goodbye, Matt. You don't know what a mistake you're making."

Matt stopped for a moment as his eyes swept the room. "And with that, she stormed out, yelling, *Good riddance*, and I never heard from her again."

"Whatever happened to her?" Yardley asked, louder than usual.

"Funny you should ask. Norio and I still work together. A few months ago, he told me she met some real estate magnate, had a whirlwind relationship, and got married."

"You sound like you're okay with it," Jason said.

"I am. I couldn't trust her again. Not like she came back because she made a mistake. She reached out because the politician ended the relationship. Like I said, no second place for me in a relationship."

"Queen Bee only," Shalene said, with a grin.

"You got it." Matt's eyes found Rachel's. "That's what our esteemed therapist always says."

"Aww. I thought she said it just to me," Jason said.

"Me." Yardley waved.

Shalene pointed to herself. "Should I add, me too?"

"All of us," Sapphire said with a stern tone.

Matt smiled without turning to Sapphire.

What's going on with her?

He noticed Rachel's eyes, brush over him and her.

Trying to figure it out, Rach?

"So, my friend, your thoughts about your mother or," Rachel's eyes flashed mischief, "trust in finding someone right for you?"

Matt's eyes grabbed hers. *Here she goes, pushing me a bit. Yup, but like the others, I know she wants good for me.*

"You going to answer her?" Sapphire asked in a fiery tone.

Not going there with her.

"Rachel, I think you're right about my mother. She wants the best for me, like you, and guess what else?" Matt leaned forward.

Keep your eyes on Rachel only.

"Yes?" Sapphire's tone bit hard.

"Listening to everyone here—" Matt nodded to everyone. *Okay, include her*—"helped me see I'm not alone."

Tap, tap, tap.

There she goes again.

"Also," Matt said with his eyes reaching Rachel again, "Madame Therapist? Right again. Something changed by sharing with a few cool people, so I think I'm ready to find a life partner."

"Brother? You're cool yourself." Jason got up, offering a fist bump. "And looking for a life partner," Jason sat rubbing his chin, "something I'm considering too."

"Me too, again," Shalene said, bursting into laughter.

"Well, I already have one. I hope he still wants me," Yardley said, crossing her fingers.

"Yardley, I can't imagine he wouldn't," Matt said.

Yardley threw him a kiss.

Sapphire jumped up. "I hate to breakup this happy-fest, but I need to run." Sapphire waved to each member—except Matt. "See ya, everyone, for the last act." And swoosh, off she went.

What in the world…

Chapter Thirty

Rachel—May 17th

Another beautiful spring day. Rachel sat, closing her eyes as the Uber stalled in traffic. Rachel heard the sirens blaring as the vehicle came to a dead stop. She texted Michael, telling him of the delay.

She waited until Thursday night to confirm with him about getting together. That night, he told her his idea. A picnic in the Public Garden. But he insisted she wait until Thursday to let him know.

Before he left Saturday night, he kissed her again, brushing his hand across her cheek. "We're not young, Rachel." His eyes searched hers as she bit her lip. "I say this as a man and physician. Anything can happen to us anytime."

"I know. But—"

"But what? You're afraid?"

Her lips refused to move.

"Rejection?" Michael grimaced. "Or maybe, and forgive me for crossing into your territory, fear of happiness, or guilt?"

"You'd make a good therapist." Her lips turned upward.

Michael chuckled. "Glad to see you smile." His hand held her chin again. "Yet, in all seriousness, I think you do better than I do in that area. Like I might've said before, you can teach someone how to perform surgery. Ah, but to navigate the crevices of the mind takes a special person."

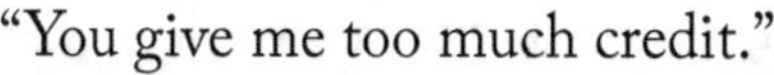

"You give me too much credit."

"No, I'm an excellent judge of character." Michael smirked. "Most of the time, except on the rare occasion, when my male animal instincts come out. *Grrrrr.*"

Rachel laughed.

"Good." He touched her nose.

Rachel gulped. Sam. Maybe someone like Sam.

"I'm optimistic, but my lady, if I may say that in these politically sensitive times, it's up to you."

Another kiss.

He walked away from her, turning around, walking backwards to the taxi, and waving.

She went inside, closing the door. The dogs scampered over to her, and she stooped down to allow them to cuddle in her arms. "Take turns. Lots of love to go around, and maybe, just maybe, you'll meet Michael. Who knows, all three of us might fall in love with him."

Her daydream was interrupted by screeching tires and brakes, pushing her forward. My goodness. Good thing for seatbelts.

"Ma'am, looks like they're clearing things."

"Great."

"Should be there soon."

Rachel closed her eyes again, ruminating on Thursday night's session. The resiliency of the human spirit never ceased to amaze her. Also, you didn't always have a sense of what would happen. Was the group a success? She might not know its effects for an extensive time, if ever.

Recently, she received a thank you note from a woman who shared that their six sessions together helped her conquer anxieties of getting married and having children. The results of the last session weren't what Rachel had expected. The woman left, telling Rachel she didn't see the point of continuing since nothing changed. When Rachel offered another referral, she declined, telling Rachel she had given her more than the others, but nothing worked.

When she left, Rachel felt bad and went over the whole scenario with Bridget and Janine. "Rachel," they said in unison, "we're not God."

"I know."

"Each of us goes through this every so often," Bridget said.

"Yup, we have to remind ourselves that we can't help everyone and don't always know even if we do," Janine said.

When she received the letter, she sighed. Another reminder of the rewarding but strange experience of being a therapist.

The group? Well, Shalene let her old self emerge after seeing the Goliath for who she is—an envious blob.

Yardley? Her ability to manage her E.D. has been remarkable. Sounds like her Daniel never gave up. Can't wait to hear more in the last session.

Jason, wow. He's willing to open his heart again. Yay! What a sweetheart. His Callie will smile from afar, applauding for her beautiful man.

Looks like he and Matt developed a bromance. Will the friendship endure beyond the group?

Fine with her. Some therapists might frown, but she wouldn't. It will happen if it's supposed to happen.

And Matt.

OMG. Who knew he'd come this far?

So happy he and Sophia worked it out. Heard great things about her skills and ability to engage clients. Can't imagine the effect the estrangement had on her. Torturous.

And for him? More than he may have admitted to anyone, including himself.

Now Matt expressed his readiness to search for a serious relationship. Another surprise.

Did he have someone in mind?

Before the last session, she thought of Sapphire.

Now?

Doesn't look like it. What a disappointment. Not only would

they make a beautiful couple, but they seemed to enjoy each other, revealing a playfulness between them.

Oh well, not for her to decide, but who knows?

You never know.

And speaking of Sapphire, so pleased for her. Not an easy feat to confront a perpetrator. Like all, they shroud their abuse in secrecy and confusion, often nurturing their victim.

Rachel shook her head. Sexual abuse?

Nothing worse than sexual abuse. Sexual, physical, and emotional abuse all rolled in one gnarled ball.

The best revenge?

Success.

Sapphire suspected all attractive men, but Matt? Like Jason, a peach, and if she considered Matt, it could provide her with that corrective experience she emphasizes to everyone.

Up to Sapphire. Only her decision. Would she remain crouched up, like a snarling, wounded child, or open herself to something different? Something better. Hope so.

Now, who are you talking about?

Michael's words echoed in her mind. Your choice, but time's marching forward.

Could he be right? Was she experiencing guilt about her own possibilities? Was she afraid of rejection? How about both?

Sam? What did he say before he died? His image loomed in front of her.

Live, my love, live. Find someone to take you on a fun adventure for the rest of your life.

No!

She recalled shaking her head vigorously, unable to halt the waterfall, blurring her vision.

Yes, he responded in his feeble voice, skinny twigs wrapping around her wrists.

No one could replace Sam.

But no one could replace anyone. Right?

You can have more than one love. Right?

How come you tell everyone else to do things you aren't doing yourself?

You know, like the client with alcohol problems treated by a therapist who denies their own alcohol abuse?

The old, *Do as I say and not as I do.*

Could she be doing the same thing with love?

Rachel sighed, looking out the window.

"Getting closer, Ma'am." The driver read her thoughts.

Now, she's going to try. What's the worst thing that could happen to her?

Alexandra asked this over and over.

Oh my God, Alexandra.

She put her hand over her mouth, to suppress the laughter bubbling in her throat. The best kept secret, speaking of secrets.

Taking the plunge for the first time at seventy-five. Who knew? Well, George Eliot's quote couldn't be more accurate about never being too late to become who or what.

Rachel cocked her head.

Why did she hide it from her?

But until this last session, what did she ever share with her?

Not much.

Rachel reflected on her own divulgences with clients.

At the start of her career, she established unbreakable walls for her clients, and something occurred that made her more at ease and less obscure with those who sought her help.

After being in the business for seven years, something that happened in one of her groups moved her to disclose.

An immediate insecurity punctured her soul.

Right away, a client thanked her, telling her it made her more approachable. The other members agreed. Since that time, she shared when she thought it made sense. Although she didn't talk about her marriage, she shared with some about her husband's death.

Now, Alexandra eased the restraints around her life.

Did it help Rachel? Yes, for a few reasons.

It made her more human, as Rachel did with her own clients long ago.

The revelation helped Rachel see that Alexandra might have more affection for her beyond the blank wall she maintained for most of their journey.

And Rachel became more reflective about her resistance to embark on a mysterious quest, not knowing the outcome.

She squirmed in her seat as the Uber decreased speed and examined her low-heeled pink shoes and fluttering pink skirt and took out her compact mirror. The face looking back, tried to hide the excitement pushing its way through old messages. She smiled at herself and fluffed the layers of curls sloping along her shoulders.

Can't believe it, but I'm ready and, squeezing her eyes tight, have a good feeling about it.

Rachel stirred as the car came to an abrupt stop. She lurched forward but was constrained by the tension of the seatbelt.

"Stupid. Watch where ya going," the driver shouted to the other driver.

He turned around to Rachel. "Sorry about that, Ma'am, but good news, we're here."

Rachel handed the driver a hefty extra amount of cash.

The driver tipped his hat. "Thank you, Ma'am. Enjoy your day."

Rachel smiled and alighted from the vehicle. She looked around but saw no Michael. *Hmmm.* He hadn't texted her back.

Delayed too?

She examined her phone to confirm if she was in the right spot.

Yes, the exact location he suggested.

While waiting, why not move a little? Rachel traversed back and forth. A few extra steps in her day could help quiet the thumping inside. She noticed people passing her. Younger and older. Some light walking or heavy jogging steps. Several clattering by on rollerblades. Many wore earphones. Others, heads down, scrolling through their devices, or with the phone attached to their ear, conversing or laughing with someone on the other end.

What would we do without our smartphones?

Even though she lived much of her life without the technological treasure, she couldn't imagine it now.

Rachel peered at her phone. No text. She listened to her voicemail to check if she had any missed calls. She didn't.

After pacing for half an hour, Rachel sat on the bench. Swirling voices whisked through her mind.

Doesn't want you.

Changed his mind.

Justine.

No, no, no.

Stop.

Slam the door on the negative messages trying to overthrow her positivity.

Something must have happened.

Rachel texted him again and waited. She set her phone down. Several seconds later, she lifted it and looked.

Nothing.

More time went by.

Okay, fifty-five minutes, then time to call another Uber.

Rachel sealed her eyes again, inhaling the perfume of the spring air. She listened to the chatter from those going past her.

Boston.

Between the colleges and medical institutions, people came from all over the world. Once here, many stayed.

She opened her eyes. Time's up. Rachel clicked her Uber app, and a moving car on the screen showed availability in five minutes. Rachel got up and walked to the curb, anticipating Uber's arrival.

Disappointment flooded her, but she remained calm.

Why should I be surprised? Look at what you hear from clients. The stories they share. How are you any different? You know what? You're not, and you gave it your best shot. At least, you tried.

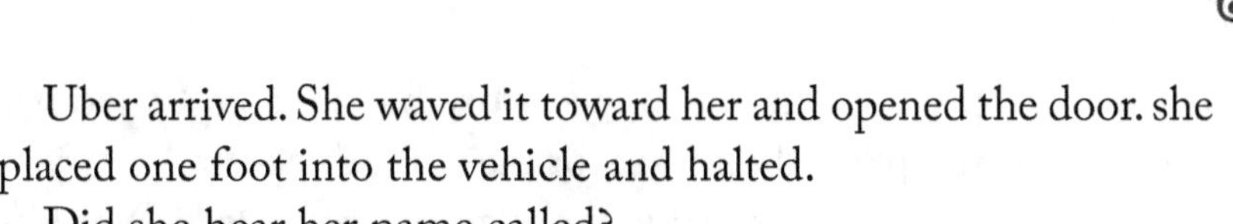

Uber arrived. She waved it toward her and opened the door. she placed one foot into the vehicle and halted.

Did she hear her name called?

It became louder.

She turned her head and could see a distant but familiar figure waving his arm and carrying what looked like a picnic basket. Tension uncorked from her as she observed him advancing toward her. A belly laugh rumbled within and soon couldn't be contained. She wrapped her arms around her body.

"Ma'am?"

"Oh, sorry, let me pay you for the inconvenience." Rachel opened her purse and pulled out some money when powerful fingers curled over hers.

She looked up into an ocean of aquamarine.

"No, I'll take care of it," Michael said, huffing. He put down the basket and handed the driver some cash. The driver grabbed it with a muffled, *Thank you*. His tires screamed as he sped away.

Michael continued huffing. "I can explain."

Rachel's eyes twinkled. "I'm excited to hear, but glad you're here."

Michael grinned, shaking his head. "So am I. You won't believe what happened, or maybe you will with all the stories you hear."

"Try me."

"Let's walk to a pleasant area as I share my tale of woe."

They strolled down the path with beautiful flowers displayed on both sides.

"You look stunning, as always."

"Thank you, as always." Rachel gazed into his admiring eyes. "And you, sir, look quite fine yourself." Rachel's eyes wandered over his form, clad in black jeans and a blazer with a white T-shirt.

"Let me indulge you with the embarrassing impediment that interrupted my punctual arrival here."

"I'm all ears."

"What could go wrong? Well, here I was driving and playing some tunes when, out of nowhere, my car died. I thought, *Okay, battery*. No problem since I carry a portable charger. I tried it—nothing. Next, I pressed a button for the roadside assistance service to come. Then I pulled out my phone to call you. Dead. Not like me to let the battery die. When the service people arrived, I asked to use their charger. Plugged my phone into their port. No signs of life. I got an Uber driver and offered him a substantial amount of money if he could get me here without killing us or anyone else. I prayed you'd wait. Dead car, dead phone, but please, no dead end here." Michael glanced at her. "Thank God."

"God answered your prayers and," she said in a wistful tone, "mine, too."

"Good." His gaze lingered for a moment. "How's this spot?"

Rachel's eye glided over the area. Clusters of picnickers sat in different sections, maintaining their own privacy from interlopers. "Perfect."

Michael removed a compact from his belt, which opened to a blanket. He laid it on the grass, bowed, and offered his hand to Rachel. "Madame, may I have the pleasure of your company in this, I hope, delicious meal, and I know, exciting journey?"

"You may," Rachel said, trying to contain the sparks igniting within her.

Michael helped her sit, then took more items from the bag at his waist—pillows inflated as they watched.

"Wow, you come prepared, doctor."

Michael chuckled before his eyes joined hers. "I try." He opened the basket, taking out glasses, a bottle of wine, a small cheese tray, plates, silverware, and gourmet sandwiches.

"Voila." He poured some wine for both. "I'd like to make a toast."

"Please do."

"To us. May this be the beginning of a new adventure."

"Yes."

They clinked glasses before sipping.

Michael put his glass down, unwrapped his sandwich, and offered Rachel a slice of cheese.

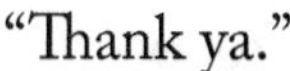

"Thank ya."

He brushed his hands and stared at Rachel. "Before you tell me your story, I want to let you know, Justine will no longer bother you."

Rachel's eyes lifted and nodded.

"I contacted her and told her in blunt language our affair didn't designate us a couple and," Michael took a sip of wine without shifting his gaze from Rachel, "we'll never be, no matter how much she tries to convince herself or anyone else otherwise."

Rachel's eyes widened. "Oh, my goodness, what did she say?"

"What could she say?"

"I guess nothing."

Michael's eyes glazed over for a moment.

Rachel closed her eyes, capturing the essence of what he told her, with ingredients of optimism and joy blending.

She opened her eyes to Michael's regarding her.

"I didn't want to interrupt your musings."

"It's okay. All pleasant after what you shared."

Michael tilted his head back and chuckled. "Good." His eyes lingered on her for a moment, causing a wave of heat to spread through her.

"Before we get into your story, let's take a bite of these sandwiches—roasted vegetables, which I believe you said would meet your palate's standards?"

"Perfect again."

Rachel unwrapped her sandwich and peered at Michael, watching him take a bite. She did the same, sitting swathed in contentment. She put her sandwich down and took a sip of wine.

"Before I begin my story, I thought about what you said."

Michael cocked an eyebrow. "What part in particular?"

"All of it."

"Good, please share your thoughts."

"Doctor, are you sure you didn't study psychiatry?

Michael grinned. "Perhaps a beautiful therapist jogged memories of my medical school rotation in psych."

"Oh, I bet you use your skills all the time." She stopped for a moment before staring at Michael. "But without digressing, let me tell you how insightful you are. I reflected on everything you said, and you're right. My history and fear of rejection melded together, with guilt playing a role around the possibility of joy again."

"Not possibility." Michael's eyes bore unto hers. "Reality." He took her hand and brought it to his lips, then to his cheek. "Beautiful Rachel." He lowered her hand but kept hold of it.

Their eyes locked for what seemed forever before the intensity caused Rachel to avert hers.

Whew.

He touched her cheek, and she blinked, before peering into the magic swimming in his glorious eyes. "Rachel, please trust me."

"I'm trying." She took his hand and stroked the palm, before examining it. Her index finger roamed over his lifeline. With a mischievous look, Rachel said, "You have a long one."

His eyes lifted. "Good. More time with you."

Enchantment wrapped around Rachel's heart. "Yes." Her eyes captured his.

For the next hour, Rachel shared everything about her family, from growing up with Leah and through the harrowing experience of their parents' deaths.

Rachel took a breath, with tears streaming down her face. Michael squeezed her hand, eyes probing hers.

"Do you feel you need to stop?" Michael said, handing her a napkin.

Rachel dabbed at her face and in a choked voice said, "You're doing it again."

Michael asked, "What do you mean? Oh." He nodded with a sheepish grin. "I'm not trying to sound like a therapist, so it must be your influence, but on a serious note, please don't feel rushed."

"I'm not." Rachel wiped her face.

"Your parents sounded very loving."

"They were."

"But your sister, not so kind, at least toward you."

"She wasn't."

Rachel talked more about what unfolded after her parents' death, and she paused as Sam's smiling face appeared in front of her. Out of nowhere, a child with a stuffed toy elephant ran by them. A sign. She shut her eyes, imagining Sam kissing her nose. She opened them, catching Michael observing her.

"Now I'll tell you about Sam. I think you would've liked each other."

Rachel told Michael about Sam, how they met, their infertility, practice, friends, and travel.

"We loved elephants, and when I saw the child with the toy elephant just now, I knew Sam sent his blessings."

"He sounds like a remarkable man, and if we met, I believe a friendship might've developed."

Rachel clutched Michael's hand. Cloaked in warmth and sweetness, Rachel brought it to her cheek.

She sighed before looking at him again. "Alright. Now, another tough part."

Michael leaned in closer to her. "Are you sure you want to continue?"

Rachel nodded, holding his hand tight. "I'll repeat what my clients say. Need to get this out."

Michael squeezed her hand. "I'm ready for as much or as little as you want to share."

Rachel nodded. "Alright. Are you familiar with parental alienation?"

"Yes, I believe so, but I hear little about it. I assume you do in your profession."

"I do, but there are good examples of it outside the therapy office. Do you recall the case of the man who abducted his children, changed his identity and theirs, and left Massachusetts to escape detection?"

"It rings a bell, but tell me more."

"It received national attention. After the mother searched for years, they located the father and two young adult children. The father lied to his children about their mother's death, but it didn't matter to them. They backed their father and wanted no relationship to the mother.

"How terrible. Did the children ever reconnect with their mother?"

"I googled for more recent information, but nothing materialized."

"What are your thoughts about it?"

"The power of loyalty and attachment, even when there's wrongdoing. Look at the Bulger brothers?"

Michael nodded.

"So parental alienation can apply to other family members. Think of these polarizing times. People withhold their children from grandparents because of opposing political views."

"I've heard a couple of those stories, which I can't understand. Quite cruel if you ask me."

"Yes, and it also can extend beyond parents and grandparents because of jealousy. Children are often used as pawns."

"Thanks for explaining, because I never considered the complexity involved in these kinds of estrangements."

"It happens more than most people realize, which made me reluctant to share my situation with you."

Rachel talked more about her sister's jealousy and her wish to keep her only child to herself.

"Believe me, I tried to connect with him, but she refused to let me be a part of his world without her or our parents present."

Michael stared deep into her eyes, and she told him everything, including the last wound inflicted at his New York showing.

"You mean to tell me, he invited you, only to exclude you from any connection to him?"

"Yes, he wanted to keep me invisible—and he did—at least in his photographs of the women in his life."

Michael shook his head.

Rachel peered at him as he looked away and sipped his wine.

Rachel allowed the ambient noise of the park to fill the space. *What's he thinking?*

After an infinite moment, he turned to her, and with knitted brows, took one of her curls and coiled it around his finger. "Beautiful lady, I'm flabbergasted by the deliberate spitefulness of your nephew," Michael pulled the curl under his nose before releasing it and putting her face in his hands, "but you—invisible? Not possible."

Rachel's cheeks blossomed, watered by streaming tears. "You, sir, not only make me feel warm inside, but I feel so alive with you." She could feel herself drowning in the sea that was his aqua-blue eyes.

Michael brushed kisses on her cheeks before lingering on her lips. "I want to move at a steady pace, but not too slow."

Rachel fanned her face. "Whew." She looked around, but people appeared preoccupied within their own circles.

Michael grinned. "What? Don't you like public displays of affection, or, as the young people say, PDAs?"

Rachel laughed. "Do you?"

"No, but I couldn't resist your allure." He paused, then added, "I have an idea."

Chapter Thirty-One

Session 10—May 27th—Rachel

No matter what went right or wrong in Rachel's life, she put it aside when she met with clients. She couldn't recall a time when her concentration sputtered to a dead halt. When she returned to her practice several weeks after Sam's death, her razor-sharp focus ensured she and her clients remained present. The events of the last five days challenged this, with a range of thoughts and feelings, airy to heavy and profound, gliding through her mind. But tonight? No. The beautiful people waiting for her would receive her undivided attention.

Rachel entered the room, pondering what she thought about the situation. A lightness sprinkled every inch of her as Matt and Sapphire sat holding hands and grinning. Their sparkle lit up the entire room and hypnotized Rachel.

She sat down and nodded. "My intuition didn't lead me astray."

"You're okay with it?" Sapphire asked.

She gazed at them for a moment before shifting toward the others. "Yes, but let me share my thoughts once I hear more about this. Before we go in-depth, how's everyone doing overall as we end our group journey together?"

Matt and Sapphire grinned at each other, hands remaining entwined, and Sapphire said, "Well, I hope you see the obvious."

"Don't talk that way to my therapist." Matt's eyes bored into Sapphire's who responded with a light punch.

"Ouch," Matt said, rubbing his arm with exaggeration.

"My therapist before yours, so I've got seniority," Sapphire quipped, lifting her chin. "So there."

Rachel gawked at them, trying to contain her bubbling expression. "Before you two continue to fight over me and share what led to this, let's check in with the others."

"I'm great." Yardley grabbed a coil from her beautiful, cascading hair, appearing more confident than Rachel ever had witnessed. "Daniel surprised me last Friday night by coming to my parents' home for Shabbat dinner." Her green eyes widened like saucers as they swept the room. "Before he left, he asked to see my father and when I asked, he laughed but wouldn't tell me what they discussed."

Rachel's heart danced, hoping it would be what Yardley wanted.

"Hey girl, do you think he might pop the question?" Shalene offered a half-smile, twisting one of her rings.

Yardley beamed. "I think so. I hope so. When he left, my father hugged me, emphasizing not to ask him questions."

"Promise you'll tell us, Yardley?" Matt asked.

"Yes, if you promise you tell the story about you two," she said in her usual quiet tone.

Matt smirked. "Got to hear from Shalene and Jason first."

"I'm fine. You, Jason?" Shalene asked, eyes snapping at him.

"Y'all, I'm mighty fine. Promise I'll share, but we're ready for you." Jason pointed to Matt and Sapphire. "Even though we know some of it."

"But Rachel doesn't," Shalene said, peering at Jason.

"Since everyone else seems to know, please tell me what I don't know." Rachel lifted her eyebrows at Matt and Sapphire.

The couple nodded as they looked at one another. Matt cleared his throat and leaned forward, taking Sapphire's hand, which caused her to giggle.

He looked at Sapphire and took a deep breath. "Sapphire and I have been talking a lot lately." He turned back to Rachel. "We've gotten to know each other and conversed outside of the sessions in the last week."

Sapphire blushed and almost talked over Matt. "Rachel, you should know that nothing more happened." Sapphire gulped. "We just knew destiny brought us here."

Rachel looked at both. "Did you think I'd disapprove?"

They glanced at each other before turning back to Rachel.

"We—weren't sure, but no disrespect, even if you did, we…" Sapphire blinked, holding her head high. "I'm sorry, Rachel, but we were going to get together, anyway."

Matt gazed at Sapphire before turning to Rachel. "Like Sapphire said, no disrespect. You helped get us together." He wiggled his eyebrows. "Maybe you were a matchmaker in another life."

Rachel's eyes crinkled. "Some therapists do become matchmakers. Not my calling, but on a serious note, I don't feel disrespected." She winked. "More about that later." She laced her hands together. "Now, please tell us how this unfolded. I observed your playfulness a few weeks ago, and thought, *Matt and Sapphire?* But after the last session?" Rachel grimaced. "I decided, *Wrong, Rachel, wrong.*"

"Right, Rachel, right." Matt laughed.

"Let me start." Sapphire glanced at Matt.

He smirked, waving his hand. "Sure. I'll interject if you miss something."

Sapphire nodded. Her eyes dazzled the room. "Ready, everyone?"

"Yes, Ma'am. We're waiting." Jason said, saluting her.

Sapphire nodded.

After she and Matt left the eighth session, she noticed a light, sweet floating sensation, like cotton candy, overtake her. When she shared it with Matt, he grabbed her hand and suggested coffee.

"We went to a local diner for coffee, and talked and talked and talked."

"And talked some more," Matt chimed in, receiving a gentle nudge from Sapphire.

Over the next few hours, Sapphire spilled everything about her fears around relationships, and with his support, she told him her plan to meet with Hugo. At midnight, he walked her to her car, hugged her, and suggested she perform one of Rachel's visualizations to prepare for the encounter.

They texted Friday, and after her confrontation with Hugo, Matt checked on her. Later in church, he showed up, and they went out for a bite to eat. Several hours later, they embraced again, and Matt asked her out for a date the next week.

"I agreed but informed him I preferred to not divulge this in the group, so I chose the aloof approach."

"She sure did, as everyone witnessed."

"I preferred not to give anything away, plus some jealousy came out about Nicole."

"After the group ended, I saw her sitting in her car," Matt interjected. "I waved, asking her what happened. She told me, and I told her, *Follow me*. We drove to that same diner, and right away, we agreed we liked each other too much to wait until the group ended.

"We've seen each other three times since the last session." Sapphire gazed at Rachel. "I know it goes against the rules for therapy, but, well," she let her hair fall over her face, before shifting one exotic eye toward Matt. "Tough. We like each other too much to say, *No-can-do* because we met in group therapy." She gripped Matt's hand and stared at Rachel.

Silence slithered into the room with another elongated moment as Rachel considered her words. She caught wide eyes, waiting for her response.

Rachel shook her head. "I can't tell you how pleased I am with this turn of events."

Matt glanced at Sapphire. "Told ya."

Sapphire brushed her hair aside, allowing a dazzle to emit from her eyes. "Oh, I'm so relieved. I thought, *It's not like he's my client,* but still."

"My dear, you're correct. He's *not* your client, so," Rachel threw up her hands, "well, so what?"

Everyone nodded, taking in what she said.

"I've seen situations where therapists do things..."

"Really?" Sapphire asked.

"Yes, they attend birthdays, weddings, baptisms, and bris ceremonies. A few have become parents, friends, and spouses of other therapists."

"Are you kidding about the last three?" Sapphire's eyes widened.

"No, I'm not," Rachel said. "It's not sanctioned, and the social workers have been most firm about relationships outside therapy. But..." Rachel waved her hand, "They've happened, and to my knowledge, no harm occurred. Human relationships are complicated. The most important issue? The therapy ends before any consideration of moving into the realm of friendship or more. Sexual relationships within the confines of the therapy? Misuse of power, and unacceptable."

Sapphire nodded her head.

"So, anything more from you two?"

Everyone shifted to Jason.

"Not now," Matt said, blue eyes, turning navy.

"Okay, Shalene, should we tell Rachel also?"

Shalene grinned, twisting her fingers.

"After we found out about those two," Jason jutting his chin toward Matt and Sapphire before pivoting back to Shalene, "I found Shalene in her favorite place—a library—and without her knowing, sat in a booth near her."

Shalene giggled, covering her mouth.

"So, there I sat, and wrote a note, passing it to some guy sitting in between us and pointing my finger at the booth next to him. I see this guy, frowning, but he handed it to Shalene. He whispered something, and I see her lean back, catching my nod and bobbing her head."

"Aren't you going to tell them what the note said?" Shalene asked, frowning.

"Oh, yeah." Jason rubbed his head. "I wrote, *Marry me... I mean date me.*"

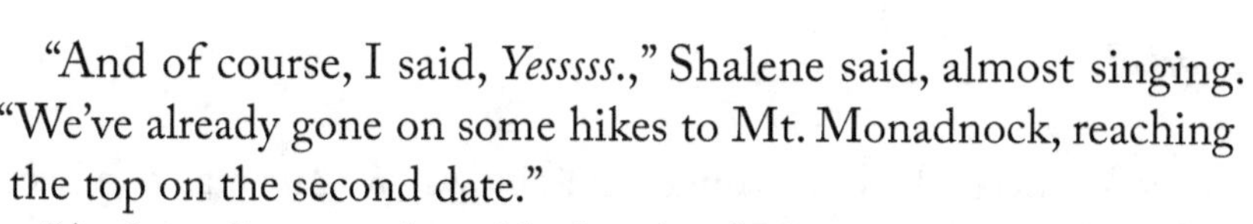

"And of course, I said, *Yesssss.*," Shalene said, almost singing. "We've already gone on some hikes to Mt. Monadnock, reaching the top on the second date."

"And we discovered we like heights." Jason glanced at Shalene.

"Yeah, I guess my almost-agoraphobia, made me want to jump so high that we're going skydiving." Shalene giggled again. "Not telling Mom and Dad until we make it down alive."

Everyone chuckled, shaking their heads.

"Yes, Ma'am, all your fault, Rachel." Jason's eyes waltzed with hers.

Shalene raised her finger. "But in a good way."

"A marvelous way," Matt said, lifting his eyebrows toward Rachel.

Rachel sighed and nodded, studying each of them and preparing the most appropriate words to emerge from her throat. "I feel like I walked into a party, and someone shouted surprise."

"You did," Yardley said. "We didn't want to tell you, but we shared our numbers a few meetings back and formed a group text, hoping you'd not care. I know we broke a few rules, but we couldn't resist and knew that if everyone agreed, *No harm*, as you would say."

"No harm at all." Rachel smiled at Yardley. "The opposite. My hopes for a corrective experience for each of you exceeded anything I could've imagined. I can't even put into words how pleased I am for you."

"Rachel, we have a couple of gifts for you, but before we share," Jason scanned the room, "we all wonder if you have cool things going on in your life?"

Rachel smiled.

"Hey, being a therapist, I get it, even though you've years over me," Sapphire said. "And I understand, I mean, *we* understand, that you keep your personal life private," Sapphire asked, "but would you be willing to...?" She squinted, offering a small space between her index finger and thumb.

Rachel gazed at all of them.

Rachel

After Michael rolled the blanket and pillows into his small compact hanging from his belt, he grabbed her hand.

"What's your idea?" Rachel asked as they strolled out of the park.

"First, come to my apartment for a late day barbeque, unless you have other plans."

"No, I have a friend walking Zsa Zsa and Gabor, so I'm free for several hours."

"Terrific, let's go back to my place and," Michael stopped, taking her chin again, "nothing beyond kissing and hugging. Like I said, I want to take things slow, kind of old-fashioned, even though I went against my rule recently."

"You're forgiven." Rachel laughed.

"Good. Never again, I promise, and I get the sense slow and steady, not too, but enough for comfort and commitment that works for me and you." He brushed her cheek again.

"Yes, I love it, and thank you for reassuring me because, well," Rachel squeezed his hand, "I would've been nervous."

He brought her hand to his lips before moving them along again.

"Tell me more about your practice."

"What do you want to know?"

"Didn't you say you're running a group?"

"I did."

"How's it going?"

"The members are amazing. I love all my clients, but these five are some of my favorites."

"Teachers have their pets. Even parents do." He swung her arm as they walked out of the park.

"Umm," Rachel said. "Human beings? We're quite the species."

Michael threw his head back and laughed. "Indeed."

"My clients, all quite successful on the outside, have each suffered some injustices."

"No one said life is fair."

"Indeed. I used to say, *a picture speaks a thousand words*, but now I emphasize an actual story lies behind the photo."

Michael nodded. "I never thought much about it." He squeezed her hand. "See, you get me to think."

"Doctor, I'm not sure about that."

"Fair enough, but you induce me to think otherwise."

Rachel looked up, smiling as the sun turned his ocean eyes green.

"Anyway, I tried helping them through individual therapy, but we came to an impasse. And although I loathed the prospect of losing them, I opted to refer them to another therapist."

"How did they respond?"

"All of them declined, and Sapphire—my client with spectacular eyes, like yours—became enraged at me."

Michael chuckled. "So much for that notion."

Rachel nodded. "Instead, they agreed to the group. All of them said they felt relief about sharing and wanted to start a new chapter, but I thought I'd see more of that sooner."

"Two months isn't a considerable amount of time."

"I know, but they've been in therapy with me for quite some time."

"What are your expectations as you wind down?"

"Good question. I hoped my fiery client and this beautiful man might come together. Their playfulness gave me hope, and based on our last meeting, I'm not so optimistic."

Michael stopped and gazed at her. "Didn't someone say sometimes the best part of the game is the last few innings?"

"Yes, I can't remember who. But it's similar in theme to the quote, *The second half of life for which the first was made.*"

"Ah, Robert Browning. Yes, something like that." His fingers tightened their grip.

"Now these people I serve are young—late twenties, early thirties. So much happened to them, they almost surrendered to a second chance for happiness. I don't know where they'll go after this last session, but I've got my fingers crossed."

"You go beyond the extra mile for your clients."

"Michael, my faith tells me that God asked me to do this work."

Michael nodded. "He did." His eyes grabbed hers. "I can tell."

She smiled. "Yes, I've given this strange calling much thought, which prompted me to tell people it's a part of my identity."

"Do most therapists share your opinion?"

"The field has become more and more secular so, maybe—but without the God part. They can view their role however they see fit, but I know God beckoned me. Sometimes people miss their calling, but if they pay close attention, they'll discover the road to take."

"Your faith shines through."

"What about you? I know you believe in God and use your healing talents to help others, so do you believe you were called?"

Michael nodded, but for a long moment he appeared to ponder her question.

"Yes? No?"

"I've never examined my desire to help others from a religious point of view, however now that you point it out, since I was ten I've wanted to be a doctor." Michael angled his head. "I stayed resolute in that desire, so maybe divine intervention encouraged me to take on a healing profession."

"I don't know the exact words, but there's a quote in the book of Jeremiah that talks about God's plan for each of us."

"You might say He planned for us to meet in this more seasoned part of life." Michael leaned into her.

Rachel snuggled back. "By the way, I forgot to tell you about my therapist, Alexandra. She's not one to reveal much, but she just shared with me she married for the first time at age seventy-five."

"Good for her." Michael lifted his eyebrows. "Never too late to find love. First time, second time, for some third time. How old is she now?"

"Eighty years old, and she told me she returned from a romantic escapade with her husband." Rachel shook her head, laughing. "Who knew?"

"What made her reveal all these details now?"

Rachel's words hung in her throat for a split second. A red wave began rising within her, and she stopped, probing Michael's eyes. "She thought her divulgence might help me take a risk and trust you—and myself."

Michael set down the basket, took her face in both hands, and kissed her lips. He grabbed a coil again and let it spring back. "Beautiful Rachel. I'm pleased you accepted Alexandra's sagacious advice."

Rachel shut her eyes and breathed in the fragrant aromas filling the space. Her skin tingled from Michael's kiss, and his powerful hand, laced with hers, provided a safe and strong anchor she never thought would present itself again.

"I wonder where our journey will take us?" Rachel asked.

"Who knows?" Michael grinned. "But I can't wait to travel the world with you to find out."

Rachel blinked at ten searching eyes. What should I tell them?

"So, you wondered about my life?"

They sat still like statues, eyes darting back and forth.

"Of course we do," Jason said with a wide grin.

"You always say you want good for us, but have you ever thought that we want good for you too?" Sapphire asked, with her chin lifted.

"Yowzah," Shalene said as she twisted her thumb ring.

Matt and Yardley nodded.

"I'd ask my usual, what would you like to know, but I won't do that."

Rachel felt eagerness rush into the room. She smiled, picturing them like adorable pups panting for their treats.

"Alright, first let me tell you how much I've learned on this journey with you."

Bobbing heads.

"Many of you know, I became a widow five years ago."

They looked at each other, shaking their heads.

"I didn't tell any of you?"

"No." Sapphire glared at her. "At least not me."

The others mumbled, *Not me.*

"Looks like none of us," Jason said.

Rachel winced. "Sorry, but if you couldn't tell, I keep very high boundaries."

"I'll say," Sapphire said, taking a sip of water.

"Now, now," Matt said, looking from Sapphire to Rachel. "Maybe she had good reason."

"I keep high boundaries, but death of a spouse?" Sapphire rolled her eyes. "Come on."

Rachel nodded. "Matt's right, but so are you Sapphire, so let me explain."

"We don't want to make you uncomfortable, so I—" Yardley shrunk. "Well, I don't know."

"If I may elaborate on Yardley's statement, we want you to reveal to us whatever you feel is worthy for us to know," Matt said with a wrinkled brow.

"Please, all of you. I'm fine, but there are reasons I didn't share with anyone about my husband's death."

They waited, wide-eyed and ready to gobble up any morsel she offered.

"Nothing ominous, I promise." She beamed. "I withheld the information from any who met with me after his death. I never, ever want to concern clients with my woes. Their, I mean, *your* needs come first."

"I get it, Rachel." Sapphire said, with softness breezing through her tone. "Sorry, I barked at you. I'd do the same things with my clients."

"I know you mean well, my dear." Rachel's eyes glistened. "But," she said, clearing her throat, "I want to go back to why I'm revealing this now. Even if you hadn't asked, I planned on sharing."

She caught Jason's dancing eyes. "You see. I told you I wished for you to become more visible. Right?"

"Yes," everyone said in unison.

"Something happened along the way."

She noticed Yardley's jade eyes intensify.

"Something very special." She glowed inside out.

"Are you going to tell us you have a honey?" Shalene asked, pulling on her ring finger.

Rachel laughed. "Ah, Shalene, you don't hold back, do you?"

"Uh-uh." Shalene rewarded Rachel with her signature one-dimpled, half-smile.

"I'm not sure he's my *honey* yet, but yes, I met a lovely man."

"Yes!" Sapphire stomped her feet, pulling on Matt's arm.

Matt's head fell back, laughing, before returning his gaze to Rachel. "Guess you made someone happy. Uh, I mean all of us are happy. Look around."

"May we ask how you met him?" Yardley peered at Rachel.

"You may. I took a Tango lesson a couple of months ago, and we met in the first class."

"And we helped, you kind of said?" Jason asked.

"I don't think I would've taken a risk without watching all of you begin the process."

"Well, Rach, I hope you receive everything you deserve, both you and...?" Matt asked.

"Michael."

"You and Michael dance your life with love and laughter."

"We'll see." Rachel's eyes sparkled at Matt and then the others. "So far it's looking good, and I hope the same for you," her head turned from Matt to the others, "and you, and you, and you, and you."

Shalene started clapping and the others joined her.

"Hey, Sapphire?" Jason raised his eyebrows.

"Oh, yes." Sapphire bent down and pulled out a beautiful, decorated box with curly, teal-colored ribbons and fans layering it. She got up and hugged Rachel. "A small token of our love and appreciation."

Rachel's eyes flooded as tears spilled onto the wrapping paper.

"Gosh, Ms. Rachel, you're going to cause me," Jason's moist chocolate eyes circled the room, "and everyone else to cry."

"Trying not to do that," Rachel said, tearing the paper and allowing her eyes to linger on the aqua Tiffany box. Her fingers grazed the satin white ribbon, lingering for a moment. *Ah, smooth like the trajectory of their near-future lives.*

"Open it."

Rachel heard Sapphire's excitement bubbling over.

"Okay." She opened the box and found an exquisite gold bangle lying inside. "Oh, my." Rachel brought her hands to her mouth, tears flowing down her face. "Too much."

"Now look inside the cuff," Sapphire said, stretching over.

Rachel opened the clasp, and she touched the elegant, engraved message. *Thank you! Love always, Jason, Matt, Sapphire, Shalene, and Yardley.*

"We didn't know whose name should go first, so agreed on alphabetical order."

Rachel continued shaking her head. "You went above and beyond."

"Nah," Matt said. "All of us make a good living, and what you gave us can't be equated into dollars."

"That's right. And didn't you say therapy's a soft science that can't be measured?" Jason lifted his eyes.

"Yes, but," Rachel shook her head, swallowing.

"Here's a tissue, Rach." Matt handed her one. "And something else." His chin lifted toward Shalene.

"Yes." Shalene twisted around and pulled out a large picture. She got out of her seat, hugged Rachel, and handed it to her. Rachel looked down at the framed photo of the five of them, with arms around each other, waving.

Rachel sniffled as she studied the photograph, then brought it to her chest. "I'm so blessed to have met the five of you. I wished the best for you but," she raised her eyes, "and I'm confident I can say this to you, I prayed God would free you from the obstacles holding you back."

"Yup. Sure can, and He blessed us with you." Jason gave a thumbs up with the three women nodding.

"Mutual admiration and reciprocal love." Rachel's eyes glittered with tears.

Rachel glanced at the clock and sighed. "I'm afraid it's time for this chapter to end."

She heard a few groans.

"I know. I hate goodbyes. But, my friends, each of you is ready for the next chapter in your remarkable Book of Life. What a story each of you will write."

She couldn't contain the unrelenting spillage coming from her eyes. Not since Sam's death—and, to a degree, Damian's betrayal—did so many tears flow.

"Now, this goes without saying, but if you need me, please text or call."

Everyone smiled with shimmering eyes.

They waited as she got her belongings, locked the door, and walked to her car. She wrapped her arms around each of them. Massive arms replacing slender, all powerful and warm like a fuzzy cloak.

Right before they departed, Jason waved his hand for a group hug, and as they embraced, someone mouthed, "Hip, hip hooray." Rachel plodded away, hearing them chat among themselves. The last words audible to her came from Shalene, asking where they should meet.

Rachel turned before getting into her car, and the five of them stood waving and throwing kisses. She put the key in the ignition and drove away. Glancing in the rearview mirror, she watched them wave until they shrank and were no longer visible.

Rachel's eyes moistened, and she whispered a silent prayer.

"Thank you, God, for allowing me to help these people see they can have a better life."

She sighed as she looked ahead, knowing how boundless everything seemed, even at night. The stars twinkled brighter than usual, a dazzling ensemble from God against the backdrop of an infinite sable sky. Perhaps a sign from Him of what's coming as she embarked on this next chapter in her own Book of Life. No matter how her story unfolded, she believed it would be engraved in glittery gold, visible for all to see.

Chapter Thirty-Two

Eighteen Months Later—A Town Outside of Boston

Bright lights flashed with the brakes of several cars squeaking as guests departed from the French country estate after celebrating the baptism of an exquisite three-month-old baby girl. One set of grandparents who planned on staying a few more days went upstairs to retire for the evening. The other two left with spouses and family members.

Matt and his wife sat in the Great Room with their baby and a small circle of friends. He sighed as he took a swallow of his cognac, glancing at the blazing fire in the floor-to-ceiling stone fireplace, then returned his focus to the gorgeous infant sleeping peacefully in her mother's arms. Sapphire looked up, scintillating eyes piercing his before both returned their attention to their precious creation.

Matt gulped as he experienced an ecstasy infusing every cell in his body. Who would have guessed that he and Sapphire would entwine themselves and create another human being?

Yeah, yeah, this occurs every minute, but when it's you, man, no words.

"Hey brother, what are you thinking about? Wait a minute, let me guess." Jason rubbed his chin, with his fiancée displaying her one-dimpled, half-smile.

Matt grinned. "Can't wait for it to happen to you two, but" Matt's eyes moved to a very pregnant Yardley and her husband, Daniel, "it looks like those two are next."

"We'll be right along, so don't you worry, Matt Ryan," Shalene said, twisting her pear-shaped engagement ring.

"We'll celebrate over and over," Sapphire said, "and as usual we need to thank Rachel, not only for helping us but also for bringing us together, forever."

"Yes, my beautiful wife and friends—visible forever."

"Brother, ya couldn't put it better, *visible forever*, putting the past behind where it belongs," Jason said with a nod, "not forgotten, but no longer immobilizing us."

Matt laced his hands together, as warmth and comfort encircled the room.

The conversation drifted to Rachel as it often did, wondering about her whereabouts. All of them received a formal letter informing them of her decision to close her practice and the contact information of a referring therapist if they needed one in the future.

When Matt opened the letter and started reading it to Sapphire, her eyes blazed. She grabbed it from his hands, almost ripping it in half.

"Come on, babe. You should understand better than anyone her reason for being so formal."

"No." Sapphire folded her arms. "She didn't have to do it this way. I can't believe it. After all these years, no call to us. I know it's been several months but," Sapphire said, whimpering, "with all we've been through with her?"

Matt shook his head. "Sapphire, you're a therapist. How would *you* have handled this?"

Her eyes narrowed. "Not like this." She threw the paper aside.

Matt wrapped his arms around her before reaching down and placing a finger under her chin. "And how do you know we won't hear from her?"

A few days later, Rachel's note arrived. She told them she planned on closing her practice and taking a cruise around the world before moving to southern Florida. Although she wouldn't check her phone often, she invited them to text her about any important events or photos they would like to share.

Matt handed her the note.

When Sapphire read it, she said, "Phew."

Matt kissed her cheek. "Told ya so." He put his hands up when Sapphire swung at him, grinning.

Within a few hours, the others texted, telling them they had also received a card.

"As usual, she provided little information," Sapphire said, gazing at her baby.

"Babe, what did you expect? She gave us more than usual at our last group meeting."

Sapphire nodded without taking her eyes off her daughter.

The others sat for a moment in relaxed silence, listening to the crackle of the fire.

"The real question is," Jason asked, "what happened to the man in her life?"

"Good question," Matt said, "but knowing Rachel, with or without him, she'll find her way."

"True," Yardley said, "but I hope she finds love again."

"I think you speak for all of us, but guess what? I've got a sense she has," Shalene said.

"You and your sixth sense, Shaleneee." Jason said, squeezing his fiancée.

Matt raised his glass.

"To Rachel, wherever you are. May you find the love you deserve. Here's some from us."

A Few Days Later

Nobody could disagree that Key West captivated tourists with one of the most beautiful sunsets in the world. People shouted *ooh and ah* when a unique, majestic painting splashed across the sky's canvas. Every late afternoon, the pier bustled with much activity as everyone strolled along the walkway awaiting the spectacle to occur.

Rachel studied the clowns skating in between people as they juggled balls to the giggles of scampering children. Her gaze shifted to the frozen statues, coming to life, an ephemeral smile jotting their face, when people dropped dollar bills in the baskets in front of them.

The fingers caressing her hand brought her attention back to the man sitting across from her. Together for several months now, his sea-changing eyes continued to mesmerize her.

"My beautiful wife, what are your thoughts?"

"Ah, my handsome husband, you continue to amaze me with your therapeutic talents."

"Well, I remain a student to the gifted woman who agreed to join me in writing this next chapter in…"

Rachel laughed. "Our Book of Life."

"Yes, something else I learned from you."

Rachel kissed her palm, then blew it at Michael.

"Caught it, and right back at you."

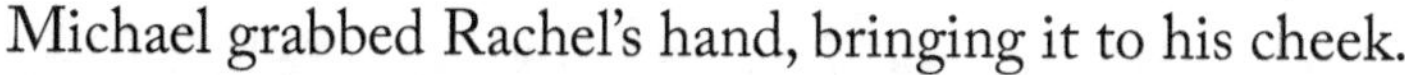

Michael grabbed Rachel's hand, bringing it to his cheek.

"Ma'am?" A server approached the table.

"Yes?" Rachel answered.

"Someone requested I deliver this note to you."

"Thank you." Rachel took the envelope addressed to her and scrutinized the elegant and familiar penmanship. Her heart jumped into her throat as she brought her hand to her chest.

Michael leaned forward. "Why don't you open it?" His eyes danced with mischief.

Rachel ripped the envelope open and read the note before looking at Michael with wide eyes.

He shook his head. "No, I didn't initiate the contact, but after listening, I encouraged the surprise."

Michael's eyes moved outward, and Rachel pivoted on her chair and followed his gaze.

A familiar figure sauntered toward them, waving with open arms.

Rachel stood and moved toward the figure, breathing in the musk aroma coming toward her and falling into powerful limbs.

The firm embrace felt like a gift wrapped in silk. She didn't want to disengage, but the noise from the crowd interrupted.

With arms linked, they turned to watch the sun lay its head down to sleep. Michael joined them, clasping Rachel's other hand. The three of them drank in the colorful masterpiece left in the sunset's wake. Rachel closed her eyes to the thunderous applause, visualizing God's pleasure for the spectators' gratitude.

A moment later, she tilted her head to the topaz-colored eyes mirroring hers. He smiled. "Oh, dear Auntie, I want so much for us to begin again."

Darlene Corbett

Darlene Corbett views herself as a lifelong learner, a pursuer of excellence, a work-in-progress, and a seeker-of-the-truth. For over thirty years, as a licensed therapist, she has helped people get unstuck.

Darlene began putting her thoughts on paper in 2011 and hasn't stopped. Her blogs can be found on such sites as Sixty and Me, BizCatalyst360, and at DarleneCorbett.com. These articles set the stage for her first book, *Stop Depriving The World of You*, published by Sound Wisdom.

Throughout her career, adjectives used to describe Darlene include, animated and effervescent, which tends to contradict the common perception of a psychotherapist.

Darlene lives in central Massachusetts with her beloved Shih Tzu, Churchill.

Visible is her first novel.